THE WEATHER HOUSE

Block Island, Rhode Island

October 1916

Based on a true story

By Gary E. Eddey

Published by

Dickens Point Publishing House
83 Skyline Drive
Morristown, NJ 07960
www.Eddey.com

Printed in the United States of America.

10 9 8 7 6 5 4 3 2 1

Interior design and layout by Just Ink Digital Design

This book was written with love and to honor
the memory of my mother, Emma Eddey,
who tried, against all odds, to matter.

To my children John and Rachel, Ann-Michele and Emily

Table of Contents

My Diary

Emma Rose

April 26, 1914 –

Annie, you saved my life yesterday. There's no two ways about it. If it weren't for you, I would have drowned there in the surf below the bluffs. The storm created such a powerful undertow—way too strong for me. We washed ashore near the lighthouse, and the next morning when they found us, you wouldn't wake up.

Why did we go sailing? We could have found another way to celebrate my 12th birthday.

And why weren't the storm warning flags flying on the lighthouse tower like they're supposed to be? Somebody should have raised them.

Mom called from the hospital today. She said you still haven't woken up. Please wake up, Annie. Please, God, make my sister better. I miss you so much.

Doctor Ricker did a good job of bandaging up my cuts and scrapes, but I'm still awful tired.

I'll write you again tomorrow.

April 27, 1914 –

Thank you for saving me, Annie.

You grabbed me with only your right arm and didn't let go. No matter how hard the waves pounded us, you wouldn't let loose of me. Annie, you were completely determined. Twice while you were holding me and swimming with your other arm, I saw planks from the shattered boat slam into you. And still you hung on. I could see it in your eyes, nothing but nothing was going to separate us. You are so strong! And you're only two years older than me. Annie, I love you.

Then that big wave came that pounded us into the surf and finally washed us ashore. That was when the mast from the boat that was bouncing up and down on the waves slammed into your head. We landed on the beach with you on top of me. Blood was coming from the back of your head. I held you tight. I kept saying your name. But you didn't respond. I was so scared.

The wind was blowing so hard, pushing the rain and sand against our faces. But I must have fallen asleep anyway. I didn't wake up until I heard the lifesaving search party calling our names the next morning. But you didn't wake up.

May 1, 1914 –

I'm still so scared. Come back and help me, Annie. I know you're awake now. But it's been five days and you're still not home from the hospital. Why, Annie? Why won't they bring you home?

I keep thinking about how they put you on the stretcher and carried you away in the back of the truck. And then the ferry made a special trip with just you from our Island to the hospital in Newport.

I can't stand how much I miss you. I hear the grown-ups talking about you all the time, but they always stop as soon as I walk into the room.

Why won't anyone tell me why you can't come home?!

MOHEGAN BLUFFS, BLOCK ISLAND, R. I.   90-46

The site where Emma and Annie washed ashore during the storm.

Prologue

I, George Washington Eddey, am the Weather Official in charge on Block Island and have been since 1908. Calling me a signal officer, a telegrapher, a weather observer, a forecaster, or a meteorologist are all quite appropriate; but in the fall of 1916 some called me a hero, a term I am sure is not accurate. It all started in October. Everyone on Block Island knew it to be an unusual month and it was extraordinary for several reasons, yet only a very few ever knew the full extent of what was taking place.

First, there was the fire, a towering inferno that engulfed the expansive Victorian Hygeia Hotel on August 28. Overlooking the New Harbor and the Great Salt Pond, this luxurious hotel sat on a prominence at the intersection of Beach and New Harbor Road. The fire burned from just before eleven p.m. until well into the next day and destroyed the entire hotel. The flames could be seen from Point Judith on the Rhode Island mainland some seventeen miles away as well as from Newport, RI and Montauk Point, Long Island and beyond. But, small favor, the Hygeia's Annex, which sits directly across the street from the main hotel, was not harmed, courtesy of northerly winds. The origin of the fire in the roof near the cupola suggested arson may be a better descriptor of the cause than simply ascribing it as accidental.

About fifty yards northwest, located diagonally across the street from the Hygeia Hotel and next door to the Annex of the Hygeia, sat the Weather House: the home to Block Island's United States Weather Bureau. The Weather House, in addition to being my office, also serves as my home. On that night my second wife and I, along with her two daughters, Annie and Emma, watched that beautiful hotel burn to the ground.

And last week another fiasco occurred, but one with no loss of life or significant property damage. It was an emergency night landing of a small plane in the surf below the one hundred and fifty-foot-high Mohegan Bluffs. The plane landed just below the Southeast Lighthouse on the southern tip of the Island. This, as it turned out, was another successful night landing of a hydroplane, albeit an emergency landing, by the twenty-four-year-old pilot, Lawrence Sperry (whose father established the Sperry Corporation to produce bombsights, fire suppression, and in-flight navigation systems for military aeroplanes.) Curiously, several days after Sperry's emergency landing, a German U-boat, the U-53, had paid a visit to the Naval War College in Newport, RI, to hand deliver a secret message to Rear Admiral Gleaver. The Naval War College was about twenty-five nautical miles from Block Island. Because the United States at that time had declared itself neutral, the German U-boat was welcomed with open arms. Shortly after that "friendly" visit, the German U-53 sank six foreign ships near the Nantucket Lightship, which Canadian and European vessels would navigate toward as they sailed to ports in New England or New York Harbor.

When Sperry's hydro-aeroplane, a Curtiss F, was refloated and towed to the New Harbor in the Great Salt Pond for repairs, it was moored a hundred yards from my office in the Weather Bureau. Two days after landing at the base of the Mohegan Bluffs and after completing repairs to the plane, Sperry piloted his Curtis F out of the Great Salt Pond to continue the flight north toward Boston. Sperry, an inventor and pilot— the first pilot to attempt a night landing and the first pilot to install a stabilizer on a plane—is one of the most celebrated pilots of our time. His is a story that is still evolving and one day, I am sure, will be told.

I witnessed all of this from my office in the Weather House—the hotel fire and, because of that emergency landing, the first flight out of the Great Salt Pond. Yet, there were two other extraordinarily notable events that transpired on Block Island this mild, weather wise, October. Those two other things—neither of which could readily be seen from the mainland, the Island, the sea, or the air, if gone undetected—could very well have changed the course of our country's history.

Gary E. Eddey

1 Block Island

"It is not down on any map; true places never are."

Moby-Dick

I am here on Block Island, in part, because the sun always casts a shadow. For the Islander of today, as in the distant past, there is little idle time; all events, weather wise or otherwise, except for the rare few, have significance.

As I tell this story, please don't expect great revelations about life. Do not expect me to explore the nature of the Great War now raging in Europe and the resulting loss of life, of which last count was in the millions. Has life lost its value? Is there an evolutionary purpose? ... I cannot answer that. And, please, understand it is difficult for me to be appallingly honest about myself and hence, by extrapolation, about the underlying motivation of some of the characters you will meet.

With that said, I present this story as it unfolded on Block Island, my adopted Island—and the home of my wife's family for about two hundred and fifty years—during a three week period in October of 1916, and hope you will indeed profit, in some small way, from my retelling the tale that lies before you.

Not quite seventy years ago, Herman Melville published a novel called *The Whale*. I am not ashamed to say that I am humored by the narrator, Ishmael, when he narrates that Nantucket is in a "real corner of the world," how it "stands there, away off shore, more lonely than the Eddystone lighthouse. Look at it," he writes, "a mere hillock, an elbow of sand; all beach without a background ... that they are so shut up, belted about, every way enclosed, surrounded, and made an utter island of and by the ocean, that to the very chairs and tables small clams will sometimes be found adhering to the backs of sea turtles. But these extravaganzas only show that Nantucket is no Illinois."

Melville writes about a romantic, isolated Nantucket, an island of whalers, those who "sleep with herds of whales swimming beneath their pillows." Perhaps he knows New Bedford too and he certainly has tremendous knowledge of an island we all know as Manhattan. But does he know Block Island?

Yes, it is true, Block Island was, and still is, an island of local farmers and fisherman; not fisherman and whalers that sail to every reach of the world, but fisherman and captains that stay and fish locally, and who farm as well. They fish for cod, swordfish, shark, tuna—including the big ones—but no whales to speak of; that *I* am aware.

If Melville thinks Nantucket was isolated, I suspect he knew nothing of Block Island, because in 1851 this Island didn't even have a proper harbor; yes it had a landing, Sands Landing; but no harbor in the traditional sense. It was an island visited by few outsiders, save a few pirates or the occasional gunship of the Royal Navy. If he did not know of Block Island, an island like Nantucket first inhabited by Indians and in 1851 *still* the home of a few Native Indian families—although not overmuch is known about them—I would not fault him, because of two very good reasons.

First, Block Island is a *local* island, as I have just explained. If one wants to explore the world, hundreds of other sailing ports would come to mind before our Island.

Second, and perhaps most surprisingly, Block Island, fifteen miles or so off the coast of its home state of Rhode Island, is an island that has a history of not being perceived as part of the United States, even when it was—and that being in the not too distant past! An island not very far from New York City, sitting in the Atlantic Ocean almost equidistant between NYC and Nantucket, not considered a part of the United States? Not possible, you think? Well, think again, because that is true and I will tell that story as well. Suffice it to say that Block Island was, and is still, a bit isolated, and when the weather is bad, almost as inaccessible today as in centuries past.

With the Great War in Europe well underway and our country's entrance into the war theater just a matter of time—despite the position of President Wilson—Block Island once again runs the risk of becoming more isolated. This past summer the Island saw visitors drop considerably, a direct effect of the war in Europe. It didn't help that the Navy War College in Newport, Rhode Island frequently paraded naval vessels near our Island; and so too did Germany, with its U-boats and support vessels occasionally surfacing near our Island.

If our country enters the war, I and most Islander's assume Block Island will be found downright useful for enemy ships—as in prior wars —perhaps even as a target. What I did not realize, until this week, is that even if we do not enter the war, our Island may be used, perhaps as a staging ground, for Germany's expansion efforts. After reading about Germany's U-boat sinking the foreign ships off Nantucket and after witnessing Sperry emergently landing his plane at night in the surf below the Southeast Lighthouse while, I believe, on a military mission, I do not need to read a confidential memo, let's say from the Assistant Secretary of the Navy, to convince me of the possibility that the effects of war, or war itself, may come to our Island in one way or another. I now had no other choice but to believe this was a distinct possibility.

And what Milton Mitchell experienced at the end of the week past removed all doubt that the Great European War would cast yet another shadow on our Island.

2 Three Mysterious Men

Milton Mitchell's original ancestor arrived on Block Island in the 1670s, about a dozen or so years after the first white settlers first began farming the Island. It was at a time when four hundred Manissean Indians called this place their home as well. To this day, we assume that Milton's ancestor, a certain Thomas Mitchell—although we are not certain of his first name—was a farmer first and a fisherman second; and today there are many Mitchell's on the Island, all of whom are descended from this one Mr. Mitchell. My wife also descends from this same man. (As well as three others who made up the original 1661 settlers.)

Last Friday, on his day off, Milton, the sixteen-year-old "messenger boy" and my assistant at the Weather Bureau, went fishing. He went alone, as he often does, a couple hundred yards west of Black Rock on the southwestern part of Block Island, the part of the island closest to the tip of Montauk Point at the tip of Long Island. Soon he reached Dicken's Point, the corner of the Island that is considered its most isolated area.

Milton loved to fish this area of the Island. Depending where one was standing, it was about one hundred and thirty feet below the top of the Mohegan Bluffs, and being that it was only a mile and a half walk up Snake Hole Road, from where he lived with his parents, it was a reasonably convenient fishing spot for him. This area has long been known as a great fishing location, especially in the late summer and fall. Sometimes Milt would help out with one of the fishing crews, or camps, that often camped out near Black Rock, usually the Murray Crew, of which I will later explain more.

After a short time had gone by, enough time to catch a few large mackerel, he started walking farther west along the shore, beyond Dicken's Point, continuing to cast with his wooden pole as he walked. There wasn't much of a beach on this part of the Island; narrow and rocky, with the surf often crashing just at the base of the now 125-foot-high bluffs. To his left, he could clearly see Montauk Point which was about eighteen miles away.

When the weather is clear, as it was on Friday, that part of the Island truly seems to be closer to Montauk and the tip of Long Island than the town of New Shoreham located in the Town Center, near the center of the Island, or even the Old Harbor with its new granite breakwater. If anything happened to you west of Black Rock, unless a fishing smack caught sight of you, it might be a couple of days before anyone would even have thought to look for you.

He was now facing due north and was able to see the most secluded part of the Island, the west beaches, and he could also see the Rhode Island mainland, about twenty-two miles away.

And then, up ahead on the beach, he noticed three well-dressed, rather tall men walking along the rocky beach. They were about a half-mile north of where he was now standing. He put his fishing rod down against the base of the bluffs and started to jog toward them.

As I mentioned, the beach on that side of the Island is narrow and, although it has plenty of white and very fine black sand, it has so many large glacial erratics and smaller round boulders that walking on it takes a lot of concentration; one can't surf cast or walk along that part of the Island very easily. Milton was most surprised to not only have seen people on this side of the Island, but that they had appeared out of nowhere, and further, he did not recognize any of the men.

They just emerged, or so it seemed, out of nowhere, walking and talking along the southwest side of the Island, an area frequented perhaps in the 1600 and 1700s by many fisherman, but today, all but vacant—except for the U. S. Lifesaving Station set up in the dunes at the end of Cooneymus Road, located about a mile north of Dicken's Point. At Conneymus Road the bluffs decrease in size to about twenty feet above the beach. A few farmhouses sit beyond the dunes but they are not visible from the water's edge.

Milt continued to jog toward the men, with every intention to catch up and say hello. Then, almost instantaneously, two things happened that he could not believe.

He saw a black Great Cormorant, a large seabird occasionally seen on Block Island, lifting off the bluff and flying a bit too low, toward the men. Just as this large seabird passed from behind, only a couple of feet over the head of the man in the middle, on its way out to sea, the man flinched, then reached inside his jacket and pulled out a handgun.

He appeared stunned to see the cormorant, and in one fluid motion, took aim and fired. The bird immediately fell to the sand just shy of the surf, still desperately flapping its wings. The man fired a second shot to finish off the bird, sending up a small tuft of feathers.

Milt was so startled that he dropped to the beach on all fours. As the man's friends congratulated him and shared a hearty laugh, Milton scrambled back to his feet. The gun had changed the situation. Saying hello was no longer in the realm of possibility. He moved as quickly and silently as possible back to his fishing gear. Milt glanced back to see if the men had perhaps seen him, but they were still laughing it up.

This pistol was unlike any he'd ever seen. It had a distinct narrow barrel and an odd squared off "L" shape, but he couldn't make anything else out.

Why was the man carrying a pistol? Did the other two have guns, as well? Probably!

When Milt was about fifty yards from his fishing gear, he looked back again. The men were walking briskly as they approached the lifesaving station.

Milton did not see any of the lifesaving crew, or surfmen as they are called, on the beach. Milton knew the surfmen for all of the lifesaving stations on the Island; two of his cousins were so employed; and many of the men were the fathers of his classmates at school. These three men did not look at all like any of the Island's surfmen.

To minimize the chances of being seen, he skirted the base of the bluffs, walking along the surf's edge only when necessary to negotiate those huge glacial erratics. *Who are they? And where the hell did they come from? What the ... are they doing here?*

Those three questions that Milt asked himself then would soon preoccupy me as well.

When Milton reached his gear, he scooped it up and glanced over his shoulder. One of the three men was now looking at him, or in his direction, with a spyglass. He spun around and ran as fast as he could toward Dicken's Point. He had to know and turned back one more time. But the three men were nowhere to be seen!

"Shit," Milt worried, "was he able to make out my face?"

3 To Be an Islander

I have become an Islander because of my position in the Weather Bureau, and because I love this place and fell in love with two women who descended from the original settlers, although not in that particular order. I have three sons, but the only one that chooses to live on the Island is my middle son, Wallace; the other two have left, one for New York and the other to Massachusetts – one to be a printer's apprentice and the other to farm. Wallace, five foot ten inches tall, and very thin, always stood as erect as humanly possible, making himself look much taller. He had a large head and a face that could be described as a bit weather beaten, even at the age of twenty-eight. My son decided early on that he wanted to stay local and make Block Island his home.

As odd as it sounds, Wallace has the personality of a raconteur, yet enjoys his solitude. He works nights at the Telephone Exchange and fishes by day. I do not mean to be insensitive toward my own son, but Wallace doesn't have that state of being that requires one to explore. By this I do not mean that he does not possess a desire to explore the real world, that characteristic he most assuredly has. Wallace loves to try new ventures; sail alone to various ports on the mainland; he braves the Atlantic to fish alone or with a small crew; he is capable, and not afraid at all, of navigating anywhere on the Eastern Seaboard, in any of the myriad of inland passages that many choose to avoid, including those in Canada, specifically Nova Scotia.

No, when I say that he doesn't want to explore I refer to something much different ... I mean he does not feel a need to explore himself. He is not an Ishmael, for example, who possesses that trait of character that is required if one is to explore oneself; as in exploring or being open to change with the experiences that exploration can offer. Simply stated, he does not have an *"Ishmaelian openness to experience."*

Block Island has many who fall into the category that Melville places Ishmael, and just as many who fall into the category in which I place my son. As we shall soon see, my two nieces appear to have that *Ishmaelian openness to experience*, but I suppose they are a bit too young for me to be so terribly certain.

The two girls I speak of are the daughters of my late wife's oldest sister, who has recently become my second wife. Now the girls have become my stepdaughters ... and my pride and joy.

To be an Islander, and to remain one, requires a state of being difficult to describe. Confident in one's self and comfortable with life in and around the sea; being local; being able to withstand long periods of harsh weather; feeling at home with, or at least tolerating, the color gray, the gray that appears when the green disappears with the arrival of the middle of fall; understanding what it means when the spring and fall borrow days from the dead of winter.

Late fall and winter can be rough on the Island, yet this October has been milder than I could ever imagine ... it is as if October is borrowing all of its days from early September.

And then there is the small Island itself, when the fields, sitting on rolling hills, are green, neatly manicured and divided by stone walls, it is especially beautiful. The sky, we like to think, is more blue than gray. The ocean wind is brisk and moist when the fog follows along, coming from all directions depending on the moving weather formations that I spend my career understanding. The hills, none over six hundred and fifty feet above sea level, now treeless (unfortunately), and the numerous ponds and the varied shore geography, this Island, perhaps not as grand as the islands of the Pacific Northwest, but nonetheless, just as majestic.

I believe there is a quality of the Block Islander not known much these days on the mainland. Those characteristics of determination and individualism combine with the apparent opposing characteristic of acceptance. Acceptance of what the Island can and cannot do for you; this is not to imply a fatalistic approach to life; rather an appreciation that everything that one does *has* significance. There is little idle time on our small Island that sits in the Atlantic Ocean. Nothing was or is easy here; there is obvious danger in many aspects of life on our Island, most notably arriving safely to the Island! These ideas may seem to be at odds with one another, but on this Island those two opposing thoughts must live side by side. This dual reality is our reality.

As difficult as this is to explain, it is just as easy for Islanders to understand. Islanders know if you have the qualities necessary to appreciate what this local Island offers and if you recognize those qualities in yourself, you stay. And if those traits of character are not in you, you try to leave. My heart goes out to those who need to leave and cannot— and also to those who wish to stay but cannot.

Those traits of character that lent themselves to remaining an Islander, were present in Wallace's father-in-law, James Murray, who currently (and for many decades past) farms and, in season, leads a land-based fishing crew. During the summer and fall of each year, he runs what we all call the Murray Crew. When the fish are not running, he returns to farming his land.

All the land-based fishing crews on the Island used thick twine netting with cork floats on the top and weighed down with lead weights to catch their fish, a technique not at all unique to Block Island, being a tradition passed down in many different cultures and civilizations for over two thousand years. These nets were set out around the schools of fish at high tide and usually at night. This was when the smaller baitfish would be feeding.

Tides, good weather, and an evening lit by a full moon would make for a great night of fishing. The Murray Camp Crew, as did the three or four other crews on the Island, would then pull the netting around the fish and onto land. When brought onto the beach, the fish were quickly packed in barrels and carted, usually with oxen or horse, into the Old Harbor area to be eventually brought to market in New York City or, salted, and kept locally.

Milton could not get his mind off the three men he had just seen. He continued to worry that the man with the telescope had seen his face. He was further concerned about the man who had shot the cormorant. Milt could not help thinking about how fast his reflexes were and how good was his aim.

He continued to run along the beach until he reached the path which led up to Snake Hole Road. When he climbed to the top of the bluffs, he walked east along the rut-filled Snake Hole Road which sat precariously close to the edge of the bluffs. Soon he was on Southeast Lighthouse Road where Wallace lived. He stopped at my son's house, but finding no one home he simply left two mackerel he had caught on a large, three-foot-high green glazed clay pot that guarded the entrance to the back door of their home. He knew my son and his wife would boil the fish (and clams) into chowder for their dinner.

Milt then walked the half mile back to his parent's home to place dinner on that table as well, but with all intentions of reporting to work as soon as possible. His parents, he found, were not home. They had just set sail for the mainland to sell two of their farm animals in New London, Connecticut.

Our responsibilities at the Weather House revolve around collecting weather data and using that information to forecast the weather. I have been allowed to provide local forecasts for about ten years, a responsibility given to few local Weather Bureau officials. We then transmit the current weather forecast to the Block Island community via weather flags, and the original data to the mainland and the main office in Washington, D.C. via the cable.

We have two other responsibilities at the Weather House, only one of which is weather related. First, in order to help tourists, and Islanders, we allow use, for a nominal fee, of our telegraphy service to communicate with those on the mainland. In the past, a significant part of the day was spent telegraphing messages to the mainland for personal and business reasons. However, now that we share the responsibility for telegraphy with the Ocean View Hotel and the Telephone Exchange, the need for this service has decreased, allowing us to spend more time on our other duties. A very important second obligation, which is weather related, is to provide brief reports to the press, such as the *New York Times* and the mainland Rhode Island papers, when the need arises. For example, when weather has impacted the course of events on or near our Island, editors of those papers routinely contact me for information that often ends up in their published stories.

I was up early at work that Saturday, changing my forecast for the weekend, when Milt interrupted me. He was not required to be at work and I was more than surprised to see him. He told me the story as it had unfolded the day before.

Milt was so nervous retelling the story that I knew there was no exaggeration in his account of what had happened. We were sitting with my two nieces in the kitchen of the Weather House, Annie in her wheelchair and Emma sitting on the floor, both focused on Mitchell's story. I was so enthralled by the story that I almost forgot my two girls were with us; I am afraid they heard things that I wished they hadn't.

When he first mentioned the three men, I thought it strange—but when I heard the part about the pistol I began worrying. Milt, being characteristically discreet, did not mention the part about the gun until the two girls had become momentarily distracted by a large schooner sailing into the inlet of the Great Salt Pond. Sailing toward the docks of the New Harbor, this fore-aft rigged ship appeared loaded with lumber. It was unusual for lumber to be brought to the New Harbor ... most loads were discharged on the other side of the Island in the Old Harbor.

From Milt's description of the gun, I thought it was a German Luger; a gun I had never seen up close before, but read about in the information bulletins of the U. S. Signal Service. It was a pistol every German officer carried into battle.

After some thought I asked Milton to take a ride out to Sandy Point and check the batteries for the telephone land cable located in our shed near the North Lighthouse. Although not yet seventeen, Milton is as reliable an assistant as I have ever hired. He has worked at the Weather House since his appointment on March 17, 1914 and I fully trusted his judgment. I remember the date but I am not sure why.

Although Sandy Point is at the other end of the Island from where Milton saw the three men, I was confident that he could check the batteries in the shed and would look around the fishing camps to see if anything unusual was happening. If new people were to blend into our Island, being temporarily employed at one of the fishing camps at the Sandy Point was a good bet.

My hunch was correct. When he returned, Milton reported the following story:

At Sandy Point, where several fishing camps continue to operate well into October, there are two government structures, the North Lighthouse and yet another U. S. Lifesaving Station. Just beyond the lifesaving station sits a third government structure, a small shack that protects the location of the submerged cable as it leaves Block Island Sound and enters the Island proper, rising from within the dunes a safe distance from the beach. The location of the small cable shack is easy to identify because that is where the telephone poles begin their long march onto the Island.

Milt was driven to Sandy Point by my brother-in-law, Arthur Ball. I had called Arthur and explained the story to him and suggested he also touch base with his cousin CC Ball who ran the general store on the Island to see if he had made the acquaintance of anyone new on the Island. I did not tell Arthur about the gun as I was not ready to share that information just yet, and although he can keep a secret, I am sure he would have mentioned that part of the story to his sister, who is, as I have already explained, my new wife.

After Arthur picked up Milton and dropped him off by the North Lighthouse, Milton said goodbye and walked out to the shack. As Milt was approaching the shed, off to his left, at a location midway between the lighthouse and the lifesaving station, appeared a man, one of the same men he had spotted on Friday! The man looked at him and instinctively Milton looked away. He continued walking out to the shack, doing his utmost to appear as if he had not noticed him. Milton was sure he was one of the "mystery men" as he called them. Leaving the beach and walking into the dunes, Milton kept his eyes on the path as he proceeded as calmly as possible to the shed.

The Block Island Weather Bureau owns and operates the telegraphic and telephonic and cable connections between Block Island and the mainland. The cables entered the Atlantic Ocean on Matunuck Beach, Rhode Island, crossed Block Island Sound, and exited the water here on Sandy Point. Hence, this shack guarded an important connection point; Both Milt and I knew that, and apparently so did that man.

Milton was now petrified. He decided he would first check the battery and cables and from his vantage point from the shed, he would then observe any and all activity at Sandy Point. If all looked calm, he would then head over to the fishing camps, passing in front of the Sandy Point Lifesaving Station to hitch a ride back to the Weather House.

When Milton reached the shack, he opened the door, went in, and quickly checked the level of the battery. He looked to see if anything had been tampered with or moved, and did not notice any disturbances. When he exited the shack and turned around, after securing the door, he looked up to see that the man was gone.

Milton was not certain where the man was; perhaps he was trying to hide in the dunes. That, Milton thought, wasn't too smart as there were frequently men moving about at the North End, with the fishing camps still active and the lighthouse keeper's family always about.

Milton saw the lighthouse keeper's wife hanging laundry on the clothesline and thought perhaps she had been noticed by the man; and that was the reason he quickly disappeared.

He did not want to complete his plan as I laid out for him, which was to make contact with the older brother of one of his friends now stationed at the Rose fishing camp. Instead, he hurried back to the road where Arthur had dropped him off thirty minutes ago, and soon caught up with the wife of one of the men in the fishing camp. Wives often drove out to the camps to visit with their husbands, usually in horse drawn carriages. Milton and the woman rode back to the beginning of Beach Street where Milton was let out; he then walked the half mile to the Weather House. He did not think he had been followed.

After Milton reviewed what had happened, I suggested that he scout out the entire Island in the morning; he would use my car, wear my cap with the broad rim and jacket to disguise himself as he looked for signs of any of the three men. Driving my car, rather than being on foot, would lessen the chances of him being seen. I was afraid now that if he would be identified again, and he clearly was identified at Sandy Point as someone who worked for the Weather House, that his life might be in danger. Although unlikely, my additional concern was that a member of the Block Island community was one of those three men; if that was the case, then my life might be in danger as well. But how to find out who they were was not going to be an easy task as Milton did not get a good look at their faces.

My son Wallace had dropped by the Weather House. After telling him the story, I asked if he would return to the west side beach where Milton had seen the "mystery men" to see if he could obtain more information. Wallace knew that area of the Island well, and knew that it was possible to land a small army there, if necessary, and not be noticed by anyone on the Island, especially in the fall or winter months.

I asked Wallace if he had seen anyone new in any of the camps recently. He didn't think so. My son was thinking out loud, "I've never seen a Luger ... the war has come to Block Island well before it has come to the mainland."

I was afraid he was right and I was now beginning to recognize that feeling of fear within myself; a feeling that starts with concern amidst uncertainty; not only the uncertainty of who the men were but the uncertainty of why they were here in the first place. Fear is not bad, not at all; it is a healthy emotion, especially when there are objects such as pistols around, and three unidentified, mysterious men.

I knew from my training in the Army that when the feeling of fear and uncertainty presented itself, in the setting of clear and present danger, it was time to try to understand what was happening. But before one reaches a full understanding of the situation, one must be kept busy. I would make sure that Milton and I, and now Wallace, would be kept busy.

I began working on a possible scenario: Could these mystery men have been involved in some way with the fire at the Hygeia? Were they the reason Sperry (who I am certain was on an assignment with our military) was near our Island last month when he landed his plane emergently at the base of the bluffs? The Hygeia Hotel fire had burned out of control. The owners of the Hygeia, the Champlin brothers, were told the fire was accidental, but could it have been arson?

I had this feeling that something else was now out of control and wondered what might be destroyed next. I was convinced of one thing— that Milton had experienced yet another event of significance on our small Island; but the question remained: "How was *this* going to cast its shadow?"

And now another questioned loomed: "Who could I trust to share this information with?" It was clear that I needed more members on our team.

But there was a more pressing issue: "Who should I be suspicious of?"

4 The Second Monday Morning of October

It is now Monday morning, the second Monday of this relatively and quite uncharacteristically mild October. I should not think like this, it goes against my training, but did the inferno that destroyed the hotel change the temperature pattern on the Island this fall? Nonsense. It may have changed the landscape but certainly not the weather.

I wasn't the only one thinking odd thoughts this morning. I could hear the two girls upstairs talking about the Luger and who was going to be shot. The girls, before and after their accident at sea, were as inquisitive and energetic as any on the Island. Fortunately, their mother was already at work and didn't hear their conversation.

Later that morning, while telegraphing the weather data to the New York Office, I made my decision who I would contact about Milton's discovery. I decided to, separately, wire Milton's story to the Brooklyn Navy Yard Weather Office using Morse code, the language of the Weather Service. This weather language broke down the wide array of weather signals into another short code, understandable to those few in our bureau. I had become so proficient in the use of the weather code that I could almost converse as if I were using a foreign language. It was in this code that I sent my query to my old colleagues at the Weather Bureau satellite office located in the Brooklyn Navy Yard.

I did not use the telephone for one very good reason: the operators in the telephone exchange would have listened in on the conversation. In the summer of 1880, when Sgt. Davis first started the Weather Station on the Island, he installed phone service to the Southeast Lighthouse so they could be notified when to raise the weather storm or warning flags on their tower. At that time, Sgt. Davis, who was my mentor, also raised the flags on Harbor Hill near the Old Harbor. Now, everyone on the

Island has phones and I raise the weather flags only on my tower, which can be seen by fisherman from both harbors equally well. The lightkeeper at the Southeast Lighthouse continues to have responsibility of raising the flags on his tower under my direction.

A few years ago, Wallace started to work the midnight shift at the Telephone Exchange for extra money. In part, through his contacts, I know the staff of that exchange very well. If he worked during the day, I would have used the phone, but not with his close friend, the young Gladys, having the day shift. It wasn't that I did not trust Gladys, just the contrary; Gladys was one of the most trustworthy and most loved young persons on the Island. My reason: I did not want her to be burdened with this type of information.

I wired instructions for the telegram that I sent to the Navy Yard Weather Office to be delivered to one of my friends in the Office of Naval Intelligence. The ONI had a small office in the New York Navy Yard, in one of the buildings near the Marine Hospital in the southeast corner of the industrial-like Navy Yard complex. The New York Navy Yard, as it is technically called, is located in Brooklyn and asks to be called the Brooklyn Navy Yard. And so I, and almost everyone else, call it that.

It wasn't long before I received a response from the Navy Yard Weather Bureau Office. I was quite surprised that the message came to me on the old Marconi Wireless device that had been installed years before and was no longer in much use. Was it the Weather Bureau staff responding, or officers in the ONI? The response was not typical of the Weather Bureau. From where the message originated was not the only question I now had. The other: Why did the message not come to me via the regular cable device or even the phone?

I would soon see how wrong I was in thinking that the transmission of data via the telephonic or telegraphic cable was indeed secure.

5 "NO ONE TO KNOW"

The wired response came in at 10:45 a.m. And other one followed at 11:00 a.m. The first response came via the cable and was generic; the second came via the wireless device and was quite a bit more graphic.

The instructions were simple, the intent clearly understood. They—and I am not sure who sent the message—were as concerned as I; and I was heartened that I had indeed made a good enough decision with whom to share my information. My fear lessened somewhat, as I had expanded my team several fold—although it would be many weeks before I truly understood how large the team had instantaneously become upon receipt of my message.

I suspected that the Navy Yard, or whatever office it was that sent the reply, was worried as well because in using the old Marconi wireless machine, they too were making sure no one could tap into the hard cable, something that was easy to do, if one knew the whereabouts of the cable boxes. They—and I suspected that to be the officers in the ONI who were using the Weather Bureaus' codes—asked me to try and determine who these men were, if possible. I was instructed to keep quiet about the transmission, including to young Milton, "No one to know..." The final message on that second transmission: "Use wireless at all times. Use cable for weather related data transmission, and for decoy only."

Prior to my being assigned to Block Island, I was stationed at the NYC Weather Bureau located at 100 Broadway, and known as '100 Broadway,' from 1904 until 1908. It is the only weather station in the United States known simply by its address. During my four years in lower Manhattan, I was occasionally reassigned temporarily to the Brooklyn Navy Yard's Weather Office. On these occasional short-term assignments, although I never worked on any ONI missions, I became friendly with a number of the Navy staff and senior officers assigned to that office.

Even after being on Block Island for the past eight years, I assumed the officers in the ONI still remembered me and would thank me for the information, albeit vague, on the three men. It is interesting that throughout my career and my work for the Weather Bureau on Block Island I never developed relationships with anyone at the Naval War College located across Block Island Sound in Newport, Rhode Island. Now with the recent report that the German U-boat had paid a friendly visit to the Naval Base in Newport, I have now another reason not to contact them about my concerns. Perhaps, because they were not part of the ONI, they would, inadvertently of course, provide information to the Germans? *No not possible*, I thought. Was Sperry working with the ONI? Yes, that was indeed probable, to my thoughts anyway.

The New York City Weather Bureau was as different an assignment as could possibly be from my current one on Block Island.

What is the difference you ask? Well, what is the difference in "going a whaling" out of Nantucket or hand lining for cod off the southeast shore of Block Island?

That NYC Weather Bureau is located on two of the highest floors of a building that at one time was the second tallest building in Manhattan. When I stand on the roof of the Weather House here, I have quite a beautiful view, but nothing like the view from the top floor of the American Surety Company building, where Weather Bureau instruments are kept, or on the roof of the building where the wind speed and direction indicators are installed.

And it was not only the view, it was the building itself. The entry doors alone to the American Surety building could very well have been taken directly from a Greek temple, and the columns surrounding the building were ionic in nature, another feature borrowed directly from the Greeks.

I would find out much later that the message I had sent earlier today was discussed with the senior leadership of the New York Weather Bureau as well as the senior ONI officers in the Navy Yard. Even my old boss was contacted immediately because a new employee at 100

Broadway had aroused the suspicions of the senior staff there. This person was a recent immigrant from Germany.

Much later I found out my message added to that concern to such a degree that the ONI contacted the Assistant Secretary for the Navy, within an hour of receiving my message, Franklin D. Roosevelt. It was common knowledge that Roosevelt, as well as most other armed forces leadership of the United States, did not agree with Wilson's neutral stance ... witness the bizarre actions of the German U-53 at the Nantucket Lightship after their "friendly" visit to the Naval War College in Newport, RI.

Why? It would be several weeks before I understood the significance, and the answer came, not from the ONI, but from someone on Block Island that I know very, very well.

But before I continue the story, I must step back and describe why there are no insignificant events on Block Island.

6 BSH vs. ASH

(Before Sheltered Harbor vs. After Sheltered Harbor)

Comparing my office in the Block Island Weather House to my old office in New York City—with its grand entrance and towering building overlooking lower Manhattan and New York Harbor and the Statue of Liberty—reminds me of the comparison between the Block Island of today with the Block Island of the last century.

S. T. Livermore wrote the first substantial history of our Island called simply, "The History of Block Island." Livermore, a Baptist minister, loved the Island and its people. In his book, he describes two Block Islands: the one he experienced in the late 1870s, and a much earlier Island; revealing how the Island, and its people, had changed.

There is no question that there was a world of difference; a comparison that can easily be explained as an Island *before a sheltered harbor of refuge* and an Island *after a sheltered harbor of refuge* (BSH vs. ASH).

After reading Livermore, it is clear that the sun shines more fully now, casting slightly fewer of those shadows on Block Island, than before the harbor of refuge was created.

I am sure the reader is aware that a topic of countless sermons, regardless of the house of worship, is the story of Jonah and the Big Fish—interpreted by some readers of the Bible as a leviathan or a whale. If there is a biblical allegory to read and learn from, Jonah isn't a bad place to start.

Any religious individual, regardless of their chosen or assigned faith, seeks to know all there is to know about obligation; about forgiveness; about God's grace; about unconditional love—for us *and* our enemies; about anger—our own and others'; and our projections of anger—toward others as well as inward to ourselves; and even about resurrection—after all, Jonah was in the whale for three days before being delivered to the safety of land.

In *Moby-Dick*, Melville devotes an entire chapter to a sermon delivered in a New Bedford Catholic Church and, of course, Jonah and the whale play a large role. Livermore also references the story of Jonah when describing the Block Island of today, the one with a "sheltered harbor of refuge"—the term used by the Army Corps of Engineers.

Before a sheltered harbor existed on our Island, the simple landing of a boat in a storm, any and every boat, was an event that had tremendous significance. With success or failure, the event always led to *living another day* vs. *death by drowning*. Talk about fear.

There is no better way to explain this than by retelling an account from Livermore. First, to set the stage, Livermore quotes from the honorable State Senator Mr. Nicholas Ball from a speech he gave to the public: "Let us see what has been done for us on this Island: The [federal] government has appropriated the sum of $265,000 for a harbor at Block Island... I have not time to enumerate the benefits afforded by the works thus paid for ... to every family upon the Island. ... considering the former risk in bringing it [fish, consumer goods] in open boats, liable to get wet on the passage; and on all our imports, the gain is in proportion to the above. .... Add to the above that the fisherman formerly caught three quintals of codfish; they get five quintals now, the fish, of course, to be as plenty in one case as in the other. Our mail comes to us now three times a week instead of once, as formerly."

And then Livermore picks up the story himself of the landing of the famous Block Island fishing boats, the *Double Enders*, and I quote directly from his book: "The greatest of all material improvements on Block Island, indeed, the mother of all others, has been the convenience of landing secured here by the construction of the Government Harbor of Refuge.

"As evidence of this, consider the following contrast: Previous to the harbor, behold that cloud coming swiftly, darkening, and accompanied by a sudden roughness of the sea that puts the fisherman's boat into great peril. He hastens from the bank homeward, but before he reaches the bay, his frail masts can hardly weather the gale. By the most skillful exertions, he skims over the enormous waves until he has neared the old landing place, but there he sees the waters leaping upon the shore and gliding back in such fury as to threaten his open boat with sinking. He dares not attempt to land. His kindred stand upon the shore in dismay. The boat is tacked this way and that way, while its inmates are pumping and bailing for their lives, and liable to be sunk any instant, while the gale increases in fury and the waves toss, dash against, and into the boat so as to make death by drowning seem inevitable. Then, in the moment of desperation, they hear the captain say: 'Boys, we shall be drowned if we stay here, so we may as well take our chances going ashore!' The vessel is now seen headed for the landing. Rapidly she glides to safety or to destruction. Eyes upon the shore fill with tears, lips quiver, and in agony, friends interpret the fearful crisis.

"There is just one way, and *only* one in which it is possible for that boat and crew to land in safety, and to escape immediate destruction. She must ride upon the shoulders of the largest of 'three brothers'—the wave that will carry her so high upon the shore that the next wave will not reach her, and thus afford the crew a moment in which to escape.

"'Steady! Steady! Not too fast,' says an old sailor on the shore.

"For if the boat gets too far upon said 'brother's' shoulders she will pitch over and be buried in an instant. Neither must the boat lag behind his shoulders, for if she does the receding wave will swamp her. Her sail is raised or lowered, by the inch, to keep balanced on that giant wave.

"'She rides! She rides!' says another, while others stand in breathless silence, and the critical instant of life or death hastens—the great wave breaks upon the shore amid the howling winds— the fisherman's boat is left there, and the crew are saved, while the 'big brother' retires to the deep, like the whale that landed Jonah.

"Such for scores of years, had been the perilous landing, at many times, on Block Island."

And there are many hundreds if not thousands of other accounts of crossing Block Island Sound from the mainland, passages that have taken over twelve hours, from Point Judith to the Old Harbor area during rough seas. The number of fisherman in peril has not been documented but the Island cemetery records those who perished while attempting to land in the days BSH.

After our sheltered harbor was constructed from granite brought in from the mainland, things changed. Arriving on Block Island ASH was no longer a potentially life-threatening experience.

Livermore's poetic language continues: "Now the boats are more safe in *going to a distance*, for if a storm arises they fly to the Harbor like doves to their windows, and such joyful expressions as have been seen there no pen can describe, as the frail boats have reached the quiet water and anchored, or tied up, in safety. There too, the steamboat moors at the wharf, and thousands visit the Island now, instead of the occasional stranger in years previous to the Harbor."

Oh, if only the Government Harbor had been constructed in Melville's time.

When the seas around Block Island are calm, when those moving weather formations are gentle upon the surface of the ocean, a safe landing can be made by anyone, anywhere on the Island— especially the west side beaches.

If those three men had landed on the most secluded part of the Island, where was their boat?

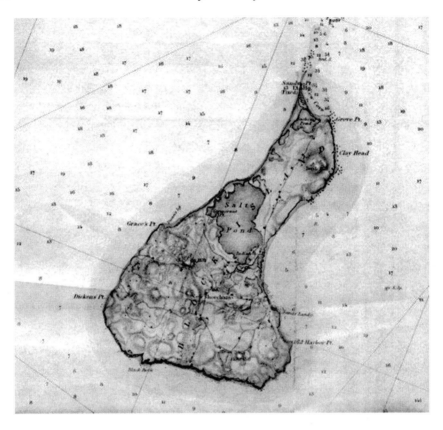

Block Island in 1857, before harbors of refuge.

7 Hiring Milton, Hiring his Ancestors

When I hired Milt two years ago to help run errands at the Weather Bureau, he had just turned fifteen. The job I offered him paid a little over $500.00 a year. He was my mother-in-law's grandnephew but was also the best friend of Wallace's youngest brother-in-law, James. Most everyone on Block Island was related to someone else on the Island—a consequence, I am sure, of being isolated from the mainland for so long.

For example, my wife's father was descended from four of the earliest settlers of the Island who settled here as far back as 1661 or 1662. And my wife's mother, Bersheba Mitchell, descends from settlers who arrived in the 1670s as well as some of the earlier settlers just mentioned. Before he died, my father-in-law once mentioned that my wife had about seventy-five direct sets of grandparents buried in the Island Cemetery. And that's just grandparents, not aunts and uncles or cousins. If you add in the aunts and uncles and the first and second cousins, God knows how many dead relatives are buried in there—perhaps just about everyone!

So as you can imagine I was well acquainted with Milton and his family and his ancestors because they were "my family" as well. He was a good youngster and as far as I could tell, a good son as well. He has done a great job at the Weather House. He never wanted to sit still, unless he was excited about something, something that really interested him. He wanted to be busy, to always do something, even if nothing needed to be accomplished. This was a great trait to have when one was fearful ... staying busy was natural for him.

In many ways Milton was like Wallace (especially when he was young). But Milt was more social, more outgoing than Wallace; who was at times quiet and withdrawn, not prone to seeking the attention of large numbers of people, but very, very personable with small groups of people. When the raconteur, the story telling aspects of Wallace was able to be expressed, for example in those small groups, he was at his liveliest. On the other hand, Milton was not a storyteller, in either small or large groups; he was far more social in a casual sense.

As one might expect, Wallace never expressed an interest in enlisting in the Army. And on the other hand, Milton did express an interest in enlisting if the United States was eventually to enter the war. He would have to wait until he turned eighteen before he could enlist, yet it appeared to me that in some small way his working for the U. S. Weather Bureau was one step in that direction. I could see his curiosity about those three men was more than just a passing interest; he was driven, as I am, to determine what their presence on our Island means.

The Great War, or the Great European War, as we are now starting to refer to it, has been underway for a few years. My contacts in NYC have been concerned about German submarines along the eastern seaboard and they have asked me to send reports of sightings of the U-boats to them immediately. When I was sure I had seen submarines off Block Island, I transmitted my findings to that office using the Weather Bureau wireless device picked up by the large antennae on Montauk Point.

Was there a connection between the three men and the German submarines? Did Milton first see the men as one or more of them walked the shore after being let out by a U-boat. The idea crossed my mind now for the first time; but as I later found out, it was the first thought in the minds of the officers of the ONI when they were handed my message by my old colleagues at the Weather Bureau.

I wanted to call my oldest sister's husband in NYC to review the events of the past several days with him, but I had to wait until the Telephone Exchange was manned by Wallace. I got along well with my brother-in-law, and many years ago convinced him to vacation on the Island, which he did by renting a small home next to the Union House Hotel. Late last night I finally had a conversation with George Weller that was both revealing and disturbing.

8 Contacts

In addition to my contacts in the Navy Yard as well as my colleagues at 100 Broadway, my sister Catherine's husband has proven to have a great deal of insight. George Weller, a lawyer, used to work for the NYC Department of the Docks and is a member of Tammany Hall. George has recently been appointed a judge in the Federal Customs Court located in lower Manhattan. My sister and her husband live on the upper west side of Manhattan on Convent Street. Their son, Royal, also a lawyer, is very interested in politics and is hopeful one day in the not too distant future, to be elected to the U. S. House of Representatives. Occasionally, they phone me with details about events before they are announced publicly, which is how I found out about the Navy's concerns about U-boat activity in Block Island Sound.

Since the accident at sea, my sister and brother-in-law have called more frequently to ask about the girls. Of all my siblings, Catherine and her husband are most worried about them. Perhaps on these frequent phone calls George has shared too much with me about the government's concerns, but he knows I keep all information confidential. For me, the trait of 'never repeating information' comes quite naturally.

George had explained to me that as of 1916 all of the major navies of the world have some form of submarine in their arsenal, yet each are trying to determine the best use of these submersibles; which is to say that their ultimate use by each respective Navy is still evolving. The Office of Naval Intelligence had discovered, mostly through British intelligence, the newer German submarines, the larger U-boats, were faster than any other submarines now in existence. And, they had further determined that some were equipped with the new torpedoes, whereas some of the smaller U-boats were known for their ability to lay mines in deep or shallow water including rivers. The newer, longer U-boats were known to have the capability to launch powerful and more accurate torpedoes, and a shuddering thought: these newer torpedoes were also believed to have sea to air capabilities.

In an earlier phone conversation with my brother-in-law, I was told that Franklin D. Roosevelt was especially concerned about the German submarines and the damage the mines and, yes, the new torpedoes, could do to our shipping lanes as well as to structures on or near the shores of rivers and our mainland.

When I heard about the sinking of the foreign vessels near the Nantucket Lightship, I was surprised, but it did all make sense, thanks to my brother-in-law's information. George was an acquaintance of Roosevelt, the source, perhaps, of some of his information.

From the time he was appointed in 1913, Roosevelt had been given wide latitude by President Wilson, a rare occurrence with Wilson, a man known for his heavy hand and rigid approach to decision making. George explained to me that Roosevelt, very quickly after being appointed to the post, became fascinated with intelligence and the ONI and has supported and argued for its growth. And in addition, he had tremendous authority because his boss, a political appointee of Wilson, deferred on many decisions to the young Roosevelt.

Our Navy has small submarines, they are slow and a third of the size of the newer German U-boats; and our torpedoes, though self-propelled, are not as powerful as the German torpedoes. Most submarines, ours and theirs, are also outfitted with one or two surface mounted deck guns. It was the deck guns that I have spotted off the coast of Block Island in the recent past—but I could not tell if they were ours, or the German subs. Routinely, I would wirelessly contact the ONI whenever I spotted mounted guns.

For centuries Block Island has been a landmark for vessels sailing from Europe. And now it must certainly be a landmark for the German submarines as well. Our Island, a mere three and one half miles wide by about seven miles long has been on all charts of this part of the world since the 1500s, if not before. It is there for all to see who have the courage to cross the Atlantic Ocean. It is not too surprising that European sailors have long stated they prefer "coming out of the sea at

Block Island" when they approach the northeastern part of the United States. The imposing light colored sandy and clay mixture of the Mohegan Bluffs are easy to see, as long as the bluffs are not shrouded in fog. Ships coming out of the sea at Block Island would then be able to sail northeast to Boston or south to NYC or Perth Amboy. With the southeast part of the Island having the Southeast Lighthouse to guide them, "coming out of the sea at Block Island" for friendly Europeans *and* hostile Germans was now easier than ever before. And to think, Melville did not even know about my Island.

9 The Marconi Device

Since the early 1900s the Block Island Weather Bureau has housed the Marconi wireless telegraphic equipment—essential for contacting passing merchant or naval ships. In fact, my station was one of the first to be so equipped, due to our strategic location in the Atlantic Ocean between NYC and Boston. Only four other stations were given the Marconi device at that time.

A year after I was reassigned to the Block Island station, I received a fair amount of notoriety because I was the first to "hear" the wireless distress signal from the *Republic* as it sank fifty miles southwest of Nantucket. That was in the winter of 1909 and represented the first time wireless communication was used in the United States for a rescue at sea.

Unfortunately, when I received that wireless communication all I could do was alert the Naval War College and the U. S. Revenue Cutter Service in Newport, and ... I did that by phone. It is not the purpose of this story but if we'd had Cutters assigned to Block Island, or even Point Judith, perhaps a faster rescue of the *Republic* would have occurred. The decision to create a safe, 'harbor of refuge' in Point Judith was a direct result of the sinking.

Were the Germans aware of the potential importance of the location of Block Island if they were to invade our country? Any German would only have to read Livermore's book on Block Island to have learned that in each war our nation has been engaged, some strategic significance, for foreign countries, has come from its location. But exactly how the German's would use the Island to their advantage in this war was difficult for me to fathom.

Over the years I would occasionally pick up wireless transmissions on the Marconi that I suspected originated from the famous Nauen wireless transmitter, located thirty or so miles northwest of Berlin. These transmissions were almost always in code and I was rarely able to decipher them, although some of Nauen's communications to German ships at sea could be understood because of the context.

For some reason I did not think it strange that our wireless communications did not contain any German numerical code, but I should have.

10 Neutrality

Although President Wilson had professed neutrality during the early years of the Great War, it was common knowledge in the military that war with Germany was around the corner. I even had advance knowledge that the War College in Newport was considering the establishment of a contact naval base in the New Harbor, in direct view of the Weather House, if the U. S. entered the war.

I know it has not been proven, but I cannot help myself from asking the question: "Would more hotels on the Island, that could potentially house sailors at a time of war, be burned?"

It is not a pleasant prospect to imagine, but I am beginning to feel that this war is yet another of those events completely out of one's control. Like the death of my first wife Nellie, or the death of Lillie's husband Samuel and her only son. Or the death of Nellie and Lillie's oldest brother Erwin, who was either killed or drowned while on an expedition to South America in the late 1880s.

And of course and most certainly, the near death of both Annie Rose and Emma Rose belong in the category of events that I refer to as "shadows cast by the sun."

How does one deal with that which is out of our control? How do we deal with days or weeks when the sun casts particularly long shadows?

The Church, and faith along with prayer, perhaps is one way to deal with this reality. Perhaps, just as it is in the sun to occasionally cast that long shadow, it is just in us to carry on; as Gilgamesh finds in his epic of life, as long as we do not give up, we can carry on. Gilgamesh was written when families were large ... although most children were dead before they were teenagers, and the few survivors rarely lived to be greater than thirty or forty. Carry on we must, that is the lesson I suppose of Gilgamesh, perhaps that is faith stated in another way. It is a good life—if you don't weaken—and certainly faith and prayer and the ability to just carry on, can provide strength to help one stay strong. If what I have just written is true and indeed is helpful for those who are still living, then how does that help those who die, at sea or in war, from infection or accidents, or for whatever reason?

Is it the memory of those who die, that lives on in us all, that helps those who die? Or is that just solace? Are we responsible to give the lives of those we know and love a life using our memory? Is that an obligation we have, and does it serve a useful purpose? I do not know.

Of all my uncertainties, of one thing I am certain: Islanders, even today, do not need a war to ask the important questions of life.

W*hy*?

Because all day-to-day events on this Island have significance; Islanders have historically been confronted with loss more frequently than others have. The weather, natural enough (so different from war), takes its revenge on Islanders in insidious ways. I cannot write well enough to describe what an Islander feels when another Islander dies, either on the Island or at sea. A sick, awful feeling deep from within comes readily to the surface, as if one is experiencing the opening of death's door oneself.

Since moving to the Island in the late 1880s (my first assignment to the Block Island station) I have felt that 'door opening' more times than I want to admit—and none more painful than when the two girls nearly drowned.

11 Coming Out of the Sea at Block Island

In centuries past, a captain of a ship sailing from Europe and coming out of the sea at Block Island would see a short, thin land mass characterized by tall, white bluffs sandwiched between the dark green vegetation above and the dark blue of the ocean below, and easily identify it as our Island. In some places, as they sailed closer, they would see the green vegetation descending halfway to the surf, a consequence of erosion of those bluffs.

If the ship came out of the sea at Block Island after 1875 it would be greeted by the majestic red brick Southeast Lighthouse resting on top of those bluffs, towering almost two hundred feet above the surf below.

The Mohegan Bluffs are indeed beautiful, from the Island or the open ocean. Sand and hard clay, eroding ever so slightly, exposing those glacial erratics; every day receding, losing land to the sea on one shore, but gaining it on the opposite end of the Island. Block Island: eroding and slowly moving north.

Recently, Wallace had moved into his partially built home on the Mohegan Bluffs. I decided to visit with him for dinner to ask him if he had seen any men, resembling the ones Milt had seen, walking the bluffs or the beach below his home. My son Wallace had a very good understanding of the Island and its fisherman, its merchants, its farmers, and its history. If anything was new, I suspect he would already know about it, and if he did not know about it, then that would have meaning also.

I wanted to test my theory on Wallace that the three men, or perhaps one or two of them, had come out of the sea at Block Island from a German U-boat.

Wallace had just completed building the exterior of his small two-story home out of wood salvaged from a dismantled smaller home, as well as the occasional lumber hauled from the sea. Using the family name, he called his home, "Eddey's Shanty;" he had the words printed in block letters and placed inside a porthole. He then mounted this porthole to the front of his home.

The view from his property overlooked the Atlantic Ocean, and if the world were flat, Wallace would be able to see Spain. His small house, and two barns—one in the front of his house and one in the back facing the Ocean—sat on almost twenty acres of land that had been given to him and his wife by Edith's father. Edith's father also owned the Murray Farm, land that sat adjacent to the large Vaill Hotel. Wallace loved the idea that when those sailors from Europe "came out of the sea at Block Island" they would be looking directly at his little home, if they could spot it through the fog.

Besides being a fisherman, Wallace was a jack-of-all-trades, drank a bit too much for my liking, and did all sorts of jobs to make a living. He was busy, doing different things; always busy, a great trait, as I have already mentioned, when fear is present. Helping here and there when necessary, drinking here and there when not so necessary.

A few years ago, he had secured a job as a part-time caretaker for a summer resident, a Judge who lived near his father-in-law's farm, and whom he became quite friendly. That house was on the bluffs also, but farther west, down toward Black Rock, and I knew that he would often walk the top of the bluffs, along Snake Hole Road, to the judge's house from time to time to check on it.

I fully expected Wallace would have noticed if any strangers were on his side of the Island.

Except for the judge's summer house, Wallace's small home, barn—and wooden outhouse—and the Vaill Hotel, there wasn't much else overlooking the bluffs on this part of the Island. I don't think I could live up there, but Wallace and Edith loved the peace and quiet. Except for their own voices, the only other sounds available to them was the surf one hundred and fifty feet below, the wind, and the occasional squawking of seagulls from above.

After I telegraphed the afternoon weather data that Milton and I had collected from the Weather House instruments, I noticed Mr. Champlin, the owner of the Hygeia Hotel, standing in the street in front of the Weather House. In a daze and appearing not to comprehend where he was, he didn't seem to notice as I walked out of my office to say hello. He continued to stare at the stone foundation of his Hotel. When I reached him I shook his hand and said, once again, how sorry I was for his loss. He nodded a gesture of thanks.

Together we walked down Beach Street closer to the burned ruins. His sadness was palpable. I knew he did not have the money to rebuild the hotel that he and his brother had purchased and recently expanded. I hadn't walked the grounds of the site in a few weeks and took this opportunity to view the remaining foundation of stones with him. The burned carcass of an old and stately hotel, now nothing more than ash and stone and charred wood, more charcoal than anything, lay under our feet.

Mr. Champlin reviewed with me what he knew about the fire. First, a cause for the fire had yet to be determined. It started late at night, on the roof possibly, and was first reported by a guest from New Jersey. The fire spread so quickly that nothing in the office was saved. The guest list was destroyed and there were no copies, so he was not sure of the name of the guest from New Jersey. He was sure, however, that the police had questioned the man at length. Of that I was not so sure.

The Champlin brothers often took photographs of their beautiful hotel from the roof of my Weather House. They even used data on Block Island weather and trends when advertising their hotel; data that I would collect for them. I always saved his Hotel's brochures and submitted them to the Weather Bureau as part of my annual reports.

When the hotel burned, we were all devastated for the loss of the building, and his livelihood; and devastated for what it took from the two brothers' hearts and souls. Fortunately, there were no serious injuries.

After about thirty minutes of talking, I asked him if he would drive me to Wallace's house, as I did not want to drive my car; that way I could continue the conversation that he clearly did not want to end. I used the excuse that my car had become quite noisy lately. My other reason for asking for the ride was that I did not want anyone, *anyone* meaning any of those three men, to think I had left the Weather House, even if it was just to visit with my son.

Something on the Island just was not right, and I was now becoming more and more convinced that what Milton had witnessed while he was fishing the other day was essential to understand. The suspicious fire (in my mind anyway); the landing of the Sperry plane last month might very well indeed have been a true accident. But I now doubted it. The three men were not at all an accident.

12 Eddey's Shanty

When Champlin dropped me off at Wallace's home I thanked him but stood by the side of the car while he continued to speak of his loss. The anguish on his face was so heart wrenching that it was as if he had lost a member of his family. I listened patiently for a few more minutes and then, when he was ready, we said goodbye and he drove off.

On the southeastern side of the house was Wallace's "front" door, even though it could only be reached by walking around to the back of the house. His real front door, the one on the front of the house that faced due west, was actually on the second story of his home and was never used. Why he built it like that I don't know; I asked him once but never got a straight answer.

I knocked on the door but no one answered. I didn't hear anyone inside so I stepped around and looked into the house from one of the back windows. His house, covered in cedar shingles painted bright white, had dark green trim to accent the windows as well as the roofline and the sides of the house. He and Edith both favored dark green.

Their two small barns were painted the same way but the outhouse remained unpainted. I never asked him why it was left bare. Most Islanders painted their outhouses, and decorated them with wooden cutouts of the moon or fish or lobster.

In the front where the nameplate "Eddey's Shanty" hung, Edith planted large clumps of beach roses. And she added those large bushes that bloomed with large purple flowers every spring … that I keep forgetting the name of … they grow wild on the bluffs just like the beach roses. Neither is harmed by the winds that often blanketed this area of the Island.

I thought it strange that I didn't hear anyone; Edith was almost always home, and if she wasn't there my son usually was home or doing something nearby.

I turned and walked toward the back of the property which faced the Atlantic Ocean. The weather was clear and you could see for miles. Off to the right was Montauk Point, the tip of Long Island eighteen miles away. It stood out clearly now, without a cloud in the sky. I stood looking at this view which went on for miles. If any of those ships sailing from Europe were coming out of the sea now, I would be staring directly at them, and they at me. But for now the view only contained small fishing smacks along with a few motor vessels, looking much smaller from my vantage point on the bluffs than they truly were.

I walked over to their well, where Wallace had installed a water pump, to have a drink. Oddly enough he did not have a difficult time securing water, even though he was close to the edge of the cliffs. All of a sudden, I was startled to see my son pop out of the outhouse. He banged the wooden door wide open. He had probably seen me walk onto his property through the cracks in the outhouse and quickly finished up his business. Although he had running water and a toilet inside, my son preferred his outhouse, even in the winter.

"Hey, Pop, what brings you up here?"

"Where's Edith?" I responded, still a bit startled by his abrupt exit from the outhouse. And then I added, just because I was annoyed with him scaring the hell out of me, "And when are you going to paint that outhouse?"

Shrugging his shoulders at my second question, he answered my first: "Over at the Vaill Hotel, visiting a guest I think."

The Vaill was a large hotel that had the only golf course on the Island. Although Wallace's property was adjacent to the hotel, the hotel itself was about a half mile away. It too overlooked the Atlantic from its perch one hundred and fifty feet above the bluffs.

We walked over to the edge of the bluffs and looked down to the sea as I asked him the same questions I had asked him previously, "Have you seen anyone new on his side of the Island?"

"No, I haven't seen anyone strange over here, but Edith's younger brother James thought he saw someone last week at the ferry that he had not previously recognized, so there is at least one person unknown to us. Do you want me to talk to him?"

"No, that's okay." I waved him off. I knew my son would have some information, even if it wasn't specifically about what I was asking.

He understood enough not to question me. "The wireless telegraphy that I received stressed that I am not to tell anyone about this—even to Milt—so you cannot say anything at all."

Wallace must have been thinking the same thing as he said softly, "I hope he did not tell James. Milt left a large mackerel for us last Friday. I suppose that was when he saw those men." I nodded in agreement.

We went inside his small home and waited for Edith to return before we ate the thick clam chowder that he had prepared earlier in the day. Clamming was plentiful all over the Island. Wallace had his favorite spot in the Great Salt Pond to clam, not too far from where the channel opened into the sea. Clam and fish chowder is served as a staple in many Island homes, especially those with cows to provide the milk base. Wallace didn't have a cow but he had access to milk from the Murray Farm.

Soon Edith walked home. She had indeed been at the Vaill, doing some sewing for the owner. We sat and had idle talk; we did not burden Edith with all of the details about the three mysterious men, except to mention that they may be potentially dangerous. Edith was not one to keep a secret.

I decided to walk over to the Vaill Hotel to hitch a ride home, so after dinner I said goodbye to my son and Edith, thanked them for the meal, and proceeded down the road. I walked slowly, no cars passed; it was late in the season so only a few guests would still be at the hotel. I thought that I would be able to find someone at the Vaill who would be able to drive me to town, with either a horse and buggy or a car. I also thought I would look around and talk to the owner to see if he had seen anything, or anyone, unusual in the past few days. I would also see if any of the few remaining guests matched the vague description of the three men. The Vaill had, like all the large hotels on the Island, a large common room where guests sat and read or talked to one another.

After I had walked about halfway to the hotel, I heard footsteps running up from behind. I was a bit scared. All sorts of things went through my head. At first, I didn't know what *the* footsteps were. *Possibly distant gunfire?* I thought. When I turned my head I saw that it was Wallace. He gave me a bit of a fright but I did not tell him I thought his footsteps sounded like distant artillery.

I was relieved it was him and did not protest. "Edith was falling asleep, moments after you left, so I thought that I would join you," he stated.

I was on edge but I was keeping that from my son. One of the basic strategies of dealing with fear is to try to keep others from experiencing your fear. Wallace and I walked the remaining quarter mile to the Vaill Hotel in silence; we had a mission, we were looking for the owner and any guests that might be outside. Wallace knew the owners of the Vaill Hotel very well; he often entertained the guests by dressing up as a sailor and telling them nautical stories. This was where he developed his reputation as being a storyteller and he was, by all accounts, a first class raconteur; and many a guest will never forget the stories he has told. Even after all these years, I love to listen to Wallace as he tells his stories of the sea, some factual, most not.

We walked into the main office of the hotel only to find the door opened and the office deserted. No one was around. We thought that that was strange and walked over to the three story main building that looked like a vastly oversized barn. One could actually see guests in their rooms since the curtains on the windows were lace, something of a tradition on the Island, as if all hotel owners imported lace from the Venetian island of Burano.

As we approached we heard a loud noise, a small explosion coming from behind us. After nearly jumping out of our skins, we realized that a car had backfired.

When we turned around the car was driving toward us, picking up speed as it approached. We jumped out of the way as the car sped past us; quickly turning around before exiting the grounds of the hotel on the same dirt road it had entered the property. It was dusk and not enough light for us to see the driver's face clearly. Was he really trying to hit my son and me?

Now I was more than on edge. But how could anyone have known that we were looking for those three men? We hadn't mentioned it to anyone, unless Milton or Arthur or CC Ball had spoken to someone on the Island already. Certainly those in the Brooklyn Navy Yard would not have told anyone on the Island. Or had they?

We couldn't find the owner, so Wallace, a little taken aback and now concerned that Edith was alone, quickly ran home. I walked in the opposite direction the three miles to my wife's home on High Street. Even though Wallace and I had cars, we often walked the four-by-seven-mile Island just like I walked the streets of New York when we lived there. I once walked the length of Manhattan, which is almost fourteen miles long, just after my father built a house on Marble Hill at the northern tip of Manhattan, but that is another story.

Now there were two additional questions I needed to answer: Who was that driver? And could it be possible that there were people besides the intended recipient of my cable messages who were now aware of who I was and what I had uncovered? If there were others that knew about those messages, then those people certainly knew that they originated from the Weather House on Block Island, and if that were the case, they now knew a lot more than I wanted them to know.

13 Payne Road

Under the circumstances, walking up and then down the very empty Payne Road on my way to High Street at night was a bit eerie; it was also a bit dusty, but there was no way a stranger to the Island would even know that this was a shortcut to High Street and the Old Harbor; or to anywhere else for that matter. It was a mile and a quarter long, with only a few buildings scattered along its path. One of those buildings was a one-room schoolhouse set down in a gully.

Payne's road reached the second highest point on the Island before descending into the Old Harbor Village by way of High Street. Sometimes there is safety in numbers, but on this road there is safety by its very nature of being an isolated, spooky and dusty road; a road occasionally traveled, and rarely walked, by people who even lived on the Island. On Payne Road, one felt alone yet quite safe.

Both Lillie and Nellie grew up on High Street, just a few minutes' walk from the ferry landing in the Old Harbor, in the house that their father built. Although Lillie and I were recently married, we often stayed in our separate homes, she on High Street and I in the U. S. Weather House on Beach Avenue. She—mere steps away from the Old Harbor on the east side of the Island and I—steps away from the New Harbor on the northwest side.

The reason we continued to stay in separate homes, at least during the week, was because of her daughter's condition and the close proximity of the school located on High Street. Annie Rose was disabled and needed a wheelchair to get about. Close to her school and the shops in the Old Harbor, that location was easier for Annie Rose and her sister, Emma Rose, to do more things on their own. The area around the Old Harbor, a few minutes' walk from Lillie's home on High Street, was now becoming more the commercial center of the Island than the Old Town Center.

Lillie and I stayed apart no more than two or three nights per week. Second marriages are like that I guess, although Annie's disability was the major deciding factor in our decision to keep both households.

Because Block Island had few trees, it was an easy reach from her front window to the roof of the Weather House across the Island. When I stood on the roof of the Weather House where some of the instruments were placed, I could see Lillie's home, and even her silhouette if the light in her bedroom was on.

It was a long walk along Payne Road and down High Street, but the moon was up and almost full; the weather crisp, but by no means cold, on this early October evening. Occasionally on the Island, in October, the weather was just grand and tonight was one of those nights. Although there was no aurora present tonight, countless stars lit up the night. Just off the horizon, as they often are in the fall, sat the wonderfully easy to identify constellations we know as Ursa Minor and Ursa Major, the little and big dipper. Mars was also quite visible. The night sky here was certainly better to appreciate than the night sky of Manhattan, even from the roof of 100 Broadway.

With darkness came a sense of serenity. I wasn't really alone on this walk home, it was a calmness that had come over me, a sense of security or safety out alone on this dirt road that almost no one traveled even in the day. I did have the fleeting thought that this was only the calm before the storm however.

It took me about twenty-five minutes to reach the end of Payne Road. I then turned left and started the long walk down High Street. There were many more houses and small buildings on High Street which descends down to the Old Harbor. Some say High Street ends at the docks, but I think it ends about one hundred yards before one reaches the wharf, at Rebecca's, the statue of a woman thought to represent women's suffrage. This statue was placed there by CC Ball's wife to mark the right of women to vote. Regardless of where High Street ends, about a quarter of a mile before it, and fifty yards before Lillie's house, stands the Masonic Hall.

I stopped and walked into the hall to see who was up this late at night. At the hall I was looking for Block Island's one and only constable, who was, as I suspected, at his usual chair next to the fireplace drinking his whiskey. Block Island never had police of any kind until recently. I told him about the driver of the vehicle at the Vaill that appeared to have driven a bit too close to Wallace and me. I did not mention anything about the three men on the beach because he could not be trusted, but I did mention that the driver of the car was a tall thin man dressed well, not that I saw him, but I thought I would use the description of one of the three men on the beach when I told him the story. He would never know what I was talking about so I thought it okay to fib a little in this instance. When I said I couldn't trust him, I was not referring to his integrity, no, not at all. He was a very good man, I simply did not believe he could do much with the information, and hence I did not want to share the entire story. For him to know just a little piece of the story was probably best.

I wasn't sure if he comprehended me at all, for he didn't even ask if I got the license plate number, which of course I didn't due to the relative darkness and the fact that the driver hadn't turned his lights on. I thanked him for his time and hoped that he wasn't too drunk to remember at least some of what I'd told him. I then left the building, crossed the street, and walked the rest of the way to Lillie's house.

Lillie was surprised that I was at her front door, especially without my car; but happily surprised.

"Why are you so dusty?" she said, reaching out with her hand to help brush me off.

"Long story. I have been waiting to tell you about this. Where are the girls?" I did not want to tell the story with the girls listening.

"Next door at the Union House. They are playing games with some of the workers," Lillie added. "Now, please tell me why you are so dusty and where is your car?"

I sat down but before I could start my story Arthur walked in the door.

Lillie's older brother, Arthur, still lived in the house his father built along with Lillie and the girls. It was Lillie and the two girls who had moved back to the family house after Lillie's first husband died in a fishing accident; his death was soon followed by another tragic death, that of her only son. Arthur was divorced, his ex-wife living on the mainland, so he enjoyed the company of his sister and his two nieces.

He continued to operate the Union House Hotel when his father died a little over ten years ago. Recently, however, Arthur was having difficulty with the business and was planning on selling the business to the quite successful Manisees Hotel. The owners of the Manisees had expressed possible interest in using the Union House as an annex for their large hotel and to provide rooms for their workers. The Union House also had access to a very productive well—one with the highest flow rate of any on the Island—that could provide endless water to launder the Manisees' sheets and towels.

"Where's your car, George?" she asked. "I didn't hear you drive up."

"I left it at the Weather House."

"Who gave you the ride over?" she continued to ask as I continued to be evasive.

Arthur began a conversation about the hotel. I sat and listened, partly to change the subject of where I had been and partly because Arthur clearly wanted, or rather needed to talk to someone. He was in financial debt and was worried about his ability to sell his late father's hotel for a decent price. It was closing for the season, with only two or three guests, and these for only a few more days. Except for the Ocean View and Manisees, gone were the days when the hotels on the Island were full, especially this late in the season.

We talked about the details of running the hotel, from collecting money from the guests to doing the laundry. He eventually got around to asking my opinion on selling the hotel. I did not know what he should do. None of it was easy and I was once and foremost quite satisfied with my career as a meteorologist with the U. S. Weather Bureau. Even though I did not make as much money, I was content. It takes a special kind of approach to life when operating a business—especially a seasonal one—that I gathered from my conversations with Arthur as well as my late father-in-law.

Arthur argued that if the United States entered the war, tourism would fall off dramatically: "Who would want to take a ferry out to the Island, with U-boats possibly patrolling the surrounding waters?"

At that point in the conversation, I realized that I had not answered Lillie when she asked why I was so dusty. When she came back into the room and wondered aloud where the girls were, I knew that I would have more time before I needed to tell my story.

"I saw them in the afternoon in front of the Weather House," Arthur said.

Lillie asked her brother if he would go try to find them. Arthur left to retrieve them as Lillie sat down to wait for the answers to her questions.

As I started to tell Lillie about the three mysterious men, we heard the laughter of her two daughters. One laugh was robust and carried well through the night air. The other, although of equal joyful feeling, was more drawn out, a harsh squeal sound, almost gasping and perhaps to many, unintelligible. The first laugh was Emma's. The second laugh perhaps unintelligible to some, yet easily recognizable to Islanders, belonged to Annie Rose.

Old Harbor Village, c 1910.
The Union House Hotel is on the left with the mansard roof.

14 The Two Girls

First, about their names. Lillie's husband Earl's last name was Rose. As time went on, Islanders and family alike started to refer to the girls as if the two names were one: Annie-Rose and Emma-Rose. When I married Lillie, they decided to keep their own last names and the first-last name combination stuck.

The two girls were always close, just like their names would imply. But they had become absolutely inseparable since the accident in the waters off the Mohegan Bluffs two springs past. They were also close in age—Annie sixteen and Emma nearly fourteen—as well as temperament; shared many interests, were good friends, yet had their own friends as well. I suppose the only thing they differed substantially in was their height: Annie was five feet ten inches tall with a powerful build—for a young girl anyway; Emma was five feet and barely an inch tall. She was not only shorter but was also somewhat smaller in frame. Why there was such a discrepancy in their heights and builds and no such discrepancy in their personalities, or their souls, well … that was well beyond my comprehension.

After the accident, as before the accident, the two sisters shared the same bed, "a cosy, loving pair."

Melville: *How it is I know not; but there is no place like a bed for confidential disclosures between friends. Man and wife, they say, there open the very bottom of their souls to each other; and some old couples often lie and chat over old times till nearly morning. Thus, then, in our hearts' honeymoon, lay I and Queequeg—a cosy, loving pair.*

I don't know that this was the best quote to begin explaining the relationship between the two girls but it seemed to fit. The one difference between Ishmael and Queequeg and the two sisters was that the two girls had been sleeping together since the time Emma was about one year old.

Every night, without exception, except for the times when one of them, or both, were ill—such as when, of course, Annie was recuperating from the accident—or they were separated by the nature of travel to and from the mainland.

The two confessed to each other, revealed to each other, explored with each other any number of things, perhaps all things; before, as well as after, the accident—confidential disclosures between friends. What I found remarkable was that they were able to expand their own happiness twofold, or greater, by sharing with each other. And also, and perhaps most importantly, they were able to dim the pain of any setback or disappointments by half or greater, when those disappointments did invariably occur.

I, and others as well, saw this friendship blossoming years ago and more often than not I would experience—perhaps witness is a better term—the two of them, together, reveling in their special friendship. I never observed any significant rivalry between the girls, even though most sisters exhibit such behavior. They are a cozy pair, perhaps drawn closer since the accident, a consequence of the event itself and the fact that the over powering personality of Annie has become somewhat tempered post-accident. Regardless, they are as inseparable now as before.

For example, several years ago before the accident, one of Annie's friends was admitted to a hospital in Providence, RI. To help the family and her friend Annie accompanied them on the ferry to the mainland. She helped keep her friend company in her wonderfully outgoing manner and stayed about a week before returning to the Island. On the return trip she was by herself; her friend would not be discharged for another two weeks Annie boarded the *George Danielson* in Providence and sailed back to the Island via Newport.

She was about twelve, not too young to travel alone, but too young, according to Emma, for her to be away from her sister for so long!

On the day the ferry was to arrive, Lillie and I watched Emma get up early, do her chores, silently, clearly preoccupied. She was quiet, except for one question.

"When is the Ferry arriving?"

The question was asked no fewer than twenty times, second only to her questioning what time it was. At last, unable to bear the wait, she slipped out of the house, without telling us where she was going and walked down to the inner basin of the landing in the Old Harbor, the first harbor of refuge on Block Island. And the harbor where the *George Danielson* docked.

I think she left the house about two hours before the ferry was to arrive. Lillie and I smiled at one another, neither of us needed to speak; nor were we surprised about what we had just witnessed.

About a half hour later, I walked down to the inner basin to see Emma sitting on an empty barrel that was positioned near the driveway leading to the Ocean View Hotel. The drive to the hotel was up a slight grade, affording her an opportune view of the Atlantic Ocean and Block Island Sound in the direction of Newport from where the ferry would arrive. She sat, her eyes glued to some spot in the open water, now unoccupied with the boat that she so craved to see, the boat that would carry her sister back to the Island and back to herself.

I did not walk up to her, purposefully keeping my distance, but I did run into CC Ball, the owner of the general store that was then located near the base of the drive that led to the Ocean View.

"She has been there for a while, George," CC said to me as I passed by his store.

"Yes, she is waiting for the ferry. Her sister is coming in from Providence." I explained to him about Annie's friend, and he said he would keep an eye on Emma. I loved CC. There were three things that always came to mind when I thought about him: first, he was very overweight; second, he had a remarkable capacity for friendship; and third, he was an accomplished merchant—and that I am sure made his late father proud.

I then returned to Lillie's home. It was comforting knowing CC would watch out for her; being the *George Danielson* would not be arriving for another ninety minutes or so, and that of course, if it was on time.

When another hour had passed Lillie and I left the house together and walked the three minutes that it took to reach the landing. As expected, Em was steadfast on her perch, although that perch was no longer a barrel, rather a wooden chair—with a soft embroidered pad—courtesy of CC. He had one of his workers bring the chair from the store for her to sit on while waiting for the ferry.

As we approached we saw Emma, gaze still fixed on the ocean, looking for the first glimmer of the small ship that would carry her sister. Within a few minutes the boat came into view, and she quickly got up, returned the chair to the general store, waved a thank you to someone inside, and ran down to the inner basin of the Old Harbor where the *George Danielson* would tie up. On that day, because the inner basin was full of fishing smacks, the ferry would have to berth at the wooden dock located at the base of the granite breakwater, on the eastern side of the Old Harbor, rather than at its dedicated location near the entrance to Ballard's.

Lillie and I followed behind, not wanting to disturb Em in her yearning to greet her sister. As the ferry came closer, Emma walked out beyond where the boat would eventually dock and climbed onto the breakwater, built because of the tireless efforts of CC Ball's father in the century past.

Closer and closer the *George Danielson* sailed. It was a boat that brought tourists to our Island, and it was a boat that brought family.

As the boat sailed closer to the entrance to the Old Harbor, Annie, leaning over the rail on the port side of the boat, spotted Emma at about the same time her sister spotted her.

If there is something finer than watching two sisters, two friends seeing each other after a period of being away, I must admit I just don't know what it could possibly be. It is at times like this that I wish I had Melville's ability to write about human emotions. Tears came to my eyes as they did Lillie; the joy in the girls was written on their faces, their smiles so wide. Witnessing unbridled joy is truly worth savoring and when it is present, fleetingly present, you know you have witnessed a special moment in a relationship. Joy, the opposite of sorrow; joy, as in to rejoice, rejoice in the relationship between the two girls. How lucky they were to have each other, of this I was certain.

As the *George Danielson* approached the wharf, they waved to each other incessantly. As we were watching the ferry, one of Lillie's late husband's sisters said hello, oblivious to what we were watching. I left

Lillie talking to her in-law and I walked out to the jetty where Emma was still standing. Almost voyeuristically, I wanted to see the emotion of the reunion close at hand. For some reason I felt that if I could see the two of them together, see their faces, I would be able to share some of that joy, and replace the tears that were now clouding my vision, thinking about the two of them.

The closer the ferry came to the dock, the greater the joy on their faces. Soon the ferry breached the Old Harbor jetty and then within a minute was in the inner basin and at the wharf, turning around to discharge its passengers. As it turned its bow to face the Atlantic Ocean, Annie ran around to the starboard side, so as not to lose eye contact with her sister.

No longer content just to wave, Annie began shouting above the noise of the engine, across the narrowing space that separated the boat from the wharf, out to her sister; she began describing the gift she brought to her from Providence. It was as if no one else mattered.

What I witnessed between the two girls was not, by any means, unique. Anyone can witness this type of reunion, anywhere there is a ferry and there is an island. Reunions like that of the two girls are played out countless times between good friends and members of families on every island, every island that has a ferry that is.

I have always thought that an arriving ferry can be a remarkable witness to what is ultimately important.

It had only been a week that the two girls had been away from each other, but it was a homecoming of sorts; these weren't always emotional events, but many were; but ever more so between two sisters who shared a bed together their entire lives. There was no room for tears of happiness between the two of them, there was too much joy. I looked over at Lillie as Annie ran off the boat toward the outstretched arms of her younger sister. Lillie looked at me and pointed her finger in the direction of Emma, who was now moving toward her sister, running with the momentum gained from jumping off the jetty and onto the wharf and into the loving embrace of her big sister.

"Look what I brought for you," Annie exclaimed. "Look in the bag." To Emma it did not matter what was in the bag brought from the mainland, all she cared about was that her sister was now home.

Old Harbor, Block Island. Docked in the Inner Basin is the *George Danielson*, the only ferry owned by the town of New Shoreham. On the left is the steamer, *The New Shoreham*.

15 Where are the girls?

"Where are the girls?" This was a common question asked frequently in Lillie's household, before the accident and after. Even with Annie's physical condition as it was, the two girls were always up to something.

For example, tonight Lillie, Arthur and I were discussing the need to start repainting some of the rooms in the Union House Hotel when, all of sudden we realized it was quite late and we didn't know what happened to the girls.

"Where are the girls?" Lillie had said abruptly, although we all thought it.

Arthur interrupted Lillie: "The last time I saw them was just after school near the Weather House, they were on their way to the beach."

"Would you please go find them?" Lillie asked.

I added, "I did see them earlier in the day also. Milton and Emma were pushing Annie out to the beach. Annie Rose wanted her 'sun time.' Come to think of it, I don't think Milt returned to work. He sure does like Annie! But I just saw them an hour ago in the back of the Union House talking to one of the remaining guests."

And then, just as I completed my sentence we heard laughter coming from High Street; the two girls sounded like they were up to their old tricks, their laughter traveling down High Street like thick fog on a cool, breezy day.

"What are they up to now! It is a bit late for them to be out," Lillie pronounced. And with that, we walked outside and toward the sounds of their laughter on this beautiful October evening that was clearly "borrowing" itself from an evening in July.

As we reached the street and looked up toward the Masonic Hall, we saw them together, Emma holding and trying to carry her sister as well as the wheelchair which was missing one of its wheels …

16 The Accident

Late May 1915

"From that hour I clove to Queequeg like a barnacle;
yea,till poor Queequeg took his last long dive."

Moby-Dick

Annie Rose took to boats as soon as she was able to climb onto them and jump off into the water. Emma Rose, nearly two years her junior, was not as adventurous about sailing or running about on the water; she preferred the land. At five foot ten Annie was much taller than her sister, and more powerful a swimmer. The first boat that Annie captained alone in the waters off Block Island was the *Nellie B* (built by my father-in-law and named after my first wife) soon after it was taken out of service as a fishing smack about four years ago. Annie was only twelve years old at that time.

Two years ago, Emma began sailing with Annie. They would sail just outside the Old Harbor and out along Crescent Beach to Clay Head and back. Soon Emma got the hang of sailing and joined her sister enthusiastically. Em was smaller and not as strong, although she could swim as far as her sister.

Two years ago, Annie received a smaller, eighteen-foot double ender and she began to sail that vessel alone. This double ender was a small pulling boat, a skiff of sorts, that could be rowed if the wind died down, although it usually took at least two to row it any distance, one on either side of the boat. Open pulling boats, on Block Island referred to as double enders, are relatively seaworthy, almost never being the cause of loss of life, especially if ketch rigged as sailboats.

One of the Dodge brothers helped Annie rig this eighteen-footer properly, and she was off and sailing alone or with people, it didn't matter. She loved being on the water.

The two girls had a lot of mischief in them, especially when together. For them risk taking was so effortless, or so it appeared. I did not especially worry about it, nor did Lillie, but in retrospect, we should have. Together, their confidence rose to levels beyond what they were individually, and although this was at once comforting, we ought to have recognized it as alarming.

The reason Block Island has two lighthouses, three lifesaving stations, one United States Weather Bureau Station and two government-funded harbors is because it can be a very dangerous place to be *near*. If you are close to the Island, in a boat, and the weather and seas turn, well you are in a most precarious location in this world.

The weather, nothing more than an ongoing collection of dynamically changing systems, can shift rather quickly, and the effects of these moving systems on the seas can be dramatic and at times quite lethal. Block Island is known for its shipwrecks and groundings; and, of course, the weather, the seas, and our location are to blame. But we are not the only area where ships go down to the sea near land; Point Judith is also another place without a protected harbor, Cape Cod also; but interestingly, Nantucket does not have the number of shipwrecks that our area has. Melville, please take note.

Block Island fisherman had used the old double-enders or ketch rigged pulling boats because they are difficult to capsize, and in the hands of a capable captain, they handle the surf, at sea or approaching a sandy cove quite easily. Rarely, if at all, does a Block Island double ender go down to the sea, while *at* sea, maybe two or three in the past few hundred years.

But it has happened, and it happened to the two sisters.

"...we gave three heavy-hearted cheers, and blindly plunged like fate into the lone Atlantic," *Moby-Dick*.

I had forecast a squall in May of two years ago, I have forgotten the exact date, and for good reason. The weather flags warning of a sudden gale were to have been raised on the tower at the Southeast Light; the girls knew enough to look for the flags and did not sail beyond the safety of the shore of the Island until they were able to see the tower. The weather flags were to have been flying, but the lighthouse staff did not raise them. They claimed I never called them.

The two set sail from Old Harbor, and around the Island until they were in view of the tower at the lighthouse; and seeing no gale warning flags, proceeded due east in the direction of Spain. The wind had picked up and the small boat responded accordingly.

It is a story that to this day I cannot bear to think about, nonetheless write about. The only aspect of this near tragedy that is comforting involves the indomitable spirit of the two sisters on that day when they saved each other. It was clear that Annie's strength saved them from certain death. Few could handle a pulling boat, mast destroyed, and all the while holding only Emma. Were it not for the grasp of her sister, Emma would have been washed overboard numerous times. Three times Annie lost her grip and had to dive overboard to bring Emma back to safety. Never did Annie give it a thought that they would not make to back to shore, until, the surf began pulverizing the boat. In the raging surf, Annie saved her sister one more time, but it would be her last effort, as Emma dragged her sister up on shore amidst the shattered remains of the boat.

And that is about all I can say. I am sorry I am unable to complete the description of the accident, but it is not for wont of trying.

The function of local bureaus is to record data to be used by the central and regional forecasting offices. In turn, local forecasts are then made public; the cold-wave flag and many other weather signal devices were introduced in 1888 by the Signal Corps "all of which were eventually reduced to a simple system of flag signals, now called *weather flags*." The August 30, 1905 edition of the Mid-Ocean described six storm warning or weather flags used for this purpose summarized below:

1. A square white flag, = clear or fair weather.

2. A square blue flag, = rain or snow.

3. A square flag with the upper half white and the lower half blue = local rain or snow.

4. A black triangular flag indicates the temperature. When placed above the number 1, 2, or 3, it indicates warmer; when below, colder; when not displayed the temperature is expected to remain about satisfactory.

5. A square, white flag with a black square in center, denotes a cold wave. During the late spring or early fall, it is also used to indicate anticipated frosts.

6. A red square flag, with a black square center denotes a major storm. It was this flag that should have been raised on the tower at the Southeast Lighthouse the day the girls sailed. Not seeing the flag on the storm-warning tower, they proceeded to sail due southeast directly toward the coming gale.

17 The Broken Wheel Chair

When Lillie, Arthur, and I walked out to High Street and looked up toward the Masonic Hall, we were greeted to a sight that would have warmed anyone's heart. In the middle of the road, the two girls were laughing so hard that they didn't seem to be able to move. Em was leaning across Annie, on top of the wheelchair, while trying to lift the large wooden front wheel that was clearly broken, almost beyond repair. We walked up the same street I had just walked down two hours ago, to find the two of them in quite a mess.

They had been visiting a friend who lived across from the Masonic Hall well off High Street. Upon their return, Annie's wheelchair caught a rut in the wooden walkway and the left wheel bent until about ready to fall off. Annie fell out of the chair and was coated in dirt, her face greeting the street in an intimate fashion. Falls for Annie out of the chair were usually accompanied by bruises on at least one part of her body, depending on the trajectory of the spill.

Em tried to bend the wheel back in line, but was unable to do so. The two of them, working together somehow, then simply dragged the chair, with Annie in it, down High Street. Progress was slow, even downhill; so slow and clumsy that they just could not stop laughing.

Although it was heartbreaking that Annie would never be able to walk again, or perhaps even talk clearly, it was joyful to see the two having so much fun, even when they were in a bit of trouble. This scene did nothing but bring another smile to my face, as it did Arthur's. I suppose when compared to the accident, nothing as minor as a broken wheelchair could possibly bother either of them.

We looked at the wheel and I removed it from the chair. Arthur had fixed the wheels before and would do it again. He picked up Annie and carried her home; I carried the wheelchair, and Emma and Lillie wheeled the broken wheel down the street. It was one of those times when my heart and my mind were content, and I would not have wanted to be anywhere else in the world. I am not, however, so sure Lillie felt that way. She had to clean both of them up and then put them to bed, a process that took up to an hour for Annie alone.

The time spent bringing the girls home and getting them ready for bed took my mind off of the problem of those three men. I knew tomorrow would bring about a decision I had to make, and I started sensing that if I were to let indecision get the better of me, it could very well be a problem. Tomorrow I was determined to expand my team.

After the girls were in bed, I asked Arthur for some of his whiskey and walked outside to sit on the porch. I had two drinks, quite uncharacteristic for me, before I made up my mind who I would add to my team. It was a decision that ultimately would turn out to be the most important decision I would ever make in my life.

18 Corn Neck Road

The next morning, as the earliest rays of the sun were making their way through the windows of Lillie's home, I quietly arose and got dressed. I tried not to wake Lillie, although I knew she would want to be up early. I bypassed the kitchen, both the food and the room, and walked through the parlor toward the front door. I noticed the two girls sleeping together, wrapped around each other, entangled, on the floor of the living room near the fireplace. After Lillie and I had fallen asleep, Emma Rose must have carried, or dragged, Annie downstairs so they could sleep by the window that had the best view of the Old Harbor and the Atlantic Ocean. When they slept downstairs it was either because it was too hot, as in a midsummer night's heat, or they were up late planning something.

I took one last long look at them sleeping soundly before leaving. As I walked down High Street, I passed the statue of Rebecca, and walked along Water Street, the heart of Old Harbor Village. Water Street is only a third of a mile long.

At the end of this short street that fronted the Old Harbor, a mighty Victorian hotel, the large New National Hotel, stood proudly fronting the harbor. And adjacent to it, sat the large Surf Hotel, that proudly sat between the Old Harbor and the beginning of Crescent Beach.

As I turned left along Dodge Street, I looked back over my shoulder to see that the sun was not quite up over the horizon, but even if it were the morning fog and haze would have kept it from my view. The other thing that may have blocked it was the large building that sits high up on the hill, the Ocean View Hotel, overlooking the inner basin. It is the most majestic hotel on the Island, even more so than the destroyed Hygeia.

At the National Hotel, Water Street changes its name and becomes Dodge Street. And about one hundred and fifty yards farther it changes its name again—this time to Ocean Ave; and after a mile and a half down the road, Ocean Avenue changes its name once again, this time to New Harbor Road. One street, four names.

At the end of the short, quarter mile Dodge Street, named after the myriad of Dodges that populated the Island from day one and an ancestor of my in-laws, comes an intersection. Normally an intersection of two crossing streets would have two names. But not on Block Island, each has, as you now can surmise, a different name: Dodge Street, Ocean Avenue, Main Street, and Corn Neck Road … and I understand Main Street is changing its name again, to Old Town Road.

Corn Neck Road follows along and out to the Ocean. Ocean Avenue does not. (Understanding the naming of these streets requires a thorough understanding of the history of the Island but that I will save for another day.) You can get to the Weather House by going straight through the intersection and continuing on Ocean Avenue, or you can turn right, continue out Corn Neck Road, and take a left onto Beach Street which was my route this morning. It took longer to go this route, but it enabled me to investigate the cable that runs off the main trunk along Beach Street, that I use to transmit my weather data to the mainland.

I walked along the course that the underground cable followed, a path I knew well, as it was my government-assigned responsibility to check the integrity of the cable on a daily basis. This morning the cable was fine.

As I approached the Weather House, I could see Milt was already at work. I walked through the gate of the white picket fence and waved.

"Hey, Mr. Eddey," he yelled, not consciously aware that most people, except the Island fisherman, were still sleeping. He had a booming voice. "Where were you last night?"

"I stayed with Lillie last night," I answered, softly. I was anxious to hear if he had seen any of the three mystery men around the Island.

I always looked up at the top of the tower standing to the right of the Weather House whenever I entered the property to make sure the flags were still in place, but also because it was a matter of pride for me. I am a meteorologist and that tower enables me to communicate my work as a forecaster to the community. I also glance at the instrument shack; it sat directly behind the tower and housed the outdoor weather equipment, except for the wind gauge which was located on the roof of the building. The expensive barometer was kept inside.

"I didn't find anything out about those men, Mr. Eddey ... except," the excitement and trepidation became evident as he talked, "Mr. Murray [Wallace's father-in-law] saw two tall men he had never seen before last month. They were walking on the west side beaches then as well. They fit the description perfectly. And he saw one of them on the landing last week. Last night I drove all over the Island looking for them, and found that they had stayed at the Spring House Hotel early in September for a few nights. I suppose it's not possible to determine if they stayed at the Hygiea before it burned?"

"Do you think anyone was suspicious of what you were doing, driving around last night?" I asked.

"No," he shook his head for emphasis. "I started out looking around the Great Salt Pond, and then walked the beach from Charleston Beach to Grace's Cove. The seaweed made for tough, slippery walking. I did not find anything except an area where the seaweed was moved over a bit, but that could have been one of the farmers gathering seaweed for planting. I don't think I saw evidence of a boat being pulled on shore, but that is what I was looking for."

We collected data from the instruments to prepare our weather report and our conversation turned to the continued high-pressure pattern holding over the Island. It was so prominent, I remarked, a hurricane would do an about face and steer clear of it.

Once inside the Weather House, we confirmed that the barometric pressure continued to rise, indicating continued great weather. No moving weather formations would disrupt this great weather pattern for the near future. Changes in pressure often drive those moving formations and knowing the direction of the barometric pressure, either up or down, is so important, no forecast can be made of any weather phenomena, without it. Changes in pressure drive moving weather formations.

Understand the significance of barometric pressure changes, and you'll recognize when the sun will cast its shadows.

The barometer was in the telegraph office, in a corner where it was safe from accidental damage or water from the often open windows in the house. Today it was clear that the pressure continued to rise as the temperature stayed steady.

I announced to Milt: "It appears that this October day will be another day borrowed from summer, just like yesterday was."

"Mr. Eddey," said Milton, "I have been reading those pamphlets about the weather since I started working with you, and I can't find any reference to the term "borrowing days" that you use frequently. Where'd it come from?"

Milton was correct, I do use that term from time to time and it is not an official weather term.

"'Borrowing days' is a phrase from the Scots," I explained. "It refers, loosely, to days in one season, such as the summer, resembling days from another season, such as the fall. I think it was originally used in a Scottish poem."

"That's all it means?"

I nodded.

I couldn't help but think how good a worker Milton was. Maybe, just maybe, I could convince him to learn more about the scientific basis for weather forecasting, so that he would stay with the Bureau. We turned our attention to the Marconi wireless device; it started to receive another transmission from the Navy. But this communication was from the Naval War College in Newport, not the Navy Yard in Brooklyn.

I deciphered the code and was slightly disturbed to read the following: "Thank you for info on three men on island ... we are aware ... do not interfere."

That was it. No explanation. Milton and I looked at one another in disbelief.

For the War College to respond to me directly there must have been some urgency. But what was that message about? It crossed my mind that the three men might be advance detail U. S. naval personnel, scouting out the west shore in preparation for the coming war and the new, albeit temporary, naval station on the Island. But that seemed unlikely, as I assumed that the War College was well aware that I knew the details of the new naval station it would create on the Island with our entry into the war against Germany.

"Mr. Eddey," Milton said, staring out the window toward the Great Salt Pond. "Mr. Eddey," he repeated, "something doesn't make sense. Are we sure we are deciphering that message properly? Could there be more meaning to it? Maybe the Marconi device is not working properly?"

I did not have an answer.

"I think there was more to that communication. Something's missing," Milton said, and then his eyes lit up. "I have an idea. I know it sounds odd, but maybe Annie Rose can sit and monitor the transmissions from the Marconi machine. Maybe she can decipher any further messages. Annie could very well understand them."

I stood and stared out the window of the Weather House too, and was aware that Milt now realized what I had the day before—we needed help.

Milton's suggestion of having my niece, now my stepdaughter, become involved by monitoring the messages, confirmed my thoughts on adding her to the team. I would call her over and keep her out of school for the next several days, but first I would have to convince Lillie.

I was sure Lillie would not want her daughter involved in this 'shadow now being cast over Block Island,' but Milt was correct. Annie would very much want to help, and to use her telegraphy skills and much more.

In retrospect, asking Annie to participate in this investigation was as important a decision as my next, which would involve the Naval War College. But at that time, I simply could not imagine how much those two decisions alone would change the course of our nation's history.

19 Mrs. Conway

Mrs. Conway was the only woman observer in the United States Weather Bureau; she was placed in charge of the Pt. Judith, R.I. station on July 1, 1891 to replace her husband. (He remained with the U. S. Signal Corps when the Weather Bureau was separated from the Army). Mrs. Conway was a superior telegraph operator and handled all government business transmitted over the Weather Bureau cable connecting Block Island and Narragansett Pier in Pt. Judith. In 1909, when I was the first to "hear" the distress call from the sinking *Republic*, the first person I called to help disseminate the urgency of the message was Mrs. Conway; I then called the Naval War College. She is a great colleague and has been helpful to me personally over the years as well.

It wasn't long after Annie had awoken from her unconsciousness, resulting from the boating accident, that she began *trying* to talk to us ... but of course she could not. The portion of the mind that allows her to talk was injured the doctors said.

But what was not injured was her desire to talk; that part of her brain appeared, early on, to be as active after the accident as before. What I mean to say is that after the accident, Annie could not communicate verbally, but she *could* communicate.

How?

It was Mrs. Conway who reminded me that Morse code could be an ideal method for her to talk with us. Years ago I had taught both girls the basics of Morse code, as I had my three sons. It was a family tradition after all. After Annie's recovery was well underway, it was easy for Mrs. Conway to re-teach her the code and Annie's first trip off the Island after the accident, courtesy of Wallace and his boat the *Anna C*, was to Mrs. Conway's office in Pt. Judith for her first refresher lesson.

One day, not too long after Mrs. Conway had thought Annie had relearned the code quite well, Annie Rose became frustrated with her mother. She was so mad that she telegraphed Mrs. Conway from my office; Mrs. Conway then, in turn, called Lillie on the phone to explain why Annie was so upset. After that, Annie wasted no time using Morse code to communicate with everyone, including her teachers at the Island school!

Morse code became, and remains, the method of choice for Annie to communicate complex thoughts and ideas. On the other hand, Mrs. Conway suggested a simpler *Yes and No communication system* for Annie to use when her requests were basic. This simple method of "yes/no" communication remains the easiest and most efficient method to communicate with her. She raises her eyes to say yes, and she moves her eyes sideways to say no.

I will never forget the first long discussion Annie had with her mother (and I) one Sunday afternoon, after her "recovery," as such as it was. She was tapping out messages to us in Morse code with her good right hand, her only extremity that remained quite useful from a physical standpoint.

"What am I going to do?" she would ask in her messages.

We sat near her as she tapped out her thoughts. She reviewed what she could no longer do, like sail or fish, or talk. I did all I could during this conversation to refrain from crying. I somehow stopped paying attention to her, focusing more on holding back my tears. But I was awakened from my anguish when Annie ended her long conversation with the words: "I want to matter." When she tapped out those words, I left the room, left Lillie and her alone, walked upstairs, and found a place where I could sit and cry.

I think we all want to matter, but those four words took on new meaning, when my then 15-year-old niece 'spoke' them. She had so much to say, just like I or you or anyone, and she had this desire to matter, now more than ever. But how? Our lives are fleeting and hers, perhaps, even more so, and yet she wanted to create something, or leave something, or do something that would long outlive her life on this Island.

Annie soon developed a hand signal to reflect that concept of wanting to matter. She raises her weak hand as much as she can, and then she places her good hand on top of the hand that doesn't work as it once did. To this day, I have adopted that hand signal, substituting my dominant hand for her good hand; I find myself using it frequently when I think of her, unconsciously I am sure.

When I enlisted, at the age of twenty-five, in the Army's Signal Service it was a time when countries wished to explore the outer bounds of our earth, including both the north and south poles. In the age of exploration, I thought then, as I do now, that the weather service would be ideal for me. It was scientific and this new *science-based profession* had civilian and military significance.

And it was a way for me to matter too. It is perhaps one of the most important truths ... we all need a purpose. And watching Annie that day made me realize how much "mattering," if that is a word, means to everyone, or nearly everyone, I suppose. I have always cherished my work with the Weather Bureau; I have a purpose, however modest.

And more than ever, Annie Rose needed to find a purpose to her now changed body and altered life. She could not explore the poles; no, she would not need to explore the North or South Pole; she had her own continent to explore. Her world, now much smaller, still needed exploration; how she would interact with it and its people had yet to be determined.

My current purpose is to uncover the intentions of those three men.

Suddenly a frightening thought occurred to me, "Could the transmission this morning, allegedly from the Naval War College, have actually come from another source?"

Marconi had long stated that he did not invent the wireless telegraph, that honor he bestowed on the German, Heinrich R. Heinz. (Others, however, bestowed that honor on a Serbian electrical engineer.) What was clear, without any disagreement, was that Marconi understood the significance of radio waves, improved and marketed the device that Heinz had developed, by clearly visualizing the wireless's potential in the commercial and military world.

How was his wireless device being used in the war effort? Again I asked myself, *Could that transmission this morning from the War College have come from another source?* The questions were now racing through my mind. And how could I communicate with the Brooklyn Navy Yard, to determine what was important, and who was behind whatever was happening?

Could German scientists have devised a method to intercept the wireless transmissions of my messages sent in Morse code and then return the messages with me thinking it was actually from the Brooklyn Navy Yard or the Naval War College? I did not have access to the newer arc radiotelephones that had been developed ten years earlier by Dr. DeForest, so I had to rely on the old Marconi Wireless that the Block Island Weather Bureau had on site since 1906.

I couldn't use the cable to send telegraphs because any number of people along the way intercepted that line. And I was afraid to use the telephone for the same reason.

There was only one thing to do.

I was now determined to communicate directly with the ONI in the Brooklyn Navy Yard without using the cable, the wireless device, or the telephone. And I knew exactly who I would send.

20 The War in Europe

At lunch, I talked with Milton and explained to him that I needed to send someone directly to the Navy Yard, and he was going to have to run the Weather House for a few hours.

I left him in charge, walked to the garage and climbed into my one-year-old Model T Ford. When I got to Corn Neck Road, I turned right and continued driving to the Old Harbor. I was thinking, *How am I going to explain to Lillie what my next step is going to be ... and why?*

But someone yelling my name interrupted my concentration.

I pulled the car off the road, onto a sandy area, not too far from the Old Harbor Lifesaving Station. The voice was that of my late father-in-law's friend, Mr. Mitchell, the owner of the Highland House, another small hotel on the Island. He ran over to my car looking startled and, in so doing, startled me.

"Hey, do you know that Annie Rose is swimming alone? She is over there ...," He pointed to the beach on the other side of the dunes. "She is in deep water near the back of the Surf Hotel. Is she allowed to do that?"

"Again! In October! No, she is not allowed to do that. Thank you." I couldn't see the beach from this part of the road. I got out of my car and ran across the street and over the seven or eight-foot-high sand dune that blocked the vision of that portion of Crescent Beach. Mr. Mitchell followed me. When we reached the top of the dune, we could see Annie in the water, alone, with her wheelchair lying on its side, being pushed about by the incoming surf.

Although she was in pretty deep water, in fact, this area of Crescent Beach was quite safe. She was trying to swim, kicking her one fairly good leg and attempting to push off the sandy bottom with the bad leg; her head at times underwater, struggling to position her mouth, by turning her neck, to breathe. She was not in distress; no, she was just working hard at whatever she was trying to accomplish this warm October day.

I was worried when I saw her, but I knew, as did she, that of all the places to swim, this was the safest on the Island; it was protected from the surf of the Atlantic Ocean, not only by the jetty of the Old Harbor, but also because of submerged glacial erratics that make up Burton's Cove. All the same, Annie shouldn't be alone; and the water was cold, even though the air wasn't.

This part of the beach was easy for her to reach. With her good leg she could push herself in the wheelchair, first down High Street and then through the town on Water Street. And after she reached Dodge Street, if she couldn't find a friend to help her, she was able to push herself down a narrow, sandy path behind the Surf Hotel, a shortcut to this area of Crescent Beach.

This path to the beach, although owned by the Surf Hotel, was used by everyone as a shortcut. During the summer, if her wheelchair got stuck in the sand, she was easily pulled to safety by any number of passersby's who were on Dodge Street or the path itself. Except this was fall and few people walked to the beach. Mr. Mitchell had seen her because he was taking a walk along the dunes, a rare outing for him, given his responsibilities at his hotel.

"What are you doing, Annie? The water is cold. It is October!" I exclaimed as I reached the surf. I took my shoes and socks off, rolled up my pants, and walked into the water to pick her up and carry her to the beach. Her head was half underwater but she was smiling.

Mr. Mitchell guided the wooden wheelchair under Annie as I placed her onto Lillie's hand-woven cushion that wasn't all that wet.

"Annie Rose!" I admonished her, not knowing what else to say.

"Is the water as cold as my feet are telling me, Annie?"

Annie raised her eyes to say yes.

She just smiled as the water dripped off her body. As cold as she was in the few parts of her body that still had feeling, she was happy.

"Did you tell your mother or sister that you were here?" I don't know why I asked because I knew the answer.

Annie Rose turned her eyes to indicate, "No."

She was able to use the accident to get away with all sorts of high crimes and misdemeanors. And we let her. It was hard to yell at Annie for trying to do the things that she once did on her own, with such ease and grace, and now with much awkwardness and great effort. It was different now, but in her mind she was the same, she was determined, she was herself, and the accident could not take away her "self." She once tapped out a Morse code message to me that it "did not matter what happened to you in life, what mattered is how you take it and deal with it." I was amazed at her maturity, her resiliency, at such a young age.

Mr. Mitchell and I pulled Annie and the wheelchair over the dunes and lifted her into the car.

Annie used her good hand to signal a "thank you" to Mr. Mitchell. He was aware of her hand signals and responded: "You are welcome," with a slight bow of his head.

Most of the Islanders were aware of how she communicated now that she was wheeling herself—or being pushed by her sister—around the Island. I often thought how great it was that Lillie had a house at the base of High Street, a location ideal for Annie. She could be independent, at least to a small extent. If Lillie lived on the west side of the Island, where Milton and Wallace lived, life would prove to be far more difficult and isolating. Even the location of the Weather House was not as convenient; and that is why Lillie continued to live there, and not move in permanently with me.

After placing the wheelchair in the trunk of the car and thanking Mr. Mitchell myself, I drove Annie back to her mother's house. I used my coat to cover her up and dry her hair and body as best I could, all in one motion. She just sat in the front seat, smiling. It wasn't the big broad smile, but it was a smile of contentment, of accomplishment. What other 15-year-old, in her condition, would have tried to swim alone?

Lillie greeted us as we pulled up to the house and immediately saw that her daughter was wet and, at the same time, was wearing her broad smile.

"Annie Rose!" Lillie yelled, as much for effect rather than as a scolding. Annie's smile became a half smile and then she turned her head. She looked away until she was convinced that her mother's voice was not one of anger or sadness, rather of concealed pride. She looked back at

Lillie and saw that tear swelling in her mother's eye; and she knew she would not be scolded.

Annie smiled again.

I explained to Lillie how Mr. Mitchell and I found her. After bringing Annie inside, I mentioned to Lilllie that I was on my way to see Wallace. I am not sure she heard me, as she did not say much.

I got back into my car and drove up High Street until, at the top, I turned right onto Payne Road. Instead of driving all the way onto his property, I parked my car about a quarter of a mile away just in case his house was being observed. I considered that I was being unnecessarily cautious, but the uncertainty of the situation had put my mind on alert; my thoughts were different now than from just a few days ago.

I was hoping Wallace was home and as I walked around to the back, which of course was his front, I saw him in the yard working on his old car.

"Hey, Pop," he called out. "You wouldn't believe this, but my car won't start. Where is your car?"

I did not want to say anything but I was beginning to believe that anything was possible, and it had only been four days since Milt's sighting of the three tall men.

At that point, my mind was made up; I had to ask a huge favor of my son.

"Wallace," I said in an obviously concerned tone of voice; so concerned that my son dropped his wrench and stared blankly, waiting for me to finish my sentence.

"Wallace," I repeated, "would you sail your boat to the Brooklyn Navy Yard? I need you to deliver a message for me ... to the Office of Naval Intelligence."

"Sure, Pop," he said without hesitation. "I'd be glad to. But why don't you just use the wireless?"

I explained why I thought a nefarious someone might be listening in on the wireless and the cable communications. He immediately understood my concern and readily agreed to set sail as soon as possible.

"I don't think you should leave just yet," I cautioned him. "Maybe at night or when the weather is foggy. Think thick pea soup fog, perhaps then you should leave."

He shot me a strange look before I explained. "I think that you and I ought to consider that we are being watched." I added, "When you are away, perhaps Edith should stay at the Vaill."

Concern draped Wallace's face as it had mine earlier in the day. He changed the subject. "Did you walk here, Pop?"

"No, I parked up in the brush at the end of Payne's path. That road is dusty." I started thinking out loud. "I will have to clean it before I take it back to the Weather House."

"What do you want me to deliver to the Navy Yard once I get there?"

"I will write out the information in an official-looking weather communication format for you to carry. You will have to hand it to one of my colleagues in the Weather Bureau either at the Navy Yard, or at one hundred Broadway. Hopefully you will be able to dock at the Brooklyn Navy Yard and deliver it there rather than having to go into Manhattan to one hundred Broadway. You should plan on docking at Dry Dock One in the Navy Yard. I will give you a packet of information that will include instructions which I will leave in the cabin of your boat later tonight. Do you think you can negotiate Hell Gate in the East River with the *Anna C*?" I knew the answer was yes, but I asked it anyway.

"Hell Gate Channel ...," he reflected. "Oh, it is every bit of a hell's gate, even at ebb tide. I forgot about that. I will have to hit the tides just right—but yes, Pop, I can make that trip to the Navy Yard in any weather!"

"I know you can. But make sure you study the tides in the East River so the *Anna C* doesn't have to strain too much against the current."

"I'll hug the shoreline as best I can if need be," Wallace nodded.

The location of Hell Gate is best appreciated by looking at a map of New York City and the East River. It is situated at the confluence of where the Harlem River flows south into the East River and out to New York Harbor and the Atlantic Ocean; but at this site, the East River also begins its flow northward into Long Island Sound through a narrow passageway that is called Hell Gate Channel. It is one of the most dangerous navigable waters in all of the United States. Hell Gate was named by the Indians that sold Manhattan to the Dutch and is considered the back door entrance to New York Harbor from Long Island Sound. It is also where the tides get all mixed up, but there is something more than the confluence of two rivers and two opposing tidal bodies of water that make it extremely treacherous to navigate for a small boat like the *Anna C.*

Hell Gate not only has the tides and fast currents, but also mid-channel rocky ledges, and a large number of underwater reefs and shoals. Each of these underwater outcroppings of New York City bedrock have names, the worst one is called Pot Rock. Mill Rock, an "above water" outcropping of bedrock, has also earned a name.

Mr. Smith, the Dock Commissioner for New York, has proposed dynamiting this area in years past, but funding has never been appropriated, of this I knew from conversations with George, my brother-in-law.

Because it connects two tidal bodies of water, namely New York Harbor proper and Long Island Sound, the East River is not so much a river as it is an estuary. This tidal pattern and its associated currents, along with the nature of the geography that make up the Hell Gate Channel, creates such a force of water that a small, underpowered boat like Wallace's *Anna C* could easily be capsized.

Wallace will have to motor down Long Island sound, avoiding the shipping traffic, especially the coal barges and steamships, to enter the East River at the tip of Randal's Island at Hell Gate, and then proceed to the end of the East River where the mouth of the various inlets of the Brooklyn Navy Yard are located.

Wallace and I agreed we would not speak to one another—by any form of communication—until he returned to Block Island. His boat was docked in the Hog Pen, a small marina in the New Harbor, which was within sight of the Weather House. I would leave the information packet on his boat no later than 8:00 p.m. tonight. He alone would decide when he was to sail. Before I left, I reminded him to suggest to Edith that she stay at the Vaill while he was away.

I walked back to my car and drove to Lillie's house where I promptly cleaned off the dust that had accumulated from my round trip ride on Payne's Road. I stepped inside to look for Lillie but no one was home. I wondered where the girls were as there was no sign of them either. Back at the Weather House, I started writing the documents for Wallace to deliver.

21 The Brooklyn Navy Yard

While the official name is the New York Naval Yard, everyone on the face of the earth calls it the Brooklyn Navy Yard, except the cartographers who designed maps or charts of the waterways around New York Harbor. The BNY has a storied past, but for now it was simply a location on the East River for my son to dock his *Anna C* and deliver some documents. But first he had to reach the docks safely.

The yard was primarily equipped to handle deep-draught vessels. I explained in the note to Wallace that there was a floating dock at the base of Dry Dock 1 that could accommodate small vessels, although he would have to negotiate the destroyer currently under construction. Last year in June of 1915 the Navy Yard had launched the USS Arizona, a 608 foot long destroyer, now being outfitted in another part of the Navy Yard. Currently on Dry Dock 1, the Navy was building the USS New Mexico, a 624 foot long battleship. I wrote all this down for Wallace so that he would not be surprised by the activity and immensity of the work in progress at that site and near where he would have to dock his boat.

Wallace knew my father was a shipbuilder. During the Civil War, he was a foreman for the Continental Ship Yard in Green Point where he worked with Erickson to help build the Monitor. But that was then and my father, Carnes, had never built vessels as massive and as complicated as the destroyers and battleships now coming off the Brooklyn Navy Yard's Dry Docks.

I grew up in Green Point, Brooklyn, but it was a different town then from what it is today. Then more dangerous, now less so because today the river is bulk headed, the East River currents tamed a bit, although they remain treacherous. Today, fortunately, not as many drownings occur as when I was living on Huron Street.

Normally we think of the shore of a river as a place of safety, or a place to swim to safely; but not the shore of the East River. It was dangerous because if you "fell off" the shore, there was a high likelihood that the river would draw you out by the force of the powerful current that pulled water away from the Brooklyn side toward the Manhattan side. This phenomenon was the case regardless of whether or not the tides in the river were pushing the flow of water north or south. Whenever I thought of walking the shore of the East River in Green Point, then and now, I always think that wearing, or holding, a life preserver is a reasonable and not at all outlandish idea.

I often wondered why Melville, in all the hundreds of pages of *Moby-Dick*, did not mention a life preserver, unless one thinks of Queequeg's coffin as one. Life preservers, to me, are as important as the crossings undertaken themselves. Why are they so inconsequential to Melville?

I completed my written instructions to Wallace, then wrote the document in code for him to hand deliver, and headed down to the Hog Pen where Wallace docked his boat, a five-minute walk from the Weather House.

I placed the papers in the cabin of the *Anna C* along with enough money for Wallace to purchase fuel and food once he arrived at New York. I included the phone number of my sister, Catherine, and her father-in-law, just in case he was unable to locate my colleagues in the Navy Yard.

I walked back to the Weather House and returned to my responsibilities as the meteorologist, and to help Milton transmit the afternoon weather data. But Milton was not there.

Where was everybody?

22 The Anna C

Milt eventually returned and brought with him the two girls and Lillie. He had left earlier with the three of them to go back to Crescent Beach. Annie had left her book on the beach when I picked her up. After we had dinner, Milt decided to stay for the night and convinced the girls to sleep on the roof instead of their bedroom on the second floor. Each would need to sleep under five blankets.

And while they were sleeping on the roof, and Lillie and I were asleep in our bedroom, the *Anna C* set sail.

The weather had turned cloudy at about midnight; Wallace recognized the weather pattern, woke his wife Edith, and dropped her off at the Vaill. He then drove his car directly to the garage at the Weather House and walked to the Hog Pen.

At approximately 1:00 a.m., when Wallace untied his boat from the dock and pushed off into the increasingly cloudy night with no brightly lit moon above, he was sure he was not observed. He quietly motored out of the Great Salt Pond and into the Atlantic Ocean toward Long Island Sound and New York City.

Early in the morning, when I saw his car in the Weather House garage, I walked over to the edge of the property line and gazed out toward the Hog Pen. Not seeing his boat at its slip, I moved my Model-T in front of his and then closed the garage doors to prevent anyone from looking inside.

Wallace was an excellent navigator and knew the passage to NYC quite well; being that the seas were not high, the only concern he harbored was navigating Hell Gate. At low tide, the main Hell Gate Channel was only about twenty-four feet deep in places and quite narrow. If the tides were flowing in either direction at full force, he would have to wait for ebb tide because his motor could not handle the power of the current. At daybreak, Wallace expected to be in the lee of Long Island, out of harm's way of the open Atlantic Ocean.

Wallace and I have had many discussions about German U-boats, and he knew how to identify a surfacing submarine. A U-boat spotting Wallace was what I was most afraid of, not Hell Gate.

When Milt and the girls awoke, damp from sleeping on the roof, I suggested he go home and tend to his responsibilities since his parents were still on the mainland. I asked him if he would continue to stay overnight at the Weather House. The girls, having not slept all that well, left the roof and returned to their bedrooms to catch another two hours of sleep.

After Milton left, and with the girls upstairs sleeping, I finally broke the news to Lillie. Although I admit I did avoid the conversation to an extent, it all happened so suddenly that I failed to explain to her why Wallace was on his way to NYC in the middle of October.

"So Wallace is WHERE?!?" Lillie exclaimed. "You sent him WHERE? Why did you do that? Does Edith know?"

Lillie was so disturbed she raised her voice so loud that I was afraid she'd wake the girls. I was a little surprised Lillie became that upset. (I guess there was a reason I liked to stay at the Weather House on occasion.)

"On the basis of such little information you sent your son on a trip, at night, to meet someone YOU HAVEN'T SEEN IN EIGHT YEARS, to ..."

"Shhhh!" I cut her off, as she was starting to yell again and I did not want her voice, which I knew was carrying out the open windows, to be heard by ears other than ours. "You must remain calm and quiet. We must all remain calm and carry on."

Little did I know that not only were the girls now awake and listening to our every word, they were already plotting how they could help. The two sisters were very smart.

"Have you told me everything?" Lillie demanded. "And is that what you were up to when you came to the house late the other night?"

I raised my eyes to say yes.

"Is that a yes? You can talk, say 'yes,' don't raise your eyes. You are not Annie Rose!" Lillie bellowed.

"Yes," I answered.

"I cannot believe you would have acted so quickly—on such limited information! It is too dangerous for him to go alone. What if there are U-boats in the sound and they follow him? What will happen then?" Lillie went on with question after question.

When her tirade was over, I explained that the greater threat was to the "entire Island" if Wallace did not go.

"HE understood that, Lillie, which is why he was willing to take the risk," I said.

"Now, do YOU understand why I did what I did?"

With that, the conversation was over. We finished eating breakfast, eggs on Lillie's day old baked bread. I got up and walked into the office with the barometer. I noticed the girls, who had now moved to the foot of the stairs leading to the bedrooms. They pretended not to notice me.

It was about 1:00 p.m. and Wallace was now approaching the eastern most tip of the North Fork of Long Island. He was fortunate to have a following sea with favorable currents and consequently had made very good time. When the October weather was good, the sea's low and the tide's in one's favor, it could be a great month to set sail. But if the weather was not good, well ... there's an old sailor's saying: "In a small boat, occasionally you can sail in October, but Never, Never do you set sail in November, the weather and seas are just too temperamental." Wallace was hoping this October would continue to borrow days from summer and not from the dead of winter.

As he motored along at a steady clip, he decided to pass Plum Island on its southern shore rather than stay out in the sound where almost all marine traffic passed. At Orient Point, he began to see local marine traffic, but did not notice anything unusual. He pulled into Orient Point to fill up on fuel using the money that I left with the documents. He wanted as near a full tank as possible as he entered the East River.

The hours went by slowly; Wallace confidently navigating the waters of Long Island Sound; he was trying to determine if he was going to reach Hell Gate at ebb tide. He made a mental game of it, recalculating everything.

When he reached City Island, he knew that he would be approaching Hell Gate at the wrong time. Should he wait off Hunt's Point near Riker's Island? He would make that decision shortly.

As he passed Fort Totten, he had officially left Long Island Sound and entered the East River. The rest of the trip would require a slow methodical navigation around the many islands and points in this most eastern portion of the river.

He kept up his steady pace. As he approached Riker's Island, he slowed his boat and eyed the two small islands beyond, North Brother's and South Brother's Islands. After the *Anna C* was abreast of these two small rock islands, Wallace could see the Hell Gate Channel. It was not as narrow as he'd remembered it. There were some vessels ahead of him, already in the channel and he was determined to follow them from a distance.

Wallace decided to enter Hell Gate from the Queens or easterly approach. He thought it safer, especially if the engine could not power itself against the strong current, which was now clearly flowing out of the East River Estuary into Long Island Sound. Wallace's eyes were getting tired; it was difficult to see ahead, with the glare of the sun directly off the bow. Wallace always wore his long brimmed cap worn low on the forehead, that helped somewhat to ease the strain on his eyes by blocking some of the glare.

At this point he was as worried about hitting debris in the river as much as about the current. The surface of the water with the glare in front of the boat made it hard to spot floating debris. The engine of the *Anna C* was getting a workout pushing hard against the advancing current.

The *Anna C* slowed even though Wallace kept it close to the shore. Ahead, he could see the upward surge of water, like a fountain, at what must have been the submerged ledge, Pot Rock. It was an unbelievable sight. Why hadn't this channel been cleared long ago? New York Harbor needed a second entrance. Any mariner sailing through the Hell Gate

Channel would ponder the question and wonder why the channel had not been totally cleared.

Just before the boat sailed under the railroad bridge that crossed from Queens onto Ward's Island, Wallace spotted what he thought was a submerged pole near the center of the channel. But when he looked again, he couldn't be sure, having lost sight of it in the glare of the sun.

"What was that?" he thought out loud. "Was that pole a submerged submarine?"

It didn't seem possible, not in the approach to this channel that was, in places, only twenty-four feet deep, and that being at high tide. For a fleeting moment, he thought about turning around to explore, but quickly the channel became the focus of all his concentration; Hell Gate was not a place to maneuver a boat, rather one needed to sail straight through and try to keep one's boat from capsizing.

Pot Rock and its temporary fountain that was created by the current twice a day loomed ahead. Wallace kept his boat well to starboard, pulling farther into the East River, slowly but surely up stream, or was it down stream? He was not long concerned and knew that the *Anna C* could make it, and within a few minutes he had passed Pot Rock to starboard and Blackwells Island was in sight. He decided to pass Blackwells Island on the inner channel where the current was much less and he could give his engine a rest of sorts. He was now in familiar territory, my own hometown being Green Point on the East River which he would soon pass on the left or to port. The Navy Yard was a few miles away and he reached that in fifteen minutes.

As he approached the massive military complex across from lower Manhattan, he turned his attention to locating Dry Dock 1, and to avoiding all tug traffic. He continued to hug the east side of the river.

Sailing into the Brooklyn Navy Yard on the *Anna C* was a humbling experience. The size of the marine objects under construction; the size of the complex itself; the massive battleships—in dry dock and in the water —and the cranes, all towering hundreds of feet above the ground, all made for a surreal experience. Yet, there was there was something odd about a construction site this massive sitting across the river from one of the most important cities in the world.

Dry Dock 1 had an easy to recognize landmark: still under construction, the destroyer, that would soon be christened the Battleship New Mexico. There were other numerous smaller navy vessels and frigates being built there as well. Although we weren't in war, it sure looked like we were preparing for it.

Within a few minutes, the little boat from Block Island would join them.

It was now dark but the lights from the yard itself allowed him to maneuver around and in the waterways of the Navy Yard easily; he found the floating dock that I had suggested. As he approached it, he became aware that the Naval Police had already spotted him. Four officers greeted my son at the small dock with guns drawn—until he was able to identify himself as a fisherman from Block Island.

He explained to the officers that he was to hand-deliver a document to the Weather Bureau Official in Charge in the Naval Yard. With guns soon tucked safely out of sight, the officers agreed to escort Wallace to the office in a small building near the Naval Hospital.

Wallace was captivated by the Navy Yard. Wallace, the *Anna C* and the battleships of the United States Navy. Now, here was future story-telling material for my son, the Block Island raconteur and sometime fisherman.

As they walked across the complex the officers showed interest in Wallace, not so much because of the document he carried, but because none of them had ever met someone from Block Island. In fact, three had never even heard of the Island. Of this, they had much in common with Melville. Their friendliness toward Wallace, though, was almost suspicious, as if the prodigal son was returning.

23 The Office of Naval Intelligence

Communication between the U. S. Weather Bureau and the U. S. Army remained strong after the weather service was transferred from the Army to the civilian Department of Agriculture in the late 1880s. When I joined the Weather Bureau it was part of the U. S. Signal Corp, a branch of the Army. After the transfer, the New York Weather Bureau established a satellite office in the Brooklyn Navy Yard and relations with the Navy developed similarly. When the Office of Naval Intelligence established a small office in the Navy Yard it was my understanding that they frequently consulted certain key weather staff (my old boss) when necessary. So it was no surprise that my son was introduced to not only weather and Naval officials, but to ONI officers as well.

After Wallace was escorted to an office in a small building not too far from the Naval Hospital, he entered a small room on the first floor and was introduced to two officers in full dress uniform, and another man dressed in a business suit. There was no representative of the Weather Bureau present, but Wallace felt comfortable and was not at all concerned. He was sure that the right people, whoever they were, would soon be reading what I had written.

The three officers reviewed the documents, none being thrown off with the use of weather codes. Within about fifteen minutes the two officers stood and said they would need to review the documents with their supervisors and left the room. Wallace was surprised by their leaving so abruptly.

The man in the business suit remained seated and asked where Wallace would be staying for the night. Wallace answered that he planned to stay on the upper west side of Manhattan with my sister and her husband in their home on Convent Street. The man wanted to know some details about them and where on the upper west side was Convent

Street—he had never heard of it. After explaining about my oldest sister, my brother-in-law and their son—his cousin Royal—the man appeared satisfied. He stood, shook Wallace's hand, and thanked him for making the effort to sail to New York City and delivering the documents. He then walked Wallace to the front of the small building where a driver was summoned.

While they were waiting for a driver, the man stated they expected him back at the Naval Yard the next day at 1:00 p.m. He was to report to the gate near the Marine Hospital and would then be brought into the complex to another building near the Naval Hospital. Wallace was assured that he would be able to meet at least one of my colleagues from the Weather Bureau, and after the meeting, would be free to return to Block Island.

Although Wallace was greeted with enthusiasm and respect, his sudden dismissal from the meeting with the naval officers, after his long ride, was a bit disconcerting. He assumed tomorrow's meeting would last longer.

Wallace was driven out the south gate of the yard to the Brooklyn Bridge subway station, about a mile and a half away, where he boarded the elevated subway train to Manhattan. Once over the bridge, he transferred to another subway, this one headed to the upper west side of Manhattan.

By the time Wallace reached Convent Street, it was very late and he was exhausted. It had taken Wallace two hours to travel from the Navy Yard to the upper west side, although thirty minutes of that time was spent locating their Convent Street home. It is not an easy street to find, especially when you don't have a car.

Wallace knocked several times on their apartment door before Catherine and her husband, George Weller, appeared. They were not as stunned to see Wallace as he had anticipated. Soon Wallace understood why.

After sitting down, but before he removed his overcoat and before he had dinner, Wallace related what had transpired on Block Island the week past. I had wanted Wallace to describe the turn of events to George in detail because George's son, Royal, now working as a prosecutor for

NYC, could help pass the word about this potentially serious event to others in government if the Weather Bureau, Navy, or the ONI were not interested in the data.

But little did I know, that even before Wallace had reached their apartment, numerous people had read my document and the man in the suit had phoned my brother-in-law and given him advanced notice that Wallace would soon be arriving at his door. And further, long before Wallace had reached Convent Avenue, officers of the ONI had contacted their superior, a certain Franklin D. Roosevelt, to review the course of events on Block Island that were detailed in my documents.

Apparently, what Milton had witnessed on Block Island had not gone unacknowledged, even before Wallace's arrival. George and Royal both knew Franklin D. Roosevelt, and they also knew that as Assistant Secretary of the Navy, he was concerned about espionage. The phone call to George and Catherine took place about thirty minutes prior to Wallace knocking on their door.

Exhausted from the day's activities, they all fell asleep rather quickly. In the morning, during an early breakfast, a phone call from a naval officer interrupted them. The caller asked to speak with Wallace. He requested that Wallace return to Brooklyn as soon as possible. George was instructed to make no other calls about the events on Block Island to anyone. A driver would meet Wallace at the Brooklyn Bridge station in one hour. He was not to be accompanied by anyone, and Wallace was told not to call me, a fact that we had, of course, already established.

24 An Afternoon Walk on Block Island

Unable to contact my son, all sorts of questions were raised in my mind. Had he been able to sail effortlessly through Hell Gate, navigate the East River currents, and enter the Brooklyn Navy Yard without incident? Did he hand-deliver the documents to the correct individual? Whom had he met—if anyone? I could only hope that all had gone well.

It had been two days since my son and the *Anna C* had left the Island. I was not expecting to hear anything via cable or telephone of course, but this morning, when I awoke, I climbed up onto the roof deck of the Weather House to see if his boat had reappeared at the Hog Pen. The smaller pulling boat that I had placed in his slip was still in the berth. If he had returned, he had docked or moored in the Great Salt Pond, out of my line of sight from the roof deck.

Over the past few days Milt and I, and the new enlistments to the team, my two nieces, have not sat idly. We started using the Marconi device again, not to send messages; rather to monitor messages intended for others. That was Annie's idea. We strung a wire from the roof of the Weather House to the top of the tower to improve reception on the wireless device. It was also Annie's idea to explore the Island on foot, and, if necessary, in the wheelchair, to discover where one or more of these three men were staying. Annie's single-mindedness and sense of determination and adventure led to a remarkable finding. I should have known better than to have thought that the two girls were not listening to every word spoken over the past week; in fact, they not only overheard us, but Annie was way ahead of us in thinking about what really was happening.

Lillie and I have long been impressed with the two girls' reasoning ability, and with their abundance of self-confidence. We have long since stopped trying to understand and anticipate their actions. Upon overhearing all that had been said by the rest of us, and putting that together with the knowledge of our country's possible entry into the European War, they initiated—on their own—what anyone in a military capacity would consider a small reconnaissance mission.

It began with an afternoon walk.

But before I tell the story of that afternoon stroll, it should be stated that, because of her accident, Annie looked to the uninitiated as if she could not understand much of anything spoken to her. She had become increasingly spastic (muscle tone had increased) in the past year, and had begun to develop contractures in her ankles and one of her wrists. Her body did appear distorted because her spine was crooked and starting to twist on itself—scoliosis her doctor said, an ancient term Hippocrates coined. To some she appeared, I am sure, however unfortunate, somewhat scary.

At times, polite but misguided strangers spoke to her in a slow, deliberate, loud manner as if she were mentally retarded and partially deaf; but at least they spoke to her and did not ignore her. Because of this, she was always polite, giving a nod with her eyes and then looking downward. Although the way the majority of people approached was hurtful and, understandably, made her a bit angry.

Yet, at the same time, Annie could be somewhat oppositional and pretend that she was indeed deaf, dumb and sometimes even blind; but that was only for effect, a play on her newfound sense of humor. But, oh to the unsuspecting! Those unfamiliar with her condition could not imagine what she was capable of accomplishing as she sat in her wheelchair observing the fisherman on their boats in the Old Harbor; or watching visitors walk off the ferry, the *George Danielson*, or listening to passersby as she sat at her favorite spot on Crescent Beach near the Surf Hotel. She learned a lot while being pushed around the Island by her sister, all the while listening intently and observing her world. The uninitiated never suspected that she was every bit as attentive to the world as the most skilled trained observer.

She realized that she could use her clinical condition to uncover a wealth of information. And with her improving skill using Morse code she could now communicate complex thoughts and ideas to anyone who could understand the language of Mr. Morse. Regardless of what she looked like in body, her spirit, resiliency, and her mind were as robust as any other young woman's was. Allow me to suggest that if Aristotle had known my niece, he would have made Resiliency a most important virtue—along with practical reasoning of course; more important, perhaps, than courage. Perhaps courage and resiliency go hand in hand; in Annie Rose, they stood side by side.

Although Annie continued to use, quite effectively, her simple yes/no form of nonverbal communication with everyone else, the communication with her sister was more complex and went far beyond the use of that simple system. They understood each other so well that although they occasionally used the yes/no system, more often they employed subtle nuances of physical movements that, I suspected, were translated into complex thoughts, directives, concepts even. Their language of movement became sentences with a grammar only they could appreciate. ("Grammar" here ought to be in quotes because only the two of them fully understood it.)

Their communication system was fluid and effective and was certainly an extension of the friendship they shared. They kept this system to themselves, not because of secrecy, but because it was part of the complex bond of sisterhood and surviving the accident. That continued bond gave their mother some solace after their near deaths. Years ago, Lillie had said she always knew that life would take these two someplace special; and after she realized how well they were able to communicate following Annie's recuperation, her initial feeling became reaffirmed.

"Where do you want me to push you, Annie?" Emma asked again, looking a bit incredulous.

Annie made an awkward verbal response and a corresponding slight movement of her head.

"I'm not pushing you up past the Spring House Hotel. That's too far, and I am tired," Emma protested.

Annie made another sound, accompanied by the same motion with her head.

"No way. We are not going up there. Yes, you're right, it's not that far, but it is a long way to *push* and the road is sandy. No!"

Again Annie was persistent. She wanted to go to a spot near the
Spring House Hotel where the bluffs on the southeast side of the Island
begin to rise gradually. It was a little over a mile, and it was uphill and
the sand and rut-filled road that led out to the bluff from Spring Street
would be tough to negotiate, perhaps even impassable, with a wheelchair.
But Annie Rose wouldn't take no for an answer. All of this she was able
to communicate to her sister within a matter of moments. Each nuance
of how she turned her head, combined with movements of her eyes
represented a different place on the Island, a different time, a different
reason. She was persistent and eventually Emma Rose relented and off
they went. It was 4:00 p.m. Em yelled to their mother that they were
going up to the Spring House to see a friend who was supposed to be
helping paint the hotel's annex, now that it was off-season.

"Okay, girls, but please be back home before dinner. Who are you
going to visit there?" Lillie asked.

But the girls were already headed down the dirt drive; past the Union
House Hotel, under the watchful eye of their Uncle Arthur, who was
sitting on the front porch of the hotel as they went by; then down High
Street, and up Spring Street and the start of the long, slow climb to their
destination. Even at this point Annie would not share the reason for this
afternoon walk or even their eventual destination. Annie saved this for
when Emma would really start complaining about pushing her up the
final hill near where she wanted to take a left and explore a side road.

"Why are we doing this again, Annie?" Emma said, as sarcastic as the
heavens will allow a fourteen-year-old girl to ask.

Annie remained silent; she was getting her way. And a ride up the hill
would mean that upon their return, they could then ride down together
in the wheelchair.

"How far do we have to go?" Emma asked for the tenth time. They
were halfway to their destination and Annie began her explanation, in her
language, that she thought she saw one of the three "mystery men" drive
up Spring Street the day before, and wanted to find out if she could see
the same car.

"Where are we going?" Emma again pleaded. After about a quarter a mile up the hill, just beyond the entrance to the Spring House Hotel grounds, Annie answered in a way that Em had to stop pushing and walk around to look at her facial expressions in order to understand.

"All the way up there? That's almost to the Southeast Light. We will never get back home for dinner! No!" Em was exaggerating, as she was often wont to do, especially when she did not want to do something. But this time she actually misunderstood Annie's communication. Annie wanted to go to Southeast Road, a dirt road halfway up Spring Street, not to the Southeast Lighthouse Road.

Annie shrugged her one shoulder that she had control of. She knew that they might very well be late for dinner, but their mother never yelled at her anymore; now that honor always went to Emma.

Southeast Road was another secluded part of Block Island, but not because it was isolated. In fact it was only a little over a mile and half from the inner basin of the Old Harbor. It appeared remote only because few homes were built on the dirt road leading out to the Atlantic. The road ended with a view from bluffs that were only a third the height of the Mohegan Bluffs. The brush was thick, never being cut back as on other parts of the Island, and hid the few small homes on this road from everyone. Even if you lived on the Island for an entire lifetime, one's business may never take you down this road, except perhaps to witness a brilliant sunrise. I have never even walked onto Southeast Road, although it ends at a place with a familiar name: Old Harbor Point.

It was to this dirt road that Annie was having her sister push her.

Three-fourths of the way to their destination, Em stopped for a rest while her sister waited patiently. To avoid any road traffic, Emma pushed the wheelchair off into the brush, a technique they found helpful to avoid any danger from passing cars or horse and buggy traffic on the narrow, dirt and sand surfaced roads of the Island. They had had too many close calls, almost getting clipped by a fast moving horse and buggy, or a car, on numerous occasions and diving into brush to avoid a collision; with Annie pushing off her good foot, the one that still had strength in it. She could dive several feet off the chair when the need arose.

Soon they were able to see the entrance to Southeast Road. As they approached, they could see new tire tracks in the road that was more sand than clay or dirt. The tracks were thin and without horse hoof impressions; these were the treads left by a car.

They headed into the road with Annie constantly "announcing" where certain spots in the brush would be good to hide if a car suddenly appeared on the road. As they approached the first sharp bend in the dirt road, the Atlantic Ocean appeared beyond the thick brush. With the sun setting on the opposite side of the Island, the water appeared very dark blue to black.

As they negotiated the next sharp bend in the road, they heard a car coming; they couldn't see it but could tell it was moving fast toward them. Annie moved her shoulder and her head, followed by her hand signal—the communication was clear but Emma did not need the instruction. Em quickly pushed the wheelchair into the thicket, trying to avoid the inevitable poison ivy. As she pushed harder, the wheelchair spokes got caught in the brush. They could hear the car, still moving fast, although not yet in sight.

Em pushed harder but the wheelchair would not move up the slight grade farther into the brush. Sensing there was not enough time, Annie rolled off the wheelchair and crawled into the brush as best she could. That enabled her sister to maneuver the wheelchair onto its side and hide it in the tall weeds. Emma hurried beside her sister, pulling her body farther away from the road; Annie, not able to maneuver her body well, simply pushed with her good leg and crawled in as best she could. With Annie well hidden and the wheelchair out of site, Emma positioned herself so that she could see the car as it passed.

When the car rounded the bend, only Em could see the men in the car clearly; it was the same car that Annie had seen at the landing. When Emma saw that there were three men, the driver and two in the back seat, it proved Annie right.

"How did you know, Annie?" Emma looked at her sister with wonderment.

Annie Rose just smiled.

As the car disappeared out of sight, Annie communicated that it would be best for Emma to run ahead—leaving her in the brush for a few minutes—to see in what direction on Spring Street they turned. Were they going back to town, or up toward the lighthouse and the west side of the Island?

Em ran back down Southeast Road to where she could see Spring Street as it winded its way back to the Old Harbor; but she could not see the road as it headed up toward the Southeast Lighthouse. She did not see the car drive down the hill to the Old Harbor area, so she was certain that they had turned left and continued up the hill to the other side of the Island. As she approached the end of the road at Spring Street, she walked slower, just in case the car had stopped, having seen them in the brush.

She did not see the car or any of the men and turned around and ran back to retrieve her sister. She pulled Annie out of the bushes and sat her in her chair. She then pushed her as fast as she dared back to Spring Street and down the hill to home.

"Annie, how did you know?" Em repeated.

Annie, deep in thought, did not answer.

Except for a short grade uphill near the front entrance to the Spring House, the ride back was entirely downhill. If the wheels of the wheelchair stayed on, it was going to be a quick ride back to the Old Harbor. The two girls loved to ride down this hill. Sitting together on the wheelchair, they coasted, laughing out loud until the occasional rut briefly jarred their momentum forward. They were quite content now that they knew that they too would contribute to the task at hand— trying to determine the 'who and why' of the three mystery men.

Annie couldn't wait until dinner when she would be able to tell her story.

"I do the talking," Annie told her sister.

"Oh, yeah! You get to tell the story and all I get to do is push you up the damn hill!"

Annie had a special sign for the love she felt for her sister: a movement of her good hand to her heart, and then up to her mouth, which she now signed.

"I love you, too," Emma said in a not so subtle, sarcastic kind of way, knowing full well that her sister had just taken the wind out of her fleeting disagreement.

When the sisters returned to their house, dinner was almost ready. As they washed up, they briefly explained to Lillie and Arthur what they had seen on Southeast Road near the bluffs. Arthur then called me from the Union House Hotel and let me know that I ought to drive over immediately for dinner at Lillie's house. He did not elaborate. Because the phone lines were not private, I assumed there was something I needed to know, so I drove over with Milton as soon as we finished the weather data transmission.

When Milt and I arrived and sat down for dinner, I realized for the first time that Lillie, Milton, Arthur, the two girls, and myself were about to try to put all the pieces of the puzzle together. The only person missing, of course, was Wallace.

Emma started the discussion. She reviewed how Annie and she had hidden in the brush at the sharp bend in the very sandy Southeast Road and watched as the car with the three men drove by. Annie then took over her explanation of why she had thought to go for a late afternoon stroll to Southeast Road in the first place.

Little did the girls know that Arthur had been watching over them. He noticed the girls go up Spring Street, and decided to follow them, staying far behind so that he could not be seen. Arthur confirmed that a car with one man in the front seat, and two in the back seat, turned left when it exited Southeast Road and went up the hill toward Mohegan Bluffs. Arthur did not think that the girls or the three men had noticed him, or each other. Arthur waited until he saw the two girls leave the road and then returned to his hotel. He, of course, had no idea what the two were trying to accomplish—until he was told the story.

"We didn't see you, Uncle Arthur," Em remarked.

Lillie thanked Arthur for looking out for them. She then looked at the girls and shook her head from side to side.

Annie simply flashed a crooked smile.

When I heard the story, it all began to make sense. They were staying near the secluded Old Harbor Point.

"I wonder if they have a horizontal transmission 'tower' there, perhaps hidden in the thick brush?" I thought out loud.

"Tomorrow we can see if any wireless signals come from that

direction, Mr. Eddey," Milton piped up.

Milt and I then reviewed our finding concerning the Marconi device. We discovered that running a wire from the roof of the Weather House to the top of Weather Flag tower could improve the sensitivity of the device's reception. Today we started receiving occasional strong signals that we could not recognize; we had wondered if those signals were in code, or another language, or both. Could they be transmitting in German?

We weren't sure how to proceed at this point except to continue to try and find out how to intercept those signals.

"Make sure you do not send any signals from the device, just receive them," Lillie suggested. "Let Annie have a listen in the morning."

I don't know why I was surprised at Lillie's comment which reflected, of course, confidence in her oldest daughter's abilities. Her point was well taken.

We finished our meal of fish chowder and all of us, except Arthur, returned to the Weather House.

Milton and I immediately ran to the roof to change the position of the antenna wire to capture any signals coming from across the Island at Old Harbor Point. As I fine-tuned the position, Milton ran downstairs and started listening to the Marconi device for any reception.

After just a few minutes, I heard him yelling.

"Mr. Eddey, Mr. Eddey, come here quick!"

25 The Return of the Anna C

When I got down to the office, Milt explained that as soon as I redirected the antenna, he began hearing a strong signal, presumably from the east side of the Island, perhaps from Old Harbor Point. I could not understand the communication but we were amazed. How did Annie know?

I went back upstairs to sit with Annie and ask her to explain in detail how she developed the premise that the mystery men were living off Southeast Road, but she had fallen asleep and Lillie wouldn't let me wake her. I rejoined Milt to listen for any further communications. The signals were strong but confusing and did not make sense. Were they in code? Soon they ended, and feeling a bit frustrated, we went to bed. We agreed that tomorrow we would have Annie sit by the device and monitor all signals.

I was up early, well before the sun and well before everyone else. It was now three days since my son had left the Island. I walked up to the roof of the Weather House, as I had done every morning since Wallace had left the Island, to look out at the Hog Pen to see if his boat was in its rightful berth. As I was gazing about the Island, I heard a familiar voice.

"Hey, Pop, what are you doing up there?"

I couldn't quite see him, but Wallace had spied me from the road and waited until he got closer to the building to call my name.

He had returned and it sounded from his cheerful voice that all was well.

I quickly descended from the roof using the narrow stairs that led to the second floor; and then down another flight to the front door where Wallace was sitting, having perched himself on the front stone stoop. I bent down and gave him a handshake, pulled him to his feet, and then a hug.

He was so exhausted, having not slept in over thirty-six hours, but was indeed in a good mood, appearing not at all cranky from the long trip.

We went inside to the office where Milton had slept, next to the Marconi device. Milt stood up abruptly when he saw Wallace; excited and surprised to see my son enter through the front door so early in the morning.

"When did you get in, Wallace?" I asked.

"About three o'clock this morning. I had to move the pulling boat and we decided to sleep on the boat for a bit. I was tired and fell right asleep, we just woke up."

"What do you mean 'we'?" Milt pounced, before I could ask the same question.

"It is a long story, but why don't you hear it from him directly," Wallace smiled slyly. "He is waiting down on the boat. He wants to stay in the cabin for a while and make sure no one sees him. I told him he could stay at my house but his boss suggested he stay at the Weather House.

"You will really like him," Wallace went on. "And so will Annie, by the way. We will have to wait until tonight when he feels comfortable leaving the boat to hear the whole story. But we can go down so you can meet him and bring him some breakfast. What do you have to eat, Pop? Is Lillie here? By the way, I caught a bigeye tuna on the way in last night. We had to stop the boat of course—we fought that fish for an hour. Can you believe it? The guy had never been fishing, so I thought I would show him how we do it on Block Island, and no sooner did I throw out the chum and then the lure with the bait, I landed a bigeye.

"It cost us some time but it was worth it. I want to sell it as soon as possible. That tuna could bring in some useful money."

Catching a bigeye tuna was something everyone dreamed of, and Wallace was no exception. He had caught several, but every time he landed another one, it was such a thrill. Myself, I have never caught one, although I have caught my share of swordfish and the smaller bluefin tuna.

"Where did you hook the bigeye, and how much do you think it weighs?" I asked my son.

"We landed it just as we were well into Block Island Sound, about ten miles north east of Gardiner's Bay. I think it only weighs about three hundred and fifty pounds, but it is a keeper." He was joking of course.

After listening to my son tell the short version of the fish story (I suppose that I will have to wait until he has had some wine before I hear the long version) I set out to make our unknown visitor and everyone else some oatmeal. I used milk from the Murray farm, rather than water; threw in some cinnamon and half a dozen apples. I made enough to feed a small army.

"I hope he likes oatmeal," I thought out loud.

I asked Wallace to explain what happened when he arrived at the Navy Yard, but just then Lillie, hearing the commotion in the kitchen, came down to greet Wallace, and took over the cooking of the oatmeal. I explained that Wallace had brought a guest with him and that guest would be staying at the Weather House, although he was now asleep in the cabin of the *Anna C.*

Wallace finally sat down; he drank some coffee and ate a small piece of cake that was a left over from the Union House Hotel kitchen from the day before, while awaiting the oatmeal.

"What happened at the Navy Yard? And who is the man on your boat?" Lillie asked, as I had minutes before.

Lillie, however, received a different answer than I.

Wallace explained that when he woke up at Catherine and George's apartment, the urgent phone call taking him back to the Naval Yard prevented him from seeing his cousin Royal. Royal had, though, contacted the ONI directly to make sure that the documents and my concerns were addressed seriously. Wallace explained that when Royal made his calls he was told that there were 'significant people' already aware of the documents and he should know that the Block Island Weather Official in Charge would be taken seriously. We all knew that Royal was positioning himself to run as a Republican for Congress in the next election although his father was a Democrat and part of the Tammany Hall machine. Royal had become friendly with LaGuardia, as well as the Governor of New York State, who was guiding his steps to elected national office. I suppose that explained why the ONI (and perhaps Roosevelt himself) was responsive to Royal's request.

When Wallace met the driver at the Brooklyn Bridge elevated subway line, he was taken directly to the Naval Yard and a building adjacent to the Marine Hospital. He was met by the same two Naval officers who had briefly spoken to him when he first arrived. The man in the suit had brought another three individuals, none of whom introduced themselves by name. The man in the suit finally introduced himself as John, a member of the ONI. I did not catch his last name.

The Naval Intelligence Officers questioned Wallace for over an hour about the information in the report. They talked about all sorts of things and speculated about the European War and whether Block Island could be used as a drop-off point for spies from Europe. Wallace said that Block Island was an easy landmark for ships "coming out of the sea from Europe" and could easily be used as a staging area for European spies. Wallace explained how desolate the Island was, especially in the winter, the season that was fast approaching.

Wallace also mentioned the strange "pipe" that he saw as he was navigating through the Hell Gate Channel. Was that a submersible? The officers believed that the channel was too shallow, being burdened with numerous underwater shoals, to allow for passage of a submarine. However, they had no explanation for what he might have seen.

After an hour the conversation turned to the matter of secrecy and being sure that no wireless, telephone, or telegraphic communication about this episode, the three mysterious men, or this meeting ever occurs. Further, the Naval Officer thought it prudent that no one from Wallace's family leave Block Island via the established ferryboats for the foreseeable future. Wallace was the exception of course since he could come and go as he pleased with his own boat. And the government would pay for his fuel!

Toward the end of the meeting, the Official in Charge of the New York City Weather Bureau entered the room, my old boss. He took instructions from the naval officer in charge and then quickly left the room for another meeting, but not before asking Wallace how I was doing and said to say hello.

The Weather Official in charge at 100 Broadway had the same question for the ONI officers as I had. Were any of the communications received at my Weather House erroneous messages?

"Did the War College send that message to the Block Island Weather station in response to Mr. Eddey's wireless communication? Or did someone else send it?" my old boss asked.

At that point, Wallace reported, the man in the suit, John—who was now in the cabin of the *Anna C*—left the meeting to contact the Naval War College in Newport for further information regarding their transmissions, if any, to Block Island. This, as it turned out, would be John's fifth call to the War College, but they were not able to answer the question this time either, and John returned to the meeting.

After much discussion, it was decided that Wallace needed to return the next day for further instructions; he was also told to be prepared to sail back to Block Island.

When the meeting was over, one of the officers walked him out to check on his boat and gave him a tour of the Navy Yard. In daylight, he saw the immensity of scale of the new battleships now being constructed. He was in awe and couldn't help but think that we would soon be at war, although on a personal note, he also thought here was more subject matter for his stories.

On the way to the dock, Wallace ran into one of the Naval Police Officers who had greeted him with a gun the previous night. The officer told him the entire force was watching out for his boat; that pleased Wallace immensely because he sure did love his *Anna C*.

Wallace asked if he could stay in the Naval Yard complex that night instead of traveling all the way back to the upper west side of Manhattan. The officers agreed and eventually found him a room on the top floor of one of the officer's homes, not too far from the Marine Hospital.

At the next day's meeting, Wallace began to appreciate the level of concern shared by the ONI, and he was pleased that it matched my own. At that meeting he was formerly introduced to John as a senior agent of the ONI.

John would be sent to investigate the situation as an intelligence agent. His cover would be a "meteorologist in training." And his mission was to help discover the significance of the three mysterious men. John's paycheck would come from the U. S. Weather Bureau and, as it turned out, the day before, when my old boss from 100 Broadway was summoned to the Naval Yard, he was instructed to send me a cable "reminding me" that I would have a meteorologist trainee assigned to me for the month of October. This would not have been unusual, as I had hosted many trainees during my tenure in the Weather Service, including on Block Island. It was hoped, of course, that the spies would intercept this communication.

The officers then explained to Wallace that there was an agent already assigned to the Island, although not on the Island itself. When the hotel had burned in August, the ONI had sent an agent to work as a deck hand on the ferry the *Block Island,* which sailed from New London, Connecticut. The *Block Island* was larger than the *George Danielson,* and conveniently, it docked in the New Harbor in the Great Salt Pond a few hundred yards from the Hog Pen.

One of the problems for the ONI was how to get John onto the Island. At first the officers thought simply to have him take the overnight steamship sailing from the Hudson River to Newport, Rhode Island, where he could then board the *George Danielson* for the two hour ride to Block Island. Wallace pointed out that the *George Danielson* was getting old and would most likely be taken out of service as the winter approached, and there was a significant risk that the boat would not run if the weather turned bad. The other option was to have John take the train to New London, Connecticut, and then board the ferry that sails from there to the Island, but that ferry, now that it was October, was only running once or twice per week and, if the weather turned, it wouldn't run at all either.

John argued Wallace ought to take him on his small boat so he could get a thorough understanding of the Island before officially "arriving." (There was also a personal reason John wanted to sail with Wallace, but I will leave that for later.)

Although there was some debate, the consensus of the ONI officers was that John needed to get to the Island as soon as possible—to begin the process of understanding the Island *and* start working with the team that I had assembled. And the fact that there were only a few ferry trips to the Island each week from the mainland, to either of the harbors, solidified the decision that John would sail on Wallace's boat.

One might wonder why the ONI did not send in their own team.

The answer, as I understand it, was that the ONI was not a large organization. In fact, most agents were recruited from business or academia, with anthropologists making up a large portion of the operatives. I knew from my time in NYC that the ONI was not well equipped and poorly funded by the Navy, and so I was not in the least bit surprised when only one agent was sent to our Island.

When Wallace pointed out that his boat was berthed close to where the *Block Island* docked in the New Harbor, the officers suggested that a day or two after John arrived, he was to secretly board the ferry and then walk off as if he had arrived as a tourist; or in this case, as a trainee with the U.S. Weather Service. The agent assigned to the ferry would be contacted and would throw John a line off the back of the boat, haul him up from a small skiff that Wallace owned, and then he could join the other disembarking passengers.

With that settled, the senior officer determined that John and Wallace should set sail from the Brooklyn Navy Yard as soon as possible; and at noon, in the shadow of the battleship *U.S.S. Arizona*, they left Dry Dock 1 for Block Island.

26 The Big Eye Tuna

When Lillie and I had finished cooking the oatmeal and warmed up some muffins, Lillie drove me down to the Hog Pen to meet and feed our new guest, who was waiting patiently in the *Anna C*. Lillie returned to her home on High Street, leaving the two girls in the Weather Office, monitoring the incoming communications.

After boarding, I went below to deliver breakfast. I was looking forward to meeting John; this young man who had accompanied Wallace back to our home, and who had his first taste of off shore fishing for tuna, quite unexpectedly, the night before. This man, who was about to understand why the sun always casts its shadow on our Island, I now handed a bowl of oatmeal.

He stood up and smiled. "Nice to meet you, sir." He shook my hand and then sat down, clutching the warm bowl between his hands as if to say, "It is quite cold in this cabin."

He was a thin man, much like Wallace, but at six feet two inches, a full five inches taller. He was pleasant enough and quite personable; he appeared happy to meet me finally. He introduced himself with his first name and soon I learned that he was a graduate of the Naval Academy and recently assigned to the ONI.

We talked inside the cabin, out of eyesight and earshot of anyone who may have been walking near the boat. We spoke first about his trip in Wallace's boat; he had not gotten seasick and enjoyed the opportunity to watch my son land the tuna. He was aware that the weather was remarkable for a mid-October sail up Long Island Sound to Block Island. We occasionally glanced outside the cabin, onto the dock, where Wallace and Milton were preparing the big eye tuna into steaks. After all, Wallace suspected that his friends thought that he must have gone "a fishin'," and now he had proof positive.

John looked to be in his late twenties or early thirties. I knew enough from my interactions with officers in the Navy Yard not to ask personal questions, but he did offer than he was not married and lived with one of his sisters in NYC. He was mature, thoughtful, and inquisitive; I got the feeling he had that 'Ishmaelian sense of discovery' like my two nieces.

It did not take me long to realize that I liked this young man and indeed, before I left the cabin, he had earned my respect as well. I will elaborate later.

Wallace interrupted us by asking where we should eat an early dinner. After a few moments, I thought it best that we sit down for dinner at Lillie's home. Milton suggested that we serve swordfish as well; he knew where to get some newly caught off one of the fishing boats. So, if Lillie agreed, we would all gather at her home, around her table for a resplendent fish dinner. I suspected that she would serve her baked bread and corn. Wallace would bring clam chowder. Swordfish, tuna, and chowder served with greens and late corn; a finer Block Island dinner may not be possible.

John and I continued our conversation while Wallace loaded the tuna in his car and drove off to try to sell it before heading home to retrieve Edith from the Vaill Hotel. He needed to take a nap. Before Wallace left, we had discussed how John would board the ferry, a request of the ONI officers. The ferry wouldn't arrive, at its earliest, until late tomorrow morning, or perhaps even later in the week. I was forecasting several days of fog, consistent with the unseasonably warm days of this October. And with the fog, providing it did not burn off before late morning, getting him on board should be a simple task, but before that, we would have to keep John's presence on the Island a secret.

Milton walked back to the Weather House and I wondered, as this was happening (including my running conversation with John), how strange all of this was beginning to appear, and all because Milton had seen three mysterious men on his day off.

John asked a question that brought me back from my thoughts. "Mr. Eddey, what is your greatest fear, now that you have had some time to think about what has happened? Do you have any further thoughts since Wallace left the Island three days ago? I will share with you some thoughts of the ONI." His pointed questions made me give him my full, undivided attention. You could easily see that John was a highly intelligent individual, reading my thoughts well in advance of perhaps my own ability to do so.

"Well," I answered. "I am most concerned about my wireless device, and if it can be used remotely by someone else to send messages. Or perhaps there is another Marconi device operating from another part of the Island, and my device is the cover?"

I continued: "I suppose also I wonder if there are Islanders, or perhaps visitors, living on the Island, who are spies for Germany.

"And because I am fairly confident the War College never sent that wireless message, this almost confirms that there is something intriguing, if not dangerous, now occurring. I do think it highly probable that espionage is happening here in the form of those three mysterious men."

I had other concerns that were more global regarding the entry of the United States into the war that I kept to myself. For example, what if Germany was planning a landing on our soil? And Block Island was somehow an integral cog in their strategy? A hitherto completely outrageous suggestion, but a thought now impossible to erase from my mind.

"We at the ONI agree with your comments, Mr. Eddey, and that is why I am here," John said resolutely. "As you know, I am assigned to your Weather Bureau as an assistant observer in training. The Weather Bureau will pay my salary and the ONI will, of course, reimburse you for all my expenses. However, I think it best that I stay undercover for as long as is possible. Perhaps we should dine quietly at the Weather House tonight, rather than a large family dinner at Lillie's. But if that is what you occasionally do as a family, then we should proceed with that plan, either at your wife's home or up the road at the Weather House."

"John, I don't think it will be difficult to hide you for the next twenty-four to thirty-six hours."

We sat in silence for a few moments. I looked out of the cabin and did not see anyone observing the boat. I explained that it was best if we ate dinner at Lillie's, as her home is set back from the road and would not be as likely to attract the attention of passersby.

He asked about details of boarding the back of the ferry when it arrived on the Island within the next few days, and told me about the agent that had previously been assigned to the ferry, the *Block Island*, out of New London. After Wallace and John completed their assigned task, he would be free to walk to the Weather House and not have to stay on the boat. We thought it best, however, that tonight he slept in the cabin.

"Is the *Block Island* a big ferry?" John asked.

"It is a side-wheel steamship. The large side wheel has the name of the boat printed across it in four feet block letters. You can't miss it. Interestingly, this is a bad year for ferries to our Island. The *George Danielson* is probably on its last leg and will be retired soon, and the ferry you are boarding is also going to be taken out of service. Your fellow agent is going to have to throw you a line to climb on board as the deck protrudes over the hull by a few feet everywhere except by the wheelhouse. I think it best to board the boat after it has docked rather than on its approach to the dock through the Great Salt Pond."

As I said goodbye, he stopped me with a final comment. "Wallace told me about the two girls … and Annie's condition. I am looking forward to meeting them. Wallace explained much of what happened, before we landed the tuna."

I nodded, appreciative that he took an interest in both of the girls.

"How did the accident happen?"

I couldn't answer him. As a consequence of John asking the question, tears were swelling inside of me. I repeated to myself, "he cared enough to ask," and I simply responded that it was hard to explain.

He said softly, "I am sorry." And then went on to explain to me, as he had to Wallace, that he had lost his youngest sister two years ago. She had been thrown from a horse about ten years past and was left with physical and mental deficits. He said that it was sometimes hard for him to talk about her accident as well.

"I am sorry too, John."

After a few moments, I jumped off the boat, holding back tears—for both stories—and returned to the Weather House. As I walked up the short incline, away from the Hog Pen, I became aware that I was grasping the empty cereal bowl firmly, as if it had somehow become a precious object.

I had weather work to do and was late with the morning transmission of weather data. As I was sending in my report to the regional office, I couldn't help but think how lucky Wallace and John were that the weather patterns or *the moving formations* of the past week resembled the mild weather of mid-August. Their sail from Brooklyn to Block Island couldn't have been better. But I knew that the weather couldn't last forever. No, that high-pressure system that was blocking the days of November from entering Block Island Sound could not stay around much longer.

One is filled with gratitude when the sun doesn't cast its shadow, and I found myself thinking, *Only time will tell if John can help lift the current shadow covering the Island.*

27 The Swordfish Dinner

I picked up John from the Hog Pen and drove to Lillie's home after sundown so no one would be able to see him, crouched down for most of the ride in the back seat. I took him the long way, avoiding the Old Harbor Village area, in order to show him the west side of the Island, and stopped briefly at the beach near the lifesaving station where Milt first saw the three men. I pointed out the lights from Montauk Point, and the approximate area of Gardiner's Bay where Wallace and he landed the tuna.

We then continued our drive around Fresh Pond, eventually passing in front of Wallace's home. John smiled when he saw the porthole on the front of the house: "Eddey's Shanty." He had never seen anything like that before, and frankly, neither have I. We then drove down Pilot Hill Road and continued down on High Street to Lillie's home. John, soon to be the "newest member" of the Weather Bureau, courtesy of Naval Intelligence, appeared to clearly enjoy his first sights of the Island, even though it was dusk.

Everyone came over at about 6:00 p.m. with Milton being the first to arrive, mostly, I am sure, to talk to the girls. He may have been a good worker but he still was a youngster at sixteen years old. John and I soon arrived and then Wallace. Arthur joined us when he saw Wallace pull into the driveway.

"Where's Edith?" I asked Wallace as he walked in the door.

"She's at the Vaill Hotel. I don't think she wanted to join us anyway because, as you know, she doesn't eat fish. When I went home to nap she was there, but when I woke up she had gone back to the Vaill to work the front desk."

When John was introduced to Lillie, he greeted her with a warm and gracious hello as if he had known her for years. They spoke for a few minutes, but soon became distracted when they heard the girls talking. Knowing full well Lillie would not mind, he ended his conversation and went over to talk to them, clearly at ease with Annie's physical condition. He towered above the girls, shook first Emma's hand and spoke her name, "Hello, Emma Rose." And then turned to her sister. "Hello, Annie Rose, it is wonderful to meet you," he said, gently grasping her slightly open right hand as he finished his introduction. "I'm John, a Lieutenant First Class with the ONI."

Annie responded with her genuine, broad smile that she gives when truly pleased.

"Annie," John said. "I understand from Mr. Eddey that you have been doing some work on this question of the three mysterious men. Can you share some of your thoughts with me later?"

Annie smiled and again raised her eyes.

Lillie sat us around the rectangular dining room table. The swordfish and tuna were served on clay plates handed down from her father's mother. The silverware, including the silver spoons, were also handed down from her family from the late 1800s. Lillie made a point to explain this to John. I had heard the story of those spoons countless times.

Milt announced: "The swordfish was caught less than twenty-four hours ago by my friend, Amos Littlefield, and his father, by hand lining, not with a harpoon. Much less damage to the fish." I wasn't sure if he was explaining that to the girls or John.

When we were seated, John began the discussion by asking me to summarize all that was known, both factual and speculative, up to the present time. As he asked the question, I couldn't help but reflect that it was less than twelve hours John had been on Island and we all felt so very comfortable with him at our table, as if he truly was a member of the family.

John looked toward the girls and, in essence, deputized them as part of the team when he asked if they would like to function as if they were on loan to the Navy? A question that made both of them sit up and nod 'yes' in agreement, although Annie's nod of yes was more pronounced than Em's. John went on to say, speaking to us as well, that they would have to abide by the code of conduct, which was to swear to secrecy. Everyone at the table nodded in agreement.

I began to outline the facts in a logical manner:

"First, three men with at least one pistol are seen on a secluded part of the Island, the west side beaches. And Milt is certain that he sees one of them again the following day at the North Lighthouse near the terminus of the cable.

"Second, the men are seen about a week later on Southeast Road by the two girls, and partially confirmed by Arthur.

"Third, Milt and I became concerned that the wireless communications received in response to my two messages, one to the Brooklyn Navy Yard and one from the War College, may not have originated there.

"Fourth, entry of the United States into the war with Germany may be inevitable.

"Fifth, Wallace takes information to the Brooklyn Navy Yard and confirms that we are not the only ones concerned.

"Finally, German U-boats are operating in the waters off Block Island, the questions of how many, and how frequently they come near to our shore is unknown.

"John, do you or anyone else want to add anything?"

"Well, what other facts do we know?" John asked, surveying everyone at the table.

Milton spoke up; he had been listening intently, but was also preoccupied with trying to impress Annie. "I think the fact that the Weather Bureau has one of the old Marconi wireless devices from ten years ago, and it still functions, should be placed on the list. If Mr. Eddey, as the official in charge, had not kept it in working order, I doubt any of us would be at the table tonight."

"Point well taken, Milton, or is it Milt?" John smiled.

"Milt or Milton," he blushed. "My mother calls me Milty."

At this point Annie got everyone's attention by raising her shoulder and nodding to her sister. "What Annie?" Em asked.

Annie was excited and wanted to contribute something that she had not previously mentioned to her sister. Emma went through a detailed questioning with Annie, using their complicated nonverbal system. After a few minutes, Em understood the essence of what she was saying and turned to us to explain. When Emma could understand the broad parameters of any conversation with her sister, it was easy to finish the conversation, although not always to Annie's liking; and that they did in front of all of us at the table.

As if cross-examining her, Emma started the questions so that we could appreciate what and why Annie was speculating. "You were down at the landing this afternoon, just sitting in your wheelchair. Is that correct?"

Annie's eyes said yes to that.

"How did you get there?"

Annie responded to us all with a hand motion signaling that she had wheeled herself down slowly in the afternoon.

"I saw you there today, you were headed to the fishing shacks across from where the ferry docked," Arthur interjected.

Annie turned her head slightly toward her Uncle and raised her eyes.

"Did you see someone?" I asked.

Yes.

"And did you hear that person say something, Annie?" John jumped in on the questioning.

John had the ability to talk to Annie, his experience and close relationship with his late sister clearly evident. I watched John closely as he went through a series of lengthy questions, for Annie. I could see he was intent on finding answers to questions, but also intent on understanding who Annie was, how she thought, while expressing his fondness for her through his level of attention. John was more than simply an accomplished professional, he was a genuine man whose life was made richer, I suspect, as a consequence of his relationship with his late sister.

John continued: "We will need to know what he was saying and to whom he was saying it, too, Annie. Do you think that you and your sister can explain it further, in more detail using Morse code tomorrow at the Weather Bureau?"

Emma answered for her sister: "Yes, I think she will need to use code to explain fully what she thinks she heard, and why she believes the three mysterious men are still on Block Island."

John had one more question. "Annie, that man you first saw at the inner basin—was he one of the three men that you saw on Southeast Road? And are you sure?"

Yes!

While we were digesting all that Annie had witnessed and concluded from her own observations, Emma was admonishing her: "Why didn't you tell me about all that?"

John knew instinctively that most people thought Annie did not have the ability to communicate with anyone—or even understand what others were saying. Strangers would continue their conversation in front of her because they just didn't think she could comprehend anything; or even if she could, she wouldn't be able to tell anyone. John was correct in his assumptions; he had seen it countless times with his sister before she died. Most would simply ignore her, before someone would even extend the courtesy of a simple hello.

"I will have to teach you some secret communication concepts tomorrow, and together we will review how to use Morse code utilizing those concepts," John said looking directly at Annie.

Annie raised her eyes. Her face now serious, appreciative of John's comments and relieved that John understood her potential for contributing to the task at hand. Perhaps Annie could indeed matter, I began thinking more and more.

The conversation changed to Wallace and his understanding of the meetings in the Naval Yard. By this time, Wallace had retired to a soft chair; drinking whiskey from a Block Island souvenir glass in one hand; the last of his meal resting most perilously on a fork in the other hand.

"One essential message that I received was that, and John's presence here now confirms this, there is very real concern about these men. The assumption is that they reflect the tip of the iceberg. The second message to me, and again John can confirm this, is that the ONI wants us to make sure these spies continue to operate on the Island unobstructed. They need to believe it is safe to operate from Block Island.

"I also learned something that wasn't said—the nonverbal communication of the officers told a story as well. They mentioned—John correct me if I am wrong—that Franklin D. Roosevelt, as acting secretary of the Navy, is very interested in espionage, very interested in Block Island, and very interested in what happened off Nantucket Lightship several weeks ago. I think *they* think these three men, and perhaps the fire at the Hygiea, are associated with Germany's wish to expand the war effort to North America. That wasn't said at the meeting, of course."

John did not respond.

"On a personal note, Pop, they wanted confirmation that you are as fast with Morse code now as when you were younger. I assured them that you were as fast and as accurate as ever. They also asked if you could learn German numerical code. I assured them that the answer was yes, so you better get busy learning their code.

"They sat quietly in their chairs when they read your comments regarding the wireless messages that the Germans send themselves, as if the messages were coming from the Weather House's Marconi device. I guess we now know that they were sending it from their own device, perhaps located, thanks to the girls, on Southeast Road."

Wallace continued, holding only the glass of whiskey in one hand, having consumed the fish from the fork in the other hand. "How is it possible that they can communicate using their machines and having the messages look like they are coming from the Weather Bureau cable? If that is true, then they have to be using a code other than their numerical code, such as the shorthand weather code that you use," Wallace finished the sentence pointing to me, Milton and Annie.

I sat quietly, thoughtfully thinking of an answer to that question. John also remained sitting quietly, despite being referenced, as it were, in each of Wallace's comments.

Milt mentioned about how the extended wire stretched to the signal flag tower seemed to do something to the incoming messages. Annie raised her eyes and her good arm to speak, but we did not notice her. (Annie would later tell me that at that point she had developed her hypothesis of how they figured out how to use Weather Bureau codes to transmit data over the wireless. If anyone picked up their messages and codes, they would not think twice, assuming it was simply the Weather House transmitting their data twice a day. And after understanding some of the German's subsequent transmissions over the next few days, she would ultimately understand the major objective of the mysterious men and their relationship to the U-boats. Annie was also, in retrospect, quite adept at understanding German numerical codes.)

John now took the opportunity to speak. "Yes, it is true ..." He appeared to be collecting his thoughts and I suspect he was most likely trying to choose his words carefully.

Looking at Wallace, he continued after half a minute of silence. "We are concerned that, well ... we do not want them to stop their communications. We want to understand them and use them to our advantage. So, yes, we want them to continue to operate on the Island. Wallace, I agree with your overall assessment. I guess it is fair to say that we have to let them work unhindered here on Block Island. They *cannot* know what we know about them. It is the only way to find out exactly what they are up to."

With German submarines sailing quietly by our shores, wireless messages transmitted from submarines to who knows where; with the ultimate purpose of planning, in some way, harm to our maritime and national interests, we all recognized that we were now part of an international espionage mission. While I was finishing this thought, Lillie and Em started clearing the table and Milt joined in to wash the dishes.

As they were cleaning up, John took charge of the final part of the dinner meeting. He outlined what he wanted the girls to do, together and alone, what he wanted Milt and I to do at the weather station the next morning, and what Wallace and he would try to accomplish starting before daybreak.

He looked at each of us as he gave us our assignments. Finally, he turned to Wallace and asked, "Where is Edith? It is important that you know where she is at all times."

Wallace nodded. And then John turned his attention to me.

"Mr. Eddey, I brought some documents given to me to study when I left the Navy Yard. My boss thought there just might be clues about who may be involved in Germany's affairs from Block Island. I left them on the *Anna C.* When we return, I would like to review these sheets with you."

"Okay, but remember, if the *Block Island* ferry runs, you are to 'officially arrive' tomorrow," I reminded John.

Wallace nodded. "If there is fog, we can get you on board before the boat docks; if not, I will make sure you get on after it ties up."

John turned to the girls and explained why he needed to disembark from the ferry.

We know, 'Mr. New Trainee,'" Em said, with a pronounced wink. "We read the cable from one hundred Broadway today." Both girls smiled proudly.

28 THE 1910 BLOCK ISLAND CENSUS

When we were back at the Weather House, John and I walked to the Hog Pen in the dark of the late evening and boarded Wallace's boat.

We climbed into the cabin where he opened an oversized, thick gray envelope. From it he unfolded and laid before me about fifteen or so large sheets of paper; he started his questioning. I recognized the sheets as government data filled out by enumerators from the census bureau.

"Mr. Eddey, I want to talk to you about the Island from a population or statistical perspective," John opened. "You know the Island well. I need, or rather we, the ONI, needs to know about the people on Block Island. We need to know how isolated you are here on the Island, and we need to know of anyone who has lived here in the recent past that could now be helping these three mysterious men. Perhaps from the mainland, perhaps from the Island itself. The census bureau brought these sheets to Wallace and me just before we left the Navy Yard—and although the data is from 1910, it was recorded officially just a few years ago. Perhaps buried in this data will be clues as to who may be sympathizing with Germany."

As I listened, my eyes were reading the census. "State of Rhode Island, County of Newport, Town of New Shoreham.' These words were handwritten in the spaces at the top left of every sheet. 'The Thirteenth Census of the United States: 1910 – Population.' I had never seen the official census sheets and was perhaps a bit over eager.

"Where is my name?" I asked John, who was familiar with how to read the data sheets.

"Well first, we can see that Wallace's name is on the front page … Here, it is." He pointed to the name 'Eddy, Wallace.' "Why is his name spelled Eddy? Isn't there an extra *e* there at the end? Shouldn't it be spelled 'Eddey'?"

"Yes," I chuckled. "Everyone leaves out the extra *e*. The census ought to read that Wallace was a night operator for the telephone exchange company ... Yes, there it is." I pointed to his name and occupation on the long sheets.

"He worked nights part-time in the Telephone Exchange. It is located on Main Street across from the path that leads to Crescent Beach, behind the Surf Hotel. It says that Wallace lived on Main Street, in a small apartment shared with a friend, located above the Telephone Exchange. It was a good job, one that paid him enough to move out of the Weather House. I think he spent almost all his money on rent. Then he started dating Edith and that story unfolded."

"There were 1,314 residents of Block Island in April of 1910," John continued. "There was one inhabitant, a baker who probably lived above his bakery. He was a German named Gericke. He and his wife worked together on the Island. What do you know about them?"

"I know that they came over from Germany in the late 1880s to New York City and moved to Block Island about nine years ago, although the exact time I am not sure. Their son, it says here, was born in New York. I do remember them, he was a classic baker, but I never knew them well. He was always working, did not attend our church ... Why?"

"We have information that there are Germans who know Block Island very well. Do they still live here, and do they have visitors, or help in their bakery, from time to time, that you do not recognize?"

"Yes, they are still here, but I don't remember any other Germans working in their bakery. It is a small shop."

"There is another young man, aged twenty-four, who was born in Connecticut but his parents are from Germany. He boards with the Littlefield's on Old Town Road. Mr. Littlefield is a fisherman. Is this individual still on the Island?"

I said that he had long since left the Island.

"I see there is one family from Japan. It looks like they own a store. Are they still here?"

I nodded.

"Well, how about the Sanchez family? They are fishermen. Is that the family I read about in the *New York Times* that won commendations from the Carnegie Foundation when the Larchmont went down in 1907?"

"Yes," I said. "They are originally from Florida, and the daughter-in-law is from Central America. Sanchez is a fisherman of the highest order. What a wonderful family. Their children are good students in the school. We are lucky they decided to settle here. And, yes, he did win a commendation, probably should have won a gold medal as well."

"Okay," John conceded. "Now, what about your entry in the census? They spelled your name wrong also. Look here ... again spelled without the extra *e*. E-d-d-y. Why can't people get that name right?"

"I don't know. People in my own Scottish family line even spell it wrong. They probably think they are English," I added wryly.

John continued and now I must admit that I was getting a bit bored with the questions.

"It states you are a clerk for the telegraph office. Why doesn't it say you are the Official Observer for the U. S. Weather Bureau? And you had another messenger boy, another assistant in the Weather Bureau back then and the census lists his occupation as working for the Telegraph Office instead of the Weather Bureau. Why does it say that?" John looked puzzled.

I wasn't sure how to answer his first question. Did I tell the enumerator, Mrs. Littlefield, to write that down, or did she just write it down for herself? I felt like John was cross-examining me. I quickly shifted from being bored to being annoyed.

"John, I don't remember if I told her to write it like that or not, but for the next census I will be sure to have them write that I am the 'Official Observer in Charge of the Weather Bureau.' But I suppose that most people come here to send and receive their telegrams, Mrs. Littlefield just wrote what she wrote, in that she, not being a fisherman, would see the Weather House as a place to receive and send telegrams.

"That is a service that the weather office on Block Island has performed for the community since its inception in 1878. When I first enlisted in the U. S. Signal Service, I was assigned here because I was a fast telegrapher. I developed that skill easily—as did my brother and sister who both work as telegraphers for the Grand Central Railroad in New York City.

"For some reason telegraphy came easy to me and I think it has come easy to Annie as well. The Weather House is seen as a link to the outside world, and that being the case even now that we have the telephone exchange. Now, come to think about it, I haven't sent any recent telegrams for the baker. I do remember last year that he sent several to Boston. I don't remember the messages though."

John sat and listened and then his eyes returned to the census data sheets.

"If the enumerator made a mistake on your occupation," he looked back up at me, "then how reliable was she with respect to those other Islanders? Except the farmers and fisherman, do you think maybe she made other mistakes?

"I see that you have three ministers: two Baptist and one Methodist. Are there any other ministers or priests or rabbis that come to the Island occasionally? Wallace mentioned that you go to the Methodist Church. I was raised a Methodist, although my grandmother is Jewish. She was from Newport."

He kept on asking the questions as if he was on an ONI exercise.

"The Island has two physicians, one dentist, two barbers, and a hairdresser. Your community also has three or four blacksmiths. Block Island has a lot of farmers, and not surprisingly, you have a lot of fisherman. Block Island also has two wagon drivers for the express. Are they all still here?"

I nodded yes.

"Do you know how many fishermen are on Block Island, Mr. Eddey?"

I shook my head and waited for the answer. Before the 1850s most inhabitants farmed the land, although everyone fished to some extent.

"In 1910 there were about 414 children on the Island. That is an approximate figure. That gives us about 900 adults. If half are men and half women, that would give us a figure of about 450 men. And of those 450 men, the Island has 164 fishermen, ten captains and pilots of merchant vessels, and throw in a few engineers on boats. Add the fish wholesalers and dealers along with the occasional fishermen, lighthouse keepers, and surfmen, and we have over 200 men engaged in the pursuit of livelihoods involving the sea, an astonishing forty-five percent of the adult male population.

"And as you have pointed out, Block Island is a local fishing community. If the boats leave the Island, their time to return to the Island is always measured in days or weeks, not in years like the Nantucket Whalers spend at sea. Am I correct in saying that contact with foreign ports is minimal, if at all?"

I nodded and added, "And that is why Block Island has had a need for a Weather Bureau, and harbors of refuge, from the beginning, because it is so local."

"Do you think any of the fishermen could be involved with these mysterious men?"

"No," I answered. "Not unless the transients who are helping with seasonal fishing are involved."

John returned to the census sheets. "Does that go for the Indians and blacks that live on the Island also?"

"Yes, of course," I answered, surprised by the intent of the question.

"I ask the question because I am curious about one other thing: the census lists a number of blacks, although no Indians."

"As far as the original Indians ... to the best of my knowledge the last Indian living on the Island died around the time of the Civil War. In 1850 when my wife's grandfather, Isaiah Ball, died, in attendance at the cemetery for his burial was one of the oldest Indians then alive. That is as much as I can tell you."

"I am curious about the blacks on the Island. How have they been treated here? I ask because you remember, of course, the wreck of the Schooner Winslow. I am still puzzled by the death of the black engineer on the Winslow the night it was pounded to pieces on the rocks. the *New York Times* reported that the black engineer was saved, but he 'decided to return to the ship' just moments before it was finally destroyed by the surf. Why would a man leave the safety of the shore and return to what can best be described as a deathbed?

"From the way the article was written, I surmised that you

contributed information for that article. That was a disturbing article and, by the way, I am not the only one disturbed by the implications in that piece." John turned quite serious, as if this was something he wanted to ask me, regardless of the reason he was sent to Block Island.

"Ah, you remember that article in the *New York Times* about the wreck of the Winslow," I cringed a bit. "Yes, they contacted me after the phone lines were repaired. That shipwreck occurred in March, two years ago in 1914. It was one hell of a storm with winds at hurricane force. They were at least eighty miles per hour if not higher. And as I mentioned in the article, the barometer stopped reading well before it hit its low for the storm. It is no wonder ships were lost that night, up and down the Eastern Seaboard.

"And yes, the death of the Winslow's Negro engineer was very disturbing. I am still troubled about his death. No one talks about it ... I suspect there is a lot of guilt. Perhaps it is a good thing that the guilt stays here for a while. There are black families that have lived on the Island for a long time, most live off Center Road near the Old Town Center, in a hollow near the highest point on the Island."

I stopped talking. I knew John was wondering what kind of Islanders we were, as anyone who read that article in the *New York Times* would wonder. Why would a person go back to the boat when it was on the verge of getting pounded to pieces on the rocks? The answer may not have been obvious to the casual reader, but to the serious reader, the only conclusion was that the engineer may very well have felt more comfortable on the ship than with the numerous Islanders who were trying to save the rest of the crew.

Not I nor Wallace were down on the beach that night when the Negro engineer asked to be taken back to the ship. Readers of the article, at the least, wondered why we did not offer a satisfying *home away from home* to him that night. For if we had, I am sure he would have stayed on shore and not asked to be taken back to the schooner clearly in peril. I knew after he died that we were all culpable, all of us, even though I was not on the beach helping with the rescue.

At times like this I would get quiet, not able to speak or think clearly, wanting to change the subject, to deny that which has already occurred.

Melville writes in his *Moby-Dick* the following which I think is appropriate to restate: *"But when a man suspects any wrong, it sometimes happens that if he be already involved in the matter, he insensibly strives to cover up his suspicions even from himself. And much this way it was with me. I said nothing, and tried to think nothing."*

John and I just stared at each other for a few minutes. He nodded. And then, apparently satisfied, folded up his papers, placed them back in the envelope and suggested we call it a night.

I left the cabin and returned to the Weather Bureau. Early the next morning, John wanted everyone to gather in the living room of the Weather House for assignments.

29 The Assignments

Before the sun had risen, John was in the kitchen of the Weather House waiting for everyone to wake up.

He gathered everyone in the kitchen to hear the instructions for each other. He had questions to ask and assignments to give.

He turned to Annie as soon as she was brought downstairs by Emma. He wanted to hear how she had figured out that the three men might be staying off the Southeast Road. He was as much interested in hearing the story as listening to how she thought through the problem. I could tell from his intensity that John was a 'morning person.'

Using her yes/no system, Emma, and Morse code, Annie explained how she stationed herself at the landing, in the inner basin of the Old Harbor, where she often sat in her wheelchair, looking for anything unusual. She often wheeled herself down to the dock to watch the fishermen unload their catch, so she knew that few, if any, would be suspicious of her presence. Annie loved to listen to the banter of the fishermen. She knew there was not much cod left in the waters off Block Island, because of decades of over-fishing from the long liners out of New Bedford, but there was some to be caught, or how else would those 165 fishermen on the Island survive?

Almost everyone who lives by the sea develops an appreciation and a healthy respect for the ocean, interpreted by some as a healthy fear. And I think that I am quite respectful, yes, even afraid of the sea. Certainly I have seen the fury of the ocean when those moving weather systems disrupt the calm. I am drawn to the ocean yet, at the same time, I do not think I could be a Captain of a fishing vessel or, as Melville was, part of the Whale Fishery. No, the ocean is too powerful for me, I prefer the land; yet, at the same time, I need to be near water.

Melville also tries to explain the unique relationship some have with the ocean. *"Yes, as everyone knows, meditation and water are wedded for ever."* The image and beauty of the ocean is almost a deity to Melville; we *"... see ourselves in all rivers and oceans. It is the image of the ungraspable phantom of life; and this is the key to it all."*

Well, for me it has been so, and for my father before me. And to Annie, well, the water has been the key to it all for her as well, in every manner possible. Her love for the water, sailing those small open pulling boats; her near drowning from the accident; saving her sister from certain death at sea; to the continued nourishment she gains from sitting in her wheelchair at the landing; being near the water is more than just sitting, observing. It is her past and her future; until she dies, the water will be her phantom of life.

After the accident, Lillie brought Annie some books to read and after a while she read book after book. Then her school teacher brought her a copy of *Moby-Dick*. I had never read his novel; I could not get through those seven hundred pages. Annie read them slowly, very slowly, but she read all 134 chapters.

I will never forget when she finished reading the book last spring. She sent me a Morse code message saying it was the best book she had ever read. Annie and Melville ... imagine that.

John was intently interested in Annie's responses. He listened as she explained how she had noticed a tall blond man she had never seen before, who did not appear to interact with anyone on the docks. The few things she heard the man say were in English. For example, the man, perhaps one of the three mystery men, asked a fisherman where he could buy some fish. Annie thought that was a strange question since the fish store was open and in plain sight, although not marked with a sign. Annie assumed that he did not want to be seen in a store, but she watched him eventually walk up to CC Ball's general store. He entered, and left within a few minutes with a bag under his arm. He then came back down to the inner basis and walked behind Ballard's restaurant and bar. No one walked behind that side of Ballard's, unless you were emptying garbage. The man never reappeared. It was too cold, obviously, to go swimming, or even to sit on the sand as the beach behind the building was quite eroded.

"So you just assumed, concluded, that from his actions you saw from the vantage point of your wheelchair that this man had walked up the beach to Old Harbor Point?" John asked.

Annie raised her eyes.

I added an explanation for John, "The stretch along the beach from Ballard's to Old Harbor Point is rarely walked, except by the members of the fishing club and some guests of the Spring House. It is hidden by the hills upon which the Spring House and Ocean View sit. And it is not a pretty beach to walk, unlike the beaches on almost any other part of the Island. John, you would have to see a topographical map of that area or walk it yourself to see why Annie thought he had left the Old Harbor area behind Ballard's to walk out to Old Harbor Point."

John nodded. "Thank you for the explanation."

Wallace had now entered the kitchen, and John said: "You and I must sail around the west side of the Island in your boat this morning. I need to see for myself if it is suitable for discharging passengers from a U-boat and, if so, where on the west side landings could it safely and secretly be done. Before we take off, can we ask Lillie to ask a realtor, discretely of course, who might be here at this time of year, perhaps renting a house. There are not many visitors in early October. We are also going to look for evidence of U-boat activity itself."

"Okay, but how are we going to look for evidence of U-boat activity?" Wallace asked.

John didn't answer the question, but turned to Milt, Annie, and me. "Now here is the hard part. I want the two of you, along with Annie, to keep monitoring your Marconi device for any transmissions that may be in the air, realizing that any transmission coming or leaving the Island would be in code, most likely German."

I interrupted John: "I have been meaning to ask a question. Do you think the communication from the War College was real?"

"We don't know," John shrugged. "But I suspect it wasn't real, which is what you supposedly thought. Correct?"

Annie raised her eyes. She hadn't heard that first communication. But after Milt explained it to her, it was that communication that first made her think someone was sending messages as if they originated from the Weather House, or being sent to the Weather House from others.

John continued: "The first thing we did after saying goodbye to Wallace that first morning in the Naval Yard when my boss reviewed your document with us, was to check the messages sent to and from this place, and to and from the Naval War College. After receiving little information, just before we left yesterday, as I was handed the gray census envelope, we were told that the ONI did send the first two responses. But there is no record whatsoever of the second message being sent from the War College. If your hunch is correct, then we must assume that someone on or near Block Island is sending, as well as monitoring, your messages. And perhaps they are using your weather cable's messages to actually communicate to ships in the vicinity of Block Island, including their U-boats when surfacing, day or night."

With that statement, Annie raised her eyes vigorously. She pointed to Emma and made some motions with her good hand. She was trying to add something to the conversation, but stopped when John said the following: "And that would mean that we cannot use any form of communication with anyone while we are on the Island. We have to assume that they not only can intercept our messages, but they also can send messages as if they are from us … and, we wouldn't know it."

Annie calmed down after John spoke.

Emma looked at Annie and asked, "Is that what you were thinking?"

Annie raised her eyes again; and then it sunk in for all of us.

30 The Morning

It's a mutual, joint-stock world, in all meridians.
We cannibals must help these Christians.

Queequeg

It was 7:00 a.m. and the breakfast meeting was now over.

Wallace was ready for his boat ride around the west side; he loved to cruise the waters, especially when someone else was paying for the fuel. I could tell Wallace was also looking forward to spending another day on the water with John.

John was an intelligent man, very interested in this project, and I could sense he was becoming fast attached to us as a family. He had an underlying courage, similar to a sergeant who carefully watched over his troops on the front line.

With Annie, it was a similar response. When I was helping Lillie put Annie to bed last night, she asked her mother if she liked John. Lillie said she did. And when I asked Annie if she liked John, she raised her eyes and then asked me, in Morse code, to turn to a certain page in *Moby-Dick*. She had a copy in her bedroom at the Weather House as well as at Lillie's house. On the page she asked me to look at, she pointed to a sentence and indicated that she thought John was similar to Starbuck. I read the sentence out loud.

"Starbuck was no crusader after perils; in him courage was not a sentiment; but a thing simply useful to him, and always at hand upon all mortally practical occasions."

John was indeed a practical man and had been up early today, before all of us, waiting for us all and ready to do his part in the day's assignments. He was ready for whatever the day would bring.

"I want to get some bait and troll so it looks like we are working, and besides, I told Edith that I was going fishing."

"Where was Edith last night?" John asked. "Was she home when you got there?"

"Yes, she was asleep. This morning she was still asleep, but I'd mentioned that I was taking the boat out to go fishing."

"Does she work at all?"

"Yes, she helps out at the Vaill Hotel, usually working the front desk but also doing sewing repairs."

Wallace said he would tell him more about his wife on the boat, a topic that he avoided altogether with most people.

The conversation quickly changed to how Milton, Annie, and I were going to monitor the messages.

Milt started the discussion: "I think I know what we have to do. They, the Germans, have access to our weather cable messages. Somehow, they have found a way to monitor the wireless messages we send into the sky as well as the cable messages we send to Mrs. Conway in Point Judith. Those messages we send, if in a code, can then be deciphered by anyone along the route of the cable, perhaps even a member of a weather office in New York. John, is anyone concerned about Mr. Eddey's former colleagues at the weather office in New York?"

"Are you referring to those at one hundred Broadway, or in the Brooklyn Navy Yard?" I asked.

"I mean at one hundred Broadway."

I looked over at John who simply responded, "Good question."

He did not elaborate but clearly, he, or the Naval Intelligence officials, had been thinking the same thing. Could it be that someone in the Weather Office in New York City, or another city, was a spy for Germany?

I was intrigued more than ever and now felt that with John on the Island we could possibly figure this out. Although I knew it wasn't going to be easy, little did I know that it would be a member of my own family who would do the crucial "think-work."

With John slumped in the back seat so as not to be seen, I drove Wallace and John down to the Hog Pen. Wallace readied the *Anna C.* Their plan was to show John the west side of the Island, do a little fishing, and return to the Great Salt Pond around 11:30 a.m., just in time to catch the ferry—if it was indeed running from the mainland. Wallace was certain that he could spot the ferry while at sea well before it reached Block Island. John would then board the back of the ferry, as planned, shortly after it docked.

The weather was starting to get windy and they expected to fight the good fight against a choppy sea. Maybe the weather would turn and the ferry would not arrive today. They would have to wait and see.

After putting on rain gear, they motored out to the main dock in the Great Salt Pond, about one hundred and fifty yards west of the Hog Pen. On the large commercial dock just beyond where the ferry tied up, sat the fuel pump. As the *Anna C* pulled up to the fuel pump, John slipped back under the cabin and handed Wallace cash, more than enough to pay for the fuel to fill up the boat.

Wallace smiled at John running below deck. No one was on the commercial dock, a scene that would change dramatically if the ferry was to arrive on schedule from the mainland. John was constantly vigilant about seeing who was around, watching others as they watched us. His training was to survey the environment and not look as if he was indeed scanning with his eyes.

"John, I need to point something out," Wallace explained. "The ferry docks with its bow just above the fuel pump. If it arrives today, we'll see it coming from where we're sailing this morning. I'll make sure to time our arrival back to the dock so the ferry will pass us in the Great Salt Pond. I'll follow the ferry until it approaches the dock, pull up to its starboard side just after it ties up, and bring the *Anna C* alongside as if I am going to the refueling section of the dock. The boat'll be going slow, so you'll be able to climb up onto the lower deck without much difficulty. No one will see you—everyone will be on the upper decks, or on the other side of the boat facing the dock itself. I'll put you just aft of the large paddlewheel. Even if your fellow agent doesn't see you at first, you'll be able to jump on board. I'll continue up another dozen yards and refuel. Then I'll return to the Hog Pen as quickly as I can, and walk back to find you. Wait for me on the dock just as you exit the boat. There will be a lot of people just standing around talking."

John looked up from the cabin and nodded understanding.

After fueling, they pulled away from the dock and motored out to the narrow channel at the mouth of the Great Salt Pond, about one mile from the dock. After navigating the narrow channel, Wallace turned the bow of the *Anna C* southeast to begin their assignment.

Wallace understood the currents around the Island well; he knew there was a gentle current that could push his boat, or a U-boat, silently about two to three knots southeast along the west side of the Island to the exact point where Milt first spotted the three men, north of Dicken's point. Taking advantage of this current, a vessel could travel silently—slowly yes—but silently out to sea without using engines.

Wallace kept his engine at a slow rpm, but the current kept the *Anna C* at a steady speed of five knots. About fifteen minutes into their voyage, they spotted a vessel approaching. Not knowing what kind of vessel it was, Wallace got to work and started trolling for swordfish or tuna, just to make sure the passing boat knew they were out for a day on the water to fish … not to identify spies. And maybe they would be lucky and catch another giant tuna.

Wallace looked up at the approaching boat. He recognized it as a fishing trawler out of Point Judith and explained to John that it most likely was returning from a trip to the Grand Banks. It was resting low in the water, filled with fish, but odd though that it was approaching Block Island Sound from the southwest. Usually these trawlers return to Point Judith directly from the north and rarely pass close by the Island.

As the boat passed to starboard, my son explained to John that one of his ancestors, Isaiah Ball, lived near Grace's Point, directly to port. Wallace enjoyed telling visitors about his ancestors on Block Island whether they wanted to hear about them or not. John didn't quite follow the tale but nodded as if he was interested; feigning politeness was another one of his skills honed at the Naval Intelligence Academy.

As Wallace slowed the *Anna C* to a speed which would facilitate chumming the water with bait and dragging a huge hook twenty yards or so behind the boat, John stood up and pointed, "Wallace, there it is, do you see it?"

"See what?" Wallace said, startled.

"There, at two o'clock, the antenna of a U-boat. Now, look, there is the scope. No guns on this U-boat, but I am certain that is what it is. They are either watching us, or they are sending a message." John glanced at his wristwatch. "We will have to tell your father the exact time to see if it correlates with them receiving some kind of transmission or message on the wireless device at the Weather House."

Wallace was still desperately scanning the ocean's surface.

"Do you see it now?" John repeated his question.

"Yes, my God I see it, now I see it." Wallace was stunned.

"Keep fishing, we have to keep fishing, they may be looking at us and remember, act as if we are on a routine fishing trip."

As "normally" as he could muster, in light of his concern, Wallace let out the line with the large hook, just the right size for another bigeye tuna.

"Do you see anything or any person on shore that looks suspicious?" John said with a hint of nervousness.

Wallace threw up his hands. "I haven't been looking … please, I am trying to fish," he said.

They both laughed loud enough to be heard underwater; Wallace's sense of humor apparent again.

The U-boat submerged within a few minutes. They kept the *Anna C* on course for the trip around the southeast part of the Island. Their mission had been partially accomplished, and they had only been on the water for an hour. They continued to gaze at the shore and the horizon, but saw nothing of interest. Soon they were about a mile off the shore near Black Rock where they landed two yellow fin tuna, one right after the other. This was a bit strange, thought Wallace, since these tuna usually stayed in deeper water. Wallace immediately clobbered each tuna dead, cut off their heads, and then threw the heads overboard. He then set out more chum, threw out the line once again, and put the fish in a wooden chest. He estimated each fish weighed about fifty pounds.

Wallace thought out loud: "I wonder if the U-boat is stirring up the fish?"

"We only spotted one U-boat," John said. "But perhaps there are more of them. U-boats are solitary travelers unless an operation is underway. And we know that they have a support vessel in the area, given what happened last week at the Nantucket lightship."

When they motored farther along the bluffs, Wallace was able to point out the back of his barn that blocked the view of his own house, "Eddey's Shanty." The barn was sitting close to the edge and was adjacent to his small outhouse. As the boat sailed away from shore, his home itself came into view. John, a bit more relaxed, began asking my son all sorts of questions about living on the bluffs and eventually got around to asking him the exact location of the wreck of the *Winslow*.

"The wreck was not too far from my home," Wallace said.

John explained he had read the article in the *New York Times* and discussed it with me the night before. "What happened on the beach that day?"

Wallace went quiet, as Melville would predict.

"Well," Wallace changed the subject somewhat, "there are blacks who live on the Island, several families. In addition, several young Negro orphans have also been adopted by Island families as well."

"Yes, I learned that from reading the census report, although some are listed as servants," John noted.

"One of the orphans is Fred Benson, who came to the Island when only about seven years old. Now he's near twenty. Well-loved as anyone on the Island, he too is a member of one of the fishing camps at the North End, although I heard he is considering leaving the Island to become a car mechanic. Fred was adopted from that orphanage in Massachusetts by Andrew and Hannah Milliken, now in their mid-seventies. They raised him as part of their family. They live on Light House Road."

While Wallace continued to motor his boat off Black Rock, John couldn't help but think, despite the story of Fred Benson, that Block Island, like so many other communities in our country, may not have the "welcome" sign visible enough for blacks, either as tourists or, as this disaster suggests, as sailors.

Wallace and John spotted the ferry as it came into view just beyond the North Fork of Long Island. There was not much discussion between the two of them as they returned to the harbor. Wallace was able to calculate the required speed of his boat so as to reach the channel a few minutes after the *Block Island* had entered the Great Salt Pond. Wallace followed the ferry to the commercial dock, gradually closing the distance between the two vessels. John stayed hidden in the cabin until Wallace maneuvered his boat near the back of the ferry.

The lines were securing the ferry to the dock and everyone's attention was port side, John's fellow agent, standing on the starboard side, behind the paddlewheel, was ready with a rope to pull him up. His "entrance" and "exit" couldn't have gone any smoother.

While Wallace and John were sailing on the *Anna C*, I was sitting in the office of the Weather House with Milton and Annie trying to monitor potential messages over the Marconi wireless. It was clear to us that they knew we had a wireless device and we were careful to use it in as innocuous a way as possible. Several days ago, Emma had suggested that Annie send messages regularly that had little significance other than weather related issues.

I was not convinced, however, that we would be able to decipher the German's wireless transmissions—even if we could pick them up—until Annie became animated while listening to the Marconi receive signals around 9:15 a.m.

31 Emma Rose

When Emma woke up, she walked downstairs, stood for a few moments at the bottom of the stairs, where she could see her sister a bit animated beside the Marconi device in the office. But Emma walked into the kitchen through the parlor, avoiding the hallway near the office altogether. Em was quieter this morning, more so than usual and sleeping a bit later than her sister. Usually Emma Rose would always be up before her sister, to help her with dressing and readying her for the day. Today, staying in bed, although not a rare event, was a bit out of character.

While Annie was actively engaged in trying to figure out the meaning of the transmission she had just heard, Em started eating breakfast. When I walked into the kitchen to see how she was doing, Em looked up and asked if she could go to school today instead of staying at the Weather House. Although I mentioned that John had given her an assignment to complete, I did agree she could go to school—though I cautioned her not to say a word about what was going on to anyone. I did think it a bit strange, given how excited she was at first about the situation.

After pouring her a glass of milk, I returned to the office because Milt said Annie had figured out one of the words or phrases from the wireless; the dashes and dots of this Morse code message pertained to weather data near or on Block Island, or so Annie thought.

That was strange, unless Annie had gotten it wrong.

I lost track of Emma while Annie was trying to communicate to Milt and me how she had arrived at what she thought; and before I knew it, Emma Rose had walked out the front door of the Weather House. I remember vaguely hearing her say good-bye—that she would walk to school on her own, or I thought that's what I heard. I never did find out what she said.

Regardless, Emma had no intention whatsoever of going to school.

Sibling rivalry between the two rarely played itself out, but in retrospect, Emma must have noticed how interested John was in Annie's thought process. The way he gave her special attention—perhaps because of his late sister's condition—seemed to be something more than simply a familiarity with her condition. Em noticed John's approach to her sister and felt there was something more.

When Em had awoken, she sat in bed, quietly thinking, reflecting; she was determined to make her own contributions, unique and separate from those of her sister.

Under the guise of going to school, she set out for Old Harbor, walking east along Beach Avenue to Neck Road, crossed over it and onto Crescent Beach where the bathhouses were located. In October no one was there of course; she sat quietly for a few minutes on the wooden platform facing the ocean. The surf was high this morning, the tide high; she knew enough about the Island that when the weather was good and there were high seas, this reflected the ocean responding to a serious weather event hundreds of miles away. The fact that the storm was so far away, however, did not diminish the powerful effect of seas breaking onto the shore.

Emma got up and walked along the beach to its end where the Surf Hotel sat on its perch guarding the entrance to Harbor Village and the Old Harbor itself. Instead of taking the path off the beach to the right of the hotel, which led to Dodge Street, directly across from the Telephone Exchange, she thought it would minimize her chances of being noticed by anyone if she walked around the other side of the hotel, which would lead directly into the Old Harbor itself, near the fishing shacks. After negotiating this task, the degree of difficulty only understood by knowing how close the Surf Hotel comes to the water's edge here, she reached the harbor and walked alongside the old, smelly storage sheds used by the fishermen. Walking this way she could shield herself from the view of most people walking along Water Street in the heart of Old Harbor Village. She did not want to be seen by anyone, especially since she was supposed to be on her way to school.

Em had a plan: she wanted to walk out to Old Harbor Point retracing the steps of one of the three mysterious men, the way Annie had outlined it in her discussion with John.

It didn't take long before she walked briskly by the inner basin of the Old Harbor, weaving between the fishing gear strewn on the docks, noticing that her favorite ferry, the *George W. Danielson*, was resting quietly at its berth. Soon she was behind Ballard's and walking due south along the narrow, almost dangerously rocky (rocks not rounded or more forgiving like the glacial erratics found on other parts of the Island) beach on her way to Old Harbor Point.

It was more dangerous because it was now high tide, a fact she had noted when sitting on the wooden platform at the bathhouse twenty minutes earlier. The high surf was rolling in from the north Atlantic ending its run onto the rocks where she was walking. She soon realized it was not a smart decision to walk this way to Harbor Point. Without a sandy beach to cushion the force of the breakers and the fact that the bluffs, starting their eventual rise to over one hundred and fifty feet a mile away, were so close to the water's edge, this could be a dangerous walk to Harbor Point. She now understood the reason why Islander's in the 1700s stopped using this area of the Island as a harbor and it suddenly dawned on her how Old Harbor Point got its name. It was the site of the first harbor on this side of the Island. The current Old Harbor, originally called Sands Landing, was in fact the second Old Harbor. Regardless of how difficult this area was to navigate, she was determined to find out some information as quickly as possible and continued on her journey.

It was a rare event when Em would leave the house without saying goodbye to her sister, a thought she herself had as she negotiated her way among the countless sharp rocks and the breaking surf.

With the breakers coming in from the northeast, rather than the south, it made Emma's walk far more difficult than normal; it would also explain why Wallace and John were having a wonderful ride on the *Anna C* on the opposite, west side of the Island.

Emma kept on walking, now more aware than ever that she was alone; she did not see anyone, nor was she expecting to see anyone. She also knew full well that walking this way to the point left her but one or two escape routes up onto the Island. Here, because the bluffs, although not exceedingly tall, were very difficult to climb, one was confined to continue along the beach for quite a distance.

Her mission, as she determined it, was to find antenna wires stretched out horizontally along the bluffs or perhaps in the brush that these three mysterious men could be using to transmit information.

As she approached Old Harbor Point, she saw nothing strange, the bluffs leading up to the Southeast Road looked undisturbed. She remembered the description of the U-boats and looked at the ocean for any sign of surfacing submersibles but could not find any. The water, she realized, was too rough for her to see anything even if they had surfaced; an accurate thought. Old Harbor point was named long before Sand's Landing became known as Old Harbor. It was the site of one of the original "harbors" on the east side of the Island, and long since abandoned due to its treacherous submerged rocky outcroppings. Why early Islander's choose that site for an early harbor to this day baffles me.

When she reached her destination, Em decided to turn back to look at the face of the bluffs she had just walked past, retracing her steps visually; maybe she had missed those wires. As she turned around, about seventy-five yards away, following her quietly was the man she had seen driving the car several days ago.

She was scared and did not know what to do. In a panic, she turned and continued walking fast along the beach. She tried to locate a vertical "path" up the bluffs and into the brush near Southeast Road. If she could negotiate the face of the bluffs, which here were about thirty feet high, she might quickly be able to outdistance the man following her.

It would depend solely, she thought, on her ability to climb the dunes at a place where there wasn't a real path, and hopefully where an older man, heavier than she, would not be able to follow. She looked behind; the man was now running toward her.

She quickly chose a spot to start her ascent of the steep clay bluff, but after about ten feet, a third of the way to the top, she slipped and fell back, hitting her head hard on a rock partially buried in the sand.

32 The Union House Hotel

Lillie and I started living together after I had been back on the Island for about five years. Her husband and only son died around the turn of the century, two years before my first wife, and her younger sister, Nellie, died in April of 1902 when I was stationed in land-locked Abilene, Texas. From the time I met Nellie in 1887, Lillie and I had always been friends; I met Nellie before I met Lillie, but only moments before.

When I drive or walk the Island alone, I often think about Nellie, especially the days of our courtship, for me a time of love immediately found. I remember so vividly when I met her—and her sister.

In the late summer of 1887, I boarded a ship on the Hudson River side of New York Harbor that sailed up the East River into Long Island Sound. From there the boat docked at Newport, RI, and the next day I boarded the *George W. Danielson*, owned by Block Islanders themselves, for the twenty-two mile ride to the inner basin of the Old Harbor.

When I arrived at the landing, I walked up to Old Harbor Village, and reported for duty at the Weather Station which was then located on Water Street overlooking the Old Harbor. After introducing myself to Sgt. William Davis, I looked for a place to stay and found the small Union House Hotel had a room on the top floor available for a very reasonable price.

After I secured a room at the Union House and unpacked my bags, I had every intention of returning to the Weather Station, but when I went down the three flights of stairs I literally ran into two girls. These two girls were the daughters of the owner of the hotel: Lillie and Nellie.

On the very first day on the Island, I met two of the most important women in my life; first, Nellie, the girl who became my first wife, and then her sister, Lillie, who, as you know, is now my second wife.

When I first laid my eyes on Nellie, standing there next to her sister, I was immediately drawn to the way her face was shaped; not at all aware that it was her smile that brought me into her world. The two of us would talk almost every day, facilitated, of course, because I was staying in her father's hotel and she lived in a house behind the property. If we didn't meet socially at the hotel, we would see each other when she brought messages from guests to be sent as telegrams. At that time, the weather station was the only place to send a telegram. I had the fastest hands on the Island—as an expert telegrapher that is.

Nellie and I had such good times together. I remember one Sunday, on a rare day off in May 1888, on a day borrowed from July, when Nellie asked me to walk across the Island with her to the west side. Her father asked her to pick up some fresh cod that had been caught the night before from one of the fisherman who lived near Gracie's Cove. She said she would also show me the small home where her father was born, as was his father before him. Cod was used to serve guests as well as the hotel staff. He wanted to serve one family, in particular, because they had never eaten fish before.

There wasn't a direct road to the west side; rather taking a few paths connected to one another, through the fields of the farmers, avoiding a swamp or two, climbing the stone walls that separated one field from the next, was the quickest way. We must have jumped over thirty stone walls that day, a distance of about two and a half miles.

The walk was beautiful, the sky blue and clear. The blue sky appeared brighter than the clearest water I had ever seen, offset by the emerging green grass of the pastures.

We were enjoying ourselves so much that for a while we forgot about our mission.

"George, we have to turn here to get to the house where the fish are," Nellie pleaded.

"No, let us walk a bit farther to Grace's Cove and see the view. Maybe we can see the tip of Long Island if it's clear enough."

"Okay." Nellie wanted to prolong the walk as well.

When we were at the top of the sand dunes that looked down at the Atlantic Ocean to our left and the Sound to our right, we sat down and took the view as an omen from God. What a beautiful sight.

"George," Nellie said.

"What?" I asked.

She just looked at me, didn't say anything, just stared into my eyes. Her mouth opened slightly, her head moved to the side. She started breathing deeply and I continued to meet her gaze with my eyes. I was startled by the urge of love, of tenderness, of wanting to be closer to her, even though we were just a few inches apart.

We stared at each other for a few more moments before I finally reached over and gently guided Nellie toward me, into my arms and her lips to mine. I kissed her and then, without understanding why, a passionate kiss emerged. She was a bit surprised but responded quickly in the same manner.

That first kiss just would not end. For me it was a sense of wonder fulfilled; a kiss of two mouths touching was felt to the core of our souls; more than physical, it was a pure sensation of hearts and loins wanting to be together; passion combined with wonderment; which I took as a sign of love.

We had kissed before, though not in such a passionate manner; but this kiss came unannounced. It seemed endless.

On that small bluff, overlooking Grace's Cove, Nellie and I became certain we would marry.

It took us two hours to walk those five miles, to and from the hotel, but the time seemed to go by so quickly we were surprised when her father expressed annoyance with us for being late. (She never did show me her father's childhood home!)

After Nellie died in 1902, when I was stationed in Texas, I thought thankfully we had three children and believed her life would live through them and their love. I still harbor that belief.

★★★

Milt and I were trying to understand the conclusion Annie had arrived at, now that the wireless message had been deciphered. To me, there wasn't much to it but Annie was trying to make her case that these transmissions were indeed initiated from Block Island, not the mainland or Montauk Point. They were not, she was convinced, erroneous in the sense they had no purpose. Annie tapped out her thoughts on the table, letter by letter, word by word, to explain these messages were real, not intended to confuse anyone, but rather to communicate real time messages to someone. That someone was unknown.

Earlier, Lillie had called asking about the girls; at that time, I mentioned Emma had wanted to go to school. Lillie expressed annoyance because two days ago she had called the principal and explained that the girls would be out of school for a few days and now, I tell her that I let Emma return to school.

I didn't think much about Lillie's comment until thirty minutes later when Lillie called back saying that Emma Rose had not shown up at school. Lillie had walked up High Street to bring her daughter lunch and found out that Emma was not in school. She returned home quickly and called me immediately.

When Lillie explained all of that to me, I removed my focus from deciphering the messages and explained in detail what had transpired earlier in the morning.

To say that Lillie was not pleased with what I allowed to happen is an understatement, and I too became concerned. We knew only two things, Emma Rose was not in school, and she was not at the Weather House. While we were beginning to realize that Emma may very well be in danger, Wallace, John, and the *Anna C* were returning to the Great Salt Pond.

At about 1:30 p.m. Wallace and John had successfully pulled off the boarding of the *Block Island* on the starboard side. Everything had gone smoothly and as planned. After Wallace returned his boat to the Hog Pen, they met on the commercial dock and walked back to the Weather House anxious to tell us about their morning, only to find that nothing was going smoothly here.

When they entered the back door of the Weather House, we were in the midst of trying to find Emma; we did not try to hide the concern on our faces.

"Where would she go, if she didn't go to school?" John asked, as puzzled as any of us.

Anywhere on the Island was the answer.

Lillie asked Wallace to drive around the Island and look for her; she had already enlisted her brother to do the same. I assured everyone she would turn up and explained that perhaps she was feeling a bit displaced, given all the excitement. When I said the word "displaced," I could see that Annie's head dropped. She asked to be taken outside to sit on the back porch to wait for her sister's return. Annie knew her sister always entered the Weather House via the backdoor and here she would wait for her.

The rest of us stayed inside and wondered, no, worried, where she could be.

An hour later, Wallace and Arthur each returned, empty handed, but soon left the Weather House again, this time together, to search yet another one of the west side beaches.

It was about 3:30 p.m., the approximate time Emma would have returned from school. And still no sign of her.

A short time later, with Annie still sitting on the back porch, we heard someone running up to the front of the Weather House from Beach Street. It was young Fred Benson and, as he ran up the steps to the porch, he yelled that there had been a drowning.

33 The North End

Give sorrow words, the grief that does not speak whispers
the o'er-fraught heart, and bids it break.

Shakespeare

Fred was frantic as he ran up to the Weather House. Hearing his voice, we walked out the front door, fearing the worst, welcoming Fred up the stairs and onto the porch with a motion of our hands.

"Mr. Eddey ... Hi, Mrs. Rose ... I mean Mrs. Eddey," Fred said, "Mr. Eddey, a body has been found. It's a drowning. I haven't seen the body ... they have asked to see you, can you come quickly? It is so horrible, it doesn't make any sense."

My mind went blank; I dreaded his next words, it couldn't be Em, it couldn't be. Waiting for his next comment, I began thinking she had survived the accident at sea, and now this ... no, this wasn't possible.

"Oh God! No! Was it a child?" Lillie asked, barely audible, also fearing the worst.

"I don't think so," Fred responded immediately, reacting to the fear on Lillie's face. "I'm pretty sure it's not a child."

Lillie and I calmed down a notch, but were not fully convinced. We walked Fred inside to the living room at the same time Annie was wheeling herself in from the back porch. She had heard the commotion and recognized Fred's voice, although did not understand what was happening.

When Fred saw Annie, he walked over to shake her good hand and said hello, and then sat down. Both Fred and Annie were oblivious to the panic that Fred's abrupt entry had set in motion ... Fred, because he didn't know about Emma's disappearance, and Annie, because she didn't hear Fred say there was a drowning.

Fred, now seated, glanced to the right of Annie and spotted a new face standing in the back. I introduced John as a trainee of the Weather Bureau and Fred rose again, shook his hand, and sat down for a second time.

"What happened? Who died, and it's not a child?" Lillie asked once again.

Fred shook his head no.

"Thank God," Lillie said. "Was it a *woman?*"

"No, a *man* drowned," Fred answered to the collective relief of everyone, except Annie who was now frightened.

"I was out visiting the camps at the north end," Fred explained. "I was looking for Mr. Rose [a distant uncle of Lillie's] to see if he needed someone else on the crew. When I was talking to him, one of the 'lookouts' spotted something floating in the water, a hundred yards from the lifesaving station. The crew launched one of their pulling boats and brought back the body of a man.

"Mr. Rose said someone was at the cable shed last night. He wanted me to tell you that someone had been seen at the shed where the telephone lines drop into the ground, and about the drowning. When was the last time you checked to see if the cable connection was okay? Has there been problems at that shed?"

Before I had a chance to answer, John walked over, sat across from Fred, and started asking him questions. The intensity of John's questions startled me and I interrupted to soften the impact. I did not want to leave any doubt in Fred's mind that John was anything more than a "trainee."

Still recuperating from my initial panic that the drowned person could have been Emma, I let John ask the majority of the questions, but I worried more than ever the same fate could have occurred to Em. What if this wasn't a drowning, and this was something more sinister? And what if Emma had met some other horrible fate?

"Fred …" I explained, finally being able to speak. "John is in the second phase of his training, previously he was assigned to the Brooklyn Weather office where he was assigned to a supervisor in charge of war telegraphic communications. The two of us will drive out there and talk to Mr. Rose. Does anyone know who it was that drowned—an Islander or someone from the mainland?"

I asked Fred if there were any indications of violence, did the body have any marks that suggested a fight, or even gunshot wounds. Fred did not know.

After a few more minutes of questioning, John and I got up and walked into the hallway near the front door to talk. We were both relieved that the body wasn't Em but we had yet to find her; it was clear we both had let our minds wander and thought of the possibility of Emma drowning. But with these three mystery men on the Island, it didn't take much for us to think about murder rather than a drowning. The waters off that part, the west part of the North Point, are characteristically calmer than almost any other place on the Island; this despite the fact that the waters at the tip of the North Point, also called Sandy Point, could see some of the most treacherous waters on the entire Island. To me, this was a drowning that may not have been accidental.

Lillie, still beside herself with worry, got up and walked into the kitchen to serve some food to Fred while he, Milt, and Annie continued talking about what might be going on.

Fred needed to talk and he found welcoming and sympathetic ears in Milt and Annie. He stayed seated, appearing relaxed, but was scared and confused; he did not want to leave the Weather House. And thankfully, neither Milt nor Annie burdened Fred with the unknown whereabouts of Em.

But if Fred needed to talk, given all that had transpired this past week—and now with the disappearance of Em—then the same could be said of all of us at the Weather House. And soon the entire Island, after learning about the death of this man, would need someone to listen to all of us as we reflected on the disquiet of another shadow on the Island. Giving words to our sorrow would surely be the theme, I thought, of Sunday's sermons in all of the Island churches; it always was after grief found its way into our lives.

Milt wanted to join John and me when we drove out to talk to Mr. Rose, but we asked him to stay with Annie and continue to monitor transmissions on the wireless. We didn't want him exposed to a dead body at his age.

While still standing at the front door, John and I discussed Emma's situation and possible whereabouts. I couldn't help but think that she was in danger, and even spoke the unthinkable, that she may have met a similar fate as that man. We looked over at Fred talking to Milt and Annie; they all seemed calmer than a few minutes ago. We didn't think they had made the correlation of the drowning and Em's disappearance because now Annie was starting to ask Fred about his plans to study car mechanics in Detroit.

John and I walked out onto the front porch and discussed, out of earshot, what our next step should be. We both agreed we needed to drive out to Harbor Point before heading to the north end. Perhaps Em had walked out there instead of going to school. Maybe she was picked up by those mystery men as she walked to school?

As we were walking down the steps of the front porch to my car, we were startled to hear the back door of the Weather House bang open, followed by Lillie crying out.

We ran back inside.

It was Em, wet, clothes ripped, blood on her face and arms and limping; the sock on her shoeless right foot covered in blood.

34 Lobster Dinner

It had been quite a day.

After Em reappeared, bruised and scratched, right foot swollen, clothes torn and soaked ... but *alive*! We were relieved—ecstatic might be a better descriptor— but recognized it was yet another message that we were dealing with dangerous men. We also knew that she could not be left alone anymore. I will tell her story in a moment.

And John now realized that his directive from the ONI to let the three men operate on the Island unimpeded was no longer tenable. One death and Emma's frightening episode was enough to change that notion. *But not only did John not have the authority to change it, he couldn't communicate that request via cable, wireless, or phone.*

For the immediate future, we needed to keep Emma from being identified by the man who had chased her; it is possible he could place Emma Rose to our family, especially if he had been observing her for a period of time. But Emma did not think she was watched that morning, from the time she sat on the bathhouse platform to the time she was nearly caught at Old Harbor Point. Only much later did we determine that the mystery man followed her after seeing her walking on Crescent Beach near the Surf Hotel.

After Lillie went upstairs with Em to give her a bath and comfort her, John and I felt we could leave the Weather House and drive straight to Sandy Point to investigate the drowning. Milton would stay with Annie; Wallace would return to the Weather House after bringing his wife to her parent's home on the west side; none of us thought she ought to be alone anymore.

To John and I, the most important information gained was that this man *was desperate enough to run after a teenage girl,* and that spoke volumes of his, and their, intentions.

We began feeling a significant amount of pressure to determine the mission of these three men. As it turned out, the least concerning event of the day was the spotting of the U-boat off the west side by Wallace and John. So much had happened since they saw the U-boat ten hours ago.

As we were driving to Sandy Point, John asked me to raise certain questions; he didn't want to bring attention to himself, so we agreed I would do all the questioning, of both Mr. Rose and the undertaker if we were to see him. No sooner did we mention the undertaker than we drove right up to him as we approached the tip of the Island. He had already loaded the body into an enclosed funeral wagon drawn by a horse, and appeared to be in a hurry to leave. I didn't know him well, rarely speaking to him, but I got right to the point and asked if there was evidence of foul play, or even a bullet hole somewhere. Mr. Littlefield said that he did not know yet, but didn't express much surprise at my question. As he climbed onto the wagon and took up the reins, I explained to John that Littlefield was a bit quirky, not easily engaged in conversation. We said goodbye and agreed to speak in a day or two when he'd completed his final report; which I knew he would not write until after the requisite consultation with the Island physician, Dr. James.

We then walked out to the dunes on the west part of the north end, near the fishing camps, to visit with Mr. Rose. It was about a ten-minute walk. We walked in silence until John mentioned he was now carrying his firearms. He opened his jacket to reveal two pistols, one of which was a Luger!

"Don't be alarmed," John said. "I wouldn't show anyone else, although Wallace, of course, knows I have these as well as a rifle on his boat. I think tomorrow I will bring that rifle into the Weather House, if you don't mind."

I nodded, not knowing what to say. I was startled by his request and was hesitant to let him know how uncomfortable I was with it. Regardless of how much I agreed with his sense of danger, I never liked having guns around and never owned one, even when I was in the Army. I was an awful shot.

Mr. Rose was sitting next to an open fire for warmth near one of his fishing sheds. I introduced John, then we sat across from him on a large driftwood log, and asked him his thoughts.

Mr. Rose immediately told us he believed that there was a bullet hole in the abdomen of the man pulled from the sea. He did not recognize the man, due to the fact the body was grossly mangled, most likely from one or more sharks, but it could have been an Islander. We both knew that the summer and fall of 1916 was a time of numerous shark attacks in the northeastern part of the United States. Several deaths had been attributed to shark attacks in the waters off New Jersey and New York. Perhaps this was why the undertaker did not want us to view the body.

Mr. Rose's answers to our questions were succinct, to the point, and often anticipating questions before I had a chance to ask them.

We then spoke about the man who he had seen enter the cable shack the night before last. I wondered: could it have been the same man that Milt had seen?

"Was he the dead man or was he surprised by the man who was now dead?" Mr. Rose asked giving us his answer as if it were a riddle.

After a few more minutes, with no further information coming our way, we said goodbye and returned to the Weather House.

In our haste to drive out to Sandy Point, given the worry about Emma, we had yet to review the sighting of the U-boat as well as discuss, in depth, Annie's hypothesis on the source of the wireless communications, about which I still had doubts.

While we were beginning to discuss all of this, John interrupted me with a strange request.

He thought that given Emma's "excursion" to Old Harbor Point and the fact that she could be recognized if that man saw her again—that man, John reasoned, would never think that her family would parade her in the open, so he wanted to do the unexpected: have a small outside dinner at the Weather House as soon as possible. It could be a welcoming party for the "new weather trainee" and this would demonstrate we were not afraid to bring attention to ourselves as a family, and perhaps at least one of those men might see us eating outside.

Although somewhat puzzled, I did agree to John's request. Why did he want to do this? Were we not putting Emma Rose, and all of us, in more danger? However, as soon as we walked in the door, I asked Lillie to prepare a lobster feast for tomorrow night, Friday.

Just before we'd arrived back, Lillie explained, Fred had gone home. He'd talked things through enough to feel certain he would not burden his adopted parents with the sordid details of the drowning, and refrain from discussing Emma's "adventure."

Tonight our only task was to "debrief" Emma Rose and give her an opportunity to talk.

John called Emma down from her bedroom and asked her to tell her story in detail. Just then, Wallace walked in from the back and we all returned to our seats in the living room, the only room large enough to accommodate everyone comfortably, to hear Em's version of her ordeal.

Emma was cleaned up and now wearing a bright dress. She stood up and gave an animated rendition of what had happened. She told us how, and why, she walked along the beach up to Old Harbor Point and then was stunned to see the same tall blond man following close behind—who then started chasing her. For a fourteen-year-old, she spoke freely, unencumbered by her harrowing experience.

"What happened after you fell down the bluff?" John asked. Lillie had already heard the story when she was helping clean up her daughter and couldn't bear to hear it again. She left the house for a few minutes to drive to the Hog Pen to buy lobsters from one of Wallace's friends for tomorrow's dinner.

"As I started to climb the bluff, a branch I'd grabbed snapped, and I fell. I hit my head on something, and it stung like ... you know what. But I knew I couldn't think about that—I hadda get a move on. I could hear he was getting close, so I jumped up high and dug my hands deeper into the bluff pushing my fingers harder and harder every time I reached up to get a better grip. This time I moved my feet faster, digging into the clay and pushing myself up, and with every reach of my hands, I got a better grip and was able to climb higher. As I got to the top, there were branches sticking out that I could grab, although most of them broke. I also turned partially sideways to keep my butt close to the bluffs, with my face turned the other way so that man couldn't get a good look at me.

"I knew I could climb it there, I just knew I could." Turning to her sister: "Annie, remember when we used to race up those cliffs with the boys? Remember we beat them all of the time? We were lighter—the clay bluffs don't give away like it does for the heavier boys.

"And as soon as I was half way up, I knew he was having trouble and I could put some distance between him and me when I reached the top.

"I wanted to run straight for Southeast Road, but I became a bit disoriented. The brush here was taller than me, full of thorns, a thicket more difficult to run through than I had imagined. So straight ahead was out of the question, and I had to run a zigzag path. Maybe that is why I couldn't find the road—where I'd climbed the bluff I must have been *below* the road, but I thought it was the other way."

"Probably a good idea that you didn't run on the road," John interrupted.

"I kept fighting my way through the brush, keeping my head down so as not to poke my eyes out from all the branches, until I reached Spring Street—and *then* I realized I was well below Southeast Road. I turned around ... I couldn't see him but I could hear him in the brush, still following me, and I knew he was catching up.

"A horse and buggy was coming by—it was ol' man McCabe and his Missus—and I hid from them 'cause I figured they'd stop to talk to me, and that would put them in danger, too. Wallace, why does he still have a horse and buggy? He can afford a car, can't he?"

Wallace shrugged his shoulders.

"I ran across Spring Street after they passed—climbed over more thick brush, but I just kept on going, and then I came to an open field. I jumped over and then ran alongside a stone wall 'cause I knew I could not be seen from the road."

"Do you think he saw your face?" John asked.

"John, I don't think he saw me real clear. I glanced at him real quick on the beach. But I bet he could recognize my butt! He saw a lot of that."

Emma's response gave everyone the chance to relax, with the only genuine laughter I'd heard in weeks.

Annie got her sister's attention. She asked, using her hand signals, if the man was blond.

"Yes, he was blond." Emma answered.

"How did you get here, back to the Weather House? And why did it take so long?" Annie tapped out with her good hand.

"After ... I'm guessing it was about a mile—I came out of the brush at the back of the Spring House Hotel. I kept on going because it was deserted, the painters were gone, and they'd boarded up the first floor windows. I decided to cross the fields in front of the Atlantic Inn and then over to High Street. I knew he would see me as I ran through those fields but I had no other choice.

"I just had to get to the swamp on the other side of High Street before he did, 'cause even if he saw me enter it, there was no way he could catch me in there. But I didn't know if I could beat him there. Annie, remember that deep gulley in front of the Atlantic Inn we used as a cut through? The one that's always overgrown?"

Annie, hanging on every word, quickly yessed her sister.

"I was hoping he thought I was going to hide there. No way he'd know I could crawl through the massive thicket to the other end. He was too big to pass under it. Once I got through, I knew that in order for him to follow me, he would have to back track up to the front of the Atlantic Inn, and by that time I'd beat him to the swamp.

"But ..." Emma Rose stopped and looked at all of us one by one. Emma probably learned how to do a dramatic pause from listening to Wallace tell tales. When the tension in the room was about to explode, she continued, "He ran so fast that he caught up to me in the gully. My heart was pounding from fear he was going to get me as I dove under the thicket. I was just starting to crawl on my stomach under the low branches when I felt him *grab hold* of my ankle. I kicked as hard as I could, and I musta rammed his arm into one of the thorn branches, 'cause he yelled and let go for a second. But he reached for me again, only I had wiggled farther away and this time he just got my pump ... wouldn't you know it, my favorite shoe."

The room was holding its collective breath as Emma went on, "I was so scared I forgot about the pain in my legs and arms. I crawled through that thicket almost as fast as I can run ... and mostly on my belly."

"Did he try to come after you?" John asked.

"No, and I knew he couldn't make it under. Annie and I went by there a few weeks ago, and I remembered how low to the ground the thick branches were. I wasn't even sure *I* could crawl under, but it was my only hope. I couldn't outrun him, so I had to outmaneuver him."

"Then what happened?" John said, literally on the edge of his seat.

"When I came out the other side and crossed over High Street I could hear him running back up the hill to the Atlantic Inn. From there I ran right down to the large swamp. There's no way he saw me enter the swamp, and even if he did, no way could he follow me, or even know where I would exit the swamp. What is the name of that swamp anyway?"

I looked at John. "That area of the Island, not too far from the back of Lillie's house, is a no-man's land. No one enters it, too dangerous, some sink holes and a whole lot of snakes."

Wallace added that even Block Island's pastures had been taken over, choked with brush, not unlike the many pastures no longer used for farming. For Emma, this was a lifesaver.

"Like I said," Emma continued, "once in the swamp, there's no way he coulda seen me, the brush's over ten feet high all around. Then I realized my arms were bleeding, thanks to those thorns, and my foot was cut up bad and bleeding. It started swelling."

Emma looked at me and said, "And I bet I get poison ivy, too."

"What did you do then?" I asked.

"I ran down along the edge of the swamp on the other side of that small pond ... Does that pond even have a name?"

We shook our heads no.

"I ended up on Old Town Road near the mill stream, and then to Beach Avenue, and then up to our back door." Emma pinched her lips together and nodded to signify 'end of story.'

Oh, my. Lillie and I just didn't know what to think.

Turning to John, Emma asked, "Do you think there's any danger in him knowing my shoe size?"

Annie was impressed with her sister's quick thinking, and marveled that she had actually run through the swamp—no one on the Island would even think of entering that thing.

John sunk back into his chair, not knowing what to think either. He surely had never seen a family like this before.

***

With all that had happened I was not sure anyone would get a good night's sleep, but due to overwhelming fatigue, everyone slept long and hard. Even Emma, who I was concerned, would have nightmares, slept well. Having everyone talk about their activities that evening apparently helped with the stress of the moment. I looked in at the two girls, sleeping soundly, arm in arm, ten minutes after Lillie had put them to bed.

The person who slept the least was John. As much as he was concerned that Emma's life had been in danger, her pursuer's whereabouts concerned him more. He felt it his responsibility to make sure all went well, even though he knew full well that this might be the precursor to the war in Europe being brought to U.S. soil.

The next morning Milt and I returned to collecting data and forecasting the weather. All indications were that it would only be a matter of days before October would stop borrowing days from summer and begin borrowing them from the dead of winter.

Before breakfast, John and I met briefly to discuss our next steps; keeping the girls out of harm's way was the top priority. We would go ahead with the lobster dinner, starting around 4:00 p.m., as darkness was marching forward with every passing day, and hold it in the back of the Weather House as this part of the property was visible from Ocean Avenue, leading to the ferry in New Harbor.

During the day, John said he simply wanted to observe who might be coming or going on the ferries in both harbors. He anticipated that one of the men might leave the Island, especially if he was involved in the murder. I lent him my car but other than that, we had no other plans but to continue monitoring the wireless. Friday was our first day of rest.

Four o'clock came around quickly. John had returned reporting that he had not seen anyone suspicious leave the Island on the *George Danielson*, out of the Old Harbor, nor did he see anyone suspicious leave from a steamship out of the New Harbor. There was one more ferry, the *Block Island*, set to leave the Island in a few hours.

John needed someone to keep a lookout on the harbor. Em readily volunteered, still needing to rest after her previous day's experience. From her bed she had a clear view through her window to the New Harbor and the commercial dock.

Lillie then told Em she'd bring a plate of food up to her in a little while.

The mild weather was holding for one more day (I was certain that this was the last mild evening of the year) and with John satisfied more than ever that he was on the Island for good reason, we sat down to an early dinner of lobster.

Lillie was instructing John on how to get the fire pit to the right temperature.

"John, the coals are not hot enough in the pit. Can you add a few more pieces of wood? It's stacked in back of the garage," Lillie asked.

I had brought half a cord of wood back in my car last spring; Block Island doesn't have any trees left, so I had to 'import' the wood from Connecticut.

"I need the water boiling so we can steam the lobsters in this large can, set in the fire pit. Don't start the conversations until I get back." With that, Lillie kept us all at bay as she went inside to heat up water on the stove.

As she left, Annie indicated that she had to go to the bathroom, and wheeled herself into the kitchen. Em came downstairs to help her, while the rest of us sat back and waited. No one spoke a word; everyone just waiting their turn to talk.

I began thinking about what Annie had said earlier to me on one of her long Morse code messages. She was convinced she knew what was happening; that I was right all along, that we do have enough information to solve this mystery; we just had to ask the right questions.

Within about fifteen minutes, Annie and Lillie returned.

"Who wants to start? Who wants to review what happened yesterday?"

My son Wallace raised his palm slightly as if at an auction house.

"Go ahead," I nodded to him. Lillie had brought official Weather Bureau documentation sheets to take some notes of the meeting. I smiled in appreciation to her when I noticed that she was poised to write.

"Well, in addition to the fish we caught, we saw a U-boat. We spotted it off the west side and we have the exact time that we saw the antennae and small telescope. It seemed to be visible for about ten minutes and then disappeared quickly beneath the surface, right before our eyes. John, do you want to add anything?"

John shook his head no but added, "I caught my first tuna yesterday."

Everyone laughed, nervously, but genuinely understanding his excitement.

"John," I said, "I think that you have something more to say."

"I do, but I will wait for everyone else to review their activities."

"Okay," I turned to Milton, "now it is your turn and then I will add something when you are finished."

Milton responded quickly: "I think we learned a lot, but we are not sure what it means just yet. On the telegraph machine to Point Judith, we cabled the weather data in the usual weather code jargon. At the same time, we started listening on the wireless device. At first, there was nothing, but then we heard static, which got louder. Voices could be heard but we didn't think they were English. Then we heard code being transmitted."

"What time did you send your message, and what time did you listen in to the wireless? What time do you think you heard the static, and what time do you think you heard the code?" John asked.

"We sent the message about nine thirty a.m. or thereabouts, and we were listening in on the wireless constantly. We heard the static ten minutes after that. We heard what we thought was code shortly before ten." Milt looked up at me to continue the story.

"Well," John said, turning to his left, "Wallace ... we saw the periscope and antenna at about that time also. Correct?"

"Yes," Wallace answered absently. Wallace had become quiet. He had turned his attention to the small annex of the hotel next door where he thought he saw some activity just beyond the house along New Harbor Road. Em, from her perch at the upstairs window was looking in the same direction.

"I think the times are in sync," John answered his own question. "We wrote it down on the ship's log ... it's up in the office."

We started steaming the lobsters and readied the rest of the dinner. It was getting colder on the back porch, the warmth of the open pit fire felt good, making us realize how cold it was going to get once the low-pressure from Canada rolled in.

John had never had lobster before and was amazed at the entire process. Lillie, with Wallace's help, explained that steamed lobster is much, much better than boiled lobsters. And never bake them! "Most people boil them," she explained to John, "but that leaves too much water around the meat." Within minutes the lobsters were done, turning a bright red from the intense heat of the steam.

With the lobster on the plate in front of John, everyone wanted to demonstrate how to eat it. We wanted to show him how to clip off the tail from the body, we wanted to teach him how to best remove the meat from the tail; in short, we wanted to teach him the 'Block Island' method of eating lobster. Everyone wanted to give instructions to John, including Emma from her window.

But Lillie took the lead: "First you clip off the tail fins, making sure that you remove them entirely. Make sure you break them off at the base. Then break off the tail from the body of the lobster. Now comes the fun part. Put a small curved fork, upside down, in the underside of the tail, and using the leverage of the reversed fork position, pull the meat out of the shell. Done properly, all the meat will come out in one, large piece." Lillie demonstrated on two lobsters before John understood completely.

"Thank you. Eating lobster is not so difficult, as I had been told," John marveled, and then got back to running the 'dinner meeting.'

"George … your turn."

"Well, to summarize," I said, perking up, "I think we have a timeline that is peculiar. If we have it right, the U-boat surfaces. It is about nine thirty a.m. Then, within minutes, I send the weather data to Point Judith using the weather Morse code symbols like I always do at that time.

"A few minutes later we hear static on the Marconi Wireless device. At about nine forty we start picking up Morse code signals on the wireless machine. They last for about forty-five seconds. I deciphered them, and wrote the letters down as such.

"Milt and Annie, do you have any further thoughts on this?" I asked.

"We think that the U-boat was listening to our transmission and then responded to it, and sent out the Morse code signals that we heard and recorded," Milt said succinctly. "We don't know what their communication means at this point, but Annie thinks they are using, in some way, our own transmission of weather data to communicate secret messages. If we listen we can eventually figure it out."

"But …" Annie raised her eyes and spoke the one word that was easy for her to say.

Milt acknowledged her with a nod. "Annie thinks that given the time frame for what you have described and what we have heard suggests that they are using us, perhaps to camouflage or change our weather code slightly to send another completely different message.

"And, how do they get our first message? Mr. Eddey says he thinks it is very possible that they have tapped into the telegraph cable on the Island and someone had the signal sent wirelessly to the sub. The static that we hear on the Marconi machine is an indication of that transmission."

"John, what do you think of that as a possibility?" I asked.

"Well, it is quite plausible. We would not want to disturb their connection to the telegraph cable so that we can use it to fool them in the future. I think that we need to look at their transmissions carefully to determine, one: What *are* they trying to do? And two: Why have they chosen Block Island?"

After some deliberation, John confessed, "I suspect the Germans are trying to engage our country in the war."

"Or," Annie began tapping out Morse code on the table, "they are trying to do something to us that will prevent us from *ever* entering the war. That prospect is the more frightening of the two."

After I translated that last comment, we sat quietly and finished our dinner, all of us slightly humbled as we realized we were going to have to solve this problem as soon as possible.

Rye bread, along with more corn, cooked beets, and spinach completed the dinner.

Lillie took a plate of food up to Emma who continued to sit by the window, alternating her gaze between the picnic below and out to the

New Harbor commercial dock, where the ferry to the mainland had just started boarding passengers.

Just as Lillie returned to bring a piece of freshly baked cake upstairs, Emma called to John from the second story window. She'd spotted a tall blond man she believed was the one who chased her the day before. He was walking on New Harbor Road in the direction of the ferry, presumably, to board the last ferry of the day to the mainland. John ran into the Weather House and upstairs to see who Emma had identified. Wallace, instinctively, walked to his car and waited for John to come back outside. When John came out, he was wearing his coat, and I could easily guess he had both pistols on him. I scanned the area to see if others might be observing us, but couldn't see anyone.

Dinner was over. And the *Block Island* was ready to sail out of the Great Salt Pond.

As Wallace and John departed for the New Harbor and the commercial dock, I couldn't help but wonder if John was going to use his Luger? The intensity in his eyes, his focused and brisk walk to Wallace's car, Emma's story, the partially mangled body, his thoughts on the war just confessed, all seemed to me to be directing his action. He was clearly on a mission.

New Harbor and the Great Salt Pond from the Weather House. The view includes the Hog Pen in the foreground, with passengers walking from the commercial dock.

35 John's Block Island

From the second floor window, I saw Wallace drop John off at the ferry and continue driving up West Side Road. After getting out of the car, John walked the length of the commercial dock where the ferry, *The Block Island,* was tied up. He quickly boarded the side wheeled ferry after saying something to one of the deckhands, and I lost sight of him. Without a ticket, I assumed he met up with his fellow agent, but of that, I could not be sure.

John reappeared about twenty minutes later, moments before the *Block Island* pulled away from the dock. All of a sudden, almost as if he had jumped off the bow of the departing ferry, I saw him walking away from the boat. He continued walking briskly, appearing preoccupied, onto Ocean Avenue. He paused at the Hog Pen, gazing off to his left for a few moments, out to Wallace's boat, and then continued up the hill.

As he approached the back of the Weather House, I could see he was visibly shaken. I walked downstairs to greet him, but when he walked through the back door into the kitchen, it was clear he didn't want to talk. He simply looked over to me and whispered, "Em need no longer be afraid." He opened his jacket to reveal one pistol. The Luger was no longer in his possession. Without saying another word, he walked up to his room and closed the door.

I asked no questions of him, then or ever.

★★★

The next morning, Saturday, was cold; the increasing winds and cloud cover making daybreak nothing less than a blustery experience. The change in weather fit my forecast and unfortunately, fit our mood.

With a Nor'easter establishing itself and an eastwardly-moving, Canadian low-pressure moving formation aggravating the situation, I

could tell it was not going to be a good couple of days. I expected both
the Old and New Harbor ferries would now stop running for a few days,
if not the entire week, depending on the strength of the storm and the
resulting high seas. It was common practice to halt ferry service to the
mainland during major storms, especially in the fall and winter. I was
certain this would be such a storm.

What a difference a day could make. Yesterday, and all of last week,
was like August and today had the icy feel of a winter day. John would
learn, when he awoke, that Block Island can, and will, borrow days from
any month ... whenever it pleases.

This particular morning the Weather House came to life slowly. We
acted as if there was much to do, but the reality was we simply needed to
keep busy. The death, Emma's ordeal, and the sighting of one of the
mystery men boarding the ferry was not easy to erase from our minds. I
don't know why we thought we could. We would think of those events
today and almost every day for months, if not years, to come. I didn't
even want to call the undertaker. We needed a break.

None of us had slept well. Annie was the most productive and stayed
up late with Emma at her side for most of that time to monitor the
wireless. They thought they had picked up a word on the wireless that
supported Annie's notion that an attack on one of our naval ships was
imminent. *Schlachtsciff* was a word Annie had identified through Morse
code not associated with a weather transmission. And, according to her
sister, she perseverated over a word she could not at first understand—
Hellegatte. Using John's German dictionary, the word means "Bright
Husband." She thought she heard it twice during the night.

When Annie explained this to John, he thought it was suggestive of
an attack on the Naval Vessels stationed in Newport. That phrase had
been used to refer to the War College in years past; he couldn't recall
exactly but it had something to do with a reference to one of the
commanders. With U-boats circling our Island, he felt it would make
sense that the Naval War College in Narragansett Bay would be the
target.

But Annie didn't agree with John. She thought Hellegatte was a
"safeword" and that the Germans had another meaning in mind she'd yet

to figure out. Safewords are used when, or as if, a blank is inserted into a sentence; in other words, Hellegatte had no real meaning. She did think an attack was imminent, perhaps on a Schlachtsciff. The previous night, Annie had mentioned to her sister that she thought an attack on the mainland itself was a possibility. Emma mentioned this to me when she woke up, although she could not explain to my satisfaction why Annie held that belief.

Nonetheless, with the information that Annie uncovered during the night, John was anxious to speak with his supervisors. He had much to report and considered returning on the ferry. But a return trip, if one was available, would take at least two days, depending on train connections, although he could make a phone call as soon as he reached the mainland. Or, better yet, he could contact one of the special agents of the Federal Bureau of Investigation that had just opened a field office in East Providence. But with the change in the weather, leaving the Island by ferry wouldn't be possible for a few days.

No wonder, I thought, the German spy left the Island the night before—and it was the same thought Annie expressed in a message she tapped out after breakfast. She too believed the mystery man leaving the Island the night before might signify the mission—whatever it was—was about to begin. And if that were the case, then we indeed had enough information but just were not putting it all together properly.

"It must be here," Annie tapped out, referring to the data that would elucidate their ultimate mission. I must admit I was quite struck with her idea that an attack on land was not out of the question and, further, it could occur soon. She tapped out, and we all agreed to this, that the oncoming storm could provide cover for such an operation.

We were worn out. I couldn't think anymore, the episode with Emma, especially, took a lot out of me. I didn't mind my life being in danger, but not Lillie's daughters, they had been through enough in their short lives.

Except for the girls and Milton, who kept at the wireless, for the rest of us, this Saturday morning would turn out to be a day of rest. We did not plan it that way, it just evolved as such due to our exhaustion.

***

By mid-morning, John asked to be taken for a tour of the Island; he needed a respite and Lillie was more than willing to be his tour guide. The increasing velocity of the winds would soon bring large swells to the Island's beaches, a sight that mesmerizes most people, and a sight that Lillie wanted to share with John. Today I would simply collect my weather data and transmit it in my customary manner, while the teenagers would take turns listening for more clues on the wireless.

Before they left for their tour, Lillie asked—requested is probably more accurate—that tomorrow we attend church as a family, John included. Perhaps Lillie understood John's need to return to the Brooklyn Navy Yard; attending church may very well be a final family gathering of sorts. I don't know if Lillie was thinking like that, perhaps it was me projecting my feelings onto her.

Lillie and John skipped lunch, and took off shortly before noon.

Lillie started their tour in the Old Harbor Village, driving slowly past the shops and inns. John loved the architecture of the Gable's Inn and the Surf Hotel. She then drove to the inner basin where the *George Danielson* usually berthed. Not surprisingly, it had not returned from the mainland due to the increasing seas.

This was the first time John had seen the Harbor Village in daylight. He thought that the New National Hotel, standing majestically in front of the Old Harbor, rivaled the Ocean View which overlooked the same harbor but from a different direction. Lillie didn't agree; she favored the Ocean View.

John asked Lillie to stop in at CC Ball's general store. He wanted to purchase a souvenir of the Island. A few minutes later, he returned with a small, dark cobalt blue, glazed, porcelain pitcher. When Lillie saw what he brought back to the car she asked him to look on the bottom. Stamped in red ink, John saw: *Made in Germany for CC Ball.* In fact, most of CC's souvenirs were made in Germany.

"I guess I shouldn't have bought this one," John said.

Lillie laughed. On the side of the pitcher was a quite accurate drawing of the Southeast Lighthouse sitting on the Mohegan Bluffs.

Lillie drove John up to see the Spring House and its grounds. He thought this to be the finest hotel on the Island, and here, I would have to agree. As they drove up Southeast Road, John calculated that it was a good half mile to the water from Spring Street, a long way for Em to run through the brush. Lillie continued up to the majestic Southeast Lighthouse.

She drove a half mile beyond the entrance to the lighthouse before pulling off the road. Islanders had a special location to view the bluffs and the lighthouse. Lillie pulled off at this very spot as the weather was becoming more daunting. In just a few hours, visibility was now less than a few nautical miles. At this location on the top of Mohegan Bluffs, on a clear day, one could see Montauk as well as any ship coming out of the sea from Europe. John marveled at the sight from the top of the bluffs and finally understood why Wallace chose to build his small home on these same bluffs.

The rain held up for fifteen to twenty minutes, although the mist blowing in from the ocean never let up. They spotted a single, solitary fishing vessel sailing southwest toward Long Island, which was no longer visible through the fog. They stood in silence, as most everyone does who takes the time to walk out to this part of the bluffs.

I wasn't there with them, but I understand fully what they felt, we all feel it. Even in the midst of a storm, there is calm high on these bluffs. The lighthouse standing proud less than a mile to the east, Montauk Point twenty miles due west. The serenity of this perch was not, however, shared by the beach below; a one hundred and fifty foot drop to where the waves coming in from the Atlantic could pulverize a boat in a matter of minutes. I often thought the tranquility of this location was due to the very real danger far below, protected from it, yet serving as a constant reminder of the surf's power and potential for destruction.

John would never forget those precious minutes standing on the bluffs in that mild Nor'easter with Lillie. Again, hard to describe, but those who have stood in that very location, understand. Perhaps it is not possible to explain the beauty to those who have not been there.

When the rain picked up again, they got back in the car and drove to Wallace's house. By the time they arrived at "Eddey's Shanty" the rain had stopped again, and the visibility improved a bit. John wanted to finally meet Edith and see the inside of the small home that Wallace built.

Perched high on the bluffs, Wallace's home always had a different look in a storm than in broad daylight. The white shingles, eerily brighter than the heavens above, were offset by dark green shutters that blended in more with the darkening sky that gradually enveloped, enclosed, and encircled his small home. As the storm progressed, the slowly disappearing light, reflecting off the shingles, suddenly gave the appearance that Eddey's Shanty was the brightest object, a solitary source of light, on that part of the Island.

Lillie drove around to the back of the house and parked near the second barn, which sat about ten yards from the edge of the cliff. There were numerous places along Mohegan Bluffs where one could climb down to the beach, but not in this backyard. The drop-off was dramatic. Wallace would never have to worry about anyone scaling his portion of the bluffs.

When they got out of the car, John gravitated slowly toward the outhouse that was adjacent to the second barn near the edge of the cliff.

"Where … what are you looking at?" Lillie asked, a bit puzzled.

"I'd like to see Wallace's outhouse."

"What?"

"He has one, doesn't he? This is it, over here beyond the barn."

"Yes. Do you need to use it?"

"Yes, and no."

Just then, Edith emerged from her house to say hello, but refrained when she saw John opening the outhouse door.

"Why does he want to use the outhouse?" Edith asked Lillie.

"I don't know," Lillie replied. "He just asked to use it, but I don't think he really needs to." She thought his request a bit out of character.

Shortly, Wallace came outside and asked where John was.

"He's in the outhouse."

"Why is he in there? In the rain?" Wallace asked. "Didn't he go at the Weather House?"

"I don't know," Lillie said.

Just then, John opened the outhouse door and greeted the crowd of three now staring at him.

"That is a nice outhouse," John said in a dry, matter-of-fact tone.

"Yes, I suppose it is," Wallace said, raising his eyebrows.

"It has a comfortable seat and it has nice lines," John stated.

"It's only a wooden seat," Edith interjected.

"Yes, but it is comfortable," John said.

"I can agree with that, but I am not sure about the 'lines', John," Wallace said, feigning seriousness.

"I don't really see that seat as comfortable," Lillie said under her breath.

"Wallace, you know what you should do?" John said.

"With the outhouse?" Wallace asked, raising his voice an octave.

"Yes, I think you should turn it around … have it face the ocean. I hate to see that view go to waste."

"John, now you're talking … come with me." Wallace walked to the back of the outhouse. John followed.

"Oh God, let's go inside, Edith," Lillie shook her head. "This conversation is getting out of hand."

"No, Lillie, I want to stay and listen to John. Maybe he has an idea." Then, as an afterthought, Edith commented, "He is so handsome."

Lillie looked at Edith incredulously.

Just then, John realized he had not acknowledged Edith and walked back to exchange polite hellos. But John's mind was clearly on the outhouse.

"John, there is a back door, come look," Wallace beckoned him back. "I built a panel on the back that can be removed easily to look at the view of the Atlantic. You sit turned around."

Wallace took John around to the back of the outhouse and opened the rear panel that functioned as another door, exposing the seat.

"Now that is really wonderful. I want an outhouse. Wallace you are brilliant, but you ought to put hinges on that panel, or maybe just a window. No, not a window, you need a real door."

Lillie had had enough. She walked inside and soon all followed. Being that John had never lived in a home with an outhouse, it was understandable he might find it interesting, but to actually *like* it was nonsense.

John was given a brief tour of their small cottage that Wallace built with lumber from a home he helped dismantle. Once John was upstairs in the bedroom, he understood why the front entrance was on the second floor. The door opened into a small parlor outside their bedroom.

John asked Edith about working at the Vaill Hotel, more to make conversation than work related. Edith asked about the car that almost ran over her husband in the Vaill parking lot but John did not have an explanation. That was what worried Edith the most. John assured her that he did not think there would be any more trouble. After they finished a light lunch of fish chowder, Lillie and John said goodbye and continued their tour.

As Lillie drove John down Center Road, she asked if he would like to see the Island Cemetery. John nodded, not knowing what to expect.

"If you are interested in an outhouse, I suspect you will be interested in a cemetery," Lillie said wryly, shaking her head. "It does have a beautiful view, better than Wallace's outhouse!"

When she reached the entrance, Lillie drove slowly through the columns that had a sign embedded in one of them that read, simply, "Island Cemetery." Although there were several family cemeteries scattered throughout the Island, this was the cemetery where most Islanders wished to be buried. When she parked the car, the history lesson began.

"See that marker over there," Lillie said, pointing to a four-foot-high, thin white marble memorial, "that is for Isaiah Ball and his wife. They are my great-grandparents. And up the short hill about ten yards farther, are my parents' granite markers, twelve inches thick. Alongside them is my youngest sister's resting place, Sarah Cole, who died in childbirth. George's first wife, my other sister, is buried in Abilene, Texas.

"You can see the view from up here," Lillie said, changing the subject while walking up the hill, and then pointing. "There's the New Harbor, the Weather House, Crescent Beach and the North End, Sandy Point… The one thing you cannot appreciate is the large number of fresh water ponds we have on the Island."

Lillie pointed to a large monument about fifteen yards up the hill.

"Just beyond those graves ..." she directed John to an oversized, massive white granite monument that was topped with a large, highly polished black granite sphere.

"Who is buried there?" John asked, pausing to take in the expansive view, as well as marvel at the size of this marker. "This cemetery does have a remarkable view. Just extraordinary. I have never seen such a beautiful cemetery in all my life, and would never have imagined that I would actually like a cemetery."

Lillie nodded acknowledgement and continued, "That is the marker for Nicholas Ball. It's more like a monument to him—'King Ball' we used to call him. He died in 1896 and had arranged for the three-foot black marble sphere on top of the monument to be etched with the countries and continents he visited. He traveled the world as a teenager and young adult, and did one final around-the-world trip in his retirement. This small Island had a lot of influence in Washington, D.C. when Nicholas Ball was alive. In fact, in my opinion, and don't tell my husband this, I think he was the last Islander to have any significant influence in Washington. He even had influence in the White House. When President Grant visited the Island after the Civil War, Nicholas was his host. Grant only stayed on the Island a day, but there was a time when Islanders would talk about the Island as being *after* Grant or *before* Grant. Nicholas Ball's hotel even hosted several United States Supreme Court summer sessions in the mid-1880s.

"After he died, my husband wrote a short article for a Providence newspaper that summarized his contributions to our Island ... I will give you a copy ... it includes a summary of his obituary published by the *New York Times*. I think the obituary is more interesting than my husband's article."

"Why is that?"

"Well, when you read his obituary, you will understand," Lillie said. "And you will learn that the history of the Block Island Weather Bureau begins with Nicholas Ball. He was quite instrumental in getting the U. S. Army to open up a signal station on the Island in the early 1880s by laying a cable. I think the two articles will tell you more than you ever want to know about our Island."

I always thought it interesting, a bit humorous perhaps, to witness Lillie act a bit like me when giving tours of the Island and especially the cemetery. But whoever gives a tour of the cemetery, it would not be complete without a discussion of Nicholas Ball; whether you liked him or not, he was the closest thing to royalty our Island ever knew. Even the *New York Times* referred to him as "King of Block Island."

In fact, if Nicholas Ball ever fell from grace, it would be thought of as a tragedy in the Shakespearean sense. But since he never fell from grace, tragedy did not fit him at all. Or did it?

What I mean by tragedy here is the kind that Shakespeare wrote about—a person in a high social position falls from grace, figuratively and literally, to another, lower class because of any number of infallibilities. In this sense, except for Nicholas Ball, Shakespearean tragedy could not take place on Block Island.

It was Herman Melville who first introduced the idea in literature that the common man, the ordinary man or woman, could become part of a tragedy. Up to his time, a tragedy could only occur if a character fell from grace, for example, from one social or political class to a lower one. Because there is only one class on Block Island, a working, ordinary people class, only a tragedy in the Melvillian sense could take place here.

Until, however, there was Mr. Nicholas Ball.

Nicholas Ball, kind and gracious, may not have been an Aristotelian kind of man, but he was a Shakespearean man, which is to say he was no ordinary man.

When Lillie and John arrived back at the Weather House, they found the office a beehive of activity. Annie was trying to convince Milt and Em that an attack was imminent by one or more of the U-boats.

36 Breaking the Code

An attack by a U-boat was not out of the question, but why? And more important, *where?*

Still not sure what to think, I let them argue it out while I telegraphed the weather data.

John had enjoyed his short tour, or so I surmised from his smile, but he was still tired from the week and went upstairs to rest. When he came back downstairs, he mentioned Lillie had shown him the articles I had written on the Weather Bureau and my piece on Nicholas Ball. John asked a few questions about my career. How many stations had I been assigned? What was the most remarkable assignment? What was the most difficult assignment?

I told him there were many assignments when I was younger; my first wife Nellie and I were transferred all the time, sometimes five or six times a year, but only four in the last sixteen years. Often Nellie would return to Block Island and stay with her parents on High Street while I took some of the shorter assignments. I mentioned to John that I expected to finish my career here on Block Island.

Of course, he knew I was assigned to the New York City Weather Bureau at 100 Broadway. I proceeded to tell him about my assignment to the Abilene, Texas station at the turn of the century—an assignment that could very well have been to Galveston, Texas. I was surprised that he acknowledged he knew about the deadly Galveston Hurricane that had taken the life of the wife of Dr. Cline, the Weather Official in Charge of the Galveston Weather Bureau. Dr. Cline did not understand the impact the tidal surge would have on the barrier island, but then again, neither did I at that time either. I mentioned to him that I would've most likely been killed, one of the ten thousand to have died that day, if I had been assigned there instead of Abilene. John nodded he was aware I was almost assigned to that station instead of the landlocked Abilene station.

To say I was surprised that he knew about that situation is an understatement. John was glad I was assigned to the less exotic location, Abilene… at least I was still alive. I guess the ONI had done their homework before he sailed on the *Anna C.*

When Lillie came into the room, she asked John if he liked the articles, but before giving him a chance to answer, she asked another question. I was surprised by the intensity of her question.

"John," Lillie said, "do you know of Sperry, the pilot? Lawrence Sperry? He had to land his plane on the Island a little over a month ago?"

"Yes," John answered, raising his eyes as Annie would. "I do know him and have seen him around the Naval Yard many times. My father worked at the Sperry Corporation which was founded by his father. How do you know of him, or did you just read about him in the newspapers?"

"He landed his plane," Lillie continued, "in the surf below the Southeast Lighthouse last month. Did you know that? The plane was towed into the Great Salt Pond and moored near the commercial dock, just beyond the Hog Pen."

"In all the excitement, I had forgotten he had to land his plane at the base of the bluffs. Was there much damage to the hydroaeroplane?" John asked.

Overhearing Sperry's name, Emma jumped up and ran into the kitchen.

"Do you know him? Do you really know him? He is amazing. Yes, we did see the plane. It was unbelievable! We all took off from school to see the plane. It sure looked funny down on the beach, but," pointing to the Great Salt Pond, "we got a good look at it when it was towed out there for repairs," Emma said, without taking the time to breathe.

She yelled back to Annie who was still at the Marconi. "He was handsome, wasn't he, Annie?"

Annie laughed and immediately wheeled herself into the kitchen to participate in the conversation.

"There wasn't much damage to the plane. Young Sperry was the talk of the Island," I added.

"Oh man, that guy was handsome and he was real nice to Annie and me too," Emma grinned.

"Did you two really meet him? Sperry is the talk of New York also!" John said, moving his chair to make room for Annie's wheelchair. "He used to fly his aeroplane all over Manhattan. He even flew it under and then over the Brooklyn Bridge in several loops. And this past January, I understand, it was announced that he and his father were going to be in short movies, something that Hollywood is producing for the screen. I read that in the *New York Times*."

Annie tapped out a message to her sister. She wanted Emma to ask John a question.

"Annie wants to know if he really is a movie star."

"I don't know if the short movies were ever filmed, but I heard they were going to be, Annie," John answered. "But even if they aren't filmed, he is a star in another sense."

Annie became emphatic with her sister. She motioned something to Emma who then looked at John.

"Annie wants me to tell you how we met him. The plane was towed near the commercial ferry dock so it could be fixed. The day after it was moored there, I wheeled Annie down the dock so we could get a better look at the plane. We were sitting on the dock for a long time. It was so interesting looking at him and the other men working on the aeroplane... Is that how you say it, 'aeroplane'? It was the first plane we ever saw.

"After about an hour, Mr. Sperry rowed over to the dock to pick up some food. He walked by us and said hello! He was so tall. At first, we could hardly speak to him. After a few minutes, we asked him how he liked the harbor. Other people on the dock were asking him questions too, and he answered them, but he seemed to take an interest in Annie and me. He was so nice to us. I asked him if he liked Block Island and he said yes. He told us he had flown over it several times before from an airport on Long Island."

"You two were so excited, you didn't sleep that night. You both stayed up all night talking about him and his plane," Lillie laughed.

"We still talk about him," Emma said. "Don't we, Annie?"

Annie raised her eyes and smiled.

"How long did you talk to him?" John asked.

"A long time. He sat on a piling on the dock and ate his food while he talked to all of us. I think he liked us, don't you, Annie?"

Annie smiled her big, broad smile from the heart.

"Maybe one day you will meet him again," John said.

Milton came into the kitchen from the office and asked John to give an opinion on Annie's idea that an attack on land could occur at any time.

John's 'day of rest' was now officially over. At that point, Lillie mentioned she wanted to return to her home on High Street. She said that she would be back before too long, and left the Weather House through the front door.

"I think Annie has begun to understand what is actually happening. She has been excited for the past hour—although not as excited as to hear that you know about Mr. Sperry," Milt added wryly. "Annie has been sitting over her notes, reviewing the letters tapped out in Morse code. I think she has discovered the reason why they are using the weather data... which I still don't understand."

"Is that correct, Annie?" John asked.

We all were hoping for just one more piece of information that could help us complete our understanding of why the German U-boats were using Block Island as a staging area; and Annie thought she knew.

"Em has been trying to understand her, but her nonverbal language communication system, even with Em, is not sophisticated enough for her to communicate her thoughts to us," Milt said. "Emma understands from Annie that they are using the transmission of weather data as part of their code. She thinks that she has broken a portion of the code, and Em says she thinks Annie actually knows where their transmissions are going, but we can't understand what she means."

At this point, John was a bit skeptical of Annie's ability to crack the code, but we were willing to let her give it a try.

Annie, as far as all of us could understand, had discovered that the Germans were transmitting data within our 'official weather bureau cable transmission.' They appeared to be sending the very same information that I would send via cable, except they were adding a letter, or word, at the end of every other symbol. Annie explained that they were intercepting Milton and my weather transmissions and resending them themselves with their additions. When one takes the extra letters and puts them all together, it makes sense. If Annie was correct, this was proof that the mysterious men and the U-boats were indeed able to monitor every transmission we had made to the mainland.

Annie thought that the ultimate code could very well be sent directly to the Weather Office at 100 Broadway, leading us back to a concern first voiced back at the Brooklyn Navy Yard. A German spy was probably working in my old office in lower Manhattan.

"A German spy working for the Weather Bureau, Mr. Eddey, is that possible?" Milt asked.

I nodded and John answered: "Yes. Yes, it is possible, Milton."

Again, we all began thinking through scenarios and asking questions: "Why would they put an agent in the Weather Station?" Emma asked.

"Good question," John said. "Perhaps because the staff in that office often are assigned to the Brooklyn Navy Yard's office ... and who to better gain entry to the Yard than another government official. It is beginning to make sense."

Annie moved her eyes to indicate "no" to John's explanation. She made a movement with her bad hand that meant "more." But Emma could not translate anything more than that, although she tried.

Finally, Annie asked to speak to Wallace.

John looked at me, and nodded. His mind was following me and probably got there before mine did, but I could not be sure. "Mr. Eddey, why do you think Annie wants to talk to Wallace?"

I shook my head from side to side.

It was, I must admit, a little unusual for all of us to be waiting for a fifteen-year-old girl, who couldn't talk, who had a permanent injury; waiting for her pronouncement about what the case is all about; but her mind was good and we were at a loss to explain the entire course of events in a thorough and complete manner. We were willing to give her a chance; more than that, we were hoping she could figure this out.

I asked Milton if he would take my car and pick up Wallace. He readily agreed and said he wanted to drop by his house to see if his parents had returned from selling the farm animals. He knew that if they had not made it back today, the approaching Nor'easter would keep them on the mainland a few more days, unless they were to have caught a ride on one of the local fishing vessels.

A half hour later, Milt and Wallace returned, each in separate cars. Milton's parents were not yet home. He felt relieved in a way and I felt it better for him to be staying with us rather than on the west side of the Island.

Wallace walked into the office and sat beside Annie.

I explained to him about the code and that Annie had wanted to ask him some questions. Communication would be no problem. Wallace was as proficient as I in Annie's Morse code. Milt, John, Emma, and I left Wallace and Annie alone. We walked outside. Milt and I checked the signal tower and raised the cold wave flag to fly below the storm warning weather flags. John and Emma sat on the back steps looking out onto the Great Salt Pond. The temperature was now expected to drop by twenty degrees!

The rain had stopped once again so we walked down to the water's edge, Trim's Pond. The water was clear. It was low tide and the starfish and sea urchin were easily seen on the bottom. Small fish swam by incessantly. John marveled at the beauty of the water and wondered aloud why he had not wandered down along the bank of Trim's Pond before.

It was so peaceful, here alongside the lagoon, almost surreal. John thought about how Wallace's house had looked a few hours before. Here was the same light reflected from a darkened sky. It was so beautiful that we forgot Wallace and Annie were in the office working. After about thirty minutes, we walked back up to the Weather House and entered the back door, assuming we had given Wallace and Annie enough time to be alone.

We walked back inside, not expecting any great revelations, but were we ever wrong.

37 1885

When we walked back into the Weather House Annie was smiling and Wallace, seated, his back to us, was holding a small glass of whiskey. Thirty minutes ago, Annie was just short of frantic, unable to communicate her thoughts, even to her sister. And now she was relaxed and confident. It was as if Wallace and Annie had been celebrating.

"Pop, it's simple," Wallace said, turning around and looking up. "Annie could not express her thoughts until she started talking to me about the *Anna C* and my trip to the Navy Yard. When I explained how I navigated through Hell Gate she wanted me to explain more about the explosions you saw in the channel when you were living with your father, you know, the ones you talk about occasionally. Remember when you were living in Brooklyn and the Army Corps dynamited Hell Gate?"

I nodded.

"When you walked outside, all I had to do was draw a map, a chart of New York Harbor and Annie explained all that she was concerned about."

I knew immediately Wallace and Annie were referring to the explosions that I witnessed in 1885 when I was about twenty-two or twenty-three years old. I often spoke about them because they were so dramatic. At the time, my father was moving from Green Point to Marble Hill. Marble Hill was a small, almost secluded community in northern Manhattan built on a hill of white marble and granite. Marble Hill was, and still is, a part of Manhattan even though it was (originally) an island, like Ward's Island.

I explained to John, as he seemed to be unaware of what we were referring to, that in 1851, twelve years before I was born, the Army Corps of Engineers first began blasting the submerged ledges and dangerous surface rocks within Hell Gate. In 1885, the blasting resumed and all New

Yorkers witnessed those dramatic explosions. And in 1885 when my family moved to Marble Hill, we witnessed half of that marble and granite hill being blasted away to make way for a new Harlem River channel, deep and wide enough for ships to enter the Hudson River; that channel, in turn, created the island of Marble Hill. Prior to this blasting, shipping traffic was not possible on the northern part of the Harlem River.

The explosion that I remembered most vividly was the destruction of the nine-acre Flood Rock Hell Gate ledge, totally wiped away with dynamite. I was surprised to find out that Annie had developed a sign for this and Wallace knew about her sign. Emma later told me it was one of the few signs she did not share with her sister.

"Wallace, what is her sign or symbol for Hell Gate?" I asked.

"She brings up both her hands, the good hand higher than the other one, of course. When she brings them up, she widens her fingers, to signify an explosion. Sometimes this is out of her control and her fingers on her bad hand separate wildly and uncontrollably. (The doctors call this dystonia, and it is a consequence of her brain damage and not within her control.) After she does that, Annie then gives her symbol for the jetty in the Old Harbor, meaning rocks. I knew where her thoughts were leading her and what she is thinking. And after I understood her questions, she then asked about the depth of the Hell Gate channel. And as soon as she asked that question, I knew Annie had an idea that we needed to pursue."

"Amazing, she put it together," John said softly, as he stared out the window of the office. Darkness had begun to set in and the beautiful magenta sky was becoming all but impossible to see now that the clouds in advance of the storm were approaching the Island.

Without speaking any further, John, Wallace, and I were reasonably certain that Annie had put us on our final approach to solving the mystery of the intentions of the Germans and their U-boats, now lying, or floating somewhere submerged off Block Island. She had simply asked the right questions.

I looked at John. "Is it time to go back?"

"I don't know, Mr. Eddey. We need one more piece of information or else my superiors may not act on the data. What is their specific target?

One of us has to figure that out."

"I think you also have to be careful of leaving the Island, John," Wallace said. "And I don't mean because of the weather, the Nor'Easter that's getting ready to blow."

"Perhaps, Wallace. Can you borrow another boat without raising suspicions?" We all knew John was referring to Wallace borrowing a boat larger than his *Anna C.* But under almost any weather condition, Wallace would feel most comfortable at the helm of his own boat.

Wallace did not answer. Just then, the phone rang. It was his wife Edith asking when he was going to be home. She had just returned from working at the Vaill Hotel and had seen two men in their front yard; she was getting worried.

Wallace left the Weather House immediately to return home but before he drove off, John handed him his pistol. He imagined the worst. Would his wife be a victim? He drove south along Beach Avenue to the Old Town Center, and then up to Mohegan Trail, the quickest way to his home.

38 Sunday Morning

Edith could not identify the men who were standing in front of their home—a second time—before walking east in the direction of the Vaill Hotel. Just as Wallace arrived back to his home, Edith was calling the Vaill's front desk to ask if these two men were guests at the hotel. She was told that they were indeed guests ... from New York City—repeat customers and probably just out for a stroll. It didn't make sense, why hadn't she seen them when she was working at the Vaill's front desk?

As this was playing out, my wife walked in the front door of the Weather House. I was relieved. It was not hard to imagine why we were in a constant state of apprehension, but with Lillie back at the Weather House, I was finally able to concentrate, so I joined Milt and Annie at the Marconi to listen for more transmissions.

But after a few hours of not hearing anything of interest, Milton and I called it a night. Annie, however, continued listening and stayed up for several more hours, hoping to hear more clues in German or English.

While we were asleep, around two in the morning, Annie heard a transmission of several German words that would turn out to be the last piece of the puzzle that was begun by Milton two weeks ago, although it would take days for us to understand the significance of that transmission.

When we woke the next morning we were distracted by the multiple sounds of the howling winds of a classic Nor'easter brought to the Island by yet another moving formation. A symphony it wasn't, which is to say the unrelenting noise was not necessarily pleasing to the ear.

And with Lillie determined that we all go to church, Annie, unfortunately, did not get the chance to share the 2:00 a.m. transmission until much later in the day.

With this being Sunday and with the arrival of the storm, I knew it was going to be a long, long day. But how long … I had no idea.

This Nor'easter was initially forecast a week ago by the Oswego, NY weather station. The Head Weather Observer in Oswego and I had the same mentor: Sgt. Davis. And I do believe we were both trained very well indeed. Sgt. Davis quoted Ben Franklin frequently, using his term *moving formations* to describe waves of changes in pressure moving in a specified direction.

Sgt. Davis taught us that all moving formations have a purpose. Hurricanes, for example, redistribute heat from the equatorial regions to the Polar Regions, in our case, toward the North Pole. Other storms, with different names, in other parts of the world, do the same thing. Those moving formations move heat and precipitation and water.

Unfortunately, they can also leave behind quite a mess.

Just ask Dr. Cline who, in September of 1900, was the Head Weather Observer stationed in Galveston, Texas. Remember those ten thousand vacationers who lost their lives from the storm surge that he was not able to forecast? He was able to forecast the hurricane, but not the devastating wall of water that accompanied the storm. But even if he was able to forecast the storm surge, it is unlikely that everyone could have survived due to the geography of that barrier island.

Nor'easters can do damage too, from wind and rain and from storm surges, although not usually to the same extent as hurricanes.

This morning, as any morning, the very first thing I did, after slipping on my shoes, was go downstairs to check the barometer reading. It had dropped precipitously overnight, even farther than I had anticipated. I immediately walked outside to make sure the gale force storm weather flags were still flying on the tower. I briefly considered hanging the hurricane flags, but that would have required permission from Washington, D.C.

While securing the flags I noticed the antenna wire strung between the roof and the tower was still in place, although I didn't think it would last long with the wind picking up as it was. I climbed the tower to secure it as well, so it would not snap or get blown away by the wind. I've always enjoyed climbing the tower for the view, but today there was no view, just wind pounding rain into every pore on my face. Looking out over the Island, I reflected about how well everyone had performed and how important John has been to our effort. I was, I admit, quite proud of my team, and for a moment, I got lost in my thoughts to such an extent that I forgot about the pounding rain and gusting winds and that I was standing on a tower seventy feet off the ground in a very dangerous storm.

Down from the tower, soaked, I walked to the back of the Weather House just as John emerged. We walked over to the side of the building and stood in its lee, where the wind and rain couldn't reach us.

"Mr. Eddey," John said abruptly, "I think I am ready to head back to New York. We have accumulated a lot of information that they will find useful."

I nodded.

I understood John's need to return to the Navy Yard. He had been in the field long enough without communication with them—except for his brief encounter with the deckhand/agent on the ferry—and it is entirely reasonable to assume the ONI may have collected more information regarding the German spy's intentions that, put together with our data, could be enough to solve the mystery.

"I wonder if Annie heard any more clues after we went to bed last night?" John asked.

"I don't know, she was still asleep when I came down to check the barometric pressure."

We talked about Annie's hypothesis that an attack directed at naval vessels (or even a land-based target) by the U-boats—I thought perhaps in Newport—could soon occur. We had some time to intercept more communications from the three mysterious men and/or the U-boats because we knew the Nor'easter would delay all ferries from arriving for several days.

Lillie heard us talking from the upstairs bedroom window and came down to start breakfast. She woke the girls as she walked past their bedroom door. Then she yelled to John and me from the kitchen door, "Come inside and help me. I want everyone eating breakfast before going to church. John, you are coming with us, right?"

John nodded.

It wasn't a question, it was a statement. From my conversation with her yesterday, I knew how important attending today's service was for her. When issues of family importance surfaced Lillie was drawn to the comfort and safety of the fellowship found in a congregation. With John almost certainly returning to his base in Brooklyn, and our mission perhaps coming to a close, this was just such a time.

And I kept thinking it was going to be a long, long day.

I was not looking forward to getting the girls ready for church. They were the first to complain how boring the services were, especially the sermons. I must admit my mind wandered frequently as well, and I suppose most people had the same response, although few people spoke about their feelings. The exception being, of course, the two girls; they spoke freely about how long and senseless the services often seemed to them. But today they were going to have to endure the service – their mother had made up her mind we would all attend as a family, including John.

When it comes to church, other things come to my mind, including Melville's lines written for Queequeg: *'For at bottom—so he told me—he was actuated by a profound desire to learn among the Christians, the arts whereby to make his people still happier than they were; and more than that, still better than they were. But, alas! The practices of Whalemen soon convinced him that even Christians could be both miserable and wicked; infinitely more so, than all his father's heathens. Arrived at last in old Sag Harbor; and seeing what the sailors did there; and then going on to Nantucket, and seeing how they spent their wages in that place also, poor Queequeg gave it up for lost. Thought he, it's a wicked world in all meridians; I'll die a pagan.'*

As we were preparing breakfast I began thinking about how Lillie and I had changed our membership from the Baptist Church to the Methodist Church a few years ago when the Methodist Church first opened its doors—but not for the dramatic reasons suggested by Queequeg in the above passage. Rather, it was nothing more than a tradition for my family to belong to the Methodist Church. I attended the Methodist Church in Green Point, Brooklyn where I grew up, and then the Marble Hill Methodist Church when my father built a house in that northern Manhattan neighborhood. My father had attended the Woodrow Methodist Church on Staten Island where he grew up and his father before that as well, although his grandfather was in fact a Quaker. So it all seemed reasonable for us to join the new Methodist congregation when it was established in 1907.

I wasn't concerned, as was Melville, of "the need for faith—yet the hypocrisies rampant among us all." There are hypocrisies, of that I am sure, and there surely is evil, of that I am sure as well. Perhaps we are looking at it with the three men? I do not know, because I am not that gifted, but what I do know is that life is valuable and destruction and death seem so senseless, yet when it occurs we must carry on, and I suppose faith helps us do that. Faith in ourselves … and so I join the church.

Here I, as a weather observer and forecaster, try to provide information to the community, in the form of forecasts and warnings, to bring people to safety, to help them stay alive, as well as to prevent unnecessary destruction from those borrowed days. Weather, beautiful at times, ordinary most of the time, and powerfully deadly at other times. If life is not valuable, why then would we forecast?

As I mentioned the girls are not fond of rising early to attend church. But today they surprised us all; we did not get any argument—because of John's presence. After the girls woke, within minutes, they were dressed and washed. In that order. The speed at which they got ready was in itself a true miracle—perhaps the only miracle ever to occur at the Weather House or on Block Island!

Maybe it wasn't going to be such a long day after all.

Even though Reverend Dale's sermons were long and boring, he had been extraordinary with Annie—and Em—before, as well as after, the accident. Annie's phrase, "I want to matter," I think came from discussions with Reverend Dale. I am not sure exactly how it all came about, but I do know they were reading from the book of Proverbs one evening in the parlor in Lillie's home. Annie listening, as Mr. Dale read aloud. (This was one of the few times when her younger sister would not stay around and participate.) It seems two verses in Proverbs struck Annie as important given her 'new' physical situation.

Proverbs 21, Verse 3: "To do justice and judgment is more acceptable to the Lord than sacrifice." And Verse 16: "The man that wandereth out of the way of understanding shall remain in the congregation of the dead." For a period of time, shortly after the discussion between Reverend Dale and Annie, she would tap out those phrases, sometimes to Mrs. Conners in Point Judith and sometimes to me—except she would always replace the word man with woman. I initially thought that this was an exercise, an assignment given to her by the minister. I thought she was simply saying: "No, I will not be sacrificed," and "I will not be part of a congregation of the dead."

But it quickly became clear she wanted to 'matter.' It may have started with her not wanting to be in a congregation of the dead, taken literally perhaps; but she was dwelling on a purpose for her life, the one after the accident. This was not an assignment, this was not idle talk; contrary, it was as if it were a call to arms for herself, a reason to carry on. She was not going to be counted among the dead ... *while alive.* The Proverbs had a double meaning to her, one spiritual and one practical; "I want, and will, *matter.*" (Although I believe that *wanting to matter* has more to do with who Annie Rose is as an individual, these conversations with the minister certainly didn't hurt.)

That morning for breakfast we ate corn muffins, drank milk from the Murray farm, and had our oatmeal topped with sugar from the islands of the Caribbean. Annie asked to have her muffins mixed with her oatmeal; Lillie added little milk, because the thicker the preparation, the easier it was for her to swallow. Because of her risk of aspiration while eating, Annie understood the need to be patient, or not eat at all—or rather, not to be fed at all. She could not feed herself, being unable to use her hands fully, plus her propensity to choke on her food, both a long-term consequence of the neurological damage from the accident at sea. Although eating was embarrassing for her in public, she felt quite comfortable being fed with John at the table.

This morning when Annie finished her breakfast, John carried her out to the car, a gesture that she, I am sure, will never forget. They had a short conversation that I could see made Annie smile her broad smile, but to this day, I do not know what John said to her.

We drove slowly to Center Road. The rain was coming down hard, finding its way between the windows and doorframe of the car. But we didn't notice, it was the least of our concerns. What lay before us was an uncertain future. As I drove I thought about all the tragic things that had happened to our lives, especially Lillie's life. She has already lost one son and her first husband and one daughter's life changed by the accident at sea. It was our hope that today's service might comfort us all in some small manner. Or was I asking too much?

I parked the car halfway between the church and the Town Hall on rocks to avoid the mud. Instinctively, Annie, with a flip of her head, pointed to the long green hedge at the rear boundary of the church property. I knew it was her 'shorthand' reference for the concept of "separation of church and state." I was certain she wanted to impress John with her knowledge, but I am sure he did not understand this particular nonverbal communication. Annie knew I was proud she understood this aspect of our democracy, although she didn't learn it at church; rather, from her Uncle the lawyer (my sister Catherine's husband) on one of his summer vacations to the Island.

Separation of church and state was not readily accepted in colonial New England. One of Rhode Island's colonial governors, Roger Williams, wrote in the middle of the seventeenth century, just before Block Island was settled, that "a hedge, or wall of separation, between the garden of the church and the wilderness of the world" ought to exist. William's opinion was completely different from the puritans or pilgrims and, indeed, most other nation-states. I have always felt our small church supported that notion and our minister was chosen, in part, due to being agreeable with that "hedge being in place" even though it did not exist in his homeland, Great Britain. Most all Islanders, independent souls that we are, felt perfectly comfortable with William's concept, and would have it no other way! This is important to us, of that I am certain.

As we walked up to the church, we met up with Milton's parents. They had arrived late last night on a fishing boat from Groton, Connecticut and had put in at the Old Harbor. They were quite happy to see their son and from my short conversation with them, it was clear they knew nothing about what was going on at the Weather House.

The Methodist Church was a simple structure made of wood, sided with shingles painted white. The roof was covered with those same shingles left unpainted. It had a very short steeple; no more than twenty feet high, and the bell that hung in the belfry was open to the weather on all four sides. These openings were shaped like the windows in the sanctuary—five sides with a diamond shaped top. Halfway up the peak of the front, well before the eye reaches the steeple, a triangle of the same angle, but much smaller, matched the peak of the roof. I do not know the significance of this architectural embellishment but I always gazed up at it whenever I entered the church.

Two wide wooden steps led unceremoniously from a sloped, grass-filled front yard to two large wooden doors with glass windows that opened into the small Narthex. To the right of the church was a field enclosed by a stone wall used by a farmer for his livestock. To the left of the building was the churchyard, enclosed by a white wooden fence consisting of three flat boards sandwiched between two one-by-six-inch posts.

This was not a grand church of the mainland variety; it was a simple, small building for a simple Island and its peoples. A small congregation of Islanders: farmers, fisherman, laborers, and me—the sole forecaster. Lillie and I played a role in organizing the church and are most proud that it is a successful, albeit, small congregation. As we walked towards the church I saw in Lillie a sense of contentment that I had not seen in several weeks. Church for her was indeed comforting.

Usually Annie wheels herself to the back door of the church, near where the hedge started its march along the back of the property, where she can enter without having to be lifted up the two steps that the front entrance presents as an obstacle. But this morning, partly because of the torrential rains, she wheeled herself to the front door and simply waited for someone to lift her up into the church. Milton stopped talking to his parents when he saw her waiting in front of those two steps. John helped Milt lift her into the Narthex and then Annie wheeled herself halfway toward the front and parked herself in the aisle. Milt and John followed and sat down in the aisle to her left. As Lillie and I walked through the front doors, I read the announcements posted on the wall about the service. Today's sermon: "The Four lessons of the Lord's Prayer."

As we sat down behind them I wondered would there be any clues in the sermon that could help us on our quest to determine the motives of the three mystery men. John later confided that he was wondering if any of the three mystery men would be brazen enough to attend the service!

Every once in a while tears would fill my eyes when I witnessed Annie confront the little obstacles of life. I was so full of satisfaction watching Annie sitting quietly in the aisle with John and Milton alongside. I am sure Lillie felt the same. I scanned the congregation to find Emma sitting on the right side of the sanctuary. She was with some of her friends. Full of life, laughing, and fully engaged with them, she was always, instinctively, positioning herself so she could keep an eye on her sister. I then looked over at Annie, constrained by the inability to move her body but fully comfortable with her nonverbal self, she was smiling and quite content sitting next to John and Milt.

I was joyful for Annie now, yet I knew what lay ahead for her, a life perhaps, alone, a life that would have been anything but alone if it were not for the accident. But of course she had Emma, the best sister any sister could ask for. I changed my focus to the minister as he prepared to start the service. My mind usually wandered during much of a Sunday service, focusing only on the content of the sermon when it finally arrived. I hoped today's sermon would keep my interest. If not, it would be a long, long service.

I thought about how our church had been assigned its first a fully ordained minister from London, England two years after the church was established. He arrived in the United States in 1904 with his wife and came to our church in 1909. Mr. George W. Dale, now thirty-seven years old, married, still no children. I thought about when we interviewed him and how grateful I was when he accepted our position. My daydreaming and reminiscing continued throughout the service until the sermon was about to begin.

This morning, as on most Sunday mornings, Reverend Dale stood after the last reading and walked to the podium where he gathered his notes. His bible was already open to the book of Luke.

He began his sermon slowly, in a low voice with his English accent. If you closed your eyes and could not see how young he looked, any reasonable person sitting in the pews might venture to guess he was a seventy-year-old English aristocrat. He moved like an old man sometimes also, yet his youthful appearance was simply astounding.

He began with a simple question: "How many of you understand the meaning of the Lord's Prayer? Luke keeps it simple, just like those of you who live on Block Island keep it simple. In my opinion Luke breaks the prayer down into four parts, maybe five. If you want, you can look at Psalm 145 as we begin the sermon."

He paused, giving us a chance to answer the question or open our bibles to the Psalms; he continued only after he was certain no member of the congregation wished to speak.

"*Our Father, who art in heaven,*
Hallowed be thy Name."

"What do these two lines mean? What do they mean?" He often repeated himself, sometimes so much that I once asked him about it. His candid reply: "For effect ... and to give me some time to organize my next sentences."

"Well, 'Our Father' refers, of course, to our God. The one and only God who is—and whose *name*—is Hallowed, as in holy, consecrated, sacred, revered. The first line then is a pronouncement that God is of supreme importance, he is Hallowed, sacred, revered as no other, and the second line simply reinforces that not only is God holy but his *name* is as well. And there is only one God of course ... a concept that may have originated with the Egyptians."

He stopped and looked up for a moment before continuing, this time in a slow, soft, deliberate cadence:

"*Thy kingdom come.*
Thy will be done,
On Earth as it is in heaven."

"The prayer continues by introducing the concept of the Kingdom of God *on earth*. Psalm 145 talks about the glory of the Kingdom of thy God, an everlasting Kingdom. There is one God and his will ... will be done, on Earth ... as it is in Heaven."

"The next phrase requires some thought. You could reasonably think this next concept in the Lord's Prayer refers to nourishment, food, to keep us going and you wouldn't be wrong. Most theologians think it does and, of course, there are many references to Jesus feeding the poor routinely. But I think this phrase, as short as it is, means much more.

"Give us this day our daily bread."

I thought we needed our *daily bread* to give us the strength to return John to the Brooklyn Navy Yard and complete our mission.

"God will give you, if you ask, sustenance, nourishment, *of the spiritual kind*, the kind of nourishment that is the essence of faith, the nourishment that is required for one to have faith. God is near to all who call upon him; again, I read from Psalm 145. You will need faith to endure in this world, if you ..." and now he again began raising his voice, "if you haven't found that out yet then you will soon."

At this point I wasn't sure what he was talking about, but shortly he redeemed himself and I began to realize we were being introduced to a different meaning of the phrase "getting our daily bread." I was about to learn something.

"Give us our daily bread. Now, if you believe Jesus is simply referring to food, then I suspect that if Jesus lived on Block Island, he would be referring to lobsters. Do you realize that Block Islanders and mainlanders set out over six thousand lobster pots at any given time around this Island! That is extraordinary, more than any other place in the state. There is so much lobster here we could feed a nation. The point I am trying to make is that if Jesus grew up and lived on Block Island, I don't think the Lord's Prayer would include the phrase, "Give us our daily lobster."

When Reverend Dale paused for a turned away from the pulpit and walked quickly to the center of the platform. He began staring down the aisle at Annie, sitting in her wheelchair. First, he attracted Annie's attention and then bellowed: "Annie, oh God, Annie, has she endured, her faith is real, she has asked and has been given her *daily bread* and she has endured. Annie, God loves you."

I looked at Annie, afraid she would be embarrassed. I had never seen Reverend Dale single Annie out before; no, he has never tried to use her in any way, he has only been quietly supportive of her. Annie took the attention in stride; that I knew because I could see her signaling to her sister—with her bad hand—a cryptic remark, in the nonverbal language shared only between the two sisters. I thought she said, "...the Reverend is nuts," but I couldn't be sure. Em tried to refrain from laughing so I had a suspicion I was correct. I glanced at John and immediately assumed the minister was responding in this way due to his presence.

Reverend Dale walked back to stand behind his podium, where he paused, once again, as much to catch his breath as to look at us once again.

"So far what have we learned? We have learned that God and his name is Hallowed and he has a Kingdom that we must work hard to ensure it will soon be on Earth ... a Kingdom, a spiritual domain over which God reigns that can and will be ours. We have learned that the phrase 'give us your daily bread' refers to spiritual sustenance, nutritional sustenance for the spirit, and that God will give you enough, but just enough, to help you carry on."

How comforting, I thought, especially about God's Kingdom on Earth. But how much work will that entail?"

As if to answer my question he continued: "It will not come easy." But he offered no other suggestions.

And with the rain pounding against the sanctuary windows and the wind increasing in intensity Reverend Dale continued his reading of the Lord's Prayer:

"And forgive us our trespasses,
As we forgive those who trespass against us."

"It is easy to understand why this is a crucial part of the Lord's Prayer and so essential. Forgiveness. The ancient Babyloniun Talmud, which was in oral tradition when Jesus was alive, explains: 'He who forgives will himself be forgiven.'

"We know what forgiveness is, but when ought it be put into practice?"

As Reverend Dale paused, I glanced over at Annie who was again signaling something to her sister. If I am not mistaken I believe Annie was communicating that young children must learn to forgive adults; for what, I could not decipher. I wondered if Annie had a nonverbal sign for forgiveness or did she just make one up now? And how did Emma know to make eye contact with Annie?

"Forgiveness seems easy to accomplish, but it is not so. It is not a passive, reflective thought. Rather, it requires 'doing' in the sense of action with good intention. There is nothing passive about forgiveness. The recognition of when and whom to forgive is not easy. What about the leaders in Germany who are escalating the Great War? How many more have died because of the intensification of the war?" I thought to myself that I was becoming afraid of the Germans.

I repeated the phrase, "He who forgives will himself be forgiven," over and over in my mind. I liked that phrase and realized I had never heard it said like that before.

And then the three mysterious men entered my mind—and what about the sailors in the U-boats? How do you forgive them, what have they done, if anything, yet, anyway? But was this what Jesus was saying? I wasn't sure I could forgive them because, well, I never understood that part of the forgiveness obligation.

As Melville would predict, I suppose I would go silent on this topic.

I began thinking of Isaac Cline, the forecaster in Galveston, Texas who failed to forecast the severity of the 1900 Galveston Hurricane and ten thousand lives were lost. I have long struggled about how to deal with that kind of mistake in my own profession. "Ought Cline be forgiven?" I said to myself.

As I thought this through, Reverend Dale seemed to answer with a question: "How does forgiveness work in this situation? Maybe, just maybe, we will have to expand our hearts, as hard as it seems and accept those words of Jesus: *Forgive them, for they know not what they do.* I think these words ought to be an addendum to the Lord's Prayer." Now that was a sentiment I had not heard from our minister.

How wonderful a thought, I said to myself, *but what if there is real danger when feeling afraid?* At times, the weather makes me afraid, but forgiveness is not applicable to the weather. What about when a person, or a government, makes me, or anyone else, afraid? Does it apply that we ought to forgive them, or it, for they know not what they do? *No, not until we have rectified the situation*, I thought. *Only when we are certain that 'there shall be none to make us afraid,'* then, and only then, can we forgive.

I woke from my thoughts hoping that the sermon would be over, but all I saw was Reverend Dale turn away from the congregation and walk back to the platform to gaze at his notes and continue to read from the Bible. It was becoming a very long service.

He then stepped down from the platform to be *one with his congregation*. It was a common technique, to walk down to the congregation, in some churches, not seen in Catholic or Episcopalian Churches, or the New England Unitarian Congregations for that matter, where the priest or minister always stays up, sometimes high up, in the pulpit. Although smaller, the platform and pulpit in our small church is similar to the one in the Touro Synagogue in Newport; we do not, however, have such a beautiful balcony.

"Temptation. What does the prayer mean when it asks that God not lead us into temptation? Well, maybe this is a mistake in translation or transcription over the centuries, but I don't think that we should be asking him, we need to ask ourselves this question. No temptation, please God, deliver us from evil."

"And lead us not into temptation,
But deliver us from evil."

"Please deliver us from evil. There are many examples. I will choose one. Do you want to be famous? Is there anyone who does not want to be famous? Are there men who are joining the Army to be famous? Are you running for State Senate for example, to serve or just to be famous?"

I began worrying that we might not be delivered from evil if we could not figure out why those three mystery men were on the Island.

"Now, let us move on to the last part of the Lord's Prayer as we say it in our Church. Perhaps you were not aware that these last few lines of the Lord's Prayer were actually added well after the story of Luke was first told. It ends with:

For thine is the kingdom,
and the power,
and the glory,
for ever and ever.
Amen.

"The Lord's Prayer is not only a lesson on how to pray, it is a group of lessons spoken by Jesus, who learned it from the oral traditions of the Talmud and the Old Testament. The prayer can be a powerful reminder to us all, if you understand it.

"And herein ends today's lesson, on this cold, windy, and stormy Sunday in October. In next week's sermon we will discuss how faith can help with the grief that follows loss. May you all be safe and postpone any crossings you have planned to remain on the Island until the storm passes."

Everyone in the congregation knew what he was saying. A translation was not necessary: we all knew that the Island is a safe place to be on, regardless of the weather, what is dangerous is to be **near** the Island, just offshore, when those moving formations and the sea can wreak havoc.

Reverend Dale retreated to his chair on stage left. He looked tired, he felt tired, and except for shaking our hands as we walked out the front door, his day's work was finished.

As soon as he sat, the piano music started and the choir of five women rose, his wife leading the choir. This part of the service must have been choreographed, with there being no delay as he sat and the choir immediately rose and began singing. The congregation joined the choir to sing the last hymn, another tradition in our Church; the choir members, standing, stage right, now leading the service.

When the hymn finished, the congregation remained standing for the benediction, which formally closed the service. Reverend Dale made his way down the center aisle, and soon we were in line to exit the small sanctuary to greet our minister.

While standing in line to greet the minister, a few in the congregation walked over and introduced themselves to John; but most came over to say hello to Annie and Em. After shaking hands with the minister we walked outside into the rain, stood on the dirt path outside the church momentarily, waiting for Annie and her wheelchair to be carried down the steps. Pushed by her mother, with John and Milton walking alongside, we gradually made our way to the car.

Annie began thinking about the words she had deciphered at 2:00 a.m. But with the rain continuing its onslaught, she wasn't able to communicate her thoughts. She had recognized two words as German nouns and had looked up their meaning in John's German dictionary. The two words were: "Schlachtsciff" and "zerstoren." *Battleship* and *destroyed.* The word Newport came up several times in the transmission as did another word she could not translate. She decided to remain quiet because it was too difficult to nonverbally communicate all of what she wanted to say in the car. She would wait until they got home.

39 The Decision

Back in the car, John asked to be driven to Cooneymus Road before returning to the Weather House. He wanted to walk onto the beach near the west side lifesaving station one more time. He knew this was where the Atlantic Ocean met Block Island Sound, the body of water one would have to cross to return home.

Despite the rain, no one argued. I didn't mind another excursion to the west side, it gave us more time to be together in a comfortable setting, however cramped and wet my car was at that moment. As I drove, my mind drifted to us as a family. I was going to miss John and as close as I felt to him, I realized that I still did not know his last name. (Much later, Annie would mention he shared with her his last name and where he lived in Manhattan as well, a small community called Marble Hill, a place, of course, that I knew very well indeed.)

We reached our destination, a ten-minute drive from the church, parking fifty yards from the station on the rut laden road, not venturing any closer to avoid having one or more tires become stuck in the sand. Although the rain eased up a bit, the wind had not. I estimated the gusts to be in the thirty-five to forty-five mile per hour range. John wore his long jacket, which he wrapped around his lower body, and Emma, who decided to join him, walked close behind in his lee. When they reached the top of the dune, the gusts took direct aim at them both, nearly knocking Em down. John grabbed her shoulders, put her under his jacket, and then descended to the beach and out of our line of sight.

We sat in the car and waited.

They returned twenty minutes later when the rain started up again. John did not see anything unusual; visibility was a mile or two, so I was not quite sure what he expected to see. Em was laughing, about what, I don't know, perhaps about her inability to manage the strong gusts of wind gracefully.

The ride home was noteworthy for the silence, except for the bantering between the two girls, laughing about something in the morning church service and the sound of rain hitting the car. No one else spoke.

Back in the safety of the kitchen of the Weather House, Annie abruptly started explaining the transmission she heard at 2:00 a.m. Three words, two she had been able to translate. This conversation required the use of all of Annie's nonverbal strategies including her sister. After twenty minutes, we understood her thoughts, yet the clues had not allowed her to reach a final conclusion in her own mind. She wanted to see nautical charts of Block Island Sound, Long Island Sound and the East River approach to New York City.

John and I were impressed. He did not understand the meaning of the third word either: "tore," but it did not matter. We both thought Newport could very well be the target.

After that twenty-minute discussion, the decision was made.

✦✦✦

"Mr. Eddey," John said, "I think you realize ... I must get back to New York. Do you think it possible for Wallace to take me back in his boat today, or is it too dangerous?"

"I think the *Anna C* can make it ... it has a cabin that can protect itself and it can handle the swells of a storm like this one. Wallace is a good sailor and navigator. The open ocean between here and Long Island can be treacherous. It can be dangerous crossing Block Island Sound, but once in the lee of the north shore of Long Island, it will be safer. Wallace will have to look up the tide charts, especially for the East River and Hell Gate Channel. That might be problematic."

"I know this is crazy," John continued, "but do you think the girls can come along? Annie has quite a capacity to think things through. I know it is dangerous, and I know Lillie wouldn't stand for it, but I would like to ask her. Is that all right?"

Without waiting for an answer, John added, "Also, yesterday, Annie tapped out a Morse code sentence to me that I will never forget. She tapped out, 'Words matter. They matter very much. And I want to matter just like words.' I am impressed with her intelligence and especially her resiliency—as well as her relationship with her sister. Those two are remarkable together."

John thought a moment, emotions stirring within him. He looked down and then up. His nonverbal communication was clear.

"Yes. I will try to talk her mother into it. Em will want to go too and so will Milt. But I am going to need Milt to stay here."

I knew my nieces would want to continue to participate in the mission, especially if it involved traveling to New York City. This would be the first time the girls would be in the open ocean during a storm, in a boat of any size, since their near fatal accident. There was no question in my mind they would relish the opportunity, as long as they could be together.

I walked upstairs to find Lillie and asked her directly if she would agree to let Annie accompany John and Wallace back to New York City on the *Anna C*. I was expecting an argument; I thought an explanation was going to be necessary, but all she said was, "Today?"

"Yes, now."

I sat down on the bed and waited for a response. Receiving none, I explained why John had requested the girls accompany him to the Navy Yard. I could see on her face how proud she was of her daughters and I suspected she was grateful that John thought so much about them as to request their presence. Having John recognize their abilities was heartfelt, but I knew Lillie was thinking that if they went to sea and they died, she would die with them. There was no way she could live life without the two of them, of that she was as certain as I was of the changing nature of the weather.

"Even in this weather, I think it's a good idea. But I will have to go with them."

I nodded and walked downstairs to tell John.

Wallace was at home on the sea in any weather condition. Years ago, the day after my father died, Wallace borrowed a friend's new fishing boat and took us all to New York City to the funeral. The worst part of the trip wasn't negotiating the seas of Block Island Sound in winter, but rather negotiating Hell Gate. I remember that trip well, one of the few times I have been seasick.

Within a few minutes, Lillie walked down stairs and spoke directly with John.

I walked back into the kitchen where Lillie and John were still talking. He was explaining why he wanted to have Annie in attendance when he spoke about the code. I wondered if John wanted to introduce Annie to his superiors, perhaps not only for this current mission, but for future ones as well. Does Annie have enough analytic skills, hidden within that mind, to be of assistance? It was a dream, surely.

When John went upstairs to talk to the girls, I asked Milton to drive out and pick up Wallace. Within forty minutes, they were back at the Weather House.

After I explained about the transmissions and the translated words, Wallace agreed to set sail. The only decision was when, not if. The ferries weren't running, but the *Anna C* would.

John was upstairs with the girls explaining why he wanted them to meet his superiors in the ONI. When he heard Wallace's voice, he came downstairs to plan the trip back with Wallace. They determined the best time to reach the Hell Gate Channel would be about four o'clock tomorrow morning.

"At about three this afternoon, if we can take off that quickly, that will allow enough time for us to sail against the seas and the wind, sailing along the North Shore of Long Island. We will put in at Orient Point, or Sag Harbor, for more fuel, and then set sail down Long Island Sound. We will find a telephone in one of those harbors so that you can call your superiors to let them know you will be returning. Hopefully we will reach Throgs Neck Point by two a.m., well before daybreak and heave to for a while until the tides reenter the East River."

With the decision to let the two girls sail to Brooklyn, the task of planning and packing began. Wallace had already filled his boat with fuel, courtesy of John's naval allowance. Lillie began packing enough food for several days, assuming that they might have to stay on board the boat for a few days while in New York City. John reminded us all that we were now involved in espionage and no one on the Island, or anywhere, should know about the trip. He thought the ONI would ask them to stay on site when they arrived back at the Brooklyn Navy Yard.

Just then, Em carried Annie downstairs. Emma told Wallace that Annie wanted to continue their discussion from earlier—and whether or not she could look over the charts they would use to reach New York City.

I retrieved an old nautical chart from my office and John and Wallace outlined to Annie the route they would sail. When they got to the East River, Annie positioned herself directly in front of the chart which included the beginning of Long Island Sound, the East River and all its islands, down to New York Harbor at the tip of Manhattan.

She started to talk to Emma using her symbols. I thought she was asking about the inner basin of the Old Harbor, but Em responded, "Annie, are you looking for the numbers on the chart?"

Annie responded with a yes. I didn't understand that line of communication but Em knew what her sister was looking for, and it took only a few seconds now that the chart was before her.

Wallace walked over to the table and moved the chart so that the East River from Hell Gate to the tip of Manhattan was directly in front of Annie. He pointed to each section of the nautical chart.

"Are you interested in this section?" Wallace asked as he pointed to Sands Point. Annie shook her head no.

"Are you interested in this section?" John asked as he pointed to the approach to Hell Gate. Annie nodded a little. Even John knew that this meant we were close but not yet there.

So John inched his index finger down through the channel, all the while Annie continued to nod with a slow, deliberate motion of her head as if to say, "almost there."

Finally, when his finger reached the middle of Hell Gate, at times called the graveyard of the East River, Annie completed her yes by raising her eyes up to the ceiling. She then looked at her sister, giving her the sign for what I thought again meant the inner basin of the Old Harbor here on Block Island.

Emma knew otherwise.

"You want to know how deep the channel is?" Emma asked her sister. Again, Annie said yes.

At this point John jumped in; he must have been thinking along the same lines. I did not understand at all the significance of her questions. At the moment, it appeared that only Annie and John knew what the Germans were trying to do.

I sat in amazement as I watched my stepdaughter figure out what I was so desperately trying to do. John and Annie began to communicate nonverbally before our eyes, each of us just picking up bits and pieces of their communication between the two of them, using the chart as their communication device. I saw John use Annie's symbol for a U-boat several times, but other than that, I was not quite sure what was being said. I looked at Em to read the expression on her face to see if she understood what they were communicating about.

We all watched as John's placed his finger on the chart at the Hell Gate and then moved his finger down the East River until it reached the Brooklyn Navy Yard. Annie's head stopped nodding and her big broad smile appeared, as if to say her work was done.

And according to John's nod of approval, it was. He stood up and looked at me and said simply, "I think she did it."

"I don't understand," Milton said. I didn't quite understand either, but Emma and John did. Milt got up to reposition Annie, who had fallen down into her wheelchair and needed to be raised to make her more comfortable. Annie nodded a quick thanks, but her eyes and ears were on John, who she knew finally understood what she had been thinking, but could not communicate until the nautical charts became her language board.

Annie tapped out one more message, with her finger on the arm of her wheelchair. "It is not Newport."

40 Sunday Evening

High tide in the Great Salt Pond enabled one to move a small fishing boat like Wallace's from the Hog Pen to the back of the Weather House property using a shallow lagoon, a tidal pond, called Trim's Pond. Tonight, Wallace took advantage of the high tide and brought the *Anna C* to the small dock I built years ago, usable for small skiffs regardless of tide. Loading Wallace's boat here would be easier, and bring less attention, than hauling gear to the Hog Pen.

Oil and fuel, enough for two trips if necessary, were taken care of earlier in the day. Food, blankets, rain gear, and outer clothing were essential, as was Annie's wheelchair. Cork life preservers, the ones that keep the head above water, were worn at all times. Annie would wear two, one around her waist and the other around her neck. Wallace had just obtained these life preservers, being available for the first time this summer, courtesy of the Naval War College in Newport.

With the Nor'easter showing no signs of diminishing, at 4:00 a.m., an hour behind our original schedule, Milt and I untied Wallace's lines, and waved goodbye to his crew of four—John, Lillie, and the two girls. Visibility was less than a half mile, so it wasn't long before Milt and I lost sight of the boat. We stood on the bank of Trim's Pond listening to the *Anna C* motor out of the New Harbor Channel, a distance of about a mile from the commercial dock, and into the Atlantic Ocean.

On the boat, the girls quickly became comfortable. First, Emma and Lillie secured Annie, in an upright position, facing forward on the starboard side of the cabin. In this position, even with her disability, she could see straight ahead as well as to starboard, even being able to move her head out beyond the frame of the cabin, her face directly into the wind. She loved to be at sea, in any weather, to ride the waves, and tonight she expected the ride of her life and she did not want to experience the Nor'easter sitting inside the cabin. Emma harbored no such thoughts. Wearing the two life jackets provided Annie some warmth, but it also enabled her to rest against the frame of the cabin in an upright position by leaning against those life jackets.

Wallace had explained how to position Annie so she could also see inside the cabin. Her eyesight was good and she would serve as a lookout as well, standing her watch. Lillie had put a winter cap on and wrapped a scarf around Annie's neck. In this standing position, Em was reminded of the stance her sister would take on any boat before the accident. Tonight there was no fear in the girls.

John was amazed at how Annie adapted on the boat, marveled at how this trip created a situation where Annie could—almost—become her old self again. John stared at her and thought about his sister. The comparison was unavoidable for him; transference a very real feeling in John that included tension, love, and awe at the same time. The same feelings he had about his sister, before her accident as after. John watched as the ocean sprayed her face, and watched Annie enjoy all that was thrown at her—the salt water in her face, the wind driving it into her every facial pore; even the rolling of the boat occasionally knocking her head against the door frame, against the very nature of herself after the accident. Annie had had a conversation with John two days ago, in Morse code, where she stated that she viewed herself as the same person, before or after the near drowning. She could not elaborate why or how, but this morning on the *Anna C* John got his explanation.

In this gray, awful weather that shrouds time and place, Annie Rose, supported by rope, cushioned by the two life preservers that would protect her from the rolling about and protect her from drowning if she fell overboard, this Annie Rose, who would do anything, was the best demonstration of resiliency John could have imagined. Startling and satisfying John may have understood Annie's personality at the Weather House, but here on the boat, in the water, heading into a Nor'easter, he was convinced this young woman could not be held back.

If Aristotle's virtues included resiliency, Annie could be his model. Her face lit with joy in the darkness of nightfall meeting the pounding spray of the sea, against her body and her face; as soon as they hit the open ocean, her smile appeared and did not leave her face for hours. It was not her broad smile, rather, the smile of accomplishment, of conviction. The movement of her eyes, scanning the sea, reflected what her mind was thinking. John now understood Annie would try to perform her watch duty, to do her share of the workload, to keep her eyes out for danger, above or below the seas, to perform physically as she had performed intellectually in the days prior to this voyage.

John looked at the others on the boat and noticed not one of them paid any attention to Annie; they took all that he was witnessing for granted and he confirmed to himself that he had made the correct decision to ask the girls to accompany them to Brooklyn. One mile out to sea, John couldn't help but think, *What would this trip be without Annie's presence?*

A good decision perhaps, but not one free of hardship—for any of them.

Crossing the open waters west of the Island to reach Long Island Sound proved to be as difficult as any open ocean passage Wallace had ever experienced. The seas were mounting, seven, eight, and then ten feet high, the waves coming at an alarming frequency and at different angles.

Emma was the first to vocalize she wished she was underwater on the U-boats and Lillie began thinking it was a mistake to bring the girls, not long after John marveled silently about the correctness of his decision to bring them. Irony amidst a dangerous crossing.

Annie looked at Wallace, her older cousin, a captain, at his wheel, his eyes glued to the waves as they met the bow of the boat. Wallace was concentrating; everyone knew instinctively not to distract him. Helmsman and navigator—the raconteur part of his personality and the man who drank a bit too much, now nowhere to be seen. Wallace had never read Mellville's novel but if he were asked to title a chapter, I am sure he would have chosen the following phrase: "Never dream with your hand on the Helm."

★★★

But for me, at home in the safety of the Weather House, this type of situation lends itself to daydreaming; reflecting might be the better description because inattention does not describe my current state. Whenever a member of my family was at sea in conditions like the *Anna C* found herself tonight, I cannot help but dwell on the situation when my first wife Nellie and I were transferred to Texas just months before the great Galveston Hurricane of 1900. This part of my past returns over and over again whenever a significant moving weather formation travels through Block Island waters.

Early this morning was no different.

I was assigned to the Weather Station in Green Bay, Wisconsin from 1896 to 1899 transferring to a Texas station when Nellie first became ill with the disease from which she eventually died. I requested to be transferred to a warmer climate in the hopes that Nellie's health would improve; finally, in late 1898, I was informed by the Weather Bureau in Washington, D.C. that I would be transferred to a weather station in Texas the next year.

Which U.S. Weather Bureau station would I be assigned: the one on the Gulf Coast in Galveston or the one inland in Abilene? They were both in warm climates. Galveston, a summer resort town, had just opened a new station, but the more senior Weather Observer, Dr. Isaac Cline, a noted forecaster, was stationed in Abilene, Texas, and had requested a transfer to Galveston.

Dr. Cline, initially trained as a physician before becoming a forecaster, established the Abilene, Texas U. S. Signal Corps Weather Station in 1885. After being in Abilene for almost fifteen years, he and his brother, an assistant, were sent orders to transfer to the new Galveston Weather House.

So in 1899, my first wife and I moved from Green Bay, Wisconsin to Abilene.

Tragically for Dr. Cline, he and his family of three children, moved just before the great Galveston Hurricane. This was the storm that redefined our understanding of the powerful nature of a storm surge. The storm surge that accompanied the Galveston Hurricane of 1900 was massive and led to the deaths of an estimated ten thousand people, including Cline's wife and one of his daughters.

Unfortunately, my first wife died of her illness despite the transfer to the warmer climate. And after we lost our wives, we both, for different reasons of course, returned to more familiar environs, he to New Orleans and I to Block Island. Although we haven't written to each other in over a decade, I think about Dr. Cline often, usually when thoughts of Nellie and Texas cross my mind.

It is a lot to grasp. With Annie and Em almost drowning in their accident, it was too much for Lillie to bear; she had already experienced her share of tragedy with the untimely death of two sisters, Nellie and Sarah, her oldest brother Erwin, her first husband, and her only son. Loss on this Island has to be dealt with or it deals with you, and Lillie found the strength and courage to carry on and build her life anew.

I experienced my first loss on the Island just before I got married. A good friend drowned while trying to fix his boat off Old Harbor Point. I will never forget the feeling of wanting to escape the Island, as if getting off Block Island as quickly as possible would remove the awful feeling of loss the gut has the ability to not let us forget. It is hard to write about, hard to think about, but the feeling is easy to recognize.

How do you cope with these losses? Would I be able to cope if the *Anna C* went down to the sea tonight in Block Island Sound or in Hell Gate? One cannot stop those thoughts from entering the mind when living on an Island surrounded by the Atlantic. It is impossible for Islanders to keep these thoughts out of your mind. And perhaps that is why many leave our Island community behind and move to the mainland.

When I was working at 100 Broadway I attended a lecture at Columbia University with my brother-in-law. He was a lawyer but had an interest in theology. The lecture was about an epic poem called *Gilgamesh,* parts of which had recently been translated. I knew nothing about it and attended only because of my brother-in-law's interest and I enjoyed his company. The epic or story itself was estimated to be over five thousand years old.

It addresses, among other things, loss and the overwhelming grief that can enter someone's soul after such a loss, and examines the concept that there is no need to borrow from the past for one's strength; rather, just keep on plugging away as you head into the future after such loss. Under no circumstance is there ever a need to give up.

Bad weather days are to be left in the past; as long as you are still alive, they won't prevent you from carrying on. I often think it is remembering those good weather days, almost borrowing them from the past to keep the present bad days at bay. Gilgamesh doesn't agree.

In the epic, there is a passage in which Utnapishtim, a prophet, is talking to Gilgamesh: "... but now there is you. We must find something for you. How will you find eternal life to bring back to your friend Enkidu [who has died]? He pondered busily, as if it were just a matter of getting down to work or making plans for an excursion. Then he relaxed, as if there were no use in this reflection. I would grieve at all that may befall you still.... IF I DID NOT KNOW [that] you must return and bury your own loss; *and build your world anew with your own hands.*" Build your own world anew, just as Lilly did when her first husband and only son died. The prophet ends the passage with an even more astonishing statement: "I envy you your freedom."

Here Gilgamesh is asking for help and the prophet Utnapishtim tells him to get back to work, bury your own loss by working and building your world anew, and do it with your own hands; almost saying, how lucky you are to build anew!

And when the prophet adds the implausible statement: "I envy your freedom," I suspect that he is optimistic enough to see loss, however tragic, as an opportunity. It is a great life, if you don't weaken. Just get on with it all.

Anyway, I think that was the message from that lecture. Would I need to remember these lessons? No, not today, as I believed with all my heart that Wallace would be able to handle most any difficulty that may arise.

41 "Never Dream with your Hand on the Helm"

Moby-Dick

Wallace kept the *Anna C* motoring along at fourteen knots, except when the seas were high and they were lucky to be able to run against the tide at five to seven knots. Most of the waves were four to six feet high, but at times reached twelve feet. The high seas were brutal, at times submerging the bow under several feet of water and knocking the passengers around quite a bit. Annie was soaked, yet she stayed at her post for over two hours. Bailing the stern was a constant chore for John and Lillie, and at times Em.

As Annie stood her watch she became wet and cold, but wasn't hungry because she was fed and hydrated with hot milk and clam chowder from the stove of Edith. It was not a pleasant night on the open ocean but it wasn't the ordeal, psychologically, one might expect. With their minds on their mission, the rough going was more tolerable, more a challenge than an obstacle.

They reached Port Jefferson, Long Island at eight o'clock the next morning. After the boat was hit with two back-to-back large waves, Wallace decided to enter this harbor of refuge to refuel, and to rest. He was tired, his crew was tired, and the girls were a bit beat up. Throughout all of this, Wallace's mind never wandered nor was bothered by the seas. The potential danger was quite real, but he was so focused there wasn't a moment when he didn't believe he could reach the East River unscathed.

Wallace knew life was fragile in seas that had a mind of their own, and he never dreamed with his hand on the helm. Too dangerous; anyone who has been to sea in a boat like the *Anna C* during a Nor'easter understands this without an explanation, but for those who have not, no explanation is possible. I had no reservations about Wallace's abilities at sea; his level of concentration on the open ocean is unmatched. And while he may drink a bit too much on land, I have never seen him take a drink aboard his boat while at sea, or berthed for that matter, at the Hog Pen.

No, the only concern I had, even in this wicked Nor'easter, was the presence of the U-boats and whether they were aware of the *Anna C* and were following them.

Due to its naturally wide, almost rectangular harbor, Port Jefferson has been around as a harbor for a few hundred years. It is still quite active as a harbor even though its wooden shipbuilding days are long over. Sailing into the sheltered refuge, it is easy to identify the sites of the old Mather-Jones Shipyard and the Jim Bayles Shipyard, so prominent in the 1800s, now mere remnants of what they originally were.

On shore, at the center of the harbor, adjacent to Main Street, were the docks where Wallace could refuel. All his years sailing Long Island Sound, this was the first time he had ever sailed into this harbor. He hoped he would be able to fuel up, while John was more worried about finding a phone to use to call his supervisors at the ONI.

In the safety of the wide expanse of Port Jefferson, Annie asked to be put to bed in the forward cabin. Emma carried her sister; they were both exhausted. Wallace was too, and proud they had survived the rough crossing of Block Island Sound without incident. And they had made good time. Wallace decided to stay at the dock for a while and give everyone time to rest, while John walked ashore to locate a phone. He wanted to alert his superiors of their arrival later in the day.

John saw a gentleman in a store on East Main Street and asked him if he could use the phone. This man turned out to be the owner of the fuel dock; for one dollar John could place his call to New York. A little expensive, John thought, but he handed him a bill, and was pleased that the man joined Wallace to help him refuel, affording John some privacy.

When they'd entered the harbor, all traces of their mild seasickness left them. Strange thing about being seasick; experience the calm of any harbor and one feels 100 percent better, 100 percent of the time. Wallace finished refueling and everyone ate while they waited for John's return.

John had to call several members of his Naval Intelligence group before reaching one of his colleagues. He explained he must meet with everyone on the team as soon as possible, and the *Anna C* and its crew of four would arrive in the Naval Yard, failing any catastrophe, sometime in the afternoon.

John returned to the boat after refueling was completed. After about thirty minutes more to rest, Wallace backed the boat around and the *Anna C* was again battling the wind and waves of Long Island Sound. He thought they had been through the toughest part of the voyage, but was surprised when they exited the channel and he saw that the wave height was just as high as before. All hands on deck, as it were, from here to Hell Gate. It wasn't until another half hour had gone by that the large swells and wind started dying down and Wallace's anxiety began to leave him; everyone on board sensed his more relaxed feeling, assuming that the worst was behind them.

"Wallace, where did you say you thought you saw a pipe coming out of the water, which was potentially a U-boat?" John asked. "Was it this far out, or was it in the East River?"

"It was just as I was leaving the sound, I know I saw it," Wallace insisted. "Now that it is light out, Annie and Emma, make sure you keep an eye out for any metal pipe in the water. They are hard to spot, but when you see them you will know it."

Annie was back at her post, supported as before at the doorway of the cabin, her eyesight as good as it was before the accident.

The next two hours went by slowly, but there were no near misses with rogue waves, no boat traffic to deal with; this due to the fact that Wallace sailed close to the North Shore of Long Island, away from the shipping channels. The driving rain would let up periodically as if the moving formation was heading southeast and out to sea.

It was now approaching noon. Annie had decided to rest and Em took over her watch.

"Emma, secure yourself to the frame of the cabin, don't be careless, just because the seas have started to calm," Wallace cautioned her. He was tired too, and did not want the additional worry of Em washing overboard.

With the classic, small Block Island fishing boat making slow but sure progress toward New York City, everyone relaxed to some extent, the worst behind them. John took this opportunity to ask a few questions he wondered about while on Block Island. One of those questions concerned Lillie's oldest brother, Erwin, who was lost at sea at age twenty-two.

"Lillie, why was your oldest brother named Erwin? That is a name not quite familiar to me. And how did he die?"

"I don't know where the name came from," Lillie shrugged. "Wallace's oldest brother has the same name, so the name continues in the family.

"As far as your second question, we are not sure how or where he died, but we think it was at the bottom of the world, near Cape Horn at the very tip of Patagonia, which is, I am told, truly at the end of the world." Pausing, Lillie looked at Wallace: "Do you want to tell the story, Wallace, or what we think we know of it?"

"No, you tell it."

Lillie then began her version of the demise of her oldest brother: "We are not certain, but we think he died on a ship that was looking for gold. Remember, John, the large tombstone in the cemetery that I showed you? The one for Nicholas Ball, the man who you read about in the article George wrote?"

"Yes, of course, Nicholas Ball. I ran into his son, CC, the other day at his general store in the Old Harbor. Was Nicholas as large as CC?"

"Almost," Wallace interjected.

Lilly continued, "Nicholas made his first fortune in the Gold Rush of California and then returned to Block Island. After a few years of farming, he used his gold to buy the land around Sands Landing, what is now Old Harbor. On his way to California, he sailed through the Magellan Straits and saw for himself how beautiful, and I suppose dangerous, that part of the world was.

"Well, gold had not yet been found at the tip of South America when he sailed 'round Cape Horn, but in the late 1880s gold was discovered there as well, and off went my oldest brother, Erwin, to seek his fortune. My brother set sail on a whaler out of Sag Harbor which was to arrive in

Punta Arenas in the Strait of Magellan, a month and a half after leaving Long Island. He told us he intended to leave the whaler and join the small gold rush in Patagonia when he arrived. It was common, we understand, for men to abandon their whalers. Unfortunately, he never returned.

"We received one letter from him. He wrote he planned on working on another vessel and from there he was going to see the glaciers and the ice-blue waters of the lakes of Argentina. He was amazed at the size of the great bird, the Condor, and told us about walking among thousands of penguins on the beaches on the island of Tierra del Fuego. He wrote briefly about the native Indians and how tall they appeared. That letter sounded like the adventure was just beginning, but unfortunately, it ended too soon; how soon and when we will never know.

"We don't know how died, where he died, or even when he died. Was he in Argentina, or was he in Chile? Was he on a ship digging for gold, or did he die crossing the glaciers? Was he murdered? We will never know."

Lillie stopped her narrative and looked at her girls, one seated and the other still standing her watch.

"I have heard a lot about that area of the world," John said after a minute of silence. "It is so unique and wild and isolated. I read in the book, *The Voyage of the Beagle,* that the icebergs that flow down river from those glacial lakes are such a deep blue that you can't believe the color is natural. I am told by my colleagues that it all looks so unreal, almost dreamlike. Unfortunately, there are a lot of stories of death down there, nightmares; some say the area is littered with human remains, and now I must add the story of Erwin to that as well. I am sorry."

"At least he died in beautiful country," Lillie gave a sad smile, "or at least saw beautiful country before he died."

John nodded. "One of the things that interested me in college was Darwin's theory of evolution." John turned his attention to the two girls. "Darwin spent time in Patagonia and other places in the Pacific on his five-year journey. His theory of evolution evolved on that trip on the *Beagle,* although it must be said that one of his grandfathers had an early notion of the concept, and even more amazingly, it was his other grandfather that funded his trip aboard *The Beagle.*"

Annie had learned about evolution in school and listened intently as John continued his discussion.

"That voyage is one of the most famous voyages of all time. Central to his theory of evolution was the uncomfortable notion that many, many animals within a species would have to die *in order for evolution to occur.* Death may seem awful—but in the course of evolution, it is a necessary thing.

"Unfortunately, Lillie, your brother did not have any children, so he was not able to contribute to the evolving nature of man. Yet his death in many ways is simply part of the evolution of man in a very small way. Darwin spent many weeks in Tierra del Fuego, or the land of the fire, possibly on the same island where your brother died. Annie, you should read the *Voyage of the Beagle* if you get the chance."

"Why was it called 'land of the fire' if the area is so cold?" Emma asked.

"The native populations of the area set huge fires on many points near the water, and hence Magellan, I believe, named it the land of the fire. Darwin has some interesting things to say about Patagonia's inhabitants, but I shall leave that as a tantalizing thought for you to get the book and read it.

"That reminds me," John said, turning to Wallace, "you must tell your father that it was the captain of the *Beagle*, Captain Fitz Roy, who first used the term *weather forecasting.* The term wasn't an American invention. Fitz Roy established the first weather related department in the British Government, well before the United States established the weather service in the Signal Corp. I forgot to tell him that."

"I will tell him." Wallace knew me well enough to know that I would find that fact quite interesting; he was further impressed that John could tie in the story of Erwin and Patagonia with Darwin and the captain of the *Beagle,* as if it were an everyday fact of life.

There are voyages of importance in life and there are voyages of folly. The expedition of the *Beagle* certainly falls into the former; the two voyages of the Stone Fleet, for example, out of New Bedford in 1861 to block the harbors of Savannah and Charleston in our Civil War were voyages of pure folly, perhaps even bordering on madness.

True, the crew of the *Anna C* may have been a bit foolish for sailing directly into a Nor'easter, but they hoped the outcome of their voyage down Long Island Sound would one day be considered anything but folly.

42 Precious Cargo

After John finished his discussion of the *Voyage of the Beagle*, he asked Wallace if he could take over at the helm. Wallace instructed him on the finer points of steering a vessel but when John took the wheel, he was unable to keep a straight course and within ten minutes Wallace had to take back the responsibilities.

I wasn't at all surprised that John couldn't steer the boat straight. He, like almost all ONI agents, were not navy men. They were recruited from businesses and colleges, including Yale and Harvard. Real navy men, it was said, were men of honor and espionage work was beneath them! Much later I would understand how this recruitment "situation" may very well have led to a less than adequate spy network.

Lillie then took the helm, to give Wallace a rest. She was able to handle the boat, until, a rogue fourteen-foot wave hit the boat broadside and then she too quickly relinquished it back. This wave knocked everyone to the floor of the cabin, except Annie who now was retied tightly to the cabin door. John thought to himself it was a lot easier talking about a voyage than actually being on one and appreciated the work that Wallace was doing piloting his boat to New York City. He was not alone in marveling how easy Wallace made it all appear.

At noon, they reached Sands Point where Long Island Sound narrows to become the East River. Suddenly the force of the current leaving the East River became quite apparent, but fortunately the seas had diminished at this point to only two or three feet.

"I need your eyes, John." Wallace instructed John to stand watch alongside Emma who had just replaced her sister. Wallace suspected that if they were to see any signs of U-boat activity, it would be here where the sound narrowed dramatically.

The boat continued to cruise at about eight to ten knots, the current becoming more of a force of obstruction than Wallace had anticipated. He worried that if the current was slowing them down now, what would happen when they reached Hell Gate Channel? He could handle his boat in the open seas, but no boat his size could handle the vicious and unpredictable currents and eddies of Hell Gate when the tides of New York Harbor and Long Island Sound opposed each other. He knew all too well Hell Gate could indeed be a hole to hell.

His dwelling on this came to an abrupt halt when Emma broke the silence and screamed.

"Yes, I see it ... there it is," Emma yelled at the top of her voice, pointing frantically to a pipe sticking out of the water.

"Where?" John and Wallace asked simultaneously. Lillie stood up, still holding Annie. Everyone scanned the water in the direction of Emma's outstretched arm, but nobody else saw anything.

"Over there, at ten o'clock," Emma said.

Annie started getting excited. She wanted to be on deck. Lillie carried her so she could see also, but no one could see the pipe and even Em lost sight of it. Was she seeing things?

Then it reappeared and everyone saw it. And they just stared, not knowing what to say. This was confirmation, in part, that their decision to sail was not folly.

"So that is what they look like. The Germans are getting awfully close to New York," Lillie said, breaking the silence.

When Annie started nodding dramatically in response to her mother's statement, John knew exactly what she was thinking. And finally, so did everyone else on board.

"Annie, so that's why you wanted to know how deep Hell Gate Channel is at low tide," Em said, her voice still loud from the excitement or fear of seeing the U-Boat.

"Do you think," John asked the obvious question, "that this U-boat followed us from Block Island?"

"Anything is possible," Wallace answered. Over the next nautical mile, they saw the antennae reappear and then blend back into the waters of the Long Island Sound. The submarine pushed against the tide effortlessly, in contrast to the *Anna C*, which was now slowed, Wallace cutting the RPM's of the engine to decrease any transmitted noise.

At this point, Annie started yelling, making a loud guttural sound to get their attention quickly.

Everyone saw the same thing Annie had—a periscope emerging from the water a few feet aft of the black pipe.

"Get inside the cabin quickly," John ordered. Everyone moved inside and Wallace began steering the boat through the small cabin window.

"I don't want anyone to be seen by that U-boat, although it might be too late. Wallace, would it be possible to move away from the center of the channel, much closer to the shore of Long Island, just in case we have to enter one of the inlets on shore?"

Wallace nodded.

"Do you think they see us?" Lillie asked, knowing it would be impossible to know for certain.

Nobody answered her question but John and Wallace were convinced they had been spotted. Would they take them out, if they recognized the *Anna C*?

"Where is fog when you need it?" Wallace made the understatement.

"I think I can see the direction of the periscope," John said. "But I can't be sure if they, yes, yes … they are looking ahead, not to port. I think we are okay."

Wallace disagreed with John's assessment but said nothing.

"Annie, very good eyes!" John said, giving her a thumbs up. "Do you think you saw it rise out of the water?"

Annie raised her eyes, but not emphatically.

"I hope so. If Annie is correct, the U-boat is not following us," John said, relaxing a bit, "rather they're on their own mission. Keep looking out for other U-boats."

They lost track of the U-boat shortly and would never see it again. Nor did they see evidence of a second U-boat. As they were getting closer to the East River and New York City the ship traffic picked up substantially, mostly barges being pushed or pulled by tugs.

In a matter of an hour and a half, Wallace anticipated reaching Wards Island and the beginning of Hell Gate Channel. He was concerned they had been followed all along, and if so, should they put in at a port on the North Shore and travel to Brooklyn by car? Moreover, have they put everyone at the Weather House in even more danger? These were unsettling questions, now without answers. With no further sign of the U-boat, Wallace continued on and did not discuss his concerns with John.

At 1430 hours, or 2:30 p.m., the *Anna C* officially entered Hell Gate Channel. John wanted Annie to experience sailing through the Channel and had Lillie bring her back to stand, as before, secured to the frame. Both life jackets still on, Annie stood like a soldier going to battle, gazing across the bow of the boat at the wide channel with Astoria, Queens to port and Wards Island to starboard, exhausted, her spasticity now even less apparent, making it, ironically, harder to stand.

The current was not treacherous in the channel, courtesy of the Army dynamiting large sections of the rock utilizing underground tunnels in 1877 and 1878, but as soon as they approached the Gate itself, plumes of water rose out of the East River as the current forced itself around the outcroppings of ledges. The eddies created could suck a small boat underwater, drowning everyone on board as if a hole to hell suddenly opened there. A large amount of water, forced through narrow spaces, such as the situation at Hell Gate, and its increase in velocity and pressure changes is an example of Bernoulli's principle at work, a concept every weather man is taught with respect to wind and pressure changes in narrow spaces above the water line. Here its death trap was occurring below the water line.

As he navigated the channel, Wallace read out loud the depth in feet from the chart that lay before him. He used a dull light to identify the locations of the underground ledges and reefs that still remain as obstacles in the channel. While he was navigating through the ledges, Em began pondering the specifics of the U-boat invasion: "If the channel is only twenty-five-feet deep then the submarines could easily pass through this channel. But they probably would need their periscopes up. On a night with a lot of cloud cover, they could pass undetected, unless they got stuck on one of those underground ledges."

John wondered out loud: "How many times has a German spy sailed this channel in a small boat, at low tide to carefully identify the locations of these treacherous ledges?"

And then, looking at Emma, John said, "You are correct, they could easily pass undetected. Annie heard the wireless messages that convinced her Newport was not going to be the target. Two nights ago, she knew and now she is certain."

Listening to John, but not responding, Annie thought that seeing the periscope proved that we, as in a collective *we*—more than just the *Anna C* and the Weather House—are close to danger.

At night, U-boats could sail through the channel, perhaps only partially submerged, undetected, into the waters of the East River. It was a wide channel, shallow, yes, but very manageable especially at ebb tide. Remarkably, tonight had been expected to be a dark overcast night in New York, but the moving formation moved very fast out to sea. The current situation called for a change in forecast; the night sky would be clear. The Germans may not be aware of that and Annie thought there was something to take advantage of, but it was too complicated a thought to communicate to anyone.

But then, John said something, and Annie understood that he did agree with her when he said out loud, not expecting anyone to understand his thought, "Time for a false report to be issued by the weather service."

Annie let loose her broad smile and moved her hand to make sure her sister saw her response.

Wallace navigated Hell Gate effortlessly; avoiding the holes to hell too many ships failed to negotiate. He now knew that the graveyard of the East River would not take his *Anna C* and within thirty minutes they'd be secured to the same floating dock his boat had called home a few days last week in the Brooklyn Navy Yard.

With Manhattan safely to starboard and the Navy Yard fifteen minutes away to port, everyone sat, including Wallace, the first time he let himself relax and even "dream" a bit while at the helm. With everyone relaxed, the boat sailing smoothly now, almost effortlessly, John asked another question, more to kill time, than anything: "How did Block Island get its name?"

Gary E. Eddey

"It is named after Adrian Block," Wallace said, "the explorer who first identified the Island to the map makers of Europe, probably during the first of his four voyages to the area between 1610 and 1614."

John got off easy, Lillie thought, because Wallace gave him the short answer.

(If I were on board I would have provided John the long answer to the question, expanding it perhaps to answer a related question, "What or who was the first link between the isle of Manhattan and Block Island?"

Preceding the settlement of New Netherland, now known, of course, as New York City, came the exploration of the area by Henry Hudson, followed by Adrian Block. Much later, when Block Island was first being settled, in 1661 or 1662, Manhattan was in the hands of the Dutch, but changes to the leadership of that small community were soon to take place. In 1664, the forty-year rule of the Dutch would end and New Netherlands would become the domain of the English and its new name, New York, would reflect that change.

The leader of the English expedition in 1664 landed first at Coney Island and readied for the attack against the Dutch, but it never came. Why? Peter Stuyvesant was pragmatic enough to know that he would lose the battle. Stuyvesant would continue to live in New York, eventually being buried in the church he founded near his home on what is now Second Avenue near 9th Street.

Perhaps we should rely on the words of the New York Senator Chauncey M. Depew, rather than mine, to describe the connection between Manhattan and Block Island. On November 1, 1914, the *New York Times* published his article that described New York as a center of world commerce and outlined the contributions of Adrian Block in establishing New York as a center of commerce, and in it he also explains the connection between the two islands.

Captain Adrian Block "was a pioneer of civilization" and Depew credits him with the honor of being the first to establish commerce in Manhattan in the year 1614 on his *fourth* voyage to the area. The actual date is a bit earlier, but because Captain Block set up four huts for trading at approximately 39 Broadway in October 1614, that date is generally credited as the date when Holland officially recognized

Manhattan as an ideal location for commerce, about three hundred and two years ago.

Upon each of Block's voyages back to the Netherlands, his report on the land and its opportunities gained him much credibility with the Dutch. It also "dramatically renewed the efforts and enthusiasm of the Dutch for settling the island of Manhattan for commerce" and all that that entails.

Unfortunately, Block, after landing at the tip of Manhattan on his fourth voyage had a problem. He couldn't explore further or return to Europe because his ship, literally, burned into the ground. Captain Block had to build a new ship which he named *Onrust*, and for which he is given credit as the first shipbuilder on Manhattan! Oddly enough, earlier this year in May of 1916, the timbers of his boat that burned, the *Tyger*, were found in lower Manhattan at the site of an excavation for a new subway line. Amazing information that few would find interesting I am sure.

The senator writes that the *Onrush*, in the hands of Block, "sailed lightly through the perils of Hell Gate," known then, as now, as a difficult passage. Block called it *Hellegat*, which translated from the Dutch means "hole from hell." A fitting description.

For all his efforts and discoveries, Captain Adrian Block has been given only one memorial in our United States, Block Island, although in Holland he remains an important historical figure. I quote from Senator Depew: "This modest hero—whose achievements have little mention in our histories, whose only monument is Block Island, whose reward was to be made commander twelve years after, in 1624, of the whole fleet sailing between this port and Holland—was the founder of the mercantile marine of the United States."

And that is the long answer to John's question.)

As Wallace guided his boat into the inlet at Dry Dock 1, he looked northeast, his eyes focused on the floating dock where he was to tie up. Everyone else's eyes, however, were staring at the massive battleships under construction. Lillie, the two girls, and even John were mesmerized by the sight of these monstrous ships from the vantage point of being at sea level.

Wallace's eyes were quickly drawn to a small group of men, all in uniform, standing on the floating dock, as well as at the top of the dry dock, fifty feet above the floating dock. There were other officers near a hanger, covering at least two hydroaeroplanes. The officers appeared to be waiting, patiently, to welcome the crew of the *Anna C.* Wallace certainly hoped they were waiting to acknowledge them because he soon identified men at the top of the dry dock carrying firearms. This was a most unusual welcoming party. He asked John if he knew any of these men.

John finally looked away from the battleships and said yes. He pointed out his superior officer and quickly offered them a salute. A broad smile came over his face, as it did Wallace, when the officers returned the salute, signifying the official end of the run from Block Island, in a Nor'easter, to the Brooklyn Navy Yard, possibly in the shadow of a German submarine.

Although relieved, John knew that the most difficult part of the mission was just beginning. Data collection had ended, now development and implementation of the ONI's mission must begin. Annie harbored thoughts that the ONI would not understand the gravity of the threat posed, which she believed could occur as soon as tonight. To her mind, now that she had experienced crossing through Hell Gate and seeing the Brooklyn Navy Yard, the target of the U-boats had to be these monstrous ships under construction, and perhaps parts of Manhattan, and certainly not the Naval War College at Newport. She worried no one would listen to her.

What she didn't know was that John had identical concerns.

43 The Welcoming Party

The Secretary of the Navy, Josephus Daniels, and the Chief of Naval Intelligence had just flown in from Washington, D.C. to meet the small crew from Block Island. John recognized both men immediately, although he wondered why the official head of the ONI, Assistant Secretary of the Navy Franklin D. Roosevelt was not present. Nonetheless, he thought the ONI must have collected additional information. Why else would the senior leadership be greeting them at the dock?

While Wallace was maneuvering the boat toward the dock, the girls remained mesmerized by the size of the operations in the Brooklyn Navy Yard, especially the battleships that filled their eyes. Still under construction, the battleship *USS Arizona*, launched last year, was almost ready for deployment and docked adjacent to Dry Dock 1. Entering the yard from the East River, they saw the *USS Arizona* first and then came face to face with the monstrous 624 foot long *USS New Mexico* still in dry dock.

The adults on board may have been nervous about meeting the uniformed gentleman waiting patiently to throw the *Anna C* lines, but the girls were wasting no time discussing, what was obvious to them, that these battleships must be the intended target for the U-boat's powerful torpedoes.

Emma whispered to her, "Annie … these ships … are they what the Germans are looking for? Will the U-boats slip into the East River through Hell Gate and torpedo these huge ships? These battleships are huge; I have never seen anything so big. They are bigger than the buildings across the river in Manhattan!"

Annie raised her eyes to each of her sister's questions. This was the first time they had seen Manhattan, a city much larger than Providence or Boston.

"Now I understand," Em said. "When did you figure all that out? When?" Emma asked, staring in admiration, first at her sister and then back to the battleships.

Annie smiled, but before being able to answer, the boat landed hard against the dock and Annie fell out of her wheelchair where she was now seated. Emma reached out and grabbed her sister to prevent her from falling onto the deck of the boat, but it was too late; they both landed on the floor of the cabin. Laughing, and entwined on the floor, they got up and, once settled, turned their interest to the men standing on the floating dock.

Emma was excited to see these men, all in uniform; Annie shared the same thoughts but became slightly embarrassed. What would they think of her, sitting in a wheelchair, not being able to talk? She would be okay, she then thought; she had been through this time and time again; and her sister was at her side.

Two sailors helped Wallace secure the boat. Lillie was helped off by the Commanding Officer. Dressed in his formal white uniform and hat, he offered a hearty welcome to Lillie who immediately explained and apologized for the way she looked, being up all night. She was so awestruck by the contingent of officers that she momentarily forgot about her two daughters still on the boat.

The officers then asked to be introduced to the two girls.

"Where is this young lady, and her younger sister?" bellowed the Commanding Officer. The director of the ONI and the Secretary of the Navy both smiled and approached the boat.

Lillie was now certain John had sent information about the girls or these men would not have asked to meet them so quickly.

John grabbed Annie's wooden wheelchair and handed it to his boss. He then lifted Annie into the waiting arms of the commanding officer who sat her gently into it. The two officers then repositioned her so she was comfortable. Em jumped off the boat, not bothered in the least bit by a sudden rocking of the dock courtesy of a few large swells from the wake of a passing vessel out in the East River.

Everyone, except for Wallace, was led up the steep, wooden stairs to the top of the dock. Two officers carried Annie in the wheelchair, Mr.

Daniels guided Lillie up, and Emma was helped up the narrow stairs by John. Two sailors remained with Wallace and assisted him in the clean-up of the boat. Refueling would be done later in the day.

This was some welcoming party, certainly not what anyone on board the *Anna C* had expected. After a few minutes, two large motor cars appeared and they were all taken to an officer's home, a three-story brick building, near the Naval Hospital. Due to the polio epidemic that started in Brooklyn six months ago, it was decided that they should not stay on the top floor of the Naval Hospital where guests often are put up. The epidemic had run its course, but after claiming the lives of 2,300 in NYC, mostly children under the age of fourteen, it was thought prudent for the crew from Block Island to stay on the top floor of one of the officer's homes.

Waiting for them at an official officer's home—now vacant due to a temporary reassignment of a senior naval officer and his family—was a nurse from the hospital assigned to take care of the girls. She presented Annie with a new wooden wheelchair. Annie was filled with emotion, she had never expected such a kind gesture from anyone. She was sure this was at the request of John and she couldn't wait to thank him. Everyone's eyes filled with tears as Annie tried out her new wheelchair, including the nurse.

A half hour later, Wallace joined them and he also marveled at the new wheelchair. Meanwhile, John accompanied his superiors to a meeting room in a nondescript building near the hospital complex, not to be seen again for hours.

While they were resting, the Secretary of the Navy started the meeting with a question for John; they got right down to business. "Would you provide an overview of the encounters with the three men that were identified on the Island, the sightings of the U-boats near the Island, and then restate the hypothesis about the meanings of the numerous intercepted wireless communications?"

John answered the questions as clearly as he could. He reviewed everything and ended his presentation with our speculation about the purpose of the mission, including Annie's feeling that an attack on the Brooklyn Navy Yard was a possibility. He gave credit to Annie, as he had

240 Gary E. Eddey

in a previous communication to the ONI which was, of course, unknown to us.

"How did she figure all that out on such limited information?" asked the Vice Admiral who was accompanying the Secretary. After hearing the explanation, he thought that even if she were wrong, her reasoning ability was superb. They discussed the importance of deciphering codes and he thought Annie appeared to have that skill. Deciphering codes was becoming an enormously important function of the ONI and would continue to be for years to come.

"Admiral," John interjected, interrupting the discussion somewhat, "did the first ship-to-shore radio-telephone voice conversation take place between officers on the *U.S.S New Hampshire* and you in the War Department while I was on Block Island? I know the experiment was planned for last week."

John was referring to new technology that allowed wireless communication of "voice" data from ship to shore. Up to this point in time, only wireless data could be sent, such as Morse code, and now one could have a conversation using wireless technology. John knew it had the potential to change communication in the Navy, and worldwide.

"It went well. The *New Hampshire* was off the coast of Virginia when Mr. Daniels and I made the connection. It truly was remarkable. Now we can talk, as well as telegraph wirelessly, from ship to shore. This is a big improvement for our Navy and anyone else who can develop that wireless technology. Thank you for asking."

The VA was clearly pleased John had asked the question.

John nodded, but wondered, given his experience of the last two weeks, how would it be possible for that ship–to-shore voice communication to be secure? He decided to ask that follow-up question at a later time.

An hour after arriving at the officer's home, the girls and Lillie, joined by Wallace, walked over to the building where John was being debriefed. After everyone settled in, the officers began questioning the "crew from Block Island."

Mr. Daniels started by thanking John for taking the assignment. He then thanked Wallace for all his work and turned to Lillie and expressed his heartfelt thanks for allowing the girls to come on the trip. He then turned to Annie and Em and thanked them personally for their courage, attention to detail, and their ability to keep these events all secret. He impressed upon them how important it was to keep everything a secret, now and well into the future. (We all took this seriously and it is the reason I have waited so many years to tell this story.)

"Now I want to get to work. I know that you are all tired, but we must work quickly. Annie, while you, Em, and your Mom were resting, John reviewed your thoughts about what was going to happen. He wanted you to come along for several reasons, one of which was for you to experience sailing through the Hell Gate Channel. Were you awake and alert when you came through the channel?"

John quickly explained to the others Annie's yes-no system, using her eyes.

Annie, seated in the new wooden wheelchair between John and her mother, raised her eyes. She then looked at her sister, sitting next to the Secretary of the Navy. That look was Annie's sign to her sister to follow up with her thoughts as well, but Emma was too nervous to speak.

"Did you see," the VA asked, "how difficult it is to navigate Hell Gate and are you are aware of how shallow it is at low tide, no deeper than twenty-four feet?"

Annie again raised her eyes.

"And you still think that the Morse code, as you understood their code, suggested they were going to sail into the Channel?"

Annie again raised her eyes.

"And further," the VA continued, "you think ..." he paused for a moment in a deliberate way, surveying everyone in the room before completing his question, "do you think you know what they are going to do?"

The deliberate nature of the questioning did not concern Annie; rather, it comforted her as she recognized that she was being taken seriously. She looked at her sister and signaled she would need Emma's help translating her thoughts. Nervously, Em explained her sister had first thought Hell Gate figured into the picture when Wallace showed her the chart of the East River last week. And Annie became convinced when she heard a transmission in German that used the word *Holle*, which means Hell.

At this point John interrupted Em to explain to everyone that Annie had also identified a transmission that used the word Hellgatte. John thought this was a code for Newport, and although Annie thought Hellgatte was a safeword, she did not think it pertained to Newport.

"Annie," Emma spoke up, "has always believed that all references to Newport in the various transmissions were meant simply as a diversion."

At that point, Annie joined in the conversation by tapping out a word in Morse code: *Tor.*

"She wants to know what 'Tor' means in German," Emma said.

One of the officers said that it could mean 'Gate.' Annie raised her eyes and tapped out that she should have known Hellegatte referred to Hell Gate, even though the direct translation of Hellegatte means something completely different.

"Annie, I think you are going to turn out to be correct in this," Daniels said. He continued, alternating his gaze between Annie, Emma, and then John. "We think that that is plausible. We will increase patrols in the river and Long Island Sound tomorrow. We, or rather I, certainly thought Newport would be the intended target. But your ideas make as much sense as Newport. Yet, we still harbor this idea that they will only attack foreign ships in our waters as they did two weeks ago off the Nantucket Lightship.

"You all also thought that someone rotten in the Weather Bureau at one hundred Broadway was able to intercept these messages. John explained how you broke their code, Annie. We suspect that there is more to this than sabotaging the Navy Yard. Although sinking two of our largest battleships would give Germany a significant advantage and would delay, or possibly, prevent our entry into the war."

The conversation drifted to other topics among the officers, frustrating Annie.

All of a sudden, Annie became agitated.

"What is wrong?" John asked, turning his attention back to her. "Did we not focus on something?" John knew why Annie was so upset. Daniels had mentioned increasing patrols *tomorrow*. John knew that something

Annie heard on the transmissions two nights ago strongly suggested the attack could come much earlier. But how to convince everyone of this possibility would be near impossible.

With John questioning Annie, he was showing his colleagues that it was important to wait and see what flowed from Annie's mind.

"Is there something you want to add, Annie?" John asked.

Annie raised her eyes. She looked relieved and moved her left hand awkwardly down off the armrest.

"That is her signal," John explained to the Vice Admiral, "that we are not focused on the right thing. Emma, is that correct?"

Emma nodded while Annie raised her eyes in agreement.

Annie expressed frustration because she had identified on the wireless transmissions information that she was unable to communicate, but not because she was nonverbal, rather because she was having a difficult time conceptualizing and making sense of what she heard. She needed to 'talk this out.' Now, however, being in the New York Navy Yard Brooklyn, across the East River from Manhattan, she was able to put in perspective all that she had heard.

It took about fifteen minutes to communicate what she had to say. Slowly but surely, she tapped out Morse code to explain her thoughts to everyone at the table. At one point she looked at Em and asked her to talk about the U-Boats. After Emma Roses reviewed with the officers what Annie had mentioned to her previously, Annie then announced when the attack could occur.

Nobody reacted to her thought that the U-boats may come through Hell Gate tonight.

John then repeated verbally to everyone: "I think Annie means to say that the U-boats may come through the Hell Gate Channel *tonight?*"

Annie tapped out more of her thoughts: she agreed with John's statement made on the boat as they approached the East River; that a false weather report should be issued for poor visibility for the New York City area, to make the German's think that they will have cover if they intend to enter Hell Gate tonight or tomorrow. She thought the attack was to be coordinated with a forecast of bad weather. She knew from me that tonight's weather pattern was originally forecast to have a continuing low cloud cover for the New York City area. And the sudden appearance of a clear sky was entirely unexpected.

John asked for the third time: "Annie, are you convinced that Hell Gate was part of the communication?"

Annie raised her eyes. She explained slowly to Emma that she initially thought the word was Tore but later realized it was Tor.

Daniels was a bit frustrated. He questioned her again: "Annie, are you convinced that something is going to take place soon, even tonight?"

Annie, feeling more and more confident and not nearly as nervous as when the meeting first started, continued to press her point. She did not care if she was just sixteen years old, she had something to say and she was going to make her case.

John then asked again, "Are you convinced that it will take place today, tomorrow, or when? And why do you think that?"

Annie tapped out, "tonight" in Morse code on her wheelchair.

Annie then made a signal with her good hand, pulling it toward her quickly. Em interpreted that signal as meaning "*Now*, as in I want it *now*. Or it will occur *now*."

The Commanding Officer went silent. He knew it would be difficult to mount a response to an attack that might occur in less than eight hours. "Annie, I need to find out more information from you about why you think that something will occur tonight?"

Everyone was now dead serious. The mood of the meeting had turned somber, but finally Annie and John were beginning to believe that they were changing the minds of everyone in the room.

The CO changed the subject somewhat and pointed to one of his officers, "Explain to everyone what we have uncovered this past week. Share everything, especially why we think they are going to attack Newport near the Naval War College."

One of the officers, a colleague of John's who was now assigned to the CO's office at the Naval Yard, started speaking: "After we received the first communication from Mr. Eddey, we put together varied bits of information suggesting the U-boats' target may very well be Newport. They had already been welcomed last month and our surveillance of their communications suggested they would revisit the harbor, perhaps sacrificing their own crews to do so."

Looking at his CO, the officer added, "We too focused on certain transmissions but did not understand what they meant. Annie's explanation is plausible, and we will have to rethink our own conclusions..."

John interrupted: "We must acknowledge the possibility that something will happen at Hell Gate Channel, and the target may be us here at the Naval Yard. And I don't think we can ignore the possibility that an attack could occur soon, even tonight. This whole concept of warfare by submarines is not something we understand. But clearly the Germans do."

John's statement had an impact. There was silence in the room for a full minute, although it may have felt like an hour to the Block Island crew.

Daniels and the commanding officer looked at each other. Finally Daniels said, "Well, we will see. We have a weapon that we can use, tonight if need be. We can use bombs dropped from a plane or depth charges fired from the shores of Wards Island or Astoria. Does everyone agree that we need to beef up armed patrols now?"

Annie may have felt relieved; but the officers around the table were in a state of shock. John and Annie had a point to make, but it appeared that Daniels, someone who had previously been just an administrator, was taking his role seriously. He had listened to the Block Island crew all along. (He knew something that would take Annie years to understand, that the ONI did not have a grasp on the espionage situation as much as they should.)

Conversation broke out among the officers and it was clear that not everyone was in agreement that an attack could occur tonight. But, they had no choice, their focus had to shift to Hell Gate; and all available resources, despite the uncertainty of the mission's objective, would be sent to monitor and protect Hell Gate Channel and the East River up to where Long Island Sound begins. Annie's rationale, with John's support, was just too damn unsettling. They all had to listen.

The CO surprised everyone with his next comment: "The first thing we need to do is contact the *New York Times*. We want an article to run tomorrow on how we are going to experiment with new dynamite to destroy one of the submerged reefs in Hell Gate. We don't want to scare the population of New York City if we do blow up the U-boats in Hell Gate, now do we?

"The *New York Times* has run a few articles about the need to widen and dig out the channel to accommodate the larger naval ships being built in the yard, so none of this will come as a surprise to the citizens of New York."

Daniels asked John's boss to contact Naval Command in Washington. Daniels said he would inform the Assistant Secretary of the Navy, Mr. Roosevelt, and then call President Wilson. The meeting was adjourned.

John understood the significance of these calls. The crew from the Block Island Weather House had set in motion a naval mission that could very well change the course of our country's history.

Word immediately came back to Daniels that the mission had the complete backing of both Roosevelt and of course President Wilson. Increased patrols, shore lookouts, and planes were being dispatched immediately. Before this meeting, it had not been thought possible for a U-boat to navigate the channel, especially since it was only twenty-four feet deep at mean low tide, but now, thanks to the Block Island crew, all assumptions had been rethought.

After the approvals had been obtained, they met to review details of the surveillance of the East River and Hell Gate.

"John," the CO said, "there was a major fire at the end of August on Block Island, correct?"

"Yes, it was the large hotel diagonally across from the Weather House that burned to the ground. It overlooked the New Harbor where the large ferries from the mainland dock," John said. "Why do you ask? Do you think there is a connection between the fire and the three mystery men?"

"I'm not sure. Annie, did you pick up on any transmission referencing the fire?"

Annie looked to the left, moving her head with her eyes, her answer for a definite "No."

"Are you sure?" the VA asked.

Annie raised her eyes.

John's supervisor at the ONI continued the questioning: "It will be impossible to prove one way or the other, although it does seem unlikely. Block Island is well known to European sailors, and is known as a place not well guarded by the mainland; it has a long history of being abandoned during wars, and the Germans know that. Did they start the fire in the hotel? You did not see anything unusual, did you?"

"No," John answered, "but I wasn't focused on that. Mr. Eddey is close friends with one of the Champlin brothers who own the hotel. Wallace ... where is Wallace? Maybe he knows something?"

One of the officers spoke up from the hall, outside the meeting room: "I think Wallace left the room to check on his boat again; he walked back to the floating dock with one of the officers. He also wanted to see the Curtis F, the hydroaeroplane Sperry used to land on Block Island last spring."

With that, the meeting was adjourned, the crew from Block Island excused, and the commanding officer, Daniels, and the VA all left the room. Daniels then made two more calls: the first, to the head weather observer at 100 Broadway and the second, to the publisher of the *New York Times*.

Lillie and the girls left the room with John and one of his colleagues. They walked outside the building and walked over to the dry docks where they could see across the East River to Manhattan.

Outside the building, the two girls were more relaxed, relieved that the meeting was over. They felt they had indeed accomplished what they had set out to do and thought they had represented the Weather House admirably. They became playful, with Emma pushing Annie in the new wheelchair down to the dry docks. She wanted to see how fast it would go. Both of them started to laugh as Em pushed harder and harder, leaving Lillie and John behind. Soon two of the junior officers were running alongside the girls, as much to accompany them as to make sure the wheelchair did not tip. After about a hundred yards, they were convinced this one was faster.

The two junior officers running with them were friendly, and very cute, but not quite handsome. Emma instantly had a crush on the tall one. *But*, thought Emma, *neither is as handsome as Sperry*. At the meeting that had ended a short time ago, when they'd heard the name Lawrence Sperry, they instantly looked at each other and became quietly excited, hoping they would have the opportunity to see him again. Now Emma had the opportunity to find out more about Sperry. She asked the officers if they had ever met him.

"Yes," the 'cute' officer replied, "he often comes here for meetings."

"He," Em proclaimed, "is the most handsome man we have ever met!"

"You guys met him?" the officer voiced surprise.

Emma went on to tell the story of Sperry crash landing his amphibious plane in the surf below the Mohegan Bluffs; then she and Annie later met him on the commercial dock.

"He was so handsome," Em said, "we were mesmerized and just stared at him. He walked over to us and shook our hands and introduced himself. I explained who we were and I asked him if he was all right after the plane crashed. He said he was okay and thanked me for my thoughtfulness."

While Emma explained all that and more to the officers, John came up from behind, smiling. The story provided some distraction from the seriousness of the meeting that had just ended.

"You are daydreaming about meeting him and falling in love aren't you, Annie?" John teased with a laugh. "Would you like to meet him again?"

Annie turned red from embarrassment; that was indeed what she was hoping for, but she couldn't disguise her feelings as her broad wide smile from the heart appeared on her face.

John realized he hadn't seen that smile on her face in two days.

"Can we see him again, here?" Emma asked, her eyes rising just like her sister.

"Maybe."

The Vice Admiral and the Director of the ONI had returned to the group, now seated and resting at tables under an overhang outside the building's side entrance. Just as the VA approached the girls, he overheard Em's request to see Sperry once again, and responded to it with simple smile.

Everyone at the Naval Yard knew the son of the owner of the Sperry Corporation. Everyone knew him to be handsome and brilliant, someone who possessed unlimited courage. He was the inventor of the autopilot and often parked his seaplane in the Navy Yard when it wasn't on the landing strip on Governor's Island or at his home base on Long Island. He was a daredevil and, yet, an integral part of the naval air reserve. But only a few knew that he had just recently, with the help of his father, developed an aerial torpedo.

The VA wanted to evaluate Annie's ability to understand Morse code and had one of the officers in the ONI test her aptitude, her listening skills, and her Morse code skills. That request put her genuine, broad smile back on her face just as fast as the possibility of seeing Sperry once again. The VA did not want everyone sitting around during these critical hours, so he sent Annie to work.

At this time, Lillie and Emma were asked to return to the top floor of the officer's home.

John and the officers left in a car that drove them to another part of the Naval Yard where they were to plan a defense strategy. Annie's conclusion that the attack might occur as early as tonight had finally been accepted as a possibility. I learned much later from John, however, that they almost lost the argument.

Planning, and executing, a comprehensive defense against an underwater attack by German submarines was finally obtained at 2000 hours or 8:00 p.m. from President Wilson.

But would they have enough time and would they be able to identify the U-boats before they left Hell Gate? And what if Newport was indeed the target?

Lawrence Sperry first received the call to report to the Brooklyn Navy Yard at 2030 hours, 8:30 p.m.

44 Sperry and the Bombs

Anyone who enters the East River from Long Island Sound can visualize the low-lying Ward's Island and the equally low-lying part of Queens called Astoria form the boundaries of Hell Gate Channel. And from a distance, the channel may look unusually calm, despite numerous tidal-dependent eddies, but once into the gate itself ... well, hold on, because any vessel can be in for quite a ride. It is so dangerous people walking along its shores often feel afraid.

It was here the ONI would mobilize its officers, along with a contingent from the Navy and the Army Corps of Engineers, to launch an attack on the U-boats if they appeared.

At 9:30 p.m. the ONI officially asked the Navy to send officers who were experts in the detonation of explosives to Wards Island. Unfortunately, the Navy would not have their men in place for twelve hours.

The Army Corps of Engineers agreed to send their troops to Astoria, but those troops needed eighteen hours before full deployment. The engineers in the corps were the best to visualize the underwater rock and ledge formations in the channel; it was this division of the Army that had dynamited the many underwater ledges in years past utilizing underwater tunnels.

The ONI sent their officers expert in handling depth charges, developed by the Royal Navy, to Astoria as well.

The Army Corps of Engineers was also assigned the task of readying a wire cable to cross Astoria to the southern tip of Ward's Island; this to collect debris after any successful explosion. There were several such cables in storage at the Continental Iron Works Yard, located in Green Point a few miles from the Navy Yard, a shipyard that manufactured boats and other iron objects for marine and non-marine purposes.

Despite the delay in deployment, John was satisfied everyone now involved with the mission understood the serious potential for an attack on the Navy Yard. But he was even more ecstatic when he heard the response from Lawrence Sperry.

The Naval Reserve Flying Corps was almost overlooked as part of the mission. When John's boss called upon Mr. Sperry of the NRFC, it was almost an afterthought. Sperry had recently completed several practice bombing runs, one of which ended up as that night crash landing on Block Island. When asked if he foresaw a role in the mission, his answer was immediate and decisive.

"Yes."

Would he be able to drop bombs from his aeroplane over the East River and not hit land or unintended objects?

"Yes, most definitely."

Time to deployment?

"One hour, sir. I am now in Bellport. It will take approximately one hour for me to collect my gear and fly to Governor's Island or the Brooklyn Navy Yard."

When asked if the recently completed railroad bridge over the channel from Astoria to Ward's Island would interfere with his bombing runs, Sperry answered: "Not in the least bit. I will fly under it."

Within fifteen minutes, Sperry was airborne, lifting off from the small grass runway on his parents' summer estate in Bellport, Long Island. The Naval Reserve Flying Corps stored a few planes in the hanger at the Navy Yard but also on the large grass airstrip on Governor's Island. Sperry was fully aware he was to report to Governor's Island because the bombs he would drop were stored in a small building near the runway.

For this mission he would fly a slightly larger version of the Curtis F hydroaeroplane he had flown the night he landed emergently on Block Island. The larger cockpit in this plane had enough space to store eight bombs, four on each side. He would drop them by hand as his very own invention, the Sperry Autopilot, controlled the plane. He would not need a copilot.

At 11:01 p.m., he landed his own plane softly on the grass strip, and within minutes walked over to the larger Curtis and started the engine. Naval staff loaded the eight small bombs brought from the storage facility into the cockpit where normally a copilot would sit. He was ready to start the mission.

The small Governor's Island sits off the tip of Manhattan. Lookouts and patrols based from there have guarded the front entrance to New York Harbor for centuries. Across from Governor's Island, on the New Jersey side of the harbor, stands the Statue of Liberty welcoming everyone to our shores. Liberty Island welcomes while Governor's Island stands guard.

Sperry, the "Brooklyn Aviator"—as the *New York Times* often calls him—is a founding member of the United States Naval Reserve Flying Corps and every bit a showman. He lives in a townhouse with his parents and siblings, about three miles south of the Brooklyn Navy Yard on Marlborough Street near the Parade Grounds of Prospect Park. He often commutes to his father's plant in Long Island by aeroplane, taking off and landing on those very same Parade Grounds.

Two years ago, Sperry let the world see firsthand his newest invention, the autopilot. At this aeroplane competition held on the banks of the River Seine in Paris, he demonstrated the use of his gryroscopic stabilizer mounted in a specially designed Curtiss C-2 plane equipped with a hydroplane fuselage for landing, and taking off, on the Seine.

Flying with a copilot, he demonstrated in several passes over the crowd how his stabilizer, a lightweight adaptation of his father's gyroscope, could maintain level flight without the pilot's hands on the wheel. I quote from a British magazine, *The Aviator*:

"A band from the villages of Bezons and Argenteuil, spotting the aircraft of '*l'Americain*' approaching, bravely struck up 'The Star Spangled Banner.' The Curtiss C-2 flew down the river and directly in front of the judge's stand, and Sperry engaged his stabilizer device, disentangled himself from the shoulder yoke that controlled the C-2's ailerons, and passed over the crowd with arms held high. The aircraft continued on a straight and steady course and the crowd was on its feet, cheering, and shouting: '*Remarquable!*' '*Extraordinaire!*' and '*Formidable!*'"

As the article pointed out, Sperry had stunned the skeptics with his "no hands" flying.

With subsequent passes of his plane, Sperry showed the crowd the following: "During the second pass, his copilot climbed out on the starboard wing and moved about seven feet away from the fuselage. Sperry's hands were still off the controls. As Cachin moved out on the wing, the aircraft momentarily banked due to the shift of weight, but the gyroscope-equipped stabilizer immediately took over and corrected the attitudinal change, after which the Curtiss continued smoothly down the river. This time the crowd was unrestrained in its appreciation and the band delivered its supreme compliment—a vigorous rendition of 'La Marseillaise.'"

On his last pass, there was his copilot on one wing and Sperry on the other, with the pilot's seat empty. "This was a demonstration beyond the already exuberant audience's expectations. There was the aircraft, flying serenely along with both its pilot and mechanic out on the wings, waving to the spectators. The judge, René Quinton, was almost speechless and his comment mirrored the feelings of the crowd: *'Mais, c'est inouï!'* ('But that's unheard of!')."

The military observers on hand were equally stunned by Sperry's performance and when Commandant Joseph Barrès of the French Army Air Corps prevailed upon Lawrence Sperry for a ride, he witnessed Sperry's device performing an unassisted takeoff and landing.

Awarded first prize in the competition, Sperry received 50,000 francs ($10,000) and became famous overnight. His handsome young face adorned the front pages of newspapers in Paris, London and Berlin.

The *New York Times,* however, was more muted in its reception. A report covering the competition appeared in the editorial page on June 22. Sperry's invention was mentioned in these deprecatory terms: "Of stability commonly understood, no heavier than air flight vehicles will ever have even as much as that dreadfully fragile monster, the dirigible."

So much for the technical expertise of the *New York Times* staff of two years ago!

He won other competitions as well including last year's Curtis Marine Contest for flying the longest distance of anyone in the race during a specified a ten hour time period. One day he awoke and told a fellow coworker that he was going to break the distance record, and, using one of the Navy's planes stored in a floating hanger near Dry Dock

4 in the northeast section of the Brooklyn Navy Yard, he did.

Sperry had witnessed firsthand the aftermath of the sinking of the foreign vessels by the German U-boat near the Nantucket Lightship at the beginning of October, just a few days before Milton had first seen the three mysterious men. And because he was one of only a handful of Americans who understood the potential destructive wrath of the German military, John was exceedingly pleased he enthusiastically agreed to take part in the mission.

While planning for this new mission continued, that had as yet not been given a name, Annie was finishing up her assignment in the ONI transmission office.

Early in the evening, after the meeting with the Secretary of the Navy, Lillie had pushed Annie to an adjacent old building. This one looked more like a warehouse than an office building. As they walked into a room that resembled a vault, they realized that they were entering a special insulated room. It was a sound booth.

Annie was pushed by the officer next to a large speaker. John came into the room briefly with another officer they had never seen before. John introduced Ron Danny, who would be Annie's instructor and then John escorted Lillie out of the room and into another small office across the hall where she was briefed on how the Navy was responding to the potential threat to the Navy Yard.

As the officer sent Annie signals in the headphone that enveloped her left ear, Annie would signal to Em what letters were being sent. Em wrote these down and almost invariably, Annie got each of the assignments correct. Her instructor was amazed that she, although not able to communicate verbally and unable to write quickly with her good hand, she could in fact, communicate as quickly as necessary, as long as Em was there.

When the instructor asked Em to stop assisting, Annie slowed down considerably but her accuracy remained exceptional. Her "good hand" was still spastic; controlling it took much effort when creating signals from the machine.

After an hour of testing her skills, she was then given two assignments to try to crack codes previously used by the Germans.

Annie signaled to Em that she loved to do this kind of work and asked if there were any *real* codes that needed to be worked on, instead of wasting her time on these sample codes? Annie had a sign for "wasting my time" that involved a rolling of her eyes along with a shifting of her body in her seat.

The instructor called a superior and was given permission to give Annie a chance at cracking a new code. She signaled she needed her sister for the task and Em returned to sit by her side.

Astoundingly, within fifteen minutes, Annie had uncovered an element of the code previously unknown. The instructor again left the room to speak to his supervisor. Both men returned within ten minutes to find the two girls waiting nervously. The supervisor explained that he had called John and briefed him on Annie's accomplishments.

John was just as pleased to hear about Annie's performance, as much as he was to hear about Sperry's agreeing to participate in the mission. John knew Annie had skills the ONI could use, and now so did others.

Emma was asked to step outside and join Lillie for a few minutes. The supervisor wanted to ask Annie a few questions of a confidential nature that would require only yes or no answers. This conversation between the two officers and Annie would ultimately become one of the most important conversations of her life.

While all of this was going on at the Brooklyn Navy Yard, back on Block Island, Milt and I continued our duties observing and reporting the weather.

We did not attempt to do any further observations of the spies until instructed to do so. And as of yet we had heard nothing from the Navy Yard, although I am not sure how they would have contacted us since we were not using telegraphy or the phones to talk about any of this, just in case the spies had tapped the wires as we earlier suspected.

We were fully expecting not to hear from anyone in the Navy or even Wallace or Lillie. Even if we had found something, I am not sure how we would have transmitted the data to the Navy anyway. So we went back to business as usual.

Milt returned to his parent's house and I stayed alone in the Weather House. My brother in law, Arthur, visited a few times wondering how things were progressing.

We just waited and collected weather data.

I was a bit surprised to see another storm heading our way from data sent from the Green Bay, Wisconsin Weather Station. But what really did not make sense to me was a major storm in the forecasts from Washington, D.C. over New York City for the next two days. That was a surprise to me and not at all consistent with my understanding of the rapidly changing moving weather formations over New York City. Of course, I would find out much later this transmission was part of the mission and my initial assessment was indeed correct.

✫✫✫

Lillie and Emma, accompanied by John, walked back to the meeting room in the unmarked building where they had dinner served to them. Annie remained with the two officers in the transmission room for an hour longer. It was now 9:00 p.m.

During their meal, they were startled by an older gentleman in plain clothes who burst into the room and asked in a loud and concerned voice, "Where is Wallace?"

"Wallace? I guess he is on his boat," Lillie responded, wondering who this man was.

"He is not there and we need to find him. Do you think he left the Naval Yard?"

"He did not say that he was leaving the yard," John said, recognizing the man who abruptly walked in the room from photographs he had seen in the NYC newspapers. "He must be around."

"We need to locate him to move his boat!"

And with that last comment, John knew exactly what the Navy now understood, in its fullest understanding, that the U-boats were indeed a threat to the Navy Yard.

The man finally introduced himself.

"I am Louis Howe. I am sorry I barged in on your dinner. I just arrived from Washington and met briefly with everyone across the Yard. I wanted to meet both of you, so I drove over to find Wallace myself. I came up from Washington with Rear Admiral Roger Wells."

"Hello, sir," John stood up and shook his hand. John had already recognized who he was from the obvious facial scars of a childhood accident, evident on Mr. Howe's narrow and quite thin face. Mr. Howe was a lifelong trusted advisor to Mr. Roosevelt.

"Lillie," John said, turning to her, "Mr. Howe works under the Assistant Secretary of the Navy."

Lillie stood up to shake his hand.

"Mrs. Rose, I wanted to extend a thank you from Mr. Roosevelt personally for your family's contributions to this effort, especially little Emma Rose and Annie Rose. If possible, he will try to visit the Navy Yard to personally thank you in a few days, but for now, we have to find Wallace to move his boat. As you can imagine, there has been a lot of work that has taken place between the time you met this morning and now.

"We think that your data ..." Mr. Howe turned his attention to John, "and suspicions are quite correct. John, you may remember Captain Todd; he is the Director and Chief Cable Censor for the Navy. From the very beginning, after Mr. Eddey first communicated his concerns to the ONI, he has been following the cable transmissions and believes your conclusions are quite consistent with the cable transmissions that he has intercepted and evaluated. He salutes your work. Perhaps now Congress and President Wilson will understand the nature of the European War and its impact on the United States."

Mr. Howe then explained that the group had just put out an alert about a fictitious weather system rolling in to the New York area for tonight. "We are hoping, of course, the Germans will intercept this updated phony report to give them false hope of significant cloud cover over NYC tonight, enabling them to sneak into the East River undetected..."

Lillie interjected, more to make conversation than to complete Howe's sentence: "This false 'moving formation' would result in the Weather Bureau stations raising weather flags throughout Long Island Sound. It would also serve, possibly, to deter boat traffic in the eastern part of the sound."

Mr. Howe nodded in agreement. "Yes, and I also want to mention that Thomas Edison has been made aware of the episode and don't be surprised if you see him here today." Howe explained that the New Jersey inventor is the chairman of Wilson's Naval Consulting Board, as well as a close advisor to him.

Mr. Howe said goodbye and returned to his meeting; and John left the room to find Wallace to move his boat out of the Navy Yard.

The reason was obvious.

Sperry was in place on Governor's Island, his plane loaded with the appropriate cargo—bombs—waiting for instructions from the ONI office in the Navy Yard, now serving as Naval Command for this mission.

He had mapped out his flight plan to Hell Gate, flying over the Brooklyn Bridge and Manhattan Bridges and under the Railroad Bridge towering over Hell Gate Channel. He waited patiently for his instructions, standing only feet from his plane, on the grass airstrip on Governor's Island.

High tide tonight in the Hell Gate Channel would occur at 0300 hours. If Annie was correct, sailing through the channel shortly after high tide would enable the submarines to easily navigate the Hell Gate and then continue to maneuver down the East River to the Brooklyn Navy Yard. Launching floating mines and perhaps the new sea-to-air torpedoes at the ships under construction could very well be their intended target. Firepower from two submarines could potentially wreak havoc in the Navy Yard. Under the darkness and cover of an overcast sky, it was possible for them to complete their mission and then depart with the current to the main entrance of New York Harbor, between Staten Island and Brooklyn and into the Atlantic Ocean.

A brilliant plan. Would there be enough time to stop them?

45 Hell Gate Channel

Tuesday, 0300 hours

Central Command for the operation, now located in a nondescript building near the Naval Hospital in the Brooklyn Navy Yard, hoped the inaccurate weather report forecast from the Washington, D.C. office of the Weather Bureau, as transmitted to the Block Island station, would be intercepted by the Germans. Yet, at the same time, they hoped that the attack, if it were to come, would be delayed in order to give them more time to prepare to defend the East River entrance to New York Harbor.

It was 11:00 p.m. and the girls, along with Wallace, exhausted from their trip the night before and their daytime activities in the Navy Yard, fell asleep on the top floor of the officer's home minutes after lying down in their assigned beds. John had found Wallace near the dry dock where the Navy stored the aeroplanes, engaged in a conversation with one of the pilots. Wallace was instructed to move his boat. The pilots also flew the two planes to Governor's Island for safekeeping.

As they slept, the Navy did anything but. They continued their surveillance of the channel and the East River and all along Long Island Sound to Newport. The Naval War College assigned patrols to the waters off Block Island after being alerted to the operation.

Naval Officers from the ONI were on site in Astoria. A few officers from the Army Corps of Engineers were able to get into position on Ward's Island in time; they were able to position three depth charge launchers near the shore, spaced seventy-five yards apart.

And Sperry sat in the cockpit of his plane on the grass runway on Governor's Island and waited. A dozen years ago, the Wright Brothers flew their first plane at Kitty Hawk making history. Six years ago, when there were only fifty planes in the entire world, the first bombing run took place using hand grenades dropped from a plane. Tonight, Sperry would drop modified depth charges. Daniels had been pressing for more involvement of aeroplanes since he was first appointed Secretary of the Navy and Sperry was confident Daniels had made the right decision adding an air attack to this mission, even though aerial bombing runs were rarely performed. Only a few months ago Sperry himself demonstrated that the use of his stabilizer would facilitate the process, and ironically, his flight that ended with his emergency landing at night in the surf on Block Island was part of that demonstration.

From conversations Sperry had with his own father, he understood Daniels was very close to an uncle who happened to be a close friend of the Wright Brothers. Daniels was very close to this uncle, the oldest brother of Daniel's mother. This uncle had assisted the Wright Brothers at Kitty Hawk and subsequently had a major impact on Daniels' thinking about the value of aeroplanes in the military.

Sperry was sure that that relationship had a role in having him participate in this mission. Sperry wondered later to Wallace if Daniels was aware that he too was making history.

It was hoped that most, if not all, marine activity in Long Island Sound would be curtailed due to the exaggerated weather forecast report released from the Washington, D.C. office. An employee at 100 Broadway, suspected of being a German operative, was placed under heavy surveillance. If by chance he became suspicious of the fake weather report and tried to warn his superiors in the German high command, he'd be immediately arrested.

Last but not least, a press report was ready to be issued to the New York City papers—to explain any explosions necessary to sink the U-boats. The report outlined that the Army Corps had done some midnight testing in the channel in preparation to clear submerged ledges.

All of this was in place, and more, when the crew of the *Anna C* fell asleep.

At 11:10 p.m., an old Revenue Cutter, now part of the new Coast Guard, out of New London, Connecticut observed a U-boat sailing down Long Island Sound, off of New Haven, well south of Fisher's Island. As ordered, they did not give chase.

At 11:20 p.m., another U-boat was identified by a tug, *The Tasco*, also out of New London, sailing toward New York City in the sound. Wireless communication was kept to a minimum but both vessels reported their sightings to the Navy Yard using code. Keeping wireless communications to a minimum was now essential, not only with regard to this operation but to all merchant marine activity. This month alone saw a significant decrease in the Weather Bureau obtaining information from the merchant ships at sea: Because of the submarine menace brought to the world's oceans, merchant marine vessels were no longer wirelessly transmitting data about weather, hopefully decreasing the risk of discovery by German submarines. Reports from the Block Island Weather Bureau took on even greater significance as did other coastal weather and telegraph stations.

Sightings of the antennae by Naval Officers standing on the shores of Throgs Neck Point occurred at 1:00 a.m. This information was phoned to the ONI in the Navy Yard and served as the final confirmation that an attack was most definitely under way.

At this point, the Secretary of the Navy, Daniels, contacted President Wilson directly and warned him that an attack on the Navy Yard was imminent and a military response, from land and air, would occur. The President did not comment; John was told later that perhaps it was because he realized this was another blow to his position of neutrality.

At about 0120 hours, the Navy lost sight of both antennas. The U-boats had submerged and portable lights rigged on Ward's Island were turned on. The cloud cover forecast by the Weather Bureau was, of course, nonexistent.

Sperry was asked to fly a trial flight up the East River.

It was now 0138 hours.

Sperry took off and followed the East River north to Hell Gate. He realized he had a better view of the river if he kept low, and flew under both the Brooklyn and Manhattan Bridges. At high tide, there was only about 122 feet from the lower reaches of the Brooklyn Bridge and the East River. At fifty feet off the water, he had a clear picture of the river and was pleased there were no boats yet to be seen. Off to his right, all lights in the massive Navy Yard were turned on, illuminating the boats as if it were daylight, the battleships under construction standing proud.

Within minutes, he was over Hell Gate Channel and saw the brigade on Ward's Island, but did not notice the unit stationed across the channel in Astoria. He did not know if they were well camouflaged, or had not had time to get into position. The new, massive stone railroad bridge over Hell Gate Channel from Astoria to Wards Island posed a greater problem than he had anticipated due to its particular position. This practice run was important, he thought, if only to be able to negotiate it as an obstacle when dropping the bombs.

Within another minute, he was circling back around over the small islands located west of Throgs Neck Point. He was now flying about one hundred and fifty feet off the water. He had a reasonable view but did not see any evidence of the U-boats.

He returned to Governor's Island by flying over Queens and Brooklyn, so as not to bring any further notice to his practice run, if German operatives were in position to observe the channel and the river.

Back on Governor's Island, he phoned in his report to the Navy Yard. He was told to ready his payload and be prepared to drop his bombs at a moment's notice. He was alerted and warned about two Navy patrol boats that would be in the area and to avoid them. It was assumed that German spies would be observing Hell Gate and the East River. Central Command did not want Sperry to be noticed, thus there would be no more practice runs. If they had noticed his plane, it was hoped that information could not have been transmitted to the submarines in time.

Sperry was told to stand by until he received the call to take off. He refueled and waited on the grass landing strip, with a clear view of the Statue of Liberty, the tip of Manhattan and mouth of the East River.

What happened that night above, below, and on the East River at Hell Gate would take days to understand; but it was executed with precision and stunning speed at about 0325 hours.

The mission began at about 0305 hours when Sperry was ordered to lift off. Within three minutes, he was over the channel and had spotted what he thought were two antennas. Lights from the Army Corps were directed at the U-boats making his job easier than he had anticipated.

The mission ended twenty minutes later. Sperry was convinced, in his six passes over the channel, he had hit both submarines. And, as if choreographed, officers on land lobbed ten canisters of dynamite into the channel in rapid-fire progression, stopping only long enough to let Sperry fly by.

By 0335 hours Sperry had returned his plane to Governor's Island, the dynamite crews on Wards Island and Astoria were packing up; and smaller patrol boats were sent out to pick up bodies and some of the smaller debris found in the channel. A huge chain link net had been spread across the channel at 2:00 a.m. and was now collecting the larger debris, which was in turn picked up by two barges pushed by Navy tugboats. These tugs, loaded with depth charges themselves, were on their way up the East River before the explosions took place. They had only hours before daylight set in and an awakening city would observe them in action. Miraculously, by daybreak, a mere two and a half hours later, there was no trace of any activity anywhere, except for the two barges towed by Navy Yard tugs out into the Atlantic Ocean; they would dump their cargo opposite the twin towers of the New Jersey Highlands.

Some debris was seen floating in the East River by New Yorkers but no one, including anyone in the press, understood the significance of the explosions, except for the publisher and senior editor of the *New York Times*. He was asked to suppress eyewitness accounts of the event and given the reason as due to the political problems the Army Corps of engineers was having with Congress to secure funds to clear the channel of the ledges, a project estimated to cost $17 million dollars.

★★★

In the morning when Wallace, Lillie, and the girls finally awoke, they were greeted by a nurse from the Naval Hospital who brought a message from John: "Please stay put, do not leave the building until further notice."

They wondered why, had something gone wrong?

46 Later that Morning

From the windows of the top floor of the officer's home, all seemed quiet. No fires, no increase in foot or vehicular traffic, just a normal Tuesday workday. Wallace did notice workers and sailors were dressed warmly; perhaps a cold front had arrived from the northwest. There was no indication, however, that anything was amiss. Why were they being asked to stay?

At 9:00 a.m., the same breakfast served to officers from the nearby mess hall was brought to them. They ate in silence until the same nurse brought Annie a surprise gift, another new wheelchair. This one had a wooden frame reinforced with aluminum rods and the wheels were much wider. A note was attached: "From the fabricating crew in the basement." The equipment fabricators at the hospital had adapted a prototype that would make it easier for Annie to maneuver on the sandy roads and paths of Block Island. The staff at the Naval Hospital had been building wheelchairs for children who were patients at a nearby chronic care hospital. These children were paralyzed, and had almost died, from polio.

Annie and Em's interest in the new wheelchair lasted only a few short minutes until the same nurse returned yet again, this time with the morning edition of the *New York Times*.

"An officer from next door just brought over the morning newspaper. He thought you might want to read it," the nurse said as she collected the trays.

Wallace grabbed the paper and turned the pages, slowly scanning the headlines of each article. Lillie and Emma looked over his shoulder. On page seven, they found the following headlines:

"Dynamite Explosions at the Gate, off Ward's Island"

And in smaller type under the headline was a smaller headline: "A Mistake in the Middle of the Night."

The article explained dynamite had been detonated a few days earlier than planned in an attempt to dislodge one of Hell Gate's submerged ledges. No one was hurt, and the Army Corps of Engineers issued an apology for "disturbing the peace" so early in the morning. The article mentioned little else.

(The weekly newspaper for Long Island, the *Long Islander*, ran a slightly different story later in the week. That article was more questioning in its tone, but added little substance. The editor picked up the story because one of their reporters had understood Sperry was called away urgently from his family's vacation home in Bellport, but no follow-up piece appeared, and the ONI did not need to communicate with the editor.)

Wallace read the headlines out loud.

But what was the outcome of the explosions? There was no mention, of course, of that information in the article. They sat mystified.

Just after 1130 hours an officer came to bring them to the meeting room adjacent to the sound booth where Lillie had sat when her daughter was being evaluated by the transmission officers of the ONI. Annie transferred herself into her new wheelchair once they were outside and led the group to the new meeting area.

In the room, dark, without windows, sat John, his immediate supervisor in the ONI, Secretary Daniels, Rear Admiral Welles, the CO of the Naval Yard and two other officers, all, except Daniels, in full uniform. The Vice Admiral was not present.

When they entered the room, everyone stood up and gave the crew from Block Island a standing ovation, a gesture planned moments before to acknowledge the contributions of all of us. Finally, the crew from Block Island understood the mission must have been a success.

They sat down and immediately were briefed by John's boss on the importance of not mentioning this mission to anyone. An officer then reviewed with the girls methods used by spies to keep things to themselves, methods that to this day they have kept secret. Lillie thought to herself she didn't like that idea, teaching them techniques to be more secretive than they already were may be in the best interest of the country, but certainly not in her best interest!

When John was allowed to tell them what had happened in the

channel, the crew of the *Anna C* dropped their jaws. Proud their work had contributed to a successful mission—from Milton's observations, to my perseverance, to Annie's cracking the code, and so much more—they sat, stunned, as the extent of the explosions triggered by the depth charges lobbed from the shores and the bombs Sperry dropped by hand, was made clear to them. They had indeed made a difference.

They sat in silence, unable to express joy due to the seriousness of what had happened, but after a few minutes, they allowed themselves to at least smile. And Annie, as if talking to herself, repeated her hand and arm signal for *matter*, as in, "I do matter." They thought about the destruction to the Navy Yard that had been prevented. Wallace wanted more information but was told he would have to wait.

They sat and talked for about thirty minutes and then another officer walked in and delivered a message from President Wilson. He handed the message to Daniels who then handed it to the girls to read out loud. It thanked them all for their help and requested that in regard to this mission they maintain secrecy. Lillie asked to keep the message. The meeting was over when Daniels invited everyone to dinner in the Officer's Club at about 2000 hours, or 8:00 p.m.

Again, for security reasons they were asked not to leave the Navy Yard—although they could walk back and forth from the docks (they would blend in, as if they worked at the shipyard) to the building where they were now meeting. John spoke to Wallace and requested that he not go near his boat—it would have to stay where it was in Dutch Kills Creek for a while longer. "We fully expect German spies will observe our actions in and around the Navy Yard and we don't want you identified," John concluded.

The task now at hand, and one that had begun at 0330, was to clean up the debris from the channel and the East River; no one could see any debris or bodies, less their curiosity be piqued. Fortunately, the U-boats were small and when the tide reversed itself, much of the debris was easily collected from the channel with the use of the chain netting placed by the tugs. This netting was in addition to the chain link that was placed before the mission began. Before daylight emerged over Manhattan, cranes lifted the largest of the chunks of floating debris onto barges that were then barged out to the Atlantic. One large piece was brought back to the indoor buildings at the Continental Shipyard, where it would be hidden from the public long enough for Navy trucks to cart it back to the Navy Yard for inspection. The logistics of this operation were not shared.

The *New York Times* article made it easier for the day cleanup crew to finish what the two barges could not do before daybreak. Remarkably, this explosion raised no suspicions among the citizens of New York City, a city known for its inquisitive nature, except perhaps by a reporter at the *Long Islander*.

Having to be confined to the officer's home once again was not the ordeal one might think. It gave the girls time to decide what they would wear to the dinner in the Officer's Club. Although they packed extra clothes in the *Anna C*, they did not expect to be invited to a dinner with the senior officers or the Secretary of the Navy!

The nurse assigned to them offered the girls some dresses to wear, but Annie chose to wear a sailor's outfit given to her by her new friends in the transmission office. Lillie and Emma accepted the offer to wear a dress from the nurse. Wallace wore his usual clothes, washed courtesy of the naval staff.

Time went by quickly and shortly before 8:00 p.m., John came over to escort them to the dinner.

"Hey, guys …" John said with a smile. "You guys are great." He reached over to hug Annie and Emma and then proceeded to thank Wallace and Lillie. Even though John was dressed in his Navy uniform, it was the most relaxed Wallace had seen him since meeting him in the conference room two weeks ago. John had heard Annie was going to wear her sailor's outfit and John decided to dress accordingly.

"There is so much more we can now tell you about what happened early this morning. Everyone is waiting for you in the Officer's Club. The Vice Admiral's car is waiting outside to drive us across the Navy Yard. Hurry, Annie!" John joked.

Annie's broad smile returned. She signaled, "Who are we meeting?" with her hand and accompanying facial expression. Emma translated this for John.

"You are going to meet some very important people. And you are going to meet someone very, very special, perhaps a certain man you have already met. How does meeting Mr. Lawrence Sperry again sound? If you are nice to him, maybe, just maybe, he might give you a ride in his aeroplane."

Em and Annie both dropped open their mouths. They wanted to know more but couldn't ask any questions as John was ushering them toward the door. Wallace was also stunned and Lillie, looking at her two daughters, couldn't help starting to cry.

With the cover of darkness, they exited the building though the back door and were driven across the complex until the car stopped in front of another brick building, one that they had not seen before. On the way over, John poked fun at Annie for wearing a sailor's outfit. "Do you want to join the Navy?"

Annie didn't respond, but would it be possible for someone in a wheelchair to become part of the armed forces? Probably not, but dressing up like a sailor was a close second. John wondered if Annie was sending a message.

47 The Dinner

The room where the officers ate their meals was small, almost cozy, unlike other officer's dining areas Wallace had read about. No wood paneling, no view—of Manhattan or Brooklyn—although lights from the dry docks were visible to some extent. An armed guard stood at the entrance to the small room on the second floor of this nondescript brick building.

When the car reached the building, John walked ahead to talk to his boss and Daniels. The crew from Block Island entered the dining area a few minutes after John. John waved them over to where the Vice Admiral and the ONI officers were seated and then extended his hand to his right to point out Sperry, who along with his father, was seated at an adjacent table. The girls recognized Sperry immediately. John wanted Wallace and Lillie to sit with him and the Vice Admiral of the Naval Yard, Daniels, and the other senior officers. The girls were to sit at another table with Sperry, his father, and other officers from the Flying Corps Reserve.

John ushered Wallace and Lillie to the table where Secretary Daniels, Rear Admiral Usher, the Commandant of the Navy Yard, and Rear Admiral Welles of the ONI were sitting. Welles, John's immediate supervisor, got up to warmly thank Lillie and acknowledged how difficult it must have been to have her two daughters involved in this mission. His recognition of the potential danger the mission placed upon her two daughters during the past three weeks brought a smile to her face. Lillie nodded and graciously thanked him.

Sperry got up from his chair and walked over to introduce himself, for the second time of course, to Annie and Emma. He acknowledged Lillie and Wallace with a quick nod of his head and then focused on the two girls, helping seat them between him and his father. At a third table sat officers Annie recognized as the men who had evaluated her skills the day before and, at a fifth table, located near the door, sat the aides, drivers, and one armed uniformed police officer assigned to the Secretary of the Navy. Also joining them was Mr. Frederick, my old boss at 100 Broadway.

"I remember you two girls on Block Island. Do you remember me?" Sperry smiled, looking down at the girls.

"Yes, we do, sir … Mr. Sperry," Em nervously answered. Annie raised her eyes, smiled her broad smile once again, and at the same time raised her head to fix her eyes on his. Her smile was accompanied by a feeling of respect, and perhaps awe.

Sperry had previously asked John if he could sit next to Annie and Em. When the meal was finally served, John decided to change tables and join the girls, mostly to make sure Annie was fed properly, and to not place too much of a burden on her sister. He needn't have worried. Sperry understood full well how difficult it was for Annie to be fed in public. For unclear reasons he knew how to feed someone with swallowing problems, and immediately volunteered to help Annie in as 'matter of fact' manner as possible. I was amazed at the description of how he helped out.

Sperry and his father were personable, able to make anyone feel at home. Conversation at first centered on Annie's attire. "Annie, you look good in that outfit, perhaps one day it will really be yours," Sperry winked.

Her smile returned and any anxiety she still harbored meeting everyone floated to the background and out to sea. She glanced at her sister, happily engaged in conversation with Sperry's father, and she began to feel as if this were a Thanksgiving dinner. No better than a Thanksgiving dinner, because this evening would never be forgotten. It would remain a high point of her life, a story she would retell time and again, a most prominent member of her own collection of stories.

Emma had no idea she was seated next to, and engaged in conversation with, one of the most important industrialists our nation had ever produced, Sperry's father. But how was she to know, he spoke to her in a soft, grandfatherly manner, making her feel like she was part of his family. (Emma would meet this elderly man again in the future, but that is another story.)

"I remember you two on the dock in the New Harbor," Lawrence Sperry reminisced, "it was a sight I will never forget. I am delighted to see you again. And when I heard a couple of days ago that you were involved with helping solve this riddle, I couldn't have been more surprised or more proud.

"How much information can I share with these two sisters, Mr. Secretary?" Sperry said, looking over at the next table.

The response from Daniels was simple and direct: "As much as you want, except for the cleanup." The sensitive nature of removing the debris from the river was not a topic anyone wanted the girls to hear.

And so began an hour and a half dinner at the Officers Club. The Secretary, the Admirals, the CO of the Navy yard, Sperry and his father, John and his fellow officers from the ONI, two officers from the Reserve Flying Corp, one of whom had a daughter with cerebral palsy; perhaps it was from him that Sperry understood so much about feeding someone with dysphagia.

Sperry and his father, a member of the Naval Consulting Board, were also interested in how Em communicated with her sister, thinking that somehow some of their techniques would apply to hand communications while in the air. Emma tried to answer Mr. Sperry's question.

"First," Em instructed, "establish a yes and no communication system with the person. Most, like my sister, raise their eyes to say *Yes* and move them right to left to say *No*. I will teach you during the meal some of my sister's other responses, including the complicated ones, but the main thing is to first establish how to understand the signal or sign for yes and no. In an aeroplane, it could be a thumbs up for yes and a thumbs down for no.

"And then," Em continued, "try to ask only yes or no questions. Look for non-verbal clues, clues that everyone uses from time to time to communicate, even if verbal. My sister uses the same expressions."

After a few more lessons, Annie changed the topic to ask about what happened over Hell Gate Channel the night before. Emma translated: "My sister wants to know what happened from your perspective, Mr. Sperry?"

Everyone in the room, along with the girls, looked at Sperry. The room went quiet, the sounds of the city became apparent for the first time and all listened to his very detailed and suspense filled account of what happened above New York City that destroyed what was sailing below the water line. Sperry spoke with an actor's manner, most likely because he and his father, earlier in the year, had completed movie clips about their lives with one of the motion picture studios in Hollywood.

Sperry, of course, had a bird's-eye view of the entire event. One that was made even more dramatic by the weather and cloud pattern above the city, a cloud cover low enough to reflect the light from the city back down leaving a channel well lit and much brighter than could have ever been forecast by the New York Weather Office at 100 Broadway, or anyone else. His oratory ability captivated his audience, but it was much more than that or his aerial view that had ensnared his listeners. No, I imagine that it was his remarkable intellect that grasped all of what was happening—in the world, in the city, in the Navy Yard, under the water —that shone brightly at dinner as he described flying up the East River, avoiding the depth charges launched from the shores of the channel, and dropping bombs by hand, one by one, onto the U-boats.

Even the admirals sitting at the adjacent table pulled their chairs closer to listen to the dinner version of his report, somewhat exaggerated for the girls benefit most assuredly, but accurate nonetheless.

"I took off from Governor's Island at about quarter to three in the morning from the grass field. It was a bit bumpy—we will have to resurface that field soon. I could see the Battery, the tip of Manhattan clearly—the cloud cover creating a halo effect, reflecting the city lights back down to Earth from the lights still turned on in the buildings in Manhattan; enough light to provide me with enough light over the East River that I decided to fly *under* each of the four bridges.

"Up ahead, connecting Manhattan to Queens, utilizing Blackwell's Island for its towers, was the Fifty-ninth Street Bridge. I flew under the Queens side of that bridge, staying just off the water. I wanted to understand how the reflection of the night sky would appear on the water.

"Just after flying under the bridge and before I reached Ward's Island, I flew over the edge of Astoria; I dropped to about fifty feet and slowed the plane to get a better view of the channel. I was not sure I would be able to see the targets, but on the first pass, I spotted them immediately. There they were, just slightly submerged, and remarkably the silhouette of each U-boat easily visible from the plane. I could see them clearly but they appeared quite small. I wasn't sure I could hit either one of them. It was high tide and the channel looked as calm as I can ever remember it. I did not even notice any eddies. I could not see the chain from Astoria to the tip of Ward's Island, but I did notice a small group of men on each shoreline and assumed they were working on securing the chain.

"I flew a wide loop out over Riker's Island, and then slowly approached them from the north. When the U-boats reached the middle of Ward's Island, the middle of Hell Gate Channel, I dropped the bombs. With my plane on autopilot, I dropped three of them at the same time and then climbed to two hundred feet, as planned and circled back. That allowed the land troops to commence the launching of the canisters of dynamite. I am not sure if my bombs hit the submarines on that first run but on my second run, I made a direct hit on the one that was still visible. The lead U-boat was sinking by the time I circled around for the second time.

"I then turned around again, flying over Gracie Mansion, to see if I could see the U-boats. I am glad no one is living in that mansion. I came in very low when I banked to turn around, I must have been fifty feet from the top of the trees near the house. Then I flew up the channel at about one hundred and fifty feet to unload my last bomb. I dropped it where I saw some turbulence and explosions that were definitely coming from underwater.

"Again, I am not sure if I scored a direct hit, but I climbed up well out of the way of the land troop's efforts and observed even more explosions near the Astoria side of the channel. I am certain that before I returned to Governor's Island, I saw two hulls, or parts of the hulls surface, just briefly. Then the fireworks were over. Before I returned to Governor's Island, I made a final pass over the channel when the construction lights on Wards Island went dark. As I returned to Governor's Island, I flew over the cleanup barges being pushed up the river by the Navy tugboats, I guess to collect the debris."

As he said that last comment, Sperry's father tapped him on the knee to remind him not to talk about the cleanup.

"And that's the story."

And with that, Sperry ended his version and the crew from Block Island just stared in awe, with a certain amount of disbelief that the mission had gone so well.

Emma finally broke the silence with, what she hoped was a witty comment: "Mr. Sperry, when you were flying up to the Gate the first time, you may not have seen any *eddies* in the channel, but you see some now."

John laughed the loudest; he had not previously made the connection between the term used to describe the swirling of water, its resultant reverse current and turbulence, with our last name.

Everyone at the table resumed eating dinner once again as they slowly digested the story. Em noticed her sister looking at her, asking for help to be fed.

John and Sperry stepped in, however, and took turns helping Annie eat. Later, Lillie described the feeding process for her daughter as completely natural—as if we were all seated having dinner on Block Island in the comfort of our homes. During the meal, conversation continued at the table as if nothing was out of the ordinary. Annie could not eat as gracefully as others, but tonight, she did not feel conspicuous, thanks to both men. Moments before, everyone was in awe of Sperry because of his flight up the East River, and now, they were in awe of him feeding a young girl who almost drowned two years before while taking risks at sea, a trait of character Sperry understood very well. Annie focused and worked hard to make sure she would not choke on anything fed to her, yet it wasn't lost on her that she was being fed by a tandem team of two of the most handsome men a young girl could ever hope to meet.

Emma, sitting on the other side of the table, was able to eat her own dinner without having to help her sister. She was quietly grateful that John and Sperry were so helpful and Lillie, who sat observing all of this from the next table, had difficulty holding back her tears as she witnessed the tender, yet casual manner of the two men now feeding her oldest daughter.

Once during the meal Annie aspirated and choked as she laughed at a humorous comment made by Sperry; but tonight that didn't bother her, as it provided material for further interactions between Annie and those feeding her. Later, back on Block Island, Annie explained to me in a lengthy Morse code message that that dinner in the officer's club was the best night of her life.

When the meal ended, the Vice Admiral spoke about the importance of keeping this event a secret for years to come. German spies were operating on Block Island, New York City and most likely areas in New England around Newport and Bedford, Massachusetts and the ONI wanted it to appear we knew nothing of their presence. John had concerns about this arrangement but chose to talk about it privately with the VA at a later time.

ONI wanted to avoid, at all costs, the appearance of a successful mission. He explained the official word in diplomatic circles would be as follows: The U-boats were caught in a chain net at the beginning of Hell Gate and the explosions, if there was ever a question from citizens or the press, were not a part of the channel widening effort; rather from the subs colliding with each other. Under no circumstances was there ever to be mention of the U. S. Navy or Sperry's plane being involved. It was thought unlikely that Germany would send more U-boats to try to attack the Navy Yard. The Navy would now institute routine patrols in coastal waters, and the "element of surprise" was gone forever.

Wallace brought up the return trip to Block Island, and inquired when he could retrieve his boat. Rear Admiral Welles detailed a plan formulated by the ONI: "The *Anna C* will be taken to a commercial ship yard for extensive repairs, to winterize, and enclose the cabin completely. New decking and railings for safety; even creating a well for Annie to sit in her wheelchair. The boat will be returned by workers from a commercial shipyard. This will provide a good cover to return the boat to Block Island and to send along new spy equipment for secret installation at the Weather House.

"Details of the plan will be worked out," Welles continued, "including telephone and telegram communications from the Weather House to the shipyard we assign to do the work. We are sure the German spies will see your boat had repairs after it is returned to Block Island."

Wallace nodded in agreement. He liked the idea that his boat would get a major overhaul, and at no cost to himself.

"If we don't use my boat to return, how do get back?" Wallace asked.

"Train to Providence and then ferry," Welles said.

Wallace nodded.

Sperry then stood up, glanced at Lillie, and took a step in the direction of Danielson and Welles. He asked, "Would it be alright if I flew the two girls back to Block Island? Do I have permission to fly them in the new larger Curtis?"

When he asked the question, the girls dropped their jaws, as did their mother, but for different reasons.

Welles's answer was an immediate yes, as if it had been rehearsed: "In two days' time."

The Aviator from Brooklyn looked at Lillie. "Okay, in two days, if the weather is good, I will return to the Navy Yard and fly them home.

"I will come back here and pick you two up and we will then walk over to Dry Dock 3 and take off. I just happen to know a great landing spot in the Great Salt Pond. I never thought I'd be returning to Block Island so soon. And I must admit to you two, it has been an absolute pleasure to see you again." Sperry thought that an early morning flight, leaving the Navy Yard no later than midmorning and touching down in the Great Salt Pond before noon, would be a good flight plan. Everyone was certain that the Germans would not risk a trip back to Block Island to drop off any more "mystery men."

The Secretary of the Navy concluded the dinner with some brief comments to his own staff, although he included a reference for the girls, as if they were working for the ONI. He thanked everyone once again and turned to John: "I will send a messenger from the Naval War College in Newport, on the ferry, to Block Island tomorrow morning to let Mr. Eddey know everyone is all right and have him briefed on the current situation, including Mr. Sperry's offer to fly them home. That is the least the Navy can do for the girls.

"Mr. Roosevelt had hoped he would have been able to arrive from Washington in time for this dinner, but he was detained. It is still possible that he will be able to arrive in NYC before you fly home," he added, nodding in Annie's direction. "Mr. Roosevelt expresses his grateful thanks to all of you in this room."

Turning to John, he continued: "John, we also need to work out how we are going to continue to use the cable to send false messages to Mr. Eddey at the Weather Bureau to let the Germans 'eavesdrop' on our conversations. We want them to believe, of course, that we do not know they are listening. Instructions will have to be hand delivered to Mr. Eddey. Captain Todd will help with these details. Perhaps that information can be ready for Wallace to bring to his father tomorrow. Are there any more questions? If not then thank you very much."

John nodded and wrote down some notes on a piece of paper.

Annie signaled she had a question.

"Yes, Annie, what is it that you want to ask?" Daniels said, first looking at Annie and then changing his gaze to Em after she started explaining her sister's question.

Annie asked Em to inquire if the ONI had any new information on the Hygeia Hotel fire. She used her bad hand turned out and up and her good arm raised straight, her symbol for flames. Her symbol or sign for the Hygeia was a short version of Champlin, the last name of my friends who had owned the Hotel.

While the girls were framing the question, John began explaining to Sperry how Annie was communicating her question. By this time, Sperry could fully appreciate how the two understood what each was thinking, plus how much work went into the nonverbal system between the two sisters. Sperry had already been working on a nonverbal form of communication that pilots could use with their copilots while in the air. He reflected on his first meeting with these two amazing girls after his emergency landing, and now he was sitting having dinner with them, as much in awe of them as they of him. John smiled knowingly at Sperry's interest, proud that he was able to witness the girls abilities demonstrated to his superiors.

"We are still not sure about that fire." The Vice Admiral paused a moment to decide how much he wanted to reveal. He looked at Daniels.

Daniels answered the question. "The fire started at 11:00 p.m. That we know." Daniels realized his audience was everyone in the room, not just the girls, and as if being officially debriefed, Daniels motioned to close the door of the dining room and stood up. Everyone's eyes were glued on him. NYC had experienced two sabotages in the past year alone, courtesy of the Germans: fires were set at Black Tom Island and the Kingsland munitions factory that destroyed valuable war related resources.

Turning to the girls, Daniels said, "This past July, the Navy held war games a few miles off Block Island. Do you remember seeing the battleships?"

Annie raised her eyes and Emma nodded.

"And then came the fire that burned the beautiful and large Hygeia Hotel to the ground. We think the fire was possibly sabotage. The hotel had such a strategic view of the opening of the Great Salt Pond and the Atlantic Ocean, and it would have served as an ideal base for U.S. naval operations.

"The records of the guests that stayed there are being thoroughly reviewed by my staff to determine if anyone who was at the hotel does not have a confirmed address. But that may not be entirely helpful, as there was a large gathering of people that night in the lobby, making it easy for anyone on the Island to enter the hotel. It would be a terrible thing if sabotage was the case … and God forbid, if more hotels are targeted. But I am afraid that I cannot tell you more."

The girls were satisfied with that explanation and realized it all went beyond Block Island. And then Emma asked about who was the murder victim, found in the water near the North Lighthouse. It was a question I did not think had an answer, but Captain Todd, the Chief Cable Censor in the ONI, answered the question.

"We intercepted a wireless transmission from one of the subs a few days after the death was reported. The man was an operative on the Island, one of the three 'Mystery Men.' According to the intercepted cable, the Germans had discovered he was using the mission as a means to defect to the U.S., and request asylum. He was ordered 'terminated' and was killed by his fellow spy, who we shall refer to as 'Mystery Man number one'. And he——number one——thanks to John, and our operative -slash-deckhand, will not be returning to Block Island.

"So," Todd continued, "that leaves one mystery man, number three, on the Island. But we have determined that he is strictly a communications specialist, with no combat training. Thus, he does not pose a threat to any of you. We'll allow him to continue to operate on Block Island so long as he is an asset to us."

Daniels interrupted and looked at Lillie, "But if that changes, we'll send John and another agent to the Island and arrest him."

With that explanation it all made sense. The ONI knew much more than we thought it did. 'Mystery Man' number one was the man who had shot the bird. And it was he who killed 'Mystery Man' number two, and had rowed the body out and dumped it into the sea, and who had chased Emma across the Island, most likely to kill her for having seen his face. John later confided to Wallace he was aware there was one extremely dangerous man in the bunch, and was instructed to *take him out* one way or another. That is why he brought the pistols and rifle to Block Island.

It was fortuitous that 'Mystery Man' number one boarded the ferry the afternoon of the lobster dinner in the backyard of the Weather House —presumably to reconnoiter with another spy on the mainland. This provided an opportunity to have him arrested—or if he resisted, taken out at sea. We still do not know what actually happened to him.

John's original mission was accomplished that afternoon; but it became clear days before, to John, and later to ONI, that Annie had uncovered the real mission.

Daniels stood up, thanked everyone one more time, reminded them not to repeat anything, and ended the conversation by saying goodnight.

The evening over, everyone walked over, shook the hands of Wallace, Lillie and, of course, the two sisters, and left the building.

The 'crew of the *Anna C*' was driven across the Navy Yard complex to their temporary home on the top floor of the officer's home near the Naval Hospital in the VA's car, who himself drove off in a nondescript, small black Model T. Sperry and his father drove out of the Navy Yard in their own car to their home in Brooklyn, three miles away. A junior officer from the Naval Yard drove John to his home in Marble Hill where his older sister, Rachel, was waiting. Rachel would housesit for John whenever he was away for an extended period of time. In his absence, she had begun covering the fig trees with canvas sheets to protect them from the cold. She loved to cultivate those trees which helped make the yard a bit of an oasis in Manhattan. John's home was a place he had not seen in several weeks and it was in a neighborhood that I knew well. I was more than surprised to find out he lived in Marble Hill, as it was the neighborhood I lived in just before moving to Block Island. He lives less than half a mile from where my sister and older brother live in the house built by my father. I never had the chance to ask if he knew my family lived in his neighborhood *before* he first met us. What kind of coincidence is that?

After everyone had gone home, it was Annie's turn to reflect. All of this and more was witnessed by a sixteen-year-old girl from her vantage point of a wooden wheelchair. It was an evening, it was a week, it was a month she would never forget. She thought about how she was treated, so professionally by everyone and further, she met some of the most impressive people ever.

She would think about this night for the rest of her life, I know, because she would tell me often. She developed a short hand signal to communicate to her sister when she wanted anyone to know that her mind had returned to this most extraordinary time at the Brooklyn Navy Yard. It had greater significance for the two sisters than they could have ever thought possible.

Yes, they understood the importance of trying to "matter," but what they could not possibly understand at their age, was that if they themselves didn't *want* to "matter," nobody else (except perhaps one's parents) really cares.

Later that evening, Wallace and Lillie were told that they would not be able to return to Block Island the next day.

The reason would soon become clear.

48 Waiting

Early the next morning, Lillie was asked by an ONI officer if she wanted to take Emma shopping in Manhattan, now that they would not be allowed to leave the Navy Yard for at least one more day. Lillie said yes, and asked if they could be driven to B. Altman's, a beautiful department store on 18th Street in Manhattan, her most favorite place to shop in Manhattan. After being given the okay, they were driven in Mr. Howe's car to the very store where I had purchased Lillie's wedding ring. Wallace and Lillie pooled their money so that they would have enough to buy dresses for the girls.

When Lillie and Em had left the yard, and Wallace was being briefed on what shipyard would be doing the "repairs" to his boat, Annie was back in the transmission room, this time with Captain Todd in attendance, attempting to break numerical code. John came to work at the Navy Yard with his sister, Rachel, who wanted to meet Annie. They met up in the transmission room. Rachel was as gracious with Annie as her brother had been that first day they met on Block Island. I never understood why she wanted to meet Annie, other than to meet a young woman who wanted to 'matter.' Perhaps the transference of feelings from John and their own younger sister to Annie had enveloped Rachel as well. Annie was pleased Rachel had taken the time to visit with her, however short her stay in the Navy Yard was that day.

Annie expressed to Rachel how grateful she was that John had taken her seriously and treated her like an adult. It took a while for Annie to communicate those thoughts to her, but when Rachel finally understood what she was saying, she started to shed some tears.

Soon after their arrival, Annie was given a break from the grueling work in the transmission office. Captain Todd suggested they go on a brief walk around the shipyard and he led Annie, Rachel, and John on a tour of the Navy Yard to see the battleships they'd helped save. Annie was still wearing her sailor's uniform from the night before and it was doubtful that anyone would have thought that she was not an enlisted soldier, perhaps recuperating at the Naval Hospital.

Todd pushed Annie along in her wheelchair slightly ahead of John and Rachel. He had already determined she was talented in deciphering codes and may have a future in the ONI. Why? Because *he* fully believed, after listening to those same transmissions, that the attack was most assuredly going to be centered at the Newport Naval Base. He did not even think of the Brooklyn Navy Yard as a possible target!

The first time anyone lays their eyes on one of these vessels from a close vantage point, it creates a true sense of wonder. You stand before this structure, a gray horizontal steel building, in awe of its size and more so of its function. Massive, grand, incredible.

After about an hour of marveling at the sheer size of the battleships, the four returned to the transmission office where John received confirmation that Sperry would indeed be ready to fly both girls back to Block Island in two days.

The barometric pressure was holding steady and was forecast to rise, the winds would be calm, and as long as the wind was less than fifteen miles per hour, a smooth landing could be anticipated. It would be the very first landing of an aeroplane in the Great Salt Pond.

ONI made all the arrangements for Lillie and Wallace to return to the Island via train and then the ferry. They would leave first thing tomorrow morning, a day prior to the girls returning by aeroplane. John and his sister would stay overnight with the girls in the officer's home, along with the nurse from the Naval Hospital.

When Lillie returned from shopping with Em, she was told of the departure plans. She wished it were earlier in the season when they could have taken one of the Fall River Line steamships that sailed overnight from Manhattan to Newport.

Early the next morning, Wallace and Lillie were on their way to Pennsylvania Station in Manhattan to board the train to Providence. The weather was crisp and beautiful, and having only a couple light B. Altman bags to carry, they decided to walk the mile and a half to the subway stop at the base of the Brooklyn Bridge. Their other option was walking a mile north on Kent Street to the Grand Street Ferry Landing and take the ferry across the East River. But Wallace chose, as I would have, to cross the East River on the bridge that used to be called the Grand Avenue over the East River, then the East River Bridge and now, of course, the Brooklyn Bridge. They declined a final offer of a ride from the VA, said goodbye to the girls, and were off.

After boarding the subway across the bridge, they transferred to another subway at City Hall and at 35th Street exited that subway and walked east to Pennsylvania Station where they boarded the train for Providence. The aluminum-reinforced wheelchair with the wide wheels would be flown back on the plane, and the other new wheelchair would be delivered on the *Anna C* when it was returned from the shipyard. Wallace was looking forward to the train ride because the Pennsylvania Railroad would travel—via a tunnel under the East River into Queens and then back across the East River—over the new Railroad Bridge recently completed over Hell Gate Channel.

As the train approached the Hell Gate Railroad Bridge, conversation between Wallace and Lillie came to a stop. A solemn feeling, similar to attending a funeral, became apparent to each of them, as they moved closer to the window and peered down. Wallace and Lillie stared out the windows straining to see evidence, on the shores of Astoria or Wards Island, of the mission completed the night before.

"Nothing," Wallace whispered to Lillie. "Nothing."

As if to allow them a longer look, the train slowed to a crawl as it passed over the channel. Nothing below but water that appeared black with only an occasional reflection from the sun. No sign on either side of the channel of the activities of the armed forces, and Lillie thought the whole thing was just unreal. She was not the only one.

"It is amazing that this channel, almost a half mile wide, is shallow at only twenty-four feet at mean low tide, and yet so much water passing in both directions depending, of course, on the direction of the tide," Wallace continued to think out loud.

Lillie listened; she began thinking that it was this bridge that allowed them to accept what had happened two nights ago. They had sailed through the channel, but prior to seeing the waterway from the windows of the train from high on the bridge, it was not yet real, as when someone dies and you don't, or can't, believe it has happened. And then finally it sinks into one's mind that a life is lost, in this case, the loss of two U-boats and their crews.

Crossings and losses; one leads to the other so often and just as often, the other way around. I have always thought crossings are symbolic of life; and the lives of our ancestors attest to that. Crossings do more than allow for reflection, they unleash a natural state of contemplation, as was witnessed by the overwhelming poignant reaction of Wallace and Lillie as they crossed over Hell Gate on their way home.

The rest of the trip was uneventful; conversation between the two did not increase, even as time left the channel behind. Four hours later, they disembarked the train in Providence and walked a mile to board the ferry to Block Island.

***

During the day, the two girls spent their time under the watchful eye of the officers who had evaluated Annie's skills, still underdeveloped of course, in the area of transmission and understanding of codes. Rachel and John stayed with her for part of the day, and Annie once again demonstrated both an aptitude and a very real interest. Before she knew it, the day was over and they all returned to the officer's home. Em, by the way, was not as enthralled with the instructional process; her attention primarily was directed at a myriad of handsome officers in uniform, regardless of their special skill set.

That night Annie and Em tossed and turned in their beds. But, unlike Wallace and their mom, they did not have a realization of the gravity of what had taken place at Hell Gate. That would not come for many months; I assumed that that was simply a reflection of their youth. The reason they could not fall asleep was simply their anticipation of the flight back to Block Island with Sperry.

It seemed that they had just fallen asleep when they were woken up at dawn by none other than the Aviator from Brooklyn, Lawrence Sperry himself. He was wearing his flying attire and looked like he was ready to be in a motion picture, or at least that is what the girls thought.

Emma and Annie were surprised he was so comfortable with the two of them, and they with him; as if they were none other than his two younger sisters, of which he already had several. He instructed them to get dressed while he met with the CO of the Naval Yard.

"I'll meet you downstairs in thirty minutes, and then we will be off to Block Island," Sperry said. "And dress warmly, very warmly!" Sperry executed a salute, then turned and left the room.

And so, with that burst of energy, the day began. A nurse came in to help the girls with their morning preparation, dressing, washing, toileting, although not in that order. Em was very talkative, reminding her sister she wanted to sit next to Sperry when they were in the plane.

Annie rolled her eyes, a motion that was distinctly different than raising the eyes when she wanted to say yes. Her nonverbal communication could, in this instance, be understood by any sister being annoyed by a younger sister.

The nurse brought each a heavy coat and hat to wear over the clothes they wore on the *Anna C*. Both girls wished their mother had left the new dresses, to impress their pilot of course. But dressing warmly was of utmost importance.

And as the girls were preparing for their first flight, Milton and I were up early collecting weather data for our morning transmission. Wallace and Lillie had arrived last night and explained why the girls weren't with them. Wallace, back home with Edith, and Lillie upstairs in bed, were still sleeping when Em pushed her sister out the front door of the officer's home for the last time.

As they were leaving, Emma turned for one final look at the small brick building. Even at her young age, she would never forget this place or the events surrounding the past two and a half weeks. Emma pushed her sister slowly along the walkway toward the dry docks, with John and his sister close behind. They soon met up with Sperry and several other officers. The three nurses who had helped the girls over the past few days suddenly materialized to say goodbye; but also hoping, or so it appeared, for an invitation to fly with Sperry at a later time.

They walked across the yard to the plane; Emma pushed the wheelchair so that Sperry could walk side-by-side with Annie to facilitate conversation. Sperry told Annie how impressed he was with the way she deciphered the code, a conversation he wasn't able to have with her at the dinner two nights previous.

"You have a good ear for understanding code. Do you think that you are better at listening now, after your accident?" Sperry went on to suggest the possibility that the damage to certain parts of her brain freed up other parts so that she could concentrate better.

Annie rotated her good hand at the question, not entirely sure what the answer was. Often she found it hard to concentrate on certain things, but other times the concentration came easy. She was not able to explain this observation to him as they crossed the Navy Yard.

Sperry explained that they would all have to wear life preservers as well as one of the new parachutes the Navy had recently made. He did not mention that they were based on one of his recent patents. Each would also get belted into the same seat and wear headgear so as not to freeze once they were airborne.

"You two will sit to my right."

"Mr. Sperry, I thought you were going to fly us out later in the day," Em said.

"I was, but I thought that it was going to be such a beautiful day that I would take the scenic route back to your home." He smiled and so did the girls. "We have extra clothing and protection for your face and neck. It will be windy and cold once we are airborne, but the clouds will not come in from the northwest until later in the day, well after we have set down on the Great Salt Pond."

Just before they reached the dock, John and Rachel interrupted the conversation and asked Emma if she would like to take a closer look at the battleships before they leave. The girls were so enthralled with Sperry, that they did not fully appreciate they might never see John again.

After a few minutes, John and Emma left Annie and Sperry alone for a moment. As they walked toward the *USS Mexico* in dry dock, John explained that he wanted a photo of Emma and himself in front of the battleship. Emma instinctively turned around to check on her sister and saw several men in uniform approaching Sperry and Annie.

"Who are those men, John?" Emma asked.

"Those are my superior officers. You met two of them last night."

"Oh, I guess they are saying goodbye to Annie," Emma responded.

"No, Em, I think they are saying hello."

John had arranged for a photographer to take a photo of Emma and him standing in front of the *USS Mexico* and after they had posed for several photos, they returned to Annie to photograph her as well. By the time they had returned, the men had left Annie alone with just Sperry and one other officer. They continued on to the hydroaeroplane where everyone posed for one final photograph. John arranged for the photographs to document the end of the mission and to provide closure, to some degree, to having to say goodbye to two young girls, whom he got to know as family and whom he would think about almost every day for the rest of his life. Further, he understood two other things: he would indeed see Annie again, and, with the excitement of flying home, everyone would forget to say their final goodbyes.

John and one of the officers helped lift Annie and Em down the steep wooden stairs to the hanger, floating near another dock and up into the open seats of the Curtis F.

The girls were harnessed together in the seat on the right; Em in the middle, Annie on the right; the massive engine and propeller, high above their heads. They were secured with shoulder belts over padding in the front and their parachutes served as adding padding against the hard seat back. The wheelchair and some bags were placed in the back, firmly tied down, behind the wooden seats.

When nervous, everyone can hide it to some degree, but for Annie, nervousness often manifested itself as worsening spasticity; but today she was as relaxed as any time before the accident and this was extremely helpful in seating her comfortably in the plane. Emma was surprised and commented on her state. Annie simply smiled.

Sperry started the engine and John and the officers pushed the hydroaeroplane away from the dock inside the floating hanger. John waved, although the girls were too preoccupied to notice his tears.

Sitting side-by-side they waved goodbye to John and the officers and as they emerged from the hanger, Em looked back and could see that all along the top of Dry Dock Three, and from the sides of the *U. S. S. Arizona,* sailors were standing and waving. Looking back on this, it was not surprising that the workers dressed in construction outfits paid the aeroplane no attention whatsoever.

"Look Annie," Em pointed to the sailors, "they are waving at us."

Em waved back and before they knew it, Sperry had increased the revolutions of the engine and the plane started taxiing out to the East River. Conversation all but ceased as the noise of the engine drowned out their spoken words. The current in the river was moving north now, against the slight wind. The plane began taxiing out of the inlet called Wallabout Creek, and into the East River proper.

John left the hanger and walked back up the stairs to the top of the dock where Rachel and fellow officers were standing. There he joined those waving at the plane. Soon the hydroaeroplane was airborne, rising above the river, leaving him, and Brooklyn, behind.

It had been the most unique assignment he had ever been given. Assigned to the project by his superiors due to his comfortableness with individuals with physical problems, just like his late sister, he had developed a bond with this family from Block Island, and recognized a feeling of comfort—not loss—as the aeroplane gained altitude over the East River. He knew that he would see the crew from Block Island in the future.

Uncharacteristic of this professional, he began shedding a few tears and had to sit in the wheelchair for a moment and pretend he was retying his shoes, while trying to gain his composure. It was obvious to everyone he had developed such a closeness to the girls, a transference in part, to be sure, of the love and loss he once felt for his late sister. Within a few minutes, John stood and waved to the plane as it returned downriver, then lost sight of it as Sperry flew around the Battery to Liberty Island and out to the Atlantic. He needed to return to work and report for a final briefing on the mission; Franklin D. Roosevelt was now on-site.

John knew full well that this mission had provided him with several rewards in the Aristotelian sense; a mission with a surprisingly solid outcome; and perhaps the best reward, the opportunity to work with the small crew of the *Anna C*, that very well could become an extended family.

John entered the room to attend the debriefing unaware he was about to witness a rare expression of esteem and warmth from his superiors and colleagues. His fellow officers from the ONI and Naval Yard rose in unison, and gave him a standing ovation. To be given this tribute upon entering a room of colleagues is a tradition found in only a small number of professional organizations, but a true honor in any profession.

John stood just inside the doorway, fully understanding the significance of a gesture that combined kindness and respect. He walked into the room ever so slowly, he stood firm, silent, looking ahead at his fellow officers, his eyes a bit glazed over. He saluted them. "Thank you. Thank you very much," John said quietly. He thought had he not emptied his tear ducts just minutes before, most likely, he would have taken this opportunity to have done so.

The Vice Admiral stood up, offered his chair at the head of the conference table, and remained clapping as John sat in the seat just vacated. As he looked up, he saw Mr. Roosevelt sitting alongside Mr. Daniels.

49 Saying Goodbye over NYC

In under a minute, they were airborne. The plane lifted off into the wind just south of the Williamsburg Bridge, climbing slowly until the span was cleared. Sperry climbed even higher as they flew north, along the shore of Manhattan. After flying over the Queensboro Bridge he dropped in altitude to give the girls a better view of Hell Gate and circled the channel twice, using hand signals to point out where the U-boats were sunk in the middle of the channel.

After they circled back over Riker's Island, on the return trip down the East River, Sperry pointed out Gracie Mansion and Central Park with its reservoir reflecting the dancing sunlight well off to their right. Manhattan was beautiful from the sky, a sight few could ever appreciate. The two girls sat silently, amazed at what they were able to see from the plane. *This sure beats a ferry ride*, Em was thinking.

Sperry could both see and feel the joy in each of the girls; teenagers experiencing life as adults. Pure joy is an elusive concept, hard to describe, often un-witnessed, though felt deep within oneself. One is never quite sure when it will appear, but today, looking across at Annie and Em, Sperry was convinced he was witnessing pure joy. In this world of pain and loss and sorrow, it was present here, in the cockpit of the Curtis F in the form of two young girls, sitting together, secured firmly to the same seat, flying high over the East River as an eagle flies over its domain.

The plane was built by Curtis, but modified by Sperry and his father at their Long Island plant. It was a one of a kind plane, built to seat two, but three could squeeze in comfortably. In front of the two girls, partially blocking their view—and to some degree the cold air—was a new stabilizer that sat on a ledge built for the purpose. This device functioned as an autopilot, allowing the pilot to fly hands free, the stabilizer maintaining level flight for the plane.

Sperry's parachutes were his design as well, one of many patents he had already been awarded. They added a bit more warmth and were comfortable to lean back on, making the experience of flying a bit more relaxed. The girls' faces, unlike Sperry's, were covered with two wool hats, stretched over their faces and resembling socks more than hats; this to keep the cold from leaving its mark on their faces, but thin enough that he could still see their facial expressions. Sperry had cut out holes for their eyes and mouths. A thick leather hat lined with sheepskin was then tied under their chins to further protect them from the cold air. With this outerwear Sperry was sure they could handle a blast of artic air if need be. And while glancing to his right to see the girls, under all the clothing and protective gear, Sperry realized quite suddenly that he completely forgot one of the two next to him was disabled.

The process of saying goodbye to everyone on the ground had been special, yet remarkably different for the two girls. For Emma, parting with John and the other officers happened so quickly she was not sure she had even said goodbye, being that she was so excited and nervous about flying in the aeroplane. And although she did briefly wonder, when airborne, if she would ever see John again, these thoughts were overshadowed by the dramatic sights they were witnessing from the air.

The goodbye for Annie, however, was decidedly different. While Emma was walking with John to the docks, four men had approached Annie who was still with Sperry and the two other officers. These were the men that Emma saw when she turned back to look at her sister, and John remarked that they were saying "hello" to Annie, not goodbye.

It was months before Emma understood the significance of John's comment. I understood the significance when I was handed an envelope on Block Island later that morning, but there was much more to the story than that.

In the air, what captivated Annie's attention most was the deep blue of the sky behind the breaking cloud cover and the expansiveness of New York, Long Island, and Long Island Sound, all so unmistakably observable as soon as the plane climbed in altitude over New York

292   *Gary E. Eddey*

Harbor. It was simply grand—almost as grand as the request that Mr. Roosevelt had offered to her on the ground, minutes before.

It was noisy up in the air, the sound of the wind overshadowed by the noise coming from the engine mounted above the cockpit; Sperry spoke to them using hand signals as much as mouthing the words.

As they retraced their path down the East River, he pointed to the Brooklyn Bridge and asked them, via a low swooping motion of his hand, if they wanted to fly under it. Neither girl said anything, their eyes and mouths wide open, just thinking of the idea.

Before they reached the bridges, first the Williamsburg Bridge, then the Manhattan, and finally the beautiful span of the Brooklyn Bridge, Sperry tipped the wings to the left to show the girls the Brooklyn Navy Yard from the air. The battleships standing out like large, horizontal buildings, one in dry dock and the others in the water. Smaller naval craft were also below, looking much smaller in their various stages of construction. They couldn't see them but John, his boss, Mr. Roosevelt, and the President of the United States, Mr. Wilson, were down below as well; following their flight, as well as countless citizens of New York City who happened to be looking toward the sky that morning in October.

After they flew over the Williamsburg Bridge, Sperry descended quickly to about one hundred feet over the river and then sure enough, as graceful as an eagle—not that an eagle ever flew under the Manhattan and Brooklyn Bridges—Sperry piloted the plane lower and cleared each bridge with room to spare.

The girls were mesmerized; little did they know that they were the first and only females, to have ever flown under the Brooklyn Bridge. All three of them were also unaware that Sperry's father, at work early, looking out the window of his office in the Sperry Building on the East side of Manhattan, had spotted the plane with the three of them just as it flew under the bridges. *One day that type of behavior has got to be curtailed,* thought Sperry's father, a sentiment he shared with his son at dinner later that night.

Sperry continued over New York Harbor, passing the Battery to their right. He pointed out the grass airstrip on Governors Island and then banked the plane hard to the right and flew over to the Statue of Liberty.

Flying no higher than one hundred feet off the water, the girls were able to look directly into the eyes of Lady Liberty as Sperry circled the small island in a clockwise direction. After completing one circle, he piloted the Curtis F out of New York Harbor at the point where Staten Island tries to reach across the channel and touch Brooklyn, and into the Atlantic Ocean, and along the southern coast of Long Island toward Montauk Point and Block Island.

Flying in an open cockpit hydroaeroplane is an exhilarating experience, especially when experiencing it for the first time. In 1916 ... almost everyone on the planet would be experiencing it for the first time. The view, the cold air against their faces. At first the girls were in awe; then they couldn't stop laughing, marveling at the view as the wind began trying to penetrate the wool armor covering their faces. At one point over Coney Island, because Annie had to sit so low for safety and comfort due to her spasticity, Sperry banked the plane and made a complete circle to show Annie one final view of New York City that beautiful morning.

They flew over the south shore of Long Island, where Sperry pointed out his family's summer estate in Bellport, but the girls could not see it clearly. Soon they approached Montauk Point and the girls saw the lighthouse, easily recognized from the air with its one horizontal red band painted on its midsection; one of the oldest lighthouses in the United States.

And soon thereafter, they were able to see, beyond Montauk, out over the Atlantic, a land mass we all know, except for Melville of course, as Block Island. The Island had lost its characteristic green of summer and even the numerous ponds seemed darker blue than usual, even black. The Island was no longer covered in trees, obvious from as far away as Montauk; a consequence of the early settlers using the timber to build and then heat them. It has been speculated that the Island became "treeless" as early as the 1720s.

When Adrian Block first sailed by the Island in 1611, he observed many rolling hills, gently sloping toward the sea, with each and every one covered with trees. Now visible on those same hills are mostly various kinds of grasses covering those pastures, each separated by stone walls creating a sight from the sky of a carefully manicured mosaic-like farmland. But of course, the beautiful bluffs on which the Southeast Lighthouse stands, the first sight of land for those coming out of the sea at Block Island, including Mr. Block, remain as they were, albeit less some erosion. One other geographic change Block would have seen that is not present today was a long series of high sandbars well off Crescent Beach; it wasn't until 1815 when a storm carried away those sandbars that the Crescent Beach of today came into existence.

The wind was coming from the east, a favorable wind condition for landing in the Great Salt Pond, just up ahead. Emma did not want the flight to end and used hand signals to ask him if he would fly them over where he had landed in the ocean at the base of Mohegan Bluffs.

Sperry obliged her this small request as he too wanted to see the Island again from the air and revisit where he'd set down the month before at the base of the lighthouse during his emergency night landing. He also wanted the girls to point out where their accident at sea had occurred.

The girls pointed out the stretch of beach where Milton first saw the three men, Dicken's Point and then Black Rock. As they flew along the southern shore of the Island, Em pointed to Wallace's small house. "Eddey's Shanty" was easy to point out from the air because it was just west of the large Vaill Hotel. With the speed of the engine slowed, Sperry was able to verbally explain and reenact his emergency landing; and minutes later Emma showed him where Annie had saved her that fateful day, two and a half years ago.

They approached the Southeast Lighthouse, a beautiful sight from the sky, the open ocean, or the Island. And before they knew it, they were approaching Old Harbor Point. At that point, Sperry then banked the plane and started flying over the Island for the first time. Within seconds they could see the Spring House Hotel to their left, and then the Ocean View Hotel below them on their right. Because they flew directly over the Union House Hotel, they were unable to see that building or their own home behind the family hotel. They flew over Harbor Pond and then were bearing down on the Weather House, standing guard, as it has since 1903, over the New Harbor at the edge of the Great Salt Pond.

It was easy for Sperry to identify the Weather House building. It had a distinctive square shape, a flat roof with instruments resting on its surface, clapboard painted white, not pale yellow as it had when it was first built; half home, half office with a signal tower off to the side, tall enough to be seen from both harbors and a small garage that Wallace and I had recently built near Trims Pond.

Sitting like an un-welcomed neighbor diagonally across from the Weather House, visible before them, sticking out like a beached, decomposed sperm whale, was the burnt remains of the Hygeia Hotel.

As the plane passed over the Weather House, Sperry waved to say hello. He tipped the wing to provide a clear view for the two girls. Milt waved from the roof; Annie was able to see him. Wallace and Lillie stood when they heard the engine of the plane, somewhat surprised the plane approached from the east.

After circling around the Great Salt Pond, like a hawk circles in search of its prey, the hydroplane touched down in the smooth waters and glided onto a small sandy beach near Corn Neck Road. Sperry remembered this area of the Great Salt Pond was shallow, yet devoid of sandbars. It allowed him to have a soft, graceful landing, and then he could easily turn the plane around and take off for home directly into the wind. Not counting the emergency the previous month, this constituted the first *official* landing of a plane on Block Island.

I waited for the arrival of the Curtis F on the Commercial Dock, assuming Sperry would taxi over to the dock. When I saw them approaching from the east and circle the Great Salt Pond, I realized Sperry would land in the northeast section and I immediately got back in my car and drove out along Corn Neck Road to reach the landing site. I picked up Milton, Wallace, and Lillie at the Weather House and we drove together to greet them. Sperry landed in a perfect spot and had just finished taxiing onto the small, narrow sandy beach when we arrived.

As we drove up, he turned off the engine to cut the level of noise. He instructed Milton and Wallace to guide the plane up on the beach a few feet. Milton climbed onto the right wooden pontoon and reached up to help un-harness Annie and Em. Milton and Wallace un-harnessed the parachutes and lifted the girls down from the plane while Sperry secured the plane to the beach with a line he tied around a large boulder. Wallace placed Annie into the wheelchair while Lillie and I just watched the reaction of the two sisters, all bundled up with their headgear that they continued to wear, sans the masks, for the next several hours.

Sperry said hello to Wallace and Lillie and walked over. He shook my hand and thanked me for our work, addressing me as Sergeant Eddey, my title from the U. S. Signal Service that I rarely used. My immediate thought was how personable and mature he was, regardless of his age. I was impressed immediately.

"Sir, Mr. Danielson wanted me to tell you that when he received your initial telegram, everyone took notice, knowing it was from you. As you are now aware, they took your concerns seriously and sent one of their best to help you."

I nodded. "John is indeed one of the best! And you are very welcome. And thank you, and thank Mr. Danielson and everyone in Brooklyn for following through with my concerns." I looked over at the girls and continued, "And thank you for flying Annie and Emma back home. I am sure they will never forget the flight or your thoughtfulness. Just look at them, they know they have been someplace special." I turned my head and glanced at the aeroplane when I finished my sentence.

Sperry acknowledged my appreciation and then put forth the invitation for us to return to the Navy Yard next month to witness the launching of the *USS Arizona*. We were to be the guests of the CO of the Navy Yard and Mr. Daniels.

He waved Lillie over to participate in the conversation. "The battleship will set sail from the Navy Yard on November sixteenth I believe. You and your family are invited to attend the event and sit with the officers on the grandstands at the dry dock. Mr. Howe mentioned to me that Mr. Roosevelt and President Wilson will also be attending. They are looking forward to meeting all of you, although I believe Mr. Roosevelt has already met Annie."

"He has?" I exclaimed.

"Yes," Sperry said softly. He slipped me an envelope and said the contents would explain more and added that John spoke highly of 'his second family' from Block Island. I nodded and smiled, and without drawing attention, slid the envelope into my pocket.

Sperry then turned his attention back to the girls, who were busy explaining to Milton what it was like to fly in an aeroplane. He had a few questions for Milton, specifically whether he would be interested in joining the Navy. Milton immediately said yes, although he had never thought about it before.

Sperry hugged each of the girls and talked about the flight. They had many questions for him that they were unable to ask in flight. He sat on a log and answered them all patiently as Emma interpreted some of the questions from her sister. This alone was a gesture I would never forget.

After fifteen minutes, they moved in to hug him again as he stood up. Annie, and especially Em, never at a loss for words, were finding it difficult to express their gratitude and to say goodbye.

It was time for Sperry to return to Brooklyn. Declining an invitation for an early lunch at the Weather House, the girls' private pilot climbed back into the hydroaeroplane and restarted the engine as Milton and I helped turn the plane around. I could see tears in Annie's eyes; and then I noticed tears in everyone's including the pilot, as Sperry waved goodbye. Within minutes, the Brooklyn Aviator was rising over the Great Salt Pond as smoothly as a sailboat before a following wind.

While in the air, at some point over Gardiner's Bay, he changed his flight plan—something he frequently did—and instead of landing at the Naval Reserve base in Massapequa on the southern shore of Long Island, he decided to land on the grass runway of his father's estate in Bellport, Long Island. He arrived in less than forty-five minutes, less time than it took for us to load the girls in the car, drive back to the Weather House, and sit down for lunch. And by the time Wallace had returned to his home on the bluffs and joined his wife, Sperry had arrived at Long Island and was finishing dinner with his family in Bellport, letting them know about his flight with the girls. When Sperry's father arrived later in the evening from NYC, the first thing he did was suggest to his son that perhaps, just perhaps, he ought to stop flying under the East River bridges.

From time to time, my sisters, Catherine and Mary, would mail clippings from the New York and Brooklyn newspapers about Lawrence

Sperry for years to come. His accomplishments were many, yet for all those exploits, I will never forget how kind he was to the girls. For me, the short time spent on the shore of the Great Salt Pond with him was as exciting as meeting the President of the United States, a position, I suppose, Lawrence Sperry may one day hold.

Although I would never see him again, one member of my family would have the opportunity to meet him on more than one occasion.

An early Curtis F Hydroaeroplane with a single cockpit (1914).

The U.S.S. Arizona guided out of the Brooklyn Navy Yard, November 1916. 100 Broadway cannot be seen in this view but is located to the left of the Brooklyn Bridge's stanchion or tower.

50 Crescent Beach

It was over, the ending as dramatic as the beginning was uncertain; an amazing amount of work completed … from Milton's initial observations to the flight that returned the girls to Block Island, this was an extraordinary three weeks.

The final report from the ONI concluded the following: "Two U-boats thwarted, one presumably to lay mines in the East River near the Navy Yard and one to torpedo the ships already in the water, with the primary target being the *USS Arizona*; this to be accomplished by entering New York Harbor through the back door, Hell Gate, previously thought to be an impassible channel. All of this possible by using our own government weather codes to send their communications in their own code." But was that all there was to the story?

At the very least, one could look at this incident as a lesson, or a series of lessons.

Perhaps for President Wilson, it meant a move away from neutrality; for the ONI, perhaps a fuller understanding of how spies and saboteurs utilize our own existing resources to complete their missions; for the Navy, a realization that even those with physical hardships can indeed contribute; for the girls, a lesson that they too can play a role, matter by being productive.

For me, the lesson was the necessity of making decisions based on limited, often incomplete information, and to learn to feel comfortable making those decisions, despite the uncertainty. In effect, it was a lesson on how to discern or recognize when it is necessary to observe and wait for more information *before* making those decisions.

A powerful lesson, Lillie reminded me, for forecasters.

Back at the Weather House, Milton carried Annie into the kitchen and I followed with the wheelchair, recognizing that someone was missing: John. Lillie and Em simply followed us in, as if in a daze.

Everyone was tired. During the meal, Wallace repeated a comment he made early yesterday evening when I met him and Lillie at the ferry, but other than that we ate in silence.

"Pop, the officers made it clear they don't want us to give the impression that anyone is aware of the one remaining German spy on the Island. We are still going to have to be careful what we say. They wanted to hand me instructions on how to handle communications, including false communications, but they did not have them prepared before Lillie and I left Brooklyn yesterday morning. Did Sperry bring anything with him?"

I nodded. I was aware of their request, but did not disclose to anyone at the table the envelope handed to me by Sperry.

"We have to assume that they, or any of the Germans, will be able to understand and use all of our cable and wireless transmissions to and from the Island and perhaps even the telephone."

When we saw Sperry take off from the Great Salt Pond, I was quite confident our short career in Naval Intelligence was coming to an end. But when I eventually opened the envelope he handed me and read its content, I was taken aback to such an extent I became speechless. It took me a day before I mentioned the contents of the envelope to Lillie, and then only because Annie had asked Lillie if she read the letter addressed to her from the ONI.

The envelope contained a handwritten note from Secretary of the Navy, Mr. Daniels, and the director of the ONI, the Assistant Secretary of the Navy, Mr. Roosevelt. It was addressed to Lillie and simply requested her permission for Annie, since she was only sixteen years old, to join the ONI. The letter acknowledged that permission would have to be granted due to her age.

I couldn't believe my eyes. When we read the letter out loud in Annie's presence she just smiled, not her broad happy smile, but a smile nonetheless of contentment, satisfaction, and accomplishment.

Another document in the envelope summarized why the ONI thought Block Island could well have become a site for launching foreign operations, as it had during our Revolutionary War and the second revolutionary war, the War of 1812. I thought they would assign an operative here, but of course, I now knew that operative was to be Lillie's oldest daughter, with back up from John.

When it comes to the weather, I have a certain aptitude for understanding it, a skill first recognized by Sgt. Davis many years ago when I first reported for duty in 1887. Since that time, I have developed an extraordinary ability to forecast; I rarely miss a major formation change, or even a minor one, although I am the first to admit that I am not unerring. Every change in the nature of the wind, its velocity and direction, the changing barometric pressure especially; changes in temperature, cloud formations, humidity, the length of the day, and the temperature of the ocean; each and every one of these details contribute to my understanding of what lies ahead. A continuous sense of the weather and an uninterrupted understanding of its changing nature is something I simply cannot turn off ... it all comes so easily to me, much the same as telegraphy has come naturally to me.

Perhaps the officers in the ONI, especially Captain Todd and hopefully not just John, have seen in Annie similar qualities useful for their professional endeavor, forecasting, as it were, in their field of surveillance, in understanding people's behavior in a place and time that may not fit, such as activities related to spying. Certainly, I do believe her reasoning ability is a match for analyzing incomplete data and, in the past several weeks, she has also demonstrated an ability to come to conclusions, and someday make decisions, based on limited information.

***

In September 1917, eleven months after Sperry took off from the Great Salt Pond for the second time, there was another problem on the Island, or rather just off it. But this predicament *could* easily be seen, and was, by everybody. It was right there in the open, seen from the air, the Island, the water—above or below—because it was a massive battleship, the *U.S.S. Texas*. Launched in 1914, and now on its way to Europe, it ran aground just off Mansion Beach, the northern section of Crescent Beach ... in light fog *during broad daylight!*

What was the navigator thinking?

How could a battleship run aground in the middle of the day? Not possible, you'd think; well, indeed possible because there it was staring at us, stuck in the sand. Standing on the bluffs above Mansion Beach I could look directly into the eyes of the sailor standing watch in one of its tall communication towers.

Why did the *Texas* come so close to our Island when it should have been sailing out to sea to cross the Atlantic and fight in the European War?

After three days stuck, the 573-foot long battleship was finally freed from the grasp of the sandbar, a remnant of the sandbars that had been washed away in 1815. When the weather and seas allowed for it, the *Texas* was towed to the open Atlantic Ocean and then along the south shore of Long Island into New York Harbor, up the East River and finally to the Brooklyn Navy Yard for repairs to its hull. It berthed in the spot vacated by the launch of the *U. S. S. Arizona*. The Hell Gate Channel was not yet deep enough to handle this large a ship, or it would have been towed immediately to the Brooklyn Navy Yard via Long Island Sound and this point was made in numerous articles by the *New York Times* on the need for deepening the channel.

After that incident, it was a matter of only a few hours before I received a hand written note delivered to the Weather House by a sailor from the *U. S. S. Texas*. The message was from John: "May need your help. Please stand by."

I wondered why the ONI wanted us this time, but when I asked Annie, she just shrugged and tapped out that she thought she knew why it happened. I didn't realize she was already on the case and had been for several months. Although she kept her activities confidential, I did know that monitoring the transmissions of the remaining Mystery Man on the Island was her first assignment as a new ONI employee. She explained she had already reported to the ONI that the Mystery Man was communicating to someone—in her opinion a sailor on a ship— information about sandbars off the Island. Was he sending this information to the navigator on board the battleship or another crew member? Annie was sure there was indeed a German spy on the ship, and speculated that the information about the sandbars resulted in the grounding.

I asked, "If you knew espionage information was being sent, why couldn't they have prevented the grounding?"

"Sometimes," Annie explained, "things just have to happen."

Annie said that the background investigation of the crew members, that started before the battleship was towed back to the Brooklyn Navy Yard, strongly suggested that the sailor, who was in the lookout tower, was most likely the spy. Years after this episode, Annie confided in me that the man in the lookout was indeed the spy, and even Roosevelt believed he was responsible for the grounding.

Because of the grounding, the *U.S.S. Texas* was delayed a full twelve months. And Germany didn't need their U-boats to accomplish the task; they simply used our own equipment to harm us, the boat itself. Using our own resources, systems, or infrastructure to do harm was a standard blueprint in the field of sabotage, as Annie would later explain.

Life and the weather have one thing in common. Uncertainty—it is the hallmark of both. The changing nature of the weather and Annie's association with the ONI can be looked at, perhaps improbably, as an example of this uncertainty and apparent randomness. For example, if it were one year later, the U-boats may never have been able to mount their mission and we may never have had the opportunity to work with ONI because ... the following winter turned out to be the coldest and most severe Block Island had ever experienced. This prolonged cold spell left its mark in the form of ice two feet thick around much of the Island. It was unheard of for the Atlantic Ocean to remain frozen—up to a half mile off shore in some places—for such an extended period of time. If that weather pattern, an unrelenting series of low-pressure systems descending from the Arctic had occurred a year earlier the U-boats would not have been able to roam so freely, and the 'Three Mystery Men' may not have landed on our Island. And Annie may not have found her calling, although we are all certain she still would have found a way to matter.

A few days after the grounding, Milton asked for the afternoon off. He wanted to take Annie for a walk along Crescent Beach near the Surf

Hotel. Carrying a jar of milk from his parent's cows and corn muffins I
had made earlier in the day, the two set out on a walk that lasted several
hours, not because of the distance, but because of the wheelchair. A
normal fifteen-minute walk along any stretch of beach could easily turn
into a two-hour ordeal when pushing a wheelchair. He had to frequently
stop and free the sinking front wheels. The beach near the Surf Hotel,
once known as Burton's cove, is sheltered from the open ocean and the
footprints—rather, wheel prints—lasted through several cycles of tides,
unlike the beaches that surround the Island, where they would last only
as long as the next high tide.

Annie wondered how long their relationship would last. Would
Milton stay with her, remain her friend; or would he leave, like so many
of the young men who had called the Island their birthplace? And if he
stayed, would their friendship wash away with the tides too?

Annie was determined not to be determined about this. She knew she
looked 'scary' to people at times, although not to Milton, of that she was
quite sure. If Milton did stay, he would have to decide on his own. But
the question kept being repeated in her mind, as if she had no control
over it. As he struggled to push her along the beach at the water's edge,
she smiled and hoped.

Annie was suddenly curious why he had chosen this place for an
afternoon stroll. And is if reading her mind, Milt spoke softly, "Annie …
I suppose you're wondering why I brought you here … to this spot I
know is special to you?"

Annie waited; unaware she was holding her breath.

Milton gave her a shy smile as he reached for something in his
pocket. "There's a question, for as long as I can remember, I've been
wanting to ask you …"

Before Milton could finish, Annie was already raising her eyes.

Epilogue

Emma Rose

August 1941 –

The accident at sea that nearly took the life of my sister and me, clearly changed Annie Rose's life and defined mine. And although the near drowning—and the head injury she sustained when the boat was obliterated in the surf—spared my sister's intellect and spirit, it eventually claimed her life.

Years after that extraordinary October of 1916, while swimming alone at the southern end of Crescent Beach in the shadow of the Surf Hotel, my sister's seizures returned—she had not had a convulsion in years. As a result, a large amount of seawater was aspirated into her lungs, preventing oxygen from reaching her brain and she never regained consciousness. I was living in Brooklyn at the time and returned to the Island at once. Several days later, with her in my arms and my mother holding the both of us, she stopped breathing. She was thirty-three.

When she died in our arms, I understood then, as I do now, that my mother had not only lost her precious daughter, but decades earlier had lost her only son as well as my father; and in 1928, she buried my stepfather. Her anguish must have been unbearable, although when Annie died I could not imagine anyone's pain being greater than my own. I once wrote a poem about loss and titled it "Lillie's Anguish," but I was really thinking of my own pain. My mother remains a source of inspiration for me; she still lives in the house her father built.

We buried my sister at sea where our boat first capsized. It was several miles out to sea, due south of the location where we eventually came ashore at the base of Mohegan Bluffs, where the pounding surf pulverized the wooden boat and where we rescued each other, on that late afternoon, long ago, when we were teenagers. My mother did not accompany us on the boat that laid her to rest, but she understood how important the process was for her daughter to be returned to the sea; she understood my sister's life was shaped by the sea, and now would be returned to it in a way that would matter and how cathartic the process could be for all of us.

After my sister contributed to solving the mystery of the events of that October, she was asked to join the ONI as a civilian, and her seventeen-year part-time career officially began.

John was her supervisor but there was not much else I knew. Even when I moved to Brooklyn and she stayed with me for extended periods of time, she always remained quite professional, and by that I mean she kept her work private. In fact, with only two exceptions, those confidential activities were the only things she did not share fully with me.

I remember on the morning when Sperry flew us back to Block Island, John and I walked to have our photograph taken in front of the battleships. When I looked back to see my sister talking with a group of officers, I thought that that was when they were recruiting her to work with the ONI. Several years later, she explained that brief meeting was called to discuss the report Captain Todd and she had submitted the night before. Captain Todd, Annie, and one other officer in the transmission office, had concluded, after reviewing the data about the debris pulled up by the tugs, that the two U-boats sunk in Hell Gate may not have been the work of the German navy. For reasons they could not fully explain (until they deciphered the Zimmerman Telegram early in 1917) they speculated it may have been the British who set up the entire episode. Could this be possible? Why not. First, the British were pleading with President Wilson to enter the war. And, second, it was common knowledge in the military that the ONI was poorly funded and not very effective; an easy prey for the more sophisticated British spy effort.

There was one other classified issue my sister shared with me over the years: Annie never understood the Navy's reluctance to accept the dangerous nature of submarine warfare—after the war especially—and consequently, in her opinion, the Navy did not adequately prepare to defend against enemy submarines. Unfortunately, Annie and a small group of ONI operatives were proven correct when, at the beginning of WW II, hundreds of our merchant ships were sunk by German submarines—off our own coast, including in the waters just outside the front entrance to New York Harbor!

The number of innocent lives that could have been saved is staggering. Annie wondered if our government's focus on Prohibition distracted our Navy from preparing properly, a question often asked by some members of the ONI and discussed openly in the Weather House, as Rhode Island was one of only two states that refused to ratify the 18th Amendment.

Following the events in the Brooklyn Navy Yard, Milton and Annie continued their friendship. He proposed on Crescent Beach in the summer of 1917, and several months prior to his enlisting in the Army, they married at the Methodist Church. It was one of the most wonderful days of my life, and, of course, hers. To say she was happy is an understatement of biblical proportion, for her joy towered over all other aspects of her life. In her heart, she celebrated her marriage to Milton every waking moment.

In mid-1918, Milton resigned from the Block Island Weather Bureau and shipped out to fight in the Great European War. Along with many other New England recruits, he was transported by a Fall River Line steamship from Newport, RI to New York Harbor where his division boarded a transport ship to Europe. Because of Wallace's connections with the Fall River Line, my sister was able to travel with Milton on that overnight trip to NYC aboard the Priscilla, the most elegant steamship in the line. These steamships were contracted by the government to move enlisted troops from various Atlantic Ocean ports to NYC. It was the last night Annie and her husband would be together, a story that I will one day tell.

Never to return to Block Island, Milton died on a battlefield in France on October 15, 1918, three weeks before the end of the war. In 1922, a stained glass memorial window was erected in the sanctuary of the church to honor the memory and short military service of Milton Mitchell, one of 117,000 who died in our armed forces during a war that had worldwide death estimates in the 15 to 25 million range.

The story of Lawrence Sperry ended much too soon as well. On December 23, 1923, he died when the small plane he was piloting lost control in dense fog and plunged into the English Channel. If he had only listened to my uncle who preached, among other things, that flying in disregard of meteorological conditions is, at times, suicidal; perhaps, just perhaps, Mr. Sperry would still be alive. He was thirty-one years old, never to reach his full potential. His father's corporation and the one he started on his own after the Great War, to this day remain operational and highly influential.

My sister, Annie Rose, when she wasn't traveling, continued to live with our mother in the home our grandfather built behind the Union House Hotel. Annie never married again and proudly wore her gold wedding band every day until the day she died. As we now know, when she wasn't employed as a part-time telegrapher for Island hotels or the Telephone Exchange, she was working for the ONI.

Gary E. Eddey

In 1930, another memorial window was erected directly across the sanctuary from Milton's. This window honored the memory and quiet government service of George Washington Eddey. In 1887, my uncle, who became my stepfather and is the voice of this story, began his career at the Block Island Signal Station as an Assistant Observer and telegrapher. In 1908, after serving in various weather bureaus across the United States, and after losing his first wife while stationed in Texas, my uncle returned to Block Island to become the Meteorologist in Charge, ultimately serving the longest of any weather official assigned to the Island. His telegraphy skills were superior, a trait shared with his siblings and also by my sister.

After his death in 1928, I was able to view his personal papers and journal, and realized what I already suspected, that his concern for his own three children, and my sister and me, was so prominent in his daily thoughts that it became part of his character. His handwritten and typed notes submitted to the Weather Bureau served me well in retelling this story, but it was his personal reflections that inspired me to write it. After having a stroke, my uncle was forced to retire from the Weather Bureau, moved in permanently with my mother, and died two years later. He is buried in the Island Cemetery.

John went on to have a giant of a career in Naval Intelligence. He kept in contact with Annie, usually by telegraphing her short messages—in code of course—communications we now know were as much professional as they were personal. John was "family" to us; he accompanied me back to Block Island after Annie lost consciousness following her last seizure and helped me lay her to rest at sea. I am not sure where John is now, he has not responded to my last few phone calls.

As for my cousin, Wallace, when he was "running rum" during Prohibition or operating gambling junkets off the southeast shore of Block Island—much to his father's chagrin—it is all but certain that John was his guardian angel. Block Island's raconteur and sometime fisherman, died quietly in "Eddey's Shanty," the small home he built overlooking the Atlantic Ocean on Mohegan Bluffs. He died in his sleep, the result of a massive heart attack, perhaps the result of too much alcohol consumption over the years.

Emma Rose ... well, by now you know that it was me who brought to print my uncle's story. I did my best to retell his account of the events by preserving the integrity of his journal entries, adding things only when necessary to fill in the blanks and create flow. I do hope I have written the story as he would have wanted me to.

I was for a short time, like my sister, a telephone operator before moving to New York City to begin a career as a writer. I have been and remain fully appreciative that I would never have survived the accident if it were not for my sister. She saved my life. Her tenacity and courage were extraordinary and I now feel that perhaps she bordered on magnanimity. She was sure anyone could find a way to make themselves matter, regardless of what one was dealt. "It isn't what happens to you that counts," she would say, "it is how you take it."

She repeated that phrase so often she developed a hand sign for it.

It has been about a decade since my sister's death, yet I frequently, if not continuously, relive our life together. As one would expect, the enjoyable episodes, such as the flight from the Brooklyn Navy Yard back to Block Island in Sperry's Curtis F hydroaeroplane that October morning, are most satisfying to remember. Although it was autumn and no time to be in an open cockpit aeroplane that was quite a ride; it continues to bring a smile to my face. Sometimes those "not so joyful" memories return, unannounced of course, but mostly it is the wonderful memories that return over and over again. We were so fortunate to have had so many of them.

As I near the end of my own life, I do so hope there is a heaven so I can be with Annie once again. But what if there is no heaven? I suppose then the only thing that binds me to her are the memories in my mind ... and the tears, those very real tears, the physical representation of those memories ... tears that fall from my eyes even as I write this epilogue.

One night, seven or eight years before she died, my sister tapped out on the wireless device a few sentences that I wrote down and eventually memorized, word for word. When she began a message to me by tapping out my full name, I knew she was expecting me to record it on paper. We were sitting in the Weather House office; it was raining, the wind blowing hard from the north.

"Emma Rose!"

I quickly reached for a pencil.

It took a while for me to write down her words properly—I was never as adept at Morse code as she.

"Em, two things are certain; our lives are fleeting—mine shorter than yours—and then our moment will be gone. It is rare to become a legend but we can all leave a legacy. We must work hard to try to make ourselves matter—to one another, to our family, to Block Island and beyond. You have to work hard ..."

She repeated those last few words several times, until I had written them down several times. She then added: "I know of no other way..."

I knew, we all knew, she would die young, and although the two of us were in contact frequently, almost every day, courtesy of the telephone exchange where she worked—I would talk, she would listen and respond via Morse code—I wish we could have shared a few more words with one another after that last seizure. I would have told her how eternally grateful I was to have been her sister and that I too would vow to "matter". And she would have looked at me, raised her eyes in approval, and given me the sign she developed just for me: "Em, I love you so much."

And oh, how I loved her.

Acknowledgements

As all writers concerned with Block Island, I am indebted to S. T. Livermore, the author of the first substantial history of the Island published in 1877; to Charles Perry, editor of an updated 1901 version of Livermore's book; and to Robert Downie for his more recent histories and numerous commentaries of life on Block Island. I also owe a bit of gratitude to the late Bill and Marie Murray for their help bringing Block Island's history alive; as well as G. S.; and to Lawrence Epstein and, most especially, to my editor Cliff Carle, for guidance structuring the story. And, of course, to Mr. Melville.

The author acknowledges a special 'thank you' to the Matheny Book Club, under the direction of Maureen Mikan, for their suggestions and feedback.

And many thanks to all my friends for their helpful advice and excellent editorial skills. I am eternally grateful!

About the Author

Born in New Jersey near the Hudson River and currently landlocked in Morristown, New Jersey, Gary E. Eddey, a physician, descends from the original Block Island settlers. Dr. Eddey's work has appeared in the Greenpoint (Brooklyn) Gazette, several short story collections and numerous professional journals. Trained as a general academic pediatrician at New York Presbyterian Hospital, he is the Chief Medical Officer and Vice President for Medical Affairs at the Matheny Medical and Educational Center in Peapack, New Jersey. Matheny is widely recognized as a special habilitation hospital for children and adults with a multitude of chronic neurologic disabling conditions. It is also a teaching hospital of New Jersey Medical School where Dr. Eddey is an Associate Professor of Pediatrics and teaches bioethics and disability medicine in the third year Pediatric clerkship.

CPSIA information can be obtained at www.ICGtesting.com
Printed in the USA
LVOW10s1614250815

451463LV00006B/716/P